Was ever a betrayal so cruel?

Jeanne du Marchand adored her dashing young Scotsman, Douglas MacRae, and every moment in his arms was pure rapture. But when her father, the Comte du Marchand, learned she was carrying Douglas's child, Jeanne was torn from the proud youth without a word of farewell—and separated not long after from her newborn baby daughter. Jeanne feared her life was over, for all she truly cared about was lost to her.

Can the power of love prevail?

Once Douglas believed his lady's loving words—until her betrayal turned his ardor to contempt. He cannot forget even now, ten years later, when destiny brings her to his native Scotland, broken in spirit but as beautiful as before. His pride will not let him play the fool again, although memories of a past—secret, innocent, and fragile—tempt him. Can passion lead to love and forgiveness?

Avon Romantic Treasures by
Karen Ranney

So In Love • To Love a Scottish Lord
The Irresistible MacRae
When the Laird Returns
After the Kiss • My True Love
My Beloved • Upon a Wicked Time
My Wicked Fantasy

*If You've Enjoyed This Book,
Be Sure to Read These Other*
AVON ROMANTIC TREASURES

A Dark Champion *by Kinley MacGregor*
England's Perfect Hero *by Suzanne Enoch*
Guilty Pleasures *by Laura Lee Guhrke*
An Invitation to Seduction *by Lorraine Heath*
It Takes a Hero *by Elizabeth Boyle*

Coming Soon

A Wanted Man *by Susan Kay Law*

KAREN RANNEY

SO IN LOVE

BOOK FIVE OF THE HIGHLAND LORDS

An Avon Romantic Treasure

AVON BOOKS
An Imprint of HarperCollinsPublishers

AVON BOOKS
An Imprint of HarperCollins*Publishers*
10 East 53rd Street
New York, New York 10022-5299

Copyright © 2004 by Karen Ranney
ISBN: 0-380-82108-7
www.avonromance.com

First Avon Books paperback printing: July 2004

Avon Trademark Reg. U.S. Pat. Off. and in Other Countries, Marca Registrada, Hecho en U.S.A.
HarperCollins® is a registered trademark of HarperCollins Publishers Inc.

Printed in the U.S.A.

10 9 8 7 6 5 4 3 2 1

To The Fab Four:
Jeannette Herbage
Barbara Berryman
Daniel Gutierrez
Yvette Ramirez

For shared experiences, earthy wisdom, joie de vivre,
for teaching me, and helping me through dark days,
but most of all, for the gift of laughter.

Prologue

September 1782

J eanne du Marchand knew the precise moment her life
shattered. She was able to pinpoint the exact words, recall her shocked intake of breath, and feel again the swift
and frantic fluttering of her heart.

However, there was no hint of the events soon to come
on that glorious September morning. The cloudless blue
sky framed a lovely early autumn day. The breeze, carrying the scents of lavender and roses, filtered into the
house from the garden. Even the birds in the aviary were
innocent and naïve, singing a paean to a dawn already
come and gone.

Skirts swinging, she made her way down the corridor to
her father's library. One of the footmen pushed open the
floor-to-ceiling-high door, and she walked inside, waiting
silently for her father to notice her. As a child, she'd often
come to the library, at first summoned by her father for
some infraction or another. In the last few years he'd sent
for her for another reason entirely. She'd begun to think of

his questions about her lessons and her retention of them as a game and his smile a prize.

However, she'd rarely been required to report to her father lately. Nicholas, Comte du Marchand, was a very busy man and Paris itself seemed feverish with activity this autumn. Everywhere she went, Jeanne heard stories of the American war. England was losing, and France, as an ally of the young country, was ecstatic.

Their Paris home was lovely and the library one of the most beautiful rooms, with its gilt-edged ceiling frescoes and panels depicting scenes from their ancestral chateau of Vallans. The walls were painted a deep coral, a striking backdrop for the portraits of the du Marchand ancestors in their heavy gold frames. Marble columns of pale coral ringed the room, as tall as the ceiling and topped with gold acanthus leaves. A magnificent carpet lay beneath her feet, the pattern of green and gold leaves framing an oval of beige. At the end of the room a swag of coral and navy fabric attached to the ceiling framed an upholstered settee with bolsters at each end. Visitors rarely sat there, however, choosing instead one of the intricately carved chairs near her father's desk.

The books her father personally vetted were located on the second floor of this chamber, a space accessible by a staircase located at each end of the room. Normally, he sent Robert, his secretary, to fetch a volume while he remained seated behind the most dominant feature in the room, a massive desk crafted of mahogany and carved with a relief of grapes and flowers, each symbol a reminder of Vallans.

Paris might provide both cultural and political interests, but Vallans was the birthplace of the du Marchands, a fact her father never allowed anyone to forget.

Jeanne remained where she was, patiently waiting, arms behind her, bearing erect, shoulders straight, a posture she'd learned from repeated corrections when she was a child.

Her father finally glanced up and put his quill down slowly. His look wasn't the fond one he normally gave her. Nor was there any hint of pride in this glance. He crooked one finger in her direction and she knew, suddenly, why she was here. Moving to stand in front of the desk, she fingered the locket her mother had given her and willed herself to calm.

Justine must have told him.

She'd long suspected that their housekeeper was her father's mistress. Even if they did not currently share a bed, Justine went to him with every concern, and it was obvious that she possessed a great deal of power. There wasn't much that occurred in either their Paris home or at Vallans that escaped Justine.

Justine must have discovered from her maid that Jeanne was becoming ill in the morning, and that her dresses were beginning to fit too snugly.

"Is it true, daughter?" He stared fixedly at her midsection. "Are you with child?"

"Yes, Father," she said, feeling a tremor in her stomach that, thankfully, wasn't conveyed in her voice. She'd thought to hide her condition until Douglas could address him and plans could be made for their wedding.

"You are certain?" He lifted his gaze to hers.

"I am." She smiled. Even her father at his most furious could not dampen her joy.

"Then you have shamed the name of du Marchand."

His voice sounded so disinterested that he might have been commenting to a stranger about the weather. If she had been wiser, she would have been wary of the look in his eyes. Gone was the fond affection and in its place a distance she'd never before seen, as if he'd simply stopped feeling anything for her at all.

He looked down at the papers in front of him as if dismissing her. She knew better than to leave, however, until he gave her permission.

"Douglas and I will marry, Father."

Her quiet comment drew a sharp look from her father's secretary, a man who'd been present during most of her meetings with her only living parent. Robert shook his head almost imperceptibly, but she only smiled at him, used to getting her own way.

Her father's eyes, the exact shade of gray as hers, looked up disinterestedly.

"We'll marry," she said, taking another step toward the desk. "I love him, Father. Douglas comes from a good family, at least the equal of the du Marchands." She was buoyant with joy and no doubt foolish with it. But he must be made to see.

"You have shamed the du Marchand name," he said again.

It was true that she'd disobeyed countless rules in order to meet with Douglas almost every day for the last three months. She'd gone behind her chaperone's back, pretended appointments that had not existed, friends who'd not been in Paris. She'd twisted the truth until it looked like a braid. But she'd told herself that a lie for a good reason was acceptable. After they married, however, there would be no more falsehoods, no shame.

"We cannot be the first couple to have anticipated our wedding, Father," she said, smiling. "No one will know, especially if we marry soon."

She couldn't help but feel that God Himself had forgiven her even if her family priest had not. At confession, Father Haton had promised dire consequences in retaliation for her behavior with Douglas, but hell seemed so far away, especially when Douglas was near.

Now all she must do is convince her father.

He threw the quill he was using down on his desk, uncaring that it splattered droplets of ink across his documents.

"Your lover has left France, Jeanne. He's had his fill of you."

The shock she experienced was only momentary, banished by disbelief.

"It's not true," she said, and this time her father's secretary, sitting beside the desk, blanched. She should have taken her cue from him. As the minutes ticked by, her father remained silent, leaving her to feel the full brunt of his words.

"It's not true," she said again, shaking her head. "Douglas couldn't have left. He would have let me know." They were planning on meeting just this afternoon. Today she was going to tell him she was with child.

"Oh, he's gone, Jeanne," he said, his thin lips pursed in a smile. Opening a drawer, he extracted a letter and handed it to her. It was the note she'd given her maid to take to Douglas.

She felt sick. Her hands were frozen but she reached out to take the letter, gripping it tightly so that she wouldn't drop it. Resolutely, she took a deep breath and looked at her father.

"There's a good reason he isn't here," she said. "But I know he'll return."

Her father stood and rounded the desk, coming to stand in front of her. A tall man with broad shoulders, he was a very imposing figure in oratory and an even more daunting personage this morning. But she could not afford to be cowed, not when her future was at stake.

"When he comes back, we'll marry, Father. There'll be no shame to the du Marchand name."

He swung his hand back and struck her, the large crested ring on his finger biting into her skin. She made a sound, a yelp, a startled half scream that was both surprise and pain.

She took a step back, one hand going to her cheek, the other to her waist as if to protect the tiny child inside her.

"You whore," he said softly. "Do you think I'd allow you to marry an Englishman?"

"He's Scot," she said, a comment that earned her another blow.

Her father's secretary stood and gathered up some papers, leaving the room. The door made no sound as he closed it hurriedly behind him.

The joy she felt when entering the room had turned to fear, so quickly that she felt ill. She'd known of her father's xenophobia, of course, and his dislike for all things that weren't French despite the fact that he himself had married an English Duke's daughter. But she'd thought to dissuade him in Douglas's case. After all, she was his only child, his spoiled darling, and half English herself. If anyone could convince the Comte of anything, she could.

"Would you be more forgiving of my sin," she asked rashly, "if my lover had been French?"

He didn't strike her again. He only smiled a very curious smile and returned to his chair. The wide expanse of desk acted as an island between them.

"I had great hopes for you, Jeanne, but you have chosen your own future, it seems." He began writing again, dismissing her by his actions and his tone.

"What do you mean?"

He glanced up. "I am sending you home to Vallans, daughter. In the time allowed you, feel free to contemplate what you've lost by your actions. Or spend the time until you give birth dreaming of your absent lover, if you must." He smiled and dipped his quill into the inkwell again.

"And after that?" she asked. A drop of blood from the cut on her cheek rolled down her face. She angrily wiped it away, determined he would not see her flinch. "I will not marry a man of your choosing, Father." He had never made a secret of his desire for a political alliance with her as the prize.

"You will not have to, Jeanne," he said coldly. "No man of my acquaintance would have you. He'd want his bride to come unsullied to his bed, not as used as a Paris whore. You'll be taken to the Convent of Sacré-Coeur," he announced, standing once again. "To live out the remainder of your days in obedience. If you're fortunate, perhaps you'll become a woman of power and influence, but only after you manage to convince the church that you regret your sins."

"And my child?" she asked, feeling chilled to the bone. "What will happen to my child?"

As she watched him smile, she realized that he'd already made plans. The grandson or granddaughter of the Comte du Marchand would simply disappear, an annoyance that would no longer annoy.

Chapter 1

June 1792
Edinburgh, Scotland

Douglas MacRae had no idea, when he prepared for the evening, that in one moment ten years would be swept away and he would feel as lost and distraught as a young man. He had no intimation and no foreboding, when leaving his house a few hours earlier, that he might see *her*.

He stared at the woman standing in the doorway, limned by the light. An icy coldness encapsulated him, as well as a sensation of being instantly catapulted into some otherworldly place.

She was supposed to be dead.

Attired in a dark blue dress with only a hint of white at the collar and cuffs to soften the severe hue, she stood immobile, her face expressionless, holding on to the hand of a little boy. The child, his hair curling in brown ringlets, wore a suit of clothes identical to his father's down to the lace at his neck and wrists.

9

Douglas had two immediate thoughts—that Hartley's wife was a ghost from his past, and that she wasn't, evidently, still bedridden as the man had said.

The little boy rubbed at his eyes and the woman spoke to him in hushed tones. A gentle smile changed her face, lit her eyes, and softened her lips.

Suddenly it was two years ago and he was standing in the captain's cabin of his brother's ship, a scrap of a handwritten notice in his hand. Hamish had brought the news from France and he'd read it three times before making sense of the words.

"The Comte du Marchand is dead," he said aloud, the words not having the weight he expected. "And Vallans is destroyed."

"What about his daughter?" his brother had asked.

"It doesn't say." He'd laid the notice down on the table in his brother's cabin, stunned and disagreeably affected by the realization that Jeanne du Marchand must be dead as well. But it seemed that she wasn't, was she?

"Bid your father goodnight," she said tenderly to the little boy. At the sound of her voice, Douglas was immediately reminded of Paris, a shadowed garden, and the sound of summer.

The child looked timorously at the man seated next to Douglas.

"Goodnight, Papa," he said, not relinquishing Jeanne's hand. The child didn't move from his stance by the door. Nor did his host bid him come closer.

"Goodnight, Davis," Hartley said, smiling absently at his son. He managed a longer look at Jeanne.

Her auburn hair was held at the back of her head in a serviceable bun. Over it she wore an arrangement of lace and dark blue ribbon. But it was her face Douglas studied as she stood with eyes downcast, her gaze fixed on the floor.

A lovely face, one he'd kissed enough times to know the

texture of her skin, to measure the distance from the corner of her full lips across her high cheekbones to fluttering eyelashes. He'd traced the line of each winged brow with his fingertips. He'd seen a Roman coin once and the perfection of the profile had reminded him of her.

Thick spectacles now shielded her soft gray eyes, a shade that reminded him of fog and storms, and smoke from a peak fire. A voice from his memory, a laughing teasing taunt, whispered in his ear.

"I fear that I'm vain, Douglas. I could see you better if I wore them, but they are so ugly."

"Nothing you could do," he'd said, "could ever make you less beautiful in my eyes, Jeanne." His own voice had been laden with lust and youthful exuberance. But he had been in love, so desperately in love that he didn't see her as less than perfect.

She'd linked her arms around his neck and kissed him sweetly, gently.

"Then I shall always think myself beautiful, my dearest Douglas. Even if I must squint at you."

Now Jeanne's gaze traveled over him disinterestedly. Abruptly, her eyes widened as she seemed to still, her faint smile freezing in place, one hand splayed at her side.

The least she could do was appear afraid.

But perhaps she no longer had the ability to glean his thoughts as she once had. If so, she would have run from the room or begged for his forgiveness.

He would never give it.

His host flicked a finger in the child's direction and instantly the woman turned and gently pulled the boy through the doorway. Neither of them looked back, but Douglas could not stop staring in Jeanne's direction even as the door closed.

"I see you're struck dumb at the sight of my governess,"

Robert Hartley said, grinning. "I, too, feel the same when looking at Jeanne. If you discount that ugly eyewear, she's a fine morsel. Did you see those breasts?"

Douglas's hand reached out to grasp the etched crystal tumbler he was being offered, and he noted with detachment that it sparkled in the gleam of the branch of candles only a few feet from him. Warmth was curiously absent from the room, the chill so pervasive that he wondered why he'd not noticed it earlier.

Governess?

Slowly, Douglas turned his head and looked at his host. With some difficulty he managed a small smile. "Your governess is, indeed, a lovely woman."

Hartley grinned. "She'll be more than that in a few days. My wife is still abed from our youngest child's birth and a man has needs."

"And is your governess amenable to your suggestions?" How odd that Douglas's voice didn't reveal the tumult of his thoughts. Instead, it sounded steady and he appeared only barely interested in the topic at hand.

"What choice does she have? She's only a governess, after all. They may carry themselves as high and mighty, but in the end she'll do what's necessary to keep her position."

Douglas placed the glass carefully on the brass coaster beside him.

The room in which he sat was comfortable without the touches of grandiosity marking the remainder of Hartley's home. Bookcases lined the walls and the hundreds of gilt-edged books were arranged by thickness rather than topic, leading Douglas to wonder if Hartley was one of those men who furnished his library by the case, judging his reading material by weight more than content.

Some men prided themselves on being learned without any attempt at learning.

The evening had been one filled with business. Robert

Hartley was not a friend but a customer, one who wanted to engage in the importation of French textiles. Up until a few moments earlier it had been a tolerable evening.

"You should have seen her a few months ago. Scrawny little thing she was, but she's filled out nicely."

"Did you hire her yourself?" he asked and forced himself to sit back against the chair, feigning a nonchalance that he didn't feel. Instead, each of his senses was alert, his hearing attuned to the answer.

Hartley studied his glass, looking entirely too self-congratulatory. "It was my wife who brought her into the household. Evidently the girl's aunt was a friend of my wife's mother. A pity Jeanne chose to be a governess. She might have been a very sought-after courtesan with that bosom of hers."

The anger Douglas felt was a surprise, but then, he hadn't expected Jeanne to be resurrected from his past, a ghost given form. How strange that, of all the places in the world, all the cities and towns, all the houses, taverns, hovels, and huts, she would be here, in Robert Hartley's home on this one night.

He glanced toward the door, wondering at the fact that his blood was just now beginning to warm. His heart still beat in a staccato fashion, and his grip on the arm of the chair was a bit too fierce.

His host, however, seemed to have seen nothing untoward in his behavior, for which he was grateful. Douglas didn't want to explain to anyone that the sight of that one particular woman had enraged him so fully that his hands shook with the emotion.

"I understand you've been to France many times," Hartley said, pouring himself another glass of whiskey.

"I have," Douglas answered. "But my brother and his wife are the most traveled."

Hamish and Mary had decided to engage in a rescue effort in the last few years, crossing the Channel innumerable times to ferry those fleeing France to safety. He had no intention of divulging their activities to Hartley or the fact that while the English were intent upon removing Huguenots from Nova Scotia, Hamish and Mary were just as determined to populate his native country with French émigrés.

"It's a terrible thing what's happening there," Hartley said.

Strange, but the other man didn't sound all that concerned. But then, Douglas had felt the same until accompanying his brother on one of those trips to Calais. His compassion had been born the moment he'd seen the despair in the eyes of those who'd escaped France, and heard their stories.

"I suppose that any revolution has its share of brutality," Douglas said, sipping from his whiskey. "The French feel disenfranchised, which only encourages a certain radicalism."

"They're hard on their nobles, though," Hartley said, grinning. He leaned back in his chair and held his glass up to the light to admire the dark caramel color of the whiskey.

"And their king and queen," Douglas contributed, speaking of the fact that Louis XVI and his wife had been arrested the year before. France was swallowing its aristocracy, cleansing itself of nobility one person at a time.

Was that what had happened to Jeanne? Had she escaped France because she was no longer accorded the privileges of her rank? With some difficulty, Douglas focused his mind on his host and the business at hand. Until he left Robert Hartley's home, he would concentrate on being a genial guest.

Revenge could wait until later.

Chapter 2

❦

Jeanne couldn't breathe. There was a cold spot next to her heart and a pounding in her chest. She felt as if the past were a heavy stone, much like the punishment she'd received at the Convent of Sacré-Coeur. There, she'd been made to stand in the center of her cell, a series of progressively heavier rocks hung from a chain around her neck.

"Will you confess, Jeanne Catherine Alexis du Marchand?" Sister Marie-Thérèse demanded.

"I do," she'd whispered, the punishment for silence so much greater than any admission of her sins.

"You fornicated?"

A terrible word for the love she and Douglas MacRae had shared. But what would that stern-faced nun know of physical joy, of laughter in the sunlight?

"I did."

"You lusted?"

God forgive her, but she had. And did, in her nightly dreams of him. But then she woke. "I did."

"You bore a bastard?"

She placed her hands on her flat belly, feeling the eternal

15

emptiness there. "Yes," she said, keeping her head bowed.

The heavy stones were gone now, but the memory of them still pulled at her shoulders, not unlike the burdens of guilt, regret, and grief.

What was Douglas doing in Edinburgh?

Seated, he had still seemed tall, his shoulders square, his build neither slender nor overly muscled. His gaze, from eyes a deep and fathomless blue, was direct without revealing anything of the man. The groove of dimple in his cheek, however, proved that he sometimes smiled.

But not at her.

The child, Davis, was talking. Jeanne forced a weak smile to her lips, knowing that she had to answer him. Perhaps this was just a dream, and her charge was only a participant in it. But the wall was hard against her back and she could smell the perfume of the flowers in the hall and feel Davis's small hand cupped in hers.

Please, God. The prayer was the first time in years that she had actually implored the Almighty. She'd had enough of God in the convent. He hadn't saved her from Sister Marie-Thérèse. *Make him be a ghost.* But it was all too obvious that Douglas was real, and seated not twenty feet from her.

God must have been listening after all, because she somehow found the strength to continue down the hall and then up the stairs to the third floor.

"You don't look at all well, miss," Davis said, as she stopped on the landing, trying to quell her sudden nausea. The little boy looked up at her, eyes narrowed. Davis was a great worrier, his thin little face almost always drawn and pinched.

"Of course I am, Davis," she said, wishing that her heart would slow its staccato beating and her breath would come easier.

"I don't think you are, miss."

"Nonsense," she said. But she was grateful not to see any of the many maids or footmen who patrolled the hallways of the Hartley home. They would glance at her pale face and not hesitate to report her appearance to Robert Hartley.

There was nothing at all wrong with her. A fully fleshed ghost had appeared from her past, that was all.

Determinedly, she mounted the last of the steps and began to walk with lengthening strides away from the narrow back stairs and toward the nursery.

"Are you certain you're not going to be sick?"

Jeanne searched for the words that would keep the young boy from asking too many questions, none of which she could answer. She had enough to do to breathe, to put one foot in front of the other, and to continue on in the present when the past summoned her with such fervency.

She could feel the tentacles of it stretching out and entwining around her, tugging at her to remember, to recall. A touch of his hand, his breath upon her neck, the feel of his body against hers. Forbidden memories the convent had attempted to expunge all those years. Despite the many beatings, despite the mornings in which she was doused with buckets of cold water and left to stand in the chilled air, she had never told them everything.

Nor had she ever truly forgotten.

At this moment, however, she wished they had been successful, and all those occasions spread flat upon the flagstone floor of the chapel had stripped him from her mind. A memory could hurt, and that knowledge surprised her. In the convent, recollections of Douglas had kept her warm at night, kept her whole when the sisters would have splintered her soul.

Even the anger she felt at his abandonment did not ache as much as this pain.

Blessedly, she finally reached the nursery, opening the door and releasing Davis's hand. He turned and surveyed Jeanne with too much knowledge in his young eyes.

"You *are* going to be sick, aren't you? It was the fish at dinner, wasn't it? It always makes Mama ill. That's why Cook never prepares it for her anymore. I told you that if you made me eat it I'd get sick as well."

"You will not get sick, Davis," she said calmly. "Neither will I. I'm simply feeling a little fatigued."

"We didn't say goodnight to Mama," Davis said, his tone too much like a whine. On any other night she would have corrected him, but not now. Tonight all she wanted to do was put him to bed and retreat to her room.

"Your mother is sleeping and I didn't wish to disturb her." Let God make something of that lie.

Davis looked as if he didn't believe her, but Jeanne didn't care at the moment.

She helped Davis ready himself for bed and listened to his prayers with little attention. Ever since her years in the convent, she no longer prayed. Instead, she held herself tight, hands clasped in front of her, head slightly bent, an attitude of penitence or worship. Her thoughts were not on God but on Douglas.

Tucking Davis into bed, she smoothed her hand over the boy's forehead as she did every night. And, every night, Davis withdrew from her touch, not given to overt gestures of affection.

She bent and pinched off the flame of the candle beside the child's bed.

"Goodnight, Davis," she said, then stood and walked to the door.

"Goodnight, miss."

One quick glance at him and she closed the door, walking down the hall to her own chamber, a tiny room with a sloping ceiling, furnished simply with a single cot, armoire, and bureau. The young woman she'd been, the rich and spoiled aristocrat, would have been dismayed both at the small space and the scarred furniture, but the woman she was now viewed it simply as hers and accepted it as adequate for her needs. She'd done with less at the convent, and even less on the journey from France.

Walking to the window, she opened it, feeling the warm night air enter the room. There were some who said it was poisonous, and from the scent of the damp and pungent Edinburgh breeze, she could almost believe it. But a gust from the north, smelling of trees and flowers, brushed against her cheek and hinted at far-off wild places.

Removing her spectacles, she closed her eyes and vowed not to cry. Even though he'd been close enough to touch, even though he had never said a word to her, even though he treated her like a stranger, she would not cry.

A tear dampened her cheek. Mirthlessly, she chuckled at herself. Very well, she might weep for the young girl she'd been, so desperately in love that she would have challenged any of her father's edicts, and had.

She replaced her spectacle and opened her eyes, she glanced at her reflection in the night-darkened window, wondering if Douglas had recognized her at all. She had changed from the girl he'd known. Or perhaps those alterations weren't visible on the surface. Her eyes were the same color, an odd sort of gray that had always embarrassed her. Her hair was brown, with a tinge of red to it, much as it had been as a girl. While it was true her face appeared thinner and her cheekbones higher, it was no doubt due more to the deprivations of the past months than to the passage of time.

The spoiled and rebellious young girl had become a survivor, but such changes didn't show on the surface.

Her fingers toyed with the rectangular gold pendant that

was one of a few scant remnants of her past. An ugly piece of jewelry, it had belonged to her mother and was, for that reason, treasured.

Douglas had looked so prosperous sitting in Robert Hartley's library. There was a look on his face, watchful more than stern, that would caution even the most flirtatious woman from approaching him. Whereas her last memories of him had been as a smiling young man, this stranger was formidable and commanding.

Turning from the window, Jeanne performed her nightly routine of pushing the bureau in front of the door, a barricade against Hartley's nocturnal visits. A month ago he'd knocked on the door, whispering an entreaty. A week ago he'd tested the door, only to discover the furniture blocking his way. So far he'd allowed it to stand, probably because he didn't want his attempts at seduction to be overheard.

Her employer was watching her like a bird of prey. Sometimes when she came upstairs, he would stand at the landing, refusing to move as she passed. She'd feel his hand glide over the material covering her bottom, but because Davis was with her she hadn't chastised him in front of the boy. Several times when she entered the schoolroom he was there, leaving only after he'd made a show of questioning his son on his newfound knowledge, and complimenting her overmuch when little Davis repeated his daily lessons by rote.

Something would have to be done about him, and soon. Her nightly precautions wouldn't keep him at bay forever.

If she'd had another trade, another method of making her way in the world, she would never have chosen to be a governess. But she had few attributes other than her education. People, especially the Scots, simply didn't care that she was the daughter of a French Count, that her father had once been so wealthy that he'd loaned the king money, that

Vallans had boasted over three hundred rooms and countless works of art.

Nor would they care, if they had known, that she had escaped from a convent, leaving France with little more than
the clothes on her back.

It certainly hadn't mattered to Robert Hartley that she
was destitute when she'd come looking for a job, that it had
been three days since she'd last had a substantial meal.
The two questions he'd asked prior to employing her had
been simple and easily answered: Did she have any refer-
ences, and was she willing to work for a certain sum? No
to the first question, regrettably. Her years with the nuns
would not help. From the convent she'd made her way to
Scotland to be with her aunt, only to learn that her only
living relative had died a year earlier. Her uncle by marriage had no interest in opening his home to a half-French
émigré whatever the relationship. As to the latter question,
she would gladly take whatever Hartley wished to pay.

Jeanne was well aware that she was working for a
smaller wage than Hartley would have paid a Scotswoman.
But she had learned a very valuable lesson in the last ten
years. Life could be distilled to its basic elements. As long
as she was warm, dry, and had a little food, she was content. Anything more was superfluous.

Slowly, she removed her clothing, hanging each garment inside the small armoire. She was careful with her
three dresses, a legacy from a fellow émigré who had been
grateful for Jeanne's tending of her sick child.

Her fingers smoothed the fine embroidery stitches
adorning the top of the collar of one garment. As a child,
she'd been punished for her stitches. Every time she'd
taken needle to fabric, the result had been a disaster. One
of her more inventive—and kind—governesses had only
smiled and said that the tiny little spots of blood adorning
her needlework appeared like small flowers. Only later,

and quite accidentally, the same governess determined that she couldn't see well enough to sew.

But Mademoiselle Danielle had disappeared just like a succession of governesses, none of whom could adhere to her father's severe requirements that she be educated like a Jesuit while being as charming as a courtesan. The jeweler summoned by her governess had likewise been banished by her father, the glasses Jeanne needed to see properly to be taken out only when there were no visitors to their home and no chance of anyone seeing her wearing them.

Heaven forbid that the daughter of the Comte du Marchand have any flaws.

Donning her nightgown, she removed her glasses once more and washed her face and hands. Sitting on the edge of the bed, she prepared for sleep. Her ritual was one she'd begun at the Convent of Sacré-Coeur. There, the nuns had expected obedience, some outward manifestation of her inner faith. They could not know, of course, that she had none left. But she'd pretended, just in case curious eyes were looking at her through the grille set in the middle of the thick oak door. Now she folded her hands in front of her, her lips resting at her fingertips. Then she breathed her prayer in an inaudible whisper.

Please, let me die tonight. Let my heart cease beating, and my breath still. Please, do not let me see the dawn.

Tonight, however, the imploration did not come as quickly or as easily as a day ago.

She knew that there would come a time when she would be called upon to face the consequences of her actions. There would be no mercy for her, no explanation that she could possibly make, nothing that she could say that would expiate her guilt. But she'd not expected that day to be this one or the judgment to be from the one man she'd always loved.

If she were a more courageous woman, she'd march

down the stairs at this moment and ask permission to address Douglas in private. She would tell him of those months when she waited for him and he never came, and how cowardly she became. She would confess, more completely than she ever had to a single soul, how much she regretted what happened next.

Not even God could ever truly forgive her. But it might be a relief to have it over, to simply say the words to Douglas.

I am guilty of murder.

Chapter 3

D ouglas took leave from his host with less haste than he desired but probably more than was polite. The longer he listened to Hartley, the more aggravating the other man became, and when Hartley's comments returned to Jeanne, Douglas found himself growing even more annoyed. By the end of the night he was envisioning planting his fist squarely into Hartley's nose.

He dismissed his carriage, choosing instead to walk home on this damp and foggy night. He needed time to think, but before he turned the corner, Douglas glanced back at Hartley's home. A prosperous three-story brick structure, it appeared inviting with its lighted windows glowing yellow against the night.

His gaze lifted to the third floor. She was there, readying herself for bed, no doubt. Or sitting at her charge's bedside. Were those the duties of a governess? Or did she relinquish the care of the child to a nurse and dismissed all thought of him until morning? He realized his knowledge of governesses was paltry.

When he'd thought of Jeanne, it was either with irrita-

25

tion or sadness—irritation that Fate had taken her far from his punishment, and sadness that he'd been such a fool in the first place.

Now, however, he felt only hatred, an emotion so strong that it energized him. He wanted to retrace his path to Hartley's door, demand entrance, and push his way past the manservant. He would make his way up three flights of stairs to her room. She would stand in front of him as she had earlier, attired in her modest blue dress, her head bowed, her gaze on the floor. A different creature, in so many ways, from the girl he'd known.

His imagination so wanted the encounter with her that he could feel his breath grow tight at the thought of seeing her again.

Deliberately, he pushed away the memories of those earlier days. He would not recall that afternoon in the conservatory when her laughter had been a backdrop to the rainy day. Or that morning when she had lain upon a knoll with her hair spread out over the grass. He'd leaned over her with a daffodil held in his hand, tickling her chin. She'd responded by granting him a kiss for every brush of the flower's petals.

Those recollections were of a different woman, a different place. He was not the same person he had been in Paris. And Jeanne? How could he have loved someone so deeply and yet been so blind to her character?

The mist on his face was almost suffocating, the air felt so thick that he could barely breathe.

The idea of a confrontation was foolish. Besides, perhaps she wouldn't sleep alone in her third-floor room after all. Douglas wouldn't be unduly surprised if she'd already consented to be Hartley's mistress. She'd proven to be a survivor, perhaps she was also an opportunist.

The rear lanterns on his carriage glowed yellow, a nimbus of light for him to follow in the fine mist. His hair was damp, his coat sparkled with a thousand tiny droplets, yet he still stood there staring at the third-floor light. In Paris he'd done the same, watching the great house of the Comte du Marchand, waiting for dawn and Jeanne. When her signal came, he would meet her at the garden gate.

Now, determinedly, he turned and walked away.

The city matched his mood tonight, everything shuttered and silent. Lantern light would periodically pierce the darkness, but nothing could lighten the gloom for long. Edinburgh sometimes possessed a brooding quality, hunched beneath a dark, cloud-filled sky. Above all, there was the hint of history, as if these hills and narrow cobbled streets had been witness to countless human acts, some kind and compassionate, others malevolent and predatory. Edinburgh's past was replete with a history of plotting and planning. Men had died, monarchs had fallen, and fortunes had been lost or won as a result.

At night, sound carried so well that Douglas could almost imagine the slide of a dirk from its sheath or whispers in the darkness from a hundred furtive meetings, a thousand promises. There were rumors that there was a city beneath the city, whole streets where people lived out their lives in darkness and relative safety. The poor of Edinburgh were periodically rounded up and shunted to another section of the city, and some had, it was said, taken refuge in these places far from sunlight and free from taxes.

In less than fifteen minutes he was on Queen's Place. His red brick home was adorned with a white door and black shutters. Tall windows lined the first and second floors, only two of them now lit by candlelight. The third floor was embellished with half-moon windows that looked like drooping eyelids. On the roof were eight chimneys, one of them still sending tendrils of white smoke into the dark and cloud-filled night sky.

Douglas noted with some satisfaction that his home was much larger than Hartley's.

The MacRae brothers were wealthier and more influential than they had ever been. And happier? A question his brother Alisdair had asked him not that many weeks ago. Douglas had responded with a nod, introspection making him impatient. He disliked searching the contents of his soul. There were too many dark corners there to make him entirely comfortable with the task.

He waved to his coachman standing beside the curb and Stephens nodded. A moment later, the carriage was turning the corner and heading for the stables.

As he reached for the door handle, it opened in front of him. His majordomo, attired in his severe black, smiled at him and then stood aside, holding the door ajar.

"Good evening, sir."

"I thought I told you that you needn't wait up for me."

Lassiter merely smiled and closed the door behind Douglas, moving with the lithe grace of a man half his age.

"It's a horrible night outside, sir," he said. "I almost think myself home in London."

"At least it's easier to understand the English," Douglas offered. He spoke French and German and a smattering of Chinese, but occasionally the Scots dialect was more than even he could handle. Unlike his older brothers, he'd never learned Gaelic, and there were times when he felt the lack.

"Did you have an enjoyable evening, sir?"

"I had an interesting one, Lassiter. The past came back to haunt me. And you?" he asked, smiling a little. He doubted he would receive an answer. His majordomo refused any attempt at democratization of their relative positions. Lassiter would not bend from what he thought his place. Tonight, however, he surprised Douglas by replying.

"I began reading this evening after you left, sir. A most

elevating book of verse. May I compliment you on your library?"

"Most of the credit goes to my brother James," Douglas said.

"Then if you will convey my thanks as well to him, sir. I must commend him on his most eclectic taste."

He nodded, allowing Lassiter to help him off with his coat.

A spiraling mahogany staircase dominated the foyer of his home. It shot up to the second floor, then divided and wrapped around itself before reaching the third.

The first floor was comprised of the public rooms: his library, the parlor, a more intimate morning room, a large dining room that he used for entertaining, a comfortably appointed kitchen that was well ventilated to prevent the smells of cooking from reaching his guests, and various other chambers he rarely used. The bedroom suites as well as two guest rooms occupied most of the second floor. The third floor was given over to seven chambers for the servants, while above the stable were more quarters for the coachman and grooms.

A bigger home than he needed, possibly, but he'd planned for a larger family one day. Time, however, was passing, and he was no closer to making that nebulous thought a reality than he had been ten years earlier.

Douglas walked into his library, Lassiter following. In a matter of moments, the older man had the fire lit. Lassiter had many talents, all of them honed in service.

"Can I get you a glass of port, sir?" Lassiter asked.

Douglas glanced over at the sideboard and the five crystal decanters with their distinctive silver tops etched with the MacRae crest. His possessions revealed that he was a prosperous man. He was steward of the MacRae fortune in Edinburgh but his personal share of it made him wealthy enough that he'd never have to worry about an income. In addition to this Edinburgh home, he owned a small farm in the country, three ships, and a share in a racing stable. A fortune not yet equal to that of the du Marchands, but he was still young.

Lassiter evidently took his silence for assent, because he poured him a glass and returned to his side. Douglas took it with a smile.

"Go back to bed, Lassiter. I don't need coddling."

His majordomo studied him with a look that indicated he doubted Douglas's words.

"I can do very well on my own."

"But you don't have to, sir," Lassiter said. The man was English but had the obstinacy of a Scot. An instant later, obviously recognizing that he'd lost this particular battle, the old man bowed. "If you're certain, sir."

"I am."

Douglas took a sip of the port, watched as Lassiter left the room. A moment later he left as well, loosening his cravat as he walked into his library. Putting his glass down on the surface of the desk, he fumbled with the tinderbox, lighting a candle. The flickering light was not enough illumination to read, but he had entered the room only for contemplation.

He returned to the doorway, shutting the door behind him, hearing it close with a satisfying click, a sound as reassuring as a lock. He didn't employ many servants, but those who worked for him knew that his need for privacy was absolute. He was unquestionably the master in his own home.

Until this moment.

The memory of Jeanne floated into the room behind him, an incorporeal spirit that studied him with solemn gray eyes.

"What do you wish of me?"

He smiled at his own whimsy. She would never stand

before him so docilely. Her eyes would flash fire, and she'd demand to know why he'd summoned her. But then, ten years stretched between their last meeting and tonight. She'd been a wealthy nobleman's daughter the last time he'd seen her. Now she was a governess and the child standing beside her had possessed more animation.

Drawing open the drapes, he stared out at Edinburgh. The city was never truly quiet, but had a rhythm for both day and night. In the area in which he lived, carriages were encouraged not to travel after a certain hour, and straw was laid down on the road to muffle the sound of their wheels. Wealth brought comfort, including a good night's sleep.

The du Marchand wealth was legendary. What had happened in the intervening years? A story repeated a thousand times, no doubt. The last few years in France had been difficult for aristocrats.

He braced his hands on either side of the window, feeling the stiffness in his shoulders. Anger still coursed through his body. He looked into the night is if his eyes could see past the houses and the large church on the corner directly into her window.

Jeanne. Without a lot of prodding his thoughts could transport themselves back all those years ago to Paris. He'd been seventeen years old, a boy who'd fallen so desperately in love that food, sleep, even air was unnecessary to him. All he needed was the sight of Jeanne. Yet even his love hadn't been enough, had it?

He remembered the moment he'd come to tell her that his parents had arrived from Nova Scotia. He'd wanted her to meet them, prior to his asking the Comte for her hand in marriage.

Instead of Jeanne, he'd been greeted by a tall, slender woman with dark red hair. Justine.

"She isn't here," Justine said, her patrician good looks almost haughty in the dusk light.

"What do you mean, she isn't here? She has to be."

"Arrogant young whelp, aren't you?" Justine smiled at him through the iron grille of the gate. It was not a warm smile, and the amusement it revealed was no doubt at his expense.

"Where is she, Justine?" He'd held his breath for her reply, anxious in a way that he couldn't quite define.

"She won't see you," she said, her answer clipped and disinterested.

"Didn't she leave word?"

She'd only shaken her head.

"No note, no message?"

Justine only laughed. "And what message might that be, young sir? That she has nothing but love for you? That the future looks bright? You know such things are not for the two of you."

"Because I'm not French?" He'd been studying at the Sorbonne for two years, long enough that his command of the language had increased as well as his understanding of the French antipathy for anything foreign. The residents of Paris simply felt that they were superior to the rest of the world. "My family is from Nova Scotia," he'd offered, but Justine had only laughed.

"I don't care where your family is from, you stupid boy. You're not an equal in rank to Jeanne du Marchand. Not now, not ever."

He'd plunged his hands into his pockets and came up with several coins, which he thrust in Justine's direction.

"Tell me where she's gone," he said, but his demands were only met with that enigmatic smile and Justine's cool look.

"It's not worth my life to tell you, young sir. Nor does she wish to see you."

"I'd prefer to hear that from her."

"You don't believe me?" She'd given him an amused

look, one that made him decidedly uncomfortable. As if she knew a secret that he should have known.

"The Comte can have you taken away," she said. "And no one will ever see you again. Do you wish that?"

"I want to see Jeanne. I'll stay here until she comes out."

How stubborn he'd been and how idiotically intoxicated with love.

"She isn't even here," Justine said finally. "She's left Paris altogether."

He had a leaden feeling in his stomach, and the almost pitying look on her face told him she might be telling the truth.

"Where has she gone?" He'd asked the question slowly, as if to prepare himself for the answer.

Justine looked back at the house and then at him as if weighing her words. Finally, she spoke again. "I've been told to tell you that she's been sent home to Vallans. She's with child, and in disgrace."

Shock had stripped him of any words.

"She'll not see you again, young sir. The Comte du Marchand will see to that. Besides, she doesn't want anything to do with you. You've caused her nothing but pain."

Justine turned away from the iron gate, picked up her skirts, and began to walk back to the house.

"Is there nothing you can do?" he'd called out.

Justine turned and smiled at him again, a genuinely amused expression that should have warned him as to her next words. "She'll never return to Paris, young sir. After the child comes, she'll have a new life."

He'd stood in the rain for three hours, staring through the iron grille to the window where Jeanne used to signal to him. The curtains were drawn and there was no movement. No smiling face, no wave of a hand. Nothing. He slowly began to believe that she had truly left Paris—and him.

Only when the afternoon turned to night did he move away.

Now Douglas moved to his chair, sat heavily, and propped a boot on the corner of his desk. His mind wasn't occupied with the stack of papers he'd brought from his office. He would look over the agreement to purchase land in London in the morning. Memory still held him in its grasp.

She was a governess now, attired in clothing her servants wouldn't have worn a decade ago. It wasn't enough that she'd only looked at him once and then stared intently at the floor. He wanted her to suffer. Not for anything she'd done to him, but for a greater sin.

Hartley's lascivious intent might ruin his plans. *She's a fine morsel.* The words rankled, as did the lecherous tone in which they were uttered. Damn Hartley.

Douglas walked out of the library, through the darkened house, and to the back. The coachman's quarters were located above the stable. Douglas mounted the steps and knocked on the door, happy to see that Stephens hadn't begun undressing.

"Forgive me for disturbing you," he said, a comment that made his coachman smile.

"It's no problem, sir."

"I have an errand for one of the stable boys," he said. "I want this sent to Captain Manning," he added, and handed him the address.

"I'll send him right away, sir."

As he returned to the house, Douglas realized that this plan might well prove to be unwise. He had expunged Jeanne du Marchand from his life years ago. Now he should simply ignore the fact that he'd seen her, and pretend that this evening had never happened.

But he wasn't going to do that. Wise or not, he was going to take advantage of this opportunity to avenge an act of cruelty and horror.

Chapter 4

∽∾∿

In her sleep Jeanne moaned, a slight and almost inaudible protest. She tasted soot in her throat as her night-dimmed mind recalled Vallans. Not as it had been, a majestic sunlit chateau in a sweeping vista of valley, but as it had become. In her dream, she recalled the ruins of some of Vallans' chimneys, standing stark on the landscape like stolid brick giants. Below the ground, visible through gaping holes in the earth, were the dungeons and tunnels of the chateau, curiously untouched.

Gone were the tapestries that had dated back centuries, the gallery of paintings of generations of du Marchands, all the books in the great library as well as the stained-glass windows depicting the stages of the cross, and the chapel itself with its gold altar appointments.

The scene abruptly changed, as if her dream-shrouded mind could not bear the sight of such ruin. Vallans suddenly commanded the night with its hundreds of candles and lanterns. She and Douglas were there, dancing in the ballroom, their smiles intent as they gazed on each other, oblivious to the majesty around them.

Awareness came to Jeanne as she surfaced from the dream. She blinked open her eyes. Gradually, her gaze fixed on the open window. The dawn sky over Edinburgh was now a tapestry of yellow, pink, and gold hues. A new day, a new beginning.

Jeanne realized she didn't particularly want a new beginning. Instead, she wanted to exist the way she'd been living during the past ten years, without any emotion at all. But it was too late for that, wasn't it? She'd seen Douglas, and the memories would not stop flooding into her mind.

Walking to the window, she felt a heaviness that came from a disturbed night of sleep, and the effort to keep the past at bay. Standing silent, clad in her night rail, her hair arranged in one thick braid, Jeanne stared out at the view she'd seen every morning for three months. Below her were four residential streets and a square formed by their intersection. There was no traffic this early, no wagons carrying provisions to the prosperous homes, no barrow girls or street vendors. But all too soon there would be signs of life on even this affluent street.

Jeanne breathed in the scent of the morning. Flowers had been planted throughout the square, and they were blossoming now, large scarlet and yellow blooms tipping their heads gently in the breeze that swept down from the hills.

Below her, a bird landed on the windowsill and she smiled at its presence. The nine years of her imprisonment in the convent had taught her to take joy in the small things in life—a bird's song, a rainbow, a tree, the sight of a flower in bud, the simple majesty of a dawn sky.

Because she was considered an influence to be avoided, she was kept segregated in a tiny cell with one high window far away from the main structure of the convent. Her days were to be spent in contemplating her sins. On those rare occasions when she was allowed in the company of others she was ignored; an island of silence surrounded her. Talk was prohibited and even smiles were forbidden, punishment being meted out for laughter or lightheartedness as easily as for more severe infractions.

Jeanne had learned strength, however, just when she was expected to be weak. She'd begun to understand that the good sisters of Sacré Coeur were wrong. She was not that great a sinner—if so, she would have taken her own life and ended her misery. But hope, strained and tested all these years, still existed somewhere in her mind and heart.

Somehow, she would get through today and then tomorrow, and a hundred days after that, and however many God decreed she would live.

The bird flew away in a flurry of feathers. Her gaze followed him, traveling to the rooftops that dotted the skyline. Edinburgh was a prosperous city, one in which there always seemed to be some building occurring. Whole sections of the city were undergoing a transformation.

Just as she had.

She turned away from the window. Soon her charge would be up and about, eager to chatter about his dreams of the night before, and curious about his coming lessons. Once, she'd felt the same enthusiasm for the day, before that morning nearly ten years ago.

Suddenly another memory jarred her.

"Are you happy?" The memory of that question speared her, coming as it did in Douglas's voice.

"Unimaginably," she'd answered. She'd been naked, covered only in a blanket and the summer night. But she'd never felt shame with him, never hid herself from his view. Her reward for such courage had been Douglas's kisses all over her body from her ankles to her elbows and delightful places in between.

"We'll always be happy," he said, a promise that

sounded so determined that it must surely come true.

"Will we?" she'd teased. She had kissed him for his optimism, and for long moments they'd simply been lost in each other.

They had been so innocent, so enchanted in loving each other, so trusting of the world. Douglas was only a year older than she. Had the last decade changed him? Was he still as determinedly optimistic or had life taught him that it was better to be cautious than hopeful?

The man she'd seen the night before had been startlingly attractive, even more so than the boy. He'd had an aura of power, a commanding presence that might be intimidating to many. But not her. What could any person, circumstance, or occasion do to her that the Comte du Marchand and God had not already done?

She moved to stand in front of the wardrobe. The newest styles were evident in Edinburgh—one had only to stroll along the street to realize that the residents of the city were surprisingly cosmopolitan. But she was a governess and not expected to be fashionable. It was enough that her attire was clean and neat, and didn't attract the attention of Robert Hartley.

Once, she'd required the services of two maids to dress in the morning, but for nine years she'd worn only a plain smock, and she'd gradually become used to the simpler style of garment. The spoiled and somewhat willful girl who'd cozened her father into countless purchases at the modistes and mantua maker was gone. Today, she selected a plain dark green dress, adorned with a simple fringe of lace around the high neck.

She arranged her hair into a simple bun, finished the style by winding a long ivory-handled pin into it. Once, she'd worn her hair loose in full curls that fell to her shoulders. Unless she was to appear at court with her father, it was left unpowdered. When she first arrived at the convent they'd cut her hair to an inch around her scalp, ridding her, they said, of any vanity about her appearance. Over the past two years they'd allowed it to grow, perhaps to cut it as punishment again should she not adhere to some rule.

Studying herself in the mirror, she could see the effect of a troubled night on her appearance. Her gray eyes—fog eyes, Douglas had once teased—looked haunted. Her face was pale, her lips thinned.

She surveyed herself with the critical gaze of Marie-Thérèse, thinking that the nun could find no fault in her appearance. There was nothing in her dress that was out of place. The apron was spotless and pinned correctly. The three-quarter-length sleeves had a modest row of lace adorning them but nothing that might be considered showy. A matching lace fichu was tucked into her bodice and the stomacher was of the same fabric as her bodice and skirt.

Your outward appearance must match the piety of your soul. The voice belonged to Marie-Thérèse, who saw nothing good in the young girl sent in disgrace to the convent. It had been the nun's duty to strip all thoughts of licentiousness from her, to reform Jeanne's character.

How foolish to concern herself with how she looked. The only person to see her today would be Davis. If Robert Hartley sought her out, perhaps it was just as well that she appeared haggard and exhausted.

She had only one pair of earrings, a small gold set that had once belonged to a young girl she'd nursed across the Channel. As she put them on, the past flooded through her senses once again.

Douglas was kissing her, making growling sounds in his throat. She giggled and rolled toward him, her hair falling over his face.

"What are you doing?" she asked, tickling him with the ends of her hair.

"Nibbling on you, of course," he said, smiling.

"There are more substantial foods in the basket," she said, pointing to the lunch she'd brought with her. Today they'd escaped to the corner of the garden where no one could see them. The area sloped down to the river, and was secluded with several mature weeping willow trees.

"Nothing is more substantial than what I feel for you, Jeanne," Douglas said solemnly, his blue eyes intent.

The moment was precious to her, one of those memories that had the power to bring a mist of tears to her eyes. In his gaze had been love, permanency, and promise.

Forgive me, my love.

The words trembled on her lips. For the first time in a very long time Jeanne wished there were an altar in her room. She would have knelt and asked forgiveness for her very great sin. Not for loving Douglas or bearing a child but for what had happened next.

The image came to her again, as it did every day, of a very small grave mounded high with rotting leaves and surrounded by trees whose sole purpose seemed to keep out the sunlight. In her memory no birds sang. The wind didn't blow. All she could recall was the sight of that tiny mound and tasting tears. At that moment, she'd died inside.

Until last night, when she'd seen Douglas, she hadn't truly felt alive. Now what she felt was uncomfortably painful and truly frightening.

How was she to bear it?

Chapter 5

A soft knock announced the presence of Davis. Jeanne forced a smile to her face and opened the door. Her charge stood in front of her, already dressed, his normally pale face brightened with color.

"Papa has come to join us for breakfast, miss. Are you ready?"

She opened the door farther to reveal Robert Hartley standing there. Her employer smiled amiably at her, the expression revealing too many teeth.

Grabbing her shawl, she walked from the room, carefully skirting Hartley. This situation must be addressed, she realized with a sinking feeling, and soon.

"You're looking very well this morning, Jeanne," Hartley said.

"Thank you, sir," she said, easily maintaining the pose of dutiful employee as they headed for the staircase. Perhaps the Convent of Sacré-Coeur had readied her for a life of servitude. She no longer resented giving obeisance to another person or entity. Instead, she'd discovered that the freedom of her mind was more important than that of her body.

41

They walked down the stairs and into the dining room now set for breakfast. She neither made eye contact with the footmen nor appeared to notice them, and they studiously ignored her.

"You're not as thin as you were when you first came to us," Hartley said, as a footman pulled out a chair.

She smiled, and sat, thinking that starvation was a cruel diet. The journey from Vallans to the coast, a journey of a few hundred miles, had been a difficult one. There had been days at a time when there hadn't been anything to eat. But she'd concentrated, not on the privations, but on the ultimate goal—that of leaving France.

Strangely, she no longer felt French. Instead, she felt alienated, a woman without allegiance to any culture but where she lived at the moment. The Scots were just as amenable as any other group.

While they were not an entirely dour people, Jeanne wasn't certain the Scots wholeheartedly embraced the concept of good fortune. They lived almost as if they expected the inevitable tribulations and trials of life but intended to celebrate until the next misfortune arrived. Not a bad philosophy, all in all.

Davis sat, arranged his napkin. Jeanne smiled with approval, and hoped that Hartley would notice his son's earnest expression.

In a great many ways, the child reminded Jeanne of herself. She, too, had been in awe of her father and had wanted his approval. Yet nothing she could do was ever quite good enough. She'd recited a hundred poems, memorized a dozen speeches. She'd studied the Comte's writings and learned everything she could about the du Marchand name only to please him.

Now she looked at Robert Hartley and wondered if his cruelty was the equal of her father's.

The maid who served them was a young girl freshly imported from the countryside. She was awkward in her movements, as if she'd not yet become accustomed to her duties and the confinement of the Hartley home. The entire house was filled with bric-a-brac on every conceivable surface, as if Mrs. Hartley wanted to demonstrate her husband's wealth by purchasing any number of porcelain items and displaying them solely for the maids to dust. Even this family dining room was not exempt from shepherdesses, urns, and Chinese vases.

Art was cheap in Scotland, as she suspected it was as well in England. Hundreds of people were escaping from France with their possessions in bags or trunks and they used these to finance their new life.

There had been nothing left of Jeanne's past to bring with her.

Davis sat beside her quietly, the child's quiet happiness at having his father present at this meal evident even to Jeanne. To his credit, Hartley spoke to his son often, inquiring as to his studies.

The sun was streaming into the dining room, adding light to the otherwise dark and depressing furniture. Mrs. Hartley, or perhaps her husband, preferred subdued colors, shades that were inviting in candlelight but seemed too oppressive in the daytime.

"I have never seen your guest before last night," she said, toying with her silverware.

Hartley looked startled at her comment. "But then you wouldn't have, would you? My friends do not visit the nursery."

It was a rebuff, but she only smiled down at her plate. The time had passed for her to be affected by criticism.

"Does he live in Edinburgh?"

Irritation spread across his face as she raised her head and smiled directly at him. He smiled back, no doubt thinking her effort flirtatious.

"Why the interest in Douglas MacRae?"

She hadn't heard his name spoken aloud in years. Tightening her hand on her cup, Jeanne forced her smile to remain in place. "He reminds me of someone I knew in France," she said softly.

"You must learn that that life is over, Jeanne. There is nothing in France that you would recognize now."

Jeanne knew that better than he, but she kept her smile moored in place and only nodded. Hartley thought himself an arbiter of all manner of things. Such an inflated sense of self was irritating at times and a decided weakness. A lesson the nuns at Sacré-Coeur had unwittingly taught her.

"He's actually someone with whom I do business," he said, evidently attempting to soften his earlier words.

She smiled, rewarding him for his concession, and he responded with another toothy grin and a glance at her bosom.

"He's a very wealthy young man," Hartley said.

"Is he?"

She didn't care about his wealth. Instead, she wanted to know if Douglas was married, if the years had changed him, all personal questions she couldn't ask.

If anything, she should fear Douglas. How odd that Hartley, who had the power to make her existence miserable, could not incite the least spark of trepidation in her, while the man she'd adored inspired caution.

Loving Douglas had been the single most rebellious act of her life. Everything she had been, and everything she had done, and everything that had happened to her began in those three months.

Wasn't that enough of a reason to fear him?

"We were speaking of the Revolution last night," Hartley said.

She glanced over at him, surprised. "Were you?"

"A terrible circumstance. I cannot help but wonder why you left France, Jeanne. Are you an aristocrat?"

Davis and his father looked at her, waiting for her to speak.

"I've spent the past nine years of my life in a convent," she said quietly, as much of an answer that she was going to give him.

Hartley smiled, a particularly lascivious grin. "Do you miss the religious life?"

She shook her head, thinking that there were few things about it that she would miss. Yet the convent had taught her a new world, one of serenity and timelessness. She'd knelt in the dirt and weeded the garden, a penance that had become a pleasure. She was forbidden to speak, even to the sister who was assigned to watch over her. Instead, she cultivated her friends among the ladybugs and the fat caterpillars. Sometimes, on those rare occasions when she was left alone, she would let one of the bugs crawl to the end of her finger, bringing it up to her nose so that she might address her tiny companion.

"And what are you doing today?" she'd asked one pale green centipede. "Are you racing toward the carrots? You had best not do very much damage or we shall all be in trouble." Carefully, she would lower him to hide behind a frond and hoped that Fate would grant him a longer life than most centipedes were given.

She learned to find serenity within herself. Instead of concentrating on God or her sins during those interminable hours of meditation, she listened to the sound of her breathing. She felt the blood racing through her body and attempted to slow it, measured her heartbeats and calmed them until she'd achieved a curious kind of tranquillity.

How odd that those lessons were of value now. She knew that outwardly she appeared serene, despite the inward chaos of her thoughts.

"What are your plans for this morning, Davis?" Hartley asked, turning to his son.

The child looked first to Jeanne, and at her nod answered his father. "We're going to visit Mama first, sir. Then we have to study about the Romans."

"A very adventuresome morning, indeed." Hartley smiled. "Perhaps after lunch you might spare some time for an audience?" he said to Jeanne. "Around three?"

Unfortunately, she had a very good idea of the topic for this meeting. All during the act of buttering his bread and eating his oatmeal, he'd not ceased staring at her breasts.

Very well, it was time to confront Robert Hartley.

"I just thought I might consult with you on Davis's reading material," he said, smiling his toothy grin. "He cannot be allowed to remain ignorant of the world."

A little ignorance of the world might be a kindness done to the child, a comment Jeanne wisely did not voice.

Captain Manning didn't appear until well after dawn. Douglas was up and addressing his correspondence when the man was announced by Lassiter. He stood at the captain's arrival, waited until his guest was seated, and ordered breakfast to be served in his library.

"Are you still drinking cocoa in the morning, Alan?" he asked.

The older man nodded. "I don't give a whit if it stains my wooden teeth," he admitted.

A tap on the door interrupted them. Douglas called out a greeting and a young maid entered, laden with a large tray filled with a pot, two cups and saucers, and a selection of jams, toast, sausages, and jugged kippers, their tails tied together with a string. Douglas watched as she placed the tray on his desk, and thanked her.

"I need your help," he said.

Alan Manning had been a friend for nearly eight years. In fact, it was Manning who'd brought the news to Gilmuir that the flagship of the MacRae fleet had been lost at sea, knowledge that Douglas still found difficult to accept even seven years later. In his mind, his parents had been rescued and were alive somewhere. As long as they were together, Douglas knew they would survive.

Manning hadn't retired from the sea as Douglas had, but he'd recently married and for that reason had remained in Edinburgh a few weeks longer than normal. In addition, he was considering employment with the MacRaes. By agreeing to sail one of the MacRae vessels, he would forgo a greater portion of wealth at the end of each voyage, but he would also have less risk. A ship was an expensive venture. Each time a sail had to be mended, a mast repaired, or an anchor replaced, the cost was subtracted from the owner's profits. If a man owned the ship he captained, he could find himself losing a great deal of money if a voyage was plagued with bad weather or a careless crew.

"I need a favor," he said, after handing Manning a cup of his beloved cocoa. "Do you have someone you could spare? Someone you trust, who could also remain discreet?"

Captain Manning didn't say anything, but his eyes were carefully guarded. "I might. Why?"

"I want someone watched. A woman."

Manning remained silent.

"Someone from my past," Douglas added.

The captain took a sip of chocolate and smiled, closing his eyes to better savor the bitter brew. "Why not simply take her under your protection?" he asked when he opened his eyes again.

Douglas smiled. "I don't want that sort of arrangement. I just want to be apprised of her movements in case she decides to leave Edinburgh."

One eyebrow rose, but Douglas didn't answer the unvoiced question.

"Can you spare someone?"

"Where does she live?"

Douglas gave him the address, watched the second eyebrow join the first, and wondered exactly how much information he would have to impart before Manning agreed to his request.

After a moment of contemplation, he stood and walked to the far side of the room to a tall, glass-fronted cabinet. He'd never thought himself a man who believed in sentimentality, for all that he came from a family that valued ceremony and history. But his daughter had proven that assumption wrong.

Douglas opened the glass door of the cabinet and removed a tiny length of gold chain, so short that it didn't reach from the base to the end of his thumb. Walking back to the desk, he handed it to Manning.

"My brother Hamish and his wife Mary and I once rescued an infant. She was so small and malnourished that this chain could wrap around her wrist. We used it to measure her progress during the first few weeks. Most of the time we didn't know if she would live or die."

Manning stretched the chain between both hands, frowning down at it.

"My sister-in-law has a reputation as a healer, and it's because of her, I think, that Margaret survived."

"Margaret?" Manning asked, obviously surprised.

"Yes," Douglas said. He returned to the chair. "I became determined that she would never know that her mother had abandoned her."

"And the woman you want me to watch is her mother," Manning guessed.

"No," Douglas said quickly. "Not her mother. She might

have given birth to Margaret, but she never mothered her. Mary did that."

"So I'm to watch her? A protective impulse, Douglas."

"At one time I wanted to kill her," he confessed to Manning. "If she'd stood in front of me, I would have done it despite witnesses or circumstances."

"I trust time has mellowed you somewhat," Manning said.

"Somewhat," Douglas said wryly. "Up until now I've constructed a careful world for Margaret and nothing has interfered with it."

"And you think she will?"

"I don't think Jeanne du Marchand has ever spared a thought for her child."

"What if she leaves? Is my man supposed to stop her?"

"No, just let me know."

The captain shook his head, the gesture one of disapproval.

Douglas didn't care. Perhaps he had not yet formulated a plan in regards to Jeanne but he didn't want her to leave Edinburgh.

He stood, picking up the length of chain from the captain and returning it to the display case.

Margaret loved all the mementos of her early life and wanted a tale told of each item he'd saved over the years. It was she who had added to the store of treasures in the last few years. Resting on the bottom shelf were several items she'd unearthed at Gilmuir, or thought she'd outgrown. The tiny doll sitting on the bottom shelf was an example. The painted face had long since faded, and the legs and arms were loose and needed to be restuffed. But Margaret could not bear to have the doll thrown away.

Sometimes, she'd retrieve her and ask him to tell a story about when he'd first bought the doll. He'd fabricated a great many stories for his daughter, and the greatest of these had been the lie about her birth. But she would never know that the one woman who should have loved her had tossed her away.

This doll was treated with more care than Margaret had been.

Nor would his daughter ever know how foolish her own father was, unable to stop thinking about the woman he hated.

Chapter 6

When she was a child and asked to see her mother, Jeanne was often told that Hélène wasn't feeling well enough for a visit. To the child, Jeanne, the future was uncertain, an amorphous world that never materialized. "Tomorrow, your mother will feel much better. Tomorrow, perhaps she can sit in the sun. Tomorrow, little one, and she'll have breakfast with you. Will that not be fun?"

Tomorrow never came. One day, black ribbons appeared on the door and the servants began wearing black armbands. She and her father followed the priest to the chapel and watched silently as the iron grille to the crypt was unlocked. Inside the magnificently carved mahogany coffin lay her beautiful mother, but Jeanne was not to cry. According to Justine and her father, no tears were to be shed on this most mournful of days. Instead, she was to stand straight and tall and be proud that she was a du Marchand. She wept in her pillow at night, and bathed her eyes with cold water in the morning so that her maid wouldn't rush to tell Justine.

Perhaps because of childhood memories, Jeanne was

diligent about Davis's morning visits to his mother. She stood when breakfast was over, and thanked Hartley, stretching out a hand to her charge.

"We must visit your mother, Davis, before we begin our lessons."

Davis nodded. He was a dutiful child, almost nonde-script in his personality. His brown hair and brown eyes were unremarkable, as was his manner. He was neither gifted in learning nor too slow. Average would be the label Davis would carry all his life, but perhaps it would be safer than being called headstrong, wild, or evil.

The child reminded Jeanne of herself. Not in appear-ance or even in temperament, but in loneliness. Davis adored his mother as Jeanne had hers, and both women struggled to get well. In both cases the reason was the same, illness following childbirth.

They left the dining room together, making their way up the stairs to the second floor. At the door to his mother's room, Jeanne nodded to Davis and the child tapped lightly on the door. A moment later the door creaked open and Barbara, Mrs. Hartley's companion and nurse, greeted them.

"Is Mrs. Hartley well enough for Davis to bid her good morning?" Jeanne asked.

"The mistress had a good night," Barbara said, nodding and stepping aside.

Jeanne and Davis entered the room, Jeanne hesitating at the doorway until her eyes adjusted to the preternatural darkness in the room. Mrs. Hartley had not yet recovered from the birth of her latest child, another son born a month ago. The infant was thriving, being cared for by a wet nurse and nursemaid. If Mrs. Hartley ever visited her baby, Jeanne was unaware of it.

Drawing Davis forward, Jeanne urged the boy to come

and stand beside the bed. She didn't blame Davis for his
reluctance. The chamber was overpowering in its excess,
from the brocaded bedcover and hangings to the Flemish
paintings adorning the walls. Muted colors of burgundy,
emerald, gold, and sapphire assaulted the senses.

"Good morning, Mama," Davis said, sounding faint and
unlike himself. Jeanne squeezed the little boy's hand reassuringly and urged him forward. Davis glanced up at her as
if to gain one last measure of courage before dropping
Jeanne's hand and stepping up to the bed. He pulled back the
bed hanging and smiled into the darkness. "Are you feeling
better this morning?"

The voice that answered him was surprisingly robust.
"Yes, I believe I am. I've been able to eat my breakfast,
which I'm told is a very good sign."

"Did you have toast and jam, Mama? I did, and Cook
trimmed the edges of the bread for me."

"Did she?" Althea Hartley peeped out from behind one
of the bed hangings. Jeanne was startled at the woman's
beauty, as she was each time she saw the woman. Althea
was delicately blond, with a frailty that came partly from
her youth and partly from having become pregnant three
times in the last three years.

"Is your governess taking you for a walk today, pop-
pet?" she asked, glancing at Jeanne with a vague look of
confusion.

Despite the fact that Mrs. Hartley had known her aunt,
she could never seem to remember Jeanne's name, a fact
that didn't disturb her at all. The more anyone knew about
her, the more vulnerable she became. Consequently, she
cultivated an aloofness that kept the rest of the staff at a
distance. The half-life of a governess fit her perfectly. She
was neither part of the staff nor the family.

"Not until after my lessons, Mama."

She pushed back the bed hangings and stared at Jeanne. "You're from France, are you not?"

Jeanne nodded.

"Such atrocities." She glanced at her son, evidently thought better of what she was about to say, and merely shook her head.

It was just as well. What would she have responded? That, yes, there were horrible acts committed in France in the name of freedom. That people, oppressed for decades, had suddenly revolted and cast off their chains and become the masters. She knew how it felt to yearn for freedom. Yet the aristocrats of France, for the most part, had utilized their power with greater discretion, whereas the mobs had no such sensibilities.

She didn't want to talk about what she'd seen, or even what she'd experienced. Those recollections were for dark nights when she felt inclined to pity herself.

Jeanne placed her hand on Davis's head. "Say goodbye to your mother, Davis," she instructed. "Perhaps this afternoon we'll take a walk in the garden."

Where your mother can see you, and perhaps be lured into the sunshine. The thought was unspoken—governesses did not act as counselors or companions. But she met Barbara's eyes over the bed and the older woman nodded.

"That would be lovely, wouldn't it?" Althea asked, subsiding against her pillow. "Perhaps you might be convinced to do a few errands?" She turned and smiled at her companion. "I do so miss Barbara when she's gone."

"Of course, madam," Jeanne said easily and bobbed a small curtsy. An irony of Fate that she had once outranked her employer, that she'd dined with the king and played in the gardens of Versailles. Those days were gone now, set aside as if they'd never been.

"Barbara will tell you what is necessary," Althea said,

her voice trailing off as if she were too weak to complete her thought.

Jeanne took Davis's hand and turned away from the bed, hoping that Althea Hartley soon improved, if not for her sake, then her son's.

Douglas exited his home, heading for his carriage, and halted in appreciation for the scene before him. The square was ablaze with blooms, scarlet, coral, and yellow flowers bobbing in the morning light. The air was crisp, but the temperature promised to be warmer with the sun already brightening the sky.

Work, while always challenging, occasionally paled next to a beautiful day.

Winter in Edinburgh had been a damp, messy affair. Rains had pelted the city for the last two months until the inhabitants of the city had begun to fervently pray for the onset of spring. Today, their petitions looked to be granted.

Soon, the work could begin on Margaret's garden. He'd recently purchased the acreage to the west of his home. A week ago, he'd finished the plans and given them to the son of the man who'd produced miracles at Gilmuir. Ephraim had surrounded the fortress with hedges, softening the lines of the MacRae ancestral home, and creating a strolling garden where once an English fortress had stood. With any luck, his son, Malcolm, would accomplish similar feats of wonder on a terraced Edinburgh hill.

Douglas glanced up at Edinburgh Castle. Even though the structure sat in full view of the sun, there always seemed to be a dark, brooding aura to it. The square, for the most part, was quiet, the serenity interrupted periodically by carriages, but a street away there would be a bustle of activity. He had grown accustomed to the changing flavor of Edinburgh and the varied atmospheres of the city.

His life was different from that of his brothers. They were each, from Alisdair to Hamish, lords of their own domain. If Douglas was master of anything, it was the series of buildings in Leith, the ships he owned, and the countless wagons with the name MACRAE BROTHERS painted on their sides.

He'd not slept at all, but he ignored his fatigue. An hour ago, he'd bade his guest farewell somewhat cheered. Alan Manning had agreed to spare a man to watch the Hartley residence and report back to him periodically.

As Douglas entered his carriage he nodded to Stephens and began making a series of mental notes as to which tasks he wanted to accomplish first. Sitting back against the carriage, he watched the view on the way to Leith, Edinburgh's seaport.

And saw her.

Once again Jeanne was with her charge, the little boy happily walking at her side. She consulted the list in her hand, squinting slightly in the full sun.

Douglas tapped on the roof of the carriage. A moment later the driver's face appeared in the small window built for just such a purpose.

"Yes, sir?" Stephens asked.

"Pull up to the corner and wait."

Stephens closed the window and swerved the carriage out of traffic. Douglas sat back and lowered the curtain slightly so that he might observe without being seen.

For a matter of hours he'd been attempting to reconcile the memories of the Comte's daughter with that of the governess. Jeanne had been unconventional as a girl, challenging all the boundaries she'd been given, much to his delight. The youthful Douglas had been more than eager to help her explore her sensuality and more than willing to ignore any strictures he, too, had been reared to obey. They'd been wild together, headstrong, and too much in love to realize the foolishness of attempting to change society's rules simply because they seemed too restrictive.

All they'd accomplished was to create chaos around them.

He pushed away thoughts of France. Too much had happened since then for any memories, especially fond ones, to still remain. Instead, he sat and watched her, and wondered how evil could look so beautiful.

Chapter 7

J eanne took Davis's hand and together they crossed the street, heading for the shops.

"Where are we going, miss?" he asked.

She consulted her list and recited their errands. "The greengrocers to pick up some vegetables for Cook, the cobbler to pick up your father's boots, and the modistes for Barbara. Then we must have some silverware repaired."

The moment the staff had learned of her errands for Barbara, she'd been given even more tasks. She didn't mind; the day was beautiful and she was glad to be spared any thought of the coming interview with Hartley.

Davis nodded, concentrating on the pattern of bricks below his feet. He was a biddable child, almost too acquiescent. For all that he was the oldest of three brothers, he had little initiative of his own. But perhaps he would grow into it.

She rearranged their errands so that they would go to the greengrocers last. After checking that the silverware was in the bottom of the basket, she took Davis's hand and crossed the street.

Edinburgh in spring was a truly marvelous place. A

bustling city, it had its share of noise—street vendors, carriages, conversation all mingled together. The crisp breeze that blew around the corner was redolent with a perfumed scent, reminding Jeanne of the flower markets of Paris. Every time she'd seen the blooms appear she'd known that spring had come and the damp frigid winter was gone.

This area of King Street was filled with black-lacquered carriages, high-stepping horses, and well-to-do pedestrians engaging each other in conversation. She nodded at the men who tipped their hats to her, charmed with the illusion of being, for a few moments, someone other than she was. For the of time it took to walk the length of King Street, she could have been a prosperous matron of Edinburgh and Davis might have been her child.

And her husband? She pushed the thought of Douglas away, but he returned.

Why had Douglas chosen to live in Edinburgh? What had his life been like? Where had he gone after leaving Paris? Had he seen the rest of the world like he wanted when he was seventeen? All questions for which she had no answers.

She found the goldsmith's shop without any difficulty, since it faced King Street and looked to be very prosperous. CHARLES TALBOT, GOLDSMITH, was etched on the window and on a wooden sign bearing two entwined rings above the door.

A small, tinny-sounding bell rang at their entrance, summoning a man from behind a curtained alcove. His brown hair was tousled, as if he'd threaded his fingers through it. As she watched, he hurriedly dressed in a form-fitting coat. His appearance was rather incongruous, since he was still wearing a red apron. At her look, he glanced down at himself and smiled.

"I apologize," he said, "but my apprentice is out and he would otherwise have greeted you."

"I'm here on an errand for the Hartleys," she said, retrieving the silver from the bottom of the basket. "I've been told that these pieces need to be mended. Can you do the work?"

He took the silverware and examined them one by one with great care.

"I can," he said, when he'd finished studying each piece. "When do you need them returned?"

"Three days? Is that enough time?"

He nodded and smiled, but she noted that his eyes didn't change expression. They remained carefully watchful as if he were naturally distrustful, even of his patrons.

"I'll deliver them to you myself," he promised.

She gave him the Hartley address, and a moment later she and Davis were on their way.

"Where we going now, miss?" Davis asked after they left the shop, the tinny little bell singing them farewell.

She consulted her list, before glancing at his expectant face. "No doubt we'll find someplace to purchase a sweetmeat or two," she said, understanding his eagerness. She had a few coins left over from her first quarter's wages and she'd reward the child's patience with a treat before returning to the house.

"Are you very sure?" he asked breathlessly.

"I'm very sure." She smiled down at him, wondering if he would be such a worrier for the rest of his life. With her free hand she tousled his hair fondly, and smiled at him reassuringly.

"A charming picture," Douglas said.

She should have been warned, somehow. But her thoughts had been free of him for a quarter hour and no premonition had occurred to her. Had she the power to conjure him up from an unspoken wish? If so, she wanted him to vanish just as quickly. A confrontation was unwise and unwelcome.

But Douglas didn't look as if he would vanish at any moment.

He was dressed in a formal suit of clothes, a cravat wound expertly around his throat. He wore no hat, but he carried a walking stick topped with a gold knob.

She'd known the boy who'd studied at the Sorbonne, a questioning mind behind bright and shining blue eyes. The man who faced her was almost a stranger, except that she couldn't forget those months of loving him.

There was something about his half smile, something that made her want to reach out with tremulous fingers and touch the edge of it to see if it was real. Or was it only her imagination once again? Had she only dreamed him here? But the gritty feeling in her eyes proved she hadn't slept well, and Davis's hand in hers was enough to make her believe herself awake.

"Miss du Marchand," he said, bowing slightly.

"Mr. MacRae," she said, only nodding. A deliberate rudeness, but perhaps it would hasten his departure.

In her tiny cell in the convent, she'd often thought of him, the memory of the touch of his lips against her shoulder a nightly benediction. She'd heard his voice in her dreams, and felt his hand on hers in the morning light. No doubt her life would have been easier if she hadn't awakened each day missing him again. But she couldn't bear to banish the memory of him from her mind.

Sometimes it was all she had.

But now he was real, standing before her. Douglas, wearing his most fascinating smile, tender and evocative at once. His eyes tilted down at the corners, giving him an almost slumberous appearance. The skin of his face was pulled tight over his cheekbones, and even this early there was a shadow of beard on his squared chin.

She'd been passionate as a girl, fascinated with his body. "I adore how you look naked," she'd said once, giggling.

He'd rolled with her until she was under him. Using both hands, he speared them into her hair and threaded his fingers through the length of it. She always spent more time after she left him fixing her hair than her clothes, because despite her hairstyle, Douglas would insist upon it being loosened.

"You do, do you? What is it, especially, that you find entrancing?"

"Your shoulders," she said, knowing that the answer surprised him. She reached out one hand and traced a path from the well at the base of his throat along the edge of his shoulders. "They're so broad, so powerful," she said softly. "You don't look as though you could be so tender and sweet."

"Sweet?" He pressed a kiss to the end of her nose. "Is that something you should call a man?"

"Only if he brings me a flower if he hasn't seen me for a day," she said, regarding him seriously. "Or wishes to know the contents of my dreams. Only if he writes me poetry."

His cheeks had darkened, and she knew he was embarrassed at her words.

"What else about me do you love?" he asked, so obviously changing the subject that she smiled.

"Your chest," she said, teasing him. She pressed her hand flat against his chest. Sometimes she forgot how much larger he was than she and that was because of the care he took with her. Never in their loving had he been coarse or rough. She'd believed, fool that she was, that coupling was always done with tenderness.

"A fine day, is it not, Miss du Marchand?" he asked now.

He was going to pretend that they didn't know each other, that they hadn't spent months as lovers, that she hadn't been willing to give up everything she was or had been for him. Or that she hadn't been destroyed when he'd abandoned her.

"Indeed it is," she said, as accomplished at duplicity as he. Or perhaps she was more proficient, since she'd honed her skills at pretense for nine years.

"It doesn't look like it will rain."

"Indeed, it does not," she answered, wishing he would leave.

They had told each other their deepest secrets. She had held him as he shuddered in passion. She had wept on his shoulder and he had wrapped his arms around her, allowing her to express the grief for her mother that no one else had ever wished to hear. They had laughed together, her arms linked around his neck, each of them becoming so weak with amusement that they'd needed the other's support to stand.

"Have you a moment?"

"Regrettably, no." There, her voice sounded as calm as his. But not as forceful. She pressed her fingers against the base of her throat, surprised to find that she felt cold. It was fatigue, no doubt, and not fear.

He took another step forward until he stood entirely too close. To a casual observer they might appear as friends who'd met unexpectedly and were speaking of everyday matters—anything but this pulsing silence that stretched between them, interrupted only by her thoughts.

And memories.

In Paris, when she was young, he greeted her after a separation by tilting her chin up and bending down to kiss her gently on the mouth. She always stood on tiptoe and wrapped her arms around his neck, gloriously happy for the first time that day. For long minutes they would simply stand there, looking at each other, holding each other in the shaded beauty of the garden, the hours and minutes of separation finally ended as they relished being together once again.

Resolutely, she pushed those thoughts away, fingering

the locket at her throat with one hand while Davis held the other.

"I must leave," she said softly, hoping that her voice did not sound as choked to him as it did to her. "We have errands to perform."

He glanced down at Davis, smiling easily. She did not feel as capable of such amusement, or absent fondness. Here she was, standing in front of him for the first time in years, and he acted as if he didn't know her.

Four months escaped from France, three months a servant. Ten years since she'd seen him. Dear God, a lifetime had passed, but it still wasn't long enough.

Bending down, he addressed Davis. "Go and tell my coachman to open the secret door inside my carriage. You'll find some Edinburgh Rock there," Douglas said, referring to the stiff white candy made by kneading syrup by hand while it was cooling. He pointed to where his carriage stood at the corner.

Davis turned and looked at her for permission. She nodded, then watched him race to the vehicle. Abruptly, she wanted to call him back.

"Do you always keep candy in your carriage?" she asked.

"Yes," he said, surprisingly. "My daughter enjoys it."

The sudden pain she felt was as unexpected as his words.

"You have a daughter?"

She held herself so tightly that she thought the breeze might break her in two. So he had married. Life had continued for him, it seemed. She thanked Providence for the startling anger, since it was better than indulging in self-pity.

"I do."

She adjusted the basket on her arm and smiled brilliantly, and falsely, at him.

"Thank you for your kindness to Davis," she said, "but we must finish our errands."

She would have stepped aside had he not reached out and touched her arm. Not on the sleeve, but below the cuff and above the wrist of her glove, exactly where her skin was exposed. The touch of flesh to flesh was so shocking that she halted, staring down at the place where his hand rested.

"Don't touch me, please," she said, feeling as if she might choke on the words. "Please remove your hand."

Please, dear God, please step away. Turn away, leave. Get in your smart carriage and return to your wife. Your child. Leave me before I allow pity to take hold and weep in your arms. Or beg you to love me as you once did.

She lifted her gaze to his. "I must insist," she said, and the miracle was not that she was able to speak the words but that they sounded so distant, so unaffected by his touch.

"Forgive me," he said, removing his hand. "I've been intrusive. But then I'm not Hartley, am I?"

"What do you mean?"

She placed her own hand on the place he'd touched. Her arm still felt warm. She rubbed at the spot, a gesture that did not go unnoticed. His smile turned sardonic.

"Forgive me," he said again. "I only thought to offer you a solution to your dilemma."

"What dilemma might that be, Mr. MacRae?" she asked and then cursed her curiosity.

"Your employer has plans for you that do not include caring for his children."

"What do you mean?"

He hesitated for a moment and then spoke. "If you aren't his mistress now, Miss du Marchand, you soon will be."

"How do you know that?" she asked, startled not only that he was privy to Hartley's intentions but that he would speak them aloud. Evidently, the rash and reckless young man had not disappeared completely.

"Hartley bragged of it."

A shocking answer, and one for which she had no quick rejoinder. But then, she'd been cured of that habit in the convent. Speech was not only restricted, it was forbidden her for many years. She'd grown accustomed to her own thoughts but had lost the skill of conversation.

He did not seem to notice her lack as he waited patiently for her to answer him. She glanced to her right, to see Davis talking with the coachman, one cheek stuffed like a squirrel before winter.

"I escaped France on my own, Mr. MacRae," she finally said, the words evoking too much recall. "I am capable of rebuffing such offers."

"And if that isn't enough?"

"Then I shall endure the situation."

His face abruptly shuttered, the expression in his blue eyes flattened. There was nothing in his look that revealed his thoughts. How adept he'd become at hiding himself, almost as talented at the task as she. "You would consent to be Hartley's mistress?"

"If I must." Would he please leave? She was beginning to tremble, and if they remained there much longer he was certain to notice.

"I have a position," he said, surprising her. "Although not carnal in nature. You're a governess, and I have need of one."

She glanced up at him, studying his face. "Do you?" she asked, feigning disinterest.

"Will you not consider it?"

"Caring for your child?" Was this hell, and she had somehow died in the escape from France? Was this the Almighty's idea of a jest? Or was it, perhaps, one of her innumerable nightmares? No, she could feel her stomach clench and her knees weaken. That never happened in a dream.

Davis was suddenly there, tugging on her hand, pulling her back to her duties. Irritated at herself for so easily falling under the spell of the past, she turned away with no further word.

But he was not done with her, it seemed. He followed her and tapped her on the shoulder peremptorily.

She glanced at him and then away, realizing that she had never seen him angry before. He had only been a lover to her or a friend.

"You haven't answered me, Miss du Marchand."

"I have a position, Mr. MacRae. Thank you, but I believe I'll keep it."

"Even if you must become Hartley's mistress?"

Davis looked at her curiously.

She turned and faced Douglas. "There are worse things than becoming a rich man's mistress," Jeanne said in a low voice. Her gaze was suddenly intent on the cobbled street below her feet. *You never cared what happened to me ten years ago,* the girl she'd been shouted at him. *Why do you now?* The woman, however, wisely restrained her words.

She left him before he could reach out and touch her again. Hearing his footsteps behind her, she gripped Davis's hand tightly and nearly ran down the street.

Douglas MacRae, like France and all its memories, belonged in the past.

Chapter 8

～～◦◦◦～～

Douglas watched Jeanne walk rapidly away, thinking that he was three times a fool.

What had he done?

He was right: She'd changed. She'd become as arrogant as any French aristocrat. *Then I shall endure the situation.*

What the hell did *that* mean?

It was foolish to tell himself that she no longer had the power to elicit any emotion from him, because in the space of a quarter hour he'd felt irritation, anger, and curiosity. Without seeming to try, she'd pierced his self-restraint and proven that his indifference was only a façade.

She disappeared from sight and he found himself wanting to follow her and demand to know why she had stared at him as if she didn't understand his suggestion, foolish as it was.

Despite her arrogance, however, her eyes had looked tired. And her fingers had trembled on the child's shoulder. How old was the little boy? Six? Seven? The age of Hartley's son was none of his concern. Nor should he have resented the child for her casual affection toward him.

Had he lost his mind? Evidently so.

One way she hadn't changed—she was still one of those women who effortlessly attracts attention. Something about her, her stance, her poise, the look in her eyes, some indefinable essence of Jeanne made him want to study her. Her clothing wasn't outlandish; her behavior wasn't overt or brazen. If anything, she looked as if she had tried to minimize herself in her sober green dress and modest touches of lace. The bun at the nape of her neck was a hair-style an older matron might wear.

Yet she still had an odd effect on him, something he would have to guard against.

Why, however, had he offered her a position caring for the very child she'd abandoned? Had he lost all sense he possessed? He didn't want her in his home. He didn't want her in his life at all.

Why, then, this insidious curiosity? Why did he want to know what had happened to her in the ten years since they'd parted?

Halting in the middle of the road, he stared down at his feet, not seeing the cobbles but instead Jeanne du Marchand as she'd appeared only a few moments ago. She was only a pale shadow of the girl she'd been. He didn't see the wagon barreling down on him until the driver shouted, and only then moved swiftly to the other side of the street.

He made his way to his carriage, suspecting that the enigma of Jeanne du Marchand wasn't going to be an easy puzzle to solve. He'd thought himself done with the past. But at the sight of her he was the boy he'd been, innocent, hopeful, viewing the world in a way he never had since.

There was nothing about that time he'd resurrect. The innocence and the hope had been transformed to a disillusionment so deep that it had colored the rest of his life. He should forget she was in Edinburgh, forget he'd ever seen her, forget about ten years ago, and expunge all those memories he evidently still carried with him.

Entering his carriage almost angrily, he tapped on the roof so loud that there was no doubt of his mood.

"To Leith," he told Stephens, determined to purge Jeanne du Marchand from his mind.

The air smelled of soot, nothing like the air of Paris, or the sweet perfume of the Loire valley. Nicholas, Comte du Marchand, scowled at a man who smiled at him and nodded to a woman who decorously turned her head. There were so few individuals with manners left in the world.

Edinburgh did not impress him much. The greatest cities were those in France and the greatest city of all, of course, was Paris.

Since the rabble had overtaken the city, it had lost its magical charm. But he had hopes that there would come a time when reason would return once more to France, and with it the aristocracy.

Hereditary titles had been abolished and the fools in the government had actually declared war on the Austrian portion of the Holy Roman Empire. In addition, they'd arrested the King and his family last year, a hint of the increased radicalism of the government.

The journey to Edinburgh had taken him nearly a month. Nicholas found himself annoyed by the discomforts, and more determined than ever to find his daughter and recoup a small portion of his wealth. He'd learned from Justine that Jeanne was determined to leave France. From the trail he followed, it was evident that she had, indeed, done so. Survival was a du Marchand trait, it seemed.

Once in Edinburgh, however, his quest grew more difficult. Jeanne wasn't with her aunt. Evidently, his sister-in-law had died a year earlier, leaving him the further irritating task of having to search for Jeanne. A modiste, a fellow émigré, had told him that Jeanne had gotten employment. Another person shared the information that he'd given Jeanne a brush that had belonged to his dead wife. Still another told him that she'd given Jeanne a selection of her dresses in payment for caring for her sick daughter. One person led him to another, all of them émigrés and all of them too eager to exchange stories about Paris, or to ask him what he knew of missing relatives and friends.

He masked his irritation and answered as well as he could. In payment for his days of patience and hard-won tolerance, he finally located Jeanne's address.

Now he stood in front of the large and prosperous-looking structure and wondered if she'd sold the ruby after all. Or could she have married in the short time she'd been gone from France?

Providence, previously so miserly, evidently decided to reward him for his efforts. As he crossed the street, she exited the house by the side door, holding a small child's hand. She passed by him, and for a moment he wondered if she would look his way. But she seemed intent upon answering the boy's questions and didn't glance in his direction.

He followed her, curious. Not a wife, but a servant, he realized as she shifted the basket on her arm. A flush of anger raced through his body at the thought of a du Marchand in servitude. His family had commanded kings. But here she was, his errant and recalcitrant only child, attempting to shame him once again.

Nor was her appearance worthy of a du Marchand. Jeanne's hair was pulled back in a severe bun and her face was arranged in a perfectly amiable expression, a look that revealed nothing of her emotions. Her mother, Hélène, had done that often enough around him, especially during the latter years.

He almost hailed her, and then realized that she might well repudiate him on a public street. The last time he'd seen his daughter she had been in a carriage screaming at him, tears and rage twisting her features until she was a discordant creature, something only barely human.

As he watched, she took the child's hand and entered a small discreet shop. CHARLES TALBOT, GOLDSMITH, was inscribed upon the window. He waited until she was finished with her business, emerging from the shop a few minutes later. Only then did he follow her. A man spoke to her, the meeting so obviously unplanned that he hung back, watching with interest. When she walked away, he decided not to follow her. It was obvious she was attending to a servant's duties and he would not demean himself by trailing after her. There would be time enough to confront her, now that he knew for certain where she lived. No, there was another errand that interested him more than greeting his daughter.

He returned to King Street, and watched to ensure that no other customers were inside. Only then did the Comte du Marchand enter, closing and locking the door behind him.

"Are you Charles Talbot?"

The man who faced him was in his middle years and showing a paunch. His face was narrow and lined, his lips thin, and his eyebrows were curiously bushy, giving him an unkempt appearance.

"I am. May I help you, sir?" the shopkeeper asked, managing to sound obsequious while staring at him offensively.

"You had a customer a few minutes ago. A young woman with a child. What was the nature of her business?"

The man who faced him smiled thinly. "I am afraid, sir, that I'm known for the confidential nature of my dealings. I do not share the business of one customer with another." He tilted his head to the side, his rude glance not faltering. "Unless you are not going to be a customer, sir?"

Nicholas tapped his cane on the floor, irritated with this

new democracy of thought and action. But restraint, for
now, was a wiser course. He managed a smile, one that he
knew seemed friendly enough. The trick was to hide one's
thoughts, and to simply act upon them when the time was
right.

"I believe that she is a relative of mine," he said holding
out his calling card. It was only one of ten that he had left,
but the man opposite him did not need to know the degree
of his penury. By the terms of the new constitution approved by the king, Nicholas had found himself stripped
of his title, his home, his land, and his fortune. "I am late
of Paris," he added. "You must be aware of the troubles
there. Families have been separated." He waved his hand in
the air, unwilling to continue further with his charade of
grieving kin.

The man's eyes didn't soften. If anything, his gaze grew
more calculated. A born tradesman, he evidently sniffed
out a profit. Very well, Nicholas would allow him to believe that there was something in this situation for him.

"And what would the troubles in France have to do with
me?" Talbot asked, glancing down at the card. "Count?"

The tone in which he referred to his ancestral title grated
on Nicholas's nerves. He knew himself that there were
hundreds of minor nobility living in England and Scotland. Men whose familial titles were not as ancient as the
du Marchand name. But the dull-witted man evidently
didn't know the difference.

"Did she come to sell some jewelry? A stone, perhaps?"

The man's smile widened. "I couldn't tell you that one
way or the other."

Nicholas strode confidently toward the workbench, his
hand clenched around the top of his cane. Once, it had
boasted a gold-encrusted crest of his family. But he had
sold the gold a few months ago, and it was safer, at least in
Paris, to pretend that he was not an aristocrat.

"I am prepared to make the knowledge worth your while," he said softly. Those who had attended him in the past would have warned the fool that he was at his most dangerous when he was softly spoken. Any idiot could yell or shout, but managing to convey displeasure while never raising his voice took some skill.

"I am looking for a certain stone," he said. "Something · that may have been offered you by a French émigré."

The laughter his comment received was another irritant, but Nicholas cut off any response and put an amiable smile on his face. When the fool stopped laughing, he waited a few moments and then spoke again.

"Is my request so amusing, then?"

The goldsmith turned and opened a drawer in his workbench. Scooping up a handful of stones, he turned and tossed them onto the top of the glass case. Sapphires, rubies, diamonds all tumbled in a glittering array to rest against the wooden rail.

"Here, take your pick. I've been offered all of these."

Nicholas fingered the gems, pushing them into a line with the tip of his index finger. "They're paste."

"Indeed they are, and not even good representations of the originals, if I might add. Your countrymen tried to pass them off as real. I keep them to amuse myself."

"Or sell them to unsuspecting customers?" Nicholas did not doubt the goldsmith's greed. It was there in his eyes, in the way he slid his fingers over the fake jewels. When the goldsmith didn't answer his taunt, he continued, "I'm looking for a ruby. A ruby roughly in the shape of a heart," Nicholas said, maintaining his affable tone. "The Somerville Ruby."

The goldsmith looked interested, but he didn't volunteer any information.

Nicholas drew himself up, fixed one of his most imperious looks at the other man. "My wife was the daughter of the Duke of Somerville," he said. "The gem was part of her inheritance."

"I haven't seen it, Count."

Patiently, Nicholas continued. "It was taken from our possession. I believe it to be in Edinburgh."

"And the woman you asked about? Do you also believe her to have some connection with the gem?" Talbot asked casually.

"I do," Nicholas said, giving him the information grudgingly. However, there was no need for the goldsmith to know that he'd followed his daughter from France, that he would have been ignorant of her escape from the convent had it not been for his former housekeeper. Justine was as loyal to him now as she had always been, and as talented in bed. The only change the passing years had made in her had been a touch of gray in her striking red hair.

And, perhaps, a surprising reluctance for pain. In addition, she'd acquired an unhealthy obsession for religion. He'd found her at prayers one day, the image of his mistress petitioning God for forgiveness of her multitudinous sins almost amusing if it hadn't been so tedious.

"The woman I asked about is an opportunistic thief. She stole the gem."

The goldsmith regarded him for several moments, as if attempting to ascertain the truth of his statement. Nicholas managed to curtail his irritation and waited.

"The woman is employed by the Hartley family," Talbot finally offered, which only tallied with Nicholas's suspicions that his daughter had become a servant.

"And what did she want with you?"

"Why should I tell you?" There was that smirk again, that thin smile that was beginning to be a decided irritant.

"Because she is a thief," Nicholas said. Hélène had left the gem to her daughter, a legacy that had been agreed upon at their marriage. However, neither of them had anticipated that France would change or that he would be living a whisper thin distance from true penury. The ruby would keep him in some luxury until France returned to normal and he would once more be restored to his rightful place. Not scrabbling for survival in his tiny room in Paris while the magnificent house that had once been his was bequeathed to some peasant who had, no doubt, been a fishmonger a month earlier.

"Then the law will restore the gem to the rightful owner," Talbot said.

The two men regarded each other for five swings of the pendulum of the clock mounted on the wall.

The shop was small and not overtly prosperous. In France, merchants had called upon him to display their wares. In the past two years, however, he'd been forced to frequent their establishments as he'd sold one family heirloom after another in order to buy food and wood.

Vallans, the showplace of France, had been razed, leaving him without income and a lifetime of accumulated treasures. He'd managed to procure a handful of items before escaping the torch-bearing mob, and even those were rapidly dwindling.

"Then shall we make an arrangement between us?" Talbot suddenly said, his smile seeming more genuine. "I'll inform you if she attempts to sell me the ruby, while you agree to let me sell it for you."

"For a substantial commission, of course." Glancing around the shop, Nicholas wondered if Talbot's clientele was such that he already had a buyer in mind. He frankly doubted it, but he wouldn't allow his misgivings show.

"A fair commission," Talbot countered.

"Such an arrangement, of course," Nicholas said pleasantly, "is contingent upon my obtaining the ruby once again."

"I'll help you get the stone," Talbot said, extending his hand.

For a moment Nicholas regarded the other man, studying his expression while he ignored the gesture. He would be a fool to trust this man; he knew that deep in his heart. But he clasped the other man's hand and smiled anyway.

Talbot was not the only one who knew an opportunity when he saw it.

Chapter 9

━━━━━━━━━━⟡⟡━━━━━━━━━━

Jeanne stood at the window of the schoolroom, looking out at the afternoon. The sun was bright in the sky, and the window warm against her fingers.

Lessons were finished for today, and Davis had done well despite her inattention. Her mind was not on her duties, but on the conversation she'd had with Douglas.

He had a wife. And a daughter.

Could she die of envy? Or regret? She might, if the tightness in her stomach was any indication. Closing her eyes, she tried not to think of him, but it was as futile a wish as wanting to transport herself to some other place.

Douglas had a wife and a child.

She couldn't help but wonder what kind of life they had. Were they very much in love? What kind of woman was his wife? Did he tell her that he would love her and be with her forever, no matter what happened? If so, he was so much more constant to his wife than he'd ever been to her.

Jeanne could hate him for his constancy now. Where had he been when she'd needed him?

The door opened and she turned, thinking that it was

Davis returning from the water closet. Instead, it was
Robert Hartley. Not only was he early for their meeting,
but she'd not expected him to come to the schoolroom.

Moving from the window, she began stacking the books
and slates she and Davis had used in their lessons.

"You're very industrious, Jeanne," he said, leaning
against the doorjamb and watching her. "I pay the maids to
clean."

"I find that it serves as a good example to be tidy," she
said, wishing that he would go away. Although this encounter was weeks in coming, she dreaded it. "Your son is
coming along well in his numbers."

He waved a hand in the air as if dismissing her comments about Davis. Jeanne hid her irritation and continued
straightening the schoolroom.

"I hear good things about you from the rest of the staff,"
he said.

She glanced at him and then away, certain that he would
add to that remark. But he didn't, surprising her.

"That is good to hear, sir." She busied herself by taking
the slate Davis had used and placing it atop the bookcase.
Turning her back on Hartley, she prayed that he would
simply take her hint and leave.

Instead, he moved closer to her. "Are you so intent upon
pushing me away, Jeanne? You should know that it will not
affect me in the slightest."

"Then what will?" she asked, turning and facing him.

He smiled at her, a perfectly charming expression if one
didn't notice the predatory gleam in his eyes.

She thought that he might back down if she confronted
him. Instead, he seemed delighted that the subject had finally been broached.

"I can suggest a different arrangement than that of governess and employer," he said. "I can set you up with your
own house, with a carriage and a small allowance. Nothing

large, of course, but enough that you would be happy. All that I ask is that you keep yourself available for me a few nights a week. That arrangement, surely, would not be as onerous as being a governess."

"I would like to be able to hold my head up in society," she said civilly. "The post of mistress, unfortunately, would not allow me to do so."

"Does it matter what other people think, Jeanne?" he murmured. "This arrangement would be of benefit to both of us. Is society so very important to you?"

More than half her life had been spent being groomed for her place as the Comte du Marchand's daughter. She'd spent the last decade paying the price for forgetting that role. Only one man had the ability to tempt her from it again. But instead of the truth, she lied straight-faced. "Yes," she said. "The good will of society is very important to me."

"Perhaps I could convince you to ignore it." He took a step closer and she willed herself not to move. "You've filled out nicely in the last few months," he said, his gaze traveling insultingly slowly down her body.

Reaching out, he cupped her breast, smiling lightly.

She'd had experience with men like him, men who preyed on others weaker or more vulnerable than they. She held herself stiffly, and didn't move despite the fact that his thumb flicked back and forth over her nipple. Was he such a fool that he thought a woman was only a collection of parts? Either her heart must be involved or her mind before her body welcomed a man.

"Davis is of an age to be sent away to school," he said, finally moving his hand. "If I did that, Jeanne, I wouldn't require a governess for several more years."

"You must do what you think is right, sir," she said, hating him for threatening her. She had survived France; she would survive anything that happened in the future. But fear had been a constant enough companion in the last three months that it returned easily, another reason to dislike Hartley intensely.

Bullies were odious regardless of their nationality.

"Right now I think it's right that I touch you, Jeanne. What do you have to say to that?" He smoothed his hand over her bodice, let his fingers trail down to her waist.

"Davis will return in a moment," she cautioned.

"On the contrary," he said, "I've had nurse take all the children for a walk. He'll be gone some time, which gives us the opportunity to get better acquainted." He moved closer. She stepped backward until she was forced to stop because of the wall.

"It wouldn't be as bad as you think to be my mistress, Jeanne." His smile was perfectly amiable, his expression pleasant, as if he saw nothing intrinsically wrong with what he suggested. "In fact, you might find the arrangement quite pleasant."

He wasn't a bad-looking man. In fact, she might consider him handsome if his character were not so lamentable.

"You're married, sir. Have you forgotten?"

His laughter was surprising. "Of course I haven't, Jeanne. Why else would I propose putting you up in your own house?"

Hartley reached out and cupped her breast again, squeezing lightly. She shivered and stiffened.

"You should become accustomed to my touch, Jeanne, if you're to be a mistress." His eyes narrowed and the genial air he'd adopted only a moment ago slipped. In its place was the gaze of a man who knew his own power, and knew full well that she had none.

She hated him, just as she'd learned to hate Sister Marie-Thérèse, just as she'd grown to hate her father.

The first and only time she'd given herself to a man had been with love. Nothing would ever be quite as beautiful as those months in Paris, when she and Douglas had been able to steal away together. She had learned that loving Douglas physically was only an extension of what she already felt for him. She'd lost her virginity gloriously to him, and her passion had grown each time they were together until the world seemed to shimmer with it. Ten years ago she couldn't wait to be with Douglas again, each hour they were apart almost physically painful.

Hartley made pleasure sound tawdry, something to feel ashamed about. How foolish a man he was not to know that passion without emotion was lifeless.

When she didn't move, didn't rebuff his touch, he smiled. "I thought you would see the truth of the situation. The French are infinitely excitable, but they have moments of practicality."

She didn't look anywhere but at his face, keeping herself from moving only by the greatest of wills. Robert Hartley was not the first bully she'd ever encountered.

He dropped his hand while the other slid around her neck, pulling her toward him. Slowly, giving her time to move, he pressed his lips against her mouth. She kept her eyes open, focusing on his closed lids. His lips were cool, the pressure on her mouth forceful. He didn't kiss as much as mark her.

"You'll warm up in no time," he said, pulling back. He thrust his hand into her hair, dislodging the pins of her bun. "You're not a virgin, are you, Jeanne?"

At her silence, he chuckled. "I didn't think so. A man can tell. There's a certain ripeness to you."

She heard the sound of Davis returning at that moment, the intrusion welcome. She moved back just as the little boy opened the door, coming into the room with a burst of energy.

"What are you doing here?" Hartley asked, turning and frowning down at his son.

"Nurse says that it looks to rain, Father. And Robbie has a cold."

Hartley nodded, and turned to Jeanne once again. "I'll come to you tonight, Jeanne, to give you a taste of me," he whispered. "I suggest you be receptive to my visit."

A minute later he was gone, and the schoolroom was blessedly free of him. She took a deep breath. Even the air seemed cleaner.

"Are you all right, miss? You're trembling." Davis's voice seemed to come from very far away.

Twice she tried to speak, and twice nothing emerged from her lips. "Yes," she said finally managing a word. She placed her hand on the child's head, forced a smile to her lips. "I'm fine, Davis."

In that instant Jeanne made her decision.

Even if it meant being without a home or living in uncertainty, she would not be Hartley's mistress. She had already proven she was a survivor. She would not surrender now. Nor could she bear the thought of Douglas being so close, a possible witness to her humiliation.

Instead, she chose her freedom, knowing that she would have to endure whatever fate dealt her. She had done it before, she could do it again.

Chapter 10

Jeanne found that it took a special type of courage to wait for nightfall. The young girl she'd been screamed inside for Douglas to come and rescue her from this untenable situation. But the more mature Jeanne knew that there were no longer any knights in her world. She was alone and dependent upon herself.

The sound of thunder drew her to the window. A storm was approaching on the horizon, chasing the night across the sky. God would reward her courage with rain, then. She tilted her chin up to stare at the sky as if facing a Deity hiding behind the clouds.

"Scare me with thunder, punish me with rain," she softly dared.

God sent a bolt of lightning to scratch the sky.

She only smiled in response.

A few moments later, she went to the armoire, bent, and opened one of the two drawers and withdrew her valise. Stained and worn, it had held the remnants of her life on her flight from France.

Filling the case with her possessions took only a moment.

Two chemises, two dresses, a selection of well-darned stockings, her extra set of stays, and a silver hairbrush given to her.

Reaching in to the bottom of the armoire, she pulled out the book of poetry she'd rescued from the ruins of Vallans. It fell to the floor, revealing the flyleaf. There, in her schoolgirl script, she'd written her name over and over coupled with Douglas's. Jeanne Catherine Alexis du Marchand MacRae. She averted her eyes from the flyleaf, embarrassed that she'd been so utterly foolish. Another woman now bore Douglas's name.

She packed the book into the valise before reaching into the armoire again. Her fingers smoothed over a small journal, another item she'd rescued from the ruins of the library at Vallans.

When she was a little girl, she'd accidentally discovered a loose brick in the fireplace there. Over the years she'd made a habit of using it to hide those treasures she didn't want her nurse or governess to find. When she'd returned to Vallans in disgrace, to live out her confinement, everything in her room had been searched, every scrap of paper removed, every book, everything that might have reminded her of her time in Paris destroyed. But she'd already hidden the most precious of her belongings behind the loose brick.

After leaving the convent, she'd returned to Vallans simply because she had nowhere else to go. It had taken her some time to get her bearings among the ruins, but when she did, Jeanne found her way to the chimney that had once been the focal point of the library. She'd knelt there, clearing off the space in front of what had been the hearth.

Using her nails for leverage around the brick, she'd pulled it free an inch at a time. Slipping her fingers inside, she retrieved those four items she'd hidden nine years earlier. The locket her mother had given her before her death, a book of poetry given to her by Douglas after learning of her love of verse, the journal, and the greatest of her treasures, a pair of spectacles with double-hinged temple pieces and small round lenses. They fastened behind her ears with two lengths of ribbon.

These four items were proof that she was loved, by her mother, her governess, and by Douglas.

She hefted the small leather journal in her hand. For something so small, it contained enormous power to wound. Perhaps it would be wiser to wish that the journal had been consigned to the flames. She didn't want to read the words of this hopeful young woman. But she dared herself to open the book.

Page twelve:

Douglas kissed me today. I thought my heart would explode in my chest from its frantic beating. I couldn't breathe and simply lay in his arms, almost afraid. No one warned me about the power of a kiss. No one told me that it would make me feel as if my mind were separated from my body. Father Haton says that God abjures the sinner who tastes the pleasures of the flesh until marriage and I know now why. It is too difficult to stop kissing Douglas.

Another page. Twenty-four:

My feet don't touch the cobbles beneath my shoes, and my heart itself feels as if it has wings. Does love make angels of mortals, then? Do I have the power to speak to God in my new state of grace? I love him, God. I love the way he laughs, and the way his eyes crinkle when he's amused. I love the passionate way he argues a point and even his horrid accent when he speaks French. I love his family because he does, and

carrots because he does, and birds that sing because
it makes his beautiful blue eyes sparkle to hear them.

Jeanne pressed one hand flat against the page, as if to
soak up the intricate script and, by doing so, feel the emotions through the ink. Her chest hurt again with the pain
and pleasure of loving Douglas.

She couldn't read any more. She knew, without turning
to the page, what the last entry would read:

I fear my time has come and I'm both excited and
afraid. I wish there was some way to get word to
Douglas. We're about to have a child and he
should know. But if he knew, would he come to me?
My heart says yes even though there has been no
word from him. I pray that I'm a good mother, that
my father will forgive me upon seeing his grand-
child. And I know, somehow, that Douglas will re-
turn for me.

The next day she'd been sent to the convent.

Her fall from grace had been a sudden and cataclysmic
one. One moment her father was tolerant and amused. The
next, the Comte de Marchand was her jailer. They had
never restored their relationship. How could they? He had
sent her daughter away for the sake of bloodlines, for the
sake of his pride.

Packing the book into her valise, she closed it, picked it
up, and left the room.

At the head of the stairs she hesitated, listening for footsteps. At the second-floor landing she could hear the distant sound of conversation and realized that Hartley was
speaking with Althea. He was acting the doting husband
prior to coming to Jeanne's room.

Slowly, she continued down the stairs, careful not to make a sound.

The large front door was locked by seven, but she knew where the key was kept. Carefully, she reached behind the enormous blue and white Chinese vase for the small key box.

A moment later she was out the front door, locking it behind her. She tossed the key into the hedge, a delaying tactic that would guarantee no one would follow her from the house.

Although she'd already made her decision to leave, Jeanne took the four front steps reluctantly. Past the walk lined with gravel was the future, unknown, uncertain, and holding a degree of fear.

She'd already made her decision about where to go. Her aunt's husband wouldn't take her in, having already refused to do so once, but she would take refuge for a few days with a couple she'd met on the voyage across the Channel. They were the parents of the girl she'd nursed, the same ones who'd given her the three dresses. The coins she'd been willing to spend on a sweetmeat for Davis would be a small payment for their kindness. Hopefully, she'd find employment soon.

The lamps in this area of town were extinguished early in case they disturbed the residents trying to sleep. Clutching her valise close to her chest, Jeanne walked into the darkness. Above her, thunder rumbled and lightning flashed, as if God hadn't forgotten and was still affronted by her dare. Brisk wind whipped tendrils of hair from her bun and lifted her skirt above her ankles.

She could feel the sharp edges of the cobbles beneath her thin shoes, and determinedly ignored the discomfort. She'd walked nearly the whole distance from Vallans to the French coast. Wagons had been scarce on the crowded roads. The distance she needed to travel tonight was much shorter in comparison. The community of émigrés lived on the other side of Edinburgh, in a section of Old Town.

Suddenly she was grabbed from behind, arms reaching around her waist and jerking her off her feet. She screamed, but a rough hand over her mouth cut off the sound. Jeanne dropped her valise and used her fists to strike at the assailant behind her.

He swore and grabbed one of her wrists. Jeanne retaliated by kicking him. One foot connected with a leg but he didn't hesitate, grabbing her other wrist. Twisting out of his grasp, she slapped at him.

"Damn woman!"

She kicked him again before bending down and grabbing her valise and swinging it at him. It struck him in the chest with a resounding and satisfying thud.

He swore again, grabbed her and picked her up by the waist, and slung her over his shoulder. His chuckle infuriated her, and she got in one good blow using her elbow on the back of his head.

"Damn woman, will you be still?"

She heartily hoped that his shout would alert some of the neighbors, but no one emerged from the adjacent townhouses.

She debated biting him, but resorted to striking him repeatedly on the backside with her fists.

"I really don't want to do this, miss," he said. "If you don't stop struggling, I'm going to have to hit you."

"Then you're going to have to hit me," she said, kicking her legs into the air. "I'm not going to let you rape me without a struggle."

"Rape, is it? I've never raped a woman in my life," he said indignantly.

He lowered her to the ground, and she was so surprised that she stood there for a moment staring at the shape of him in the darkness. A second later, she took off, running as fast as she could. Her assailant was right behind her. An instant later he tackled her, throwing her roughly to the ground.

She lay there, winded.

"Get off me, you brute," she demanded when she could speak.

"I'm going to take you to him," he muttered. "Let him decide what to do with you."

She could barely breathe, let alone formulate a question. Like a sack of meal she was slung over his shoulder again. Backtracking a few paces, he bent and retrieved her valise and began to walk, keeping to the shadows.

Jeanne was in the ignominious position of hanging upside down, the blood rushing to her head. She struck at him with her fists, but the effort was a puny one. She still couldn't catch her breath completely, and now she was dizzy.

Less than five minutes later, her assailant dropped her unceremoniously at the base of a series of steps. She landed on her backside, staring up at him in the light of two lanterns. He was a young man, with a thin face and long brown hair. For a moment they glared at each other before he jerked his chin in the direction of the stairs.

"You're a might too heavy to carry all that way," he said, gesturing up to the front door.

She frowned at him, ignoring that insult. "What is this place?" she asked.

"Never you mind. Are you going to walk or should I get someone to help me carry you?" he asked.

"I'm not as heavy as all that," she said, annoyed.

He made a rude sound.

She stood, brushing her skirt, ignoring her sore backside. He grabbed her by the wrist and half dragged her up the steps. She debated kicking him again, but just then the door opened.

An elderly man, attired in a long dressing gown, a tasseled cap on his white hair, frowned down at both of them.

"Tell MacRae I've brought her here. She was going to run, and I didn't know what to do."

The majordomo stepped aside, revealing the one person she hadn't expected to see, didn't want to see. Douglas MacRae.

"Will you tell this person," she said, sending a sidelong glance toward her abductor, "to leave me alone? I take it I'm here at your request?"

"Actually, no," he said, moving to stand in front of the manservant.

"She was leaving the house, sir," said the young man beside her. "The captain told me I was to tell you her whereabouts. He didn't tell me that she'd be slipping away like a thief. I nearly missed her."

Douglas looked at the young man and then at Jeanne before turning to the elderly retainer. "You may retire, Lassiter," he said. "As you can see, this visitor is for me."

The majordomo looked at Douglas, then at Jeanne, no expression visible on his face. But the stiffness of his shoulders as he bowed left no doubt as to his displeasure. In an instant he'd faded away, as all upper servants were trained to do. One moment he was present, the next he was akin to invisible.

"You've shocked my servant," he said dryly, reaching out and gripping her arm. "I suggest that you come inside before you scandalize all of Edinburgh. Thank you," he said, dismissing the young man with a few coins. "You did well."

Before she could speak, before she could utter a protest,

Douglas had pushed her into the doorway and closed the door behind them. A moment later the door opened again.

"Forgot her valise, sir," the young man said, and set the case inside the door.

Douglas's eyebrows lifted as he glanced at the valise and then at Jeanne. "Planning a trip?"

"I shouldn't be here," she stated. "As you said, I might scandalize all of Edinburgh." *Not to mention your wife.* The very last person in the world she wished to meet tonight was Douglas MacRae's wife.

The thunder boomed again as Douglas glanced upward. "Will you not stay until after the storm, Miss du Marchand? Unless, of course, you have somewhere to go and a timetable to keep?" His tone was light, as if the circumstance of her appearance amused him.

She remained silent.

"Why were you leaving? Did Hartley get too amorous?"

He turned and faced her. She was wrong to think him entertained by her plight. Instead, he appeared angry. His eyes were narrowed, and his mouth thinned. Once again, she had the thought that the Douglas of her youth had matured to become a very imposing man.

Abruptly, she wanted to know everything about those years between them. What had happened to him? Where had he gone? She wanted, most of all, to know why he'd never come for her.

Had he not known how desperately she'd loved him? How much she'd grieved for his absence? For years she'd wondered if he'd died, and prayed for his soul more than for her own.

She didn't speak as he removed the shawl from her shoulders. When his hand lingered on her back, his fingers trailing to her neck, she took one cautious step forward.

"I should not be here," she said.

"Then leave," he said, his voice rough, almost rude.

She glanced at the door and then back at him.

"Or stay," he said, his voice softening.

He smiled at her, and it seemed to her that the expression held a certain daring to it, as if he challenged her with two words.

Chapter 11

"**C**ome with me," he said, offering her another choice. He turned and led the way to the parlor. He knew she was following by the brush of her slippers on the wood floor behind him.

"Is your wife not here?"

The question surprised him. So, too, the look on her face as he turned and glanced at her. She appeared as if she were preparing for an answer she didn't want to hear.

He chided himself for that foolishness and answered her. "I'm not married."

"You aren't?"

He hadn't been wrong; there was relief in her expression.

Entering the room, he waited until she followed him before sliding the door shut behind her. He hadn't noticed before that she smelled of spring flowers.

The parlor was one prepared for him by two of his brothers' wives. Riona, James's wife and Iseabal, Alisdair's wife, came often to Edinburgh even though they both lived at least a day away. Sometimes, he thought, they visited not to engage in shopping as they told him, but to ensure themselves of his well-being.

Rose silk adorned the walls, a complement to the green patterned upholstery of the sofas and chairs arrayed in front of the fireplace. He'd overseen the construction of this house, but it was his sisters-in-law who had helped make it a home.

Douglas left Jeanne standing by the door while he lit a branch of candles on the mantel. The sculpture dominating it had been created by Iseabal and depicted his mother and father standing together, their faces turned toward the distance. The work of art had been replicated for all the brothers, the better to remember Ian and Leitis.

He pointed to an overstuffed chair with rolled arms near the fire. "Won't you be seated?"

She looked as if she would demur, but finally sat on the end of the sofa. He turned and studied her, thinking that this moment was steeped in irony. Margaret often sat right there, her feet dangling as she impatiently practiced her manners. His daughter had the once effusive nature of her mother. But the woman who'd given birth to her, and abandoned her, was a pale, almost shadowy copy of the vibrant child.

For a long moment he and Jeanne simply existed in the same room, neither of them acknowledging the other. He went to the sideboard and poured a glass of brandy. He should, perhaps, offer her a cordial, a glass of mulled wine, something to take away the chill of the evening or to warm her blood.

He wasn't entirely certain he wanted her blood warmed. A cold and distant Jeanne was preferable to one who reminded him of nearly a decade ago.

They still had not acknowledged their shared past. Not a past, he amended, only a few months from his youth. An enchanted summer, perhaps, when he'd been less wise and

ready to be charmed. She had indeed fascinated him from
the first moment he'd seen her. She'd been the darling of
her father, a popular young woman on the verge of conquering Paris, a sought-after friend.

But from the instant they met, she'd given up most of
her outings, occupations, and meetings with friends to
spend time with him. He had been the sole focus of her
life, as she had been his. They'd been dangerously besotted
with one another, so in love that they'd been stupid with it.

In those months she'd always been smiling, her eyes
dancing with enthusiasm, excitement, and, later, passion.
There was no topic that she would not discuss, nothing that
she didn't want to know. They'd spent hours in debates.
He'd told her of growing up in Nova Scotia, and related
tales of his older brothers. She, too, had shared her life
with him. She grieved, still, for her mother, and he suspected she was often lonely being an only child. She had a
riotous talent for mimicry and amused him with her tales
of court life, sketching vignettes of the friends and acquaintances of her father.

Oddly enough, he'd frozen Jeanne as she'd been at sixteen, never allowing himself to consider the woman she
might have become.

She looked tired, he noted with detachment. Beneath
her eyes were pale smudges of shadow. The flush of rose
on her pale cheeks was a delicate counterpart to her bisque
complexion. She was, he thought, no more animated than
the sculpture on the mantel.

He didn't want to feel compassion for her. He couldn't
allow himself that luxury. The instant he did, the second he
became curious about her, he would fall beneath her spell,
and he wouldn't be that foolish again.

The woman in his parlor possessed no legacy from the
Jeanne of his youth. Now she sat with her hands clasped in
front of her, appearing the personification of propriety. If

anything, she was a colorless reminder of the girl he'd known. Perhaps that was just as well. Jeanne of the sparkling voice, of the easily summoned passion and bright laughter, cared for no one but herself.

"I take it Hartley is proving to be a difficulty," he said, impatient with himself and his penchant for recall. If he remembered anything, it should be the day he'd rescued Margaret.

"I've left his employ," she said, looking too sedate for the luminous promise of her eyes.

"Does he know it?" He smiled at her look of surprise. "Most servants do not leave at night, Jeanne," he said, deliberately using her name for the first time. She looked disconcerted by his familiarity. There'd been a time when she'd whispered his name, teasingly drawing out the syllables.

"I have a position," he said, hearing the words leave his lips. He returned to the sideboard, wished he were the type of man to drown himself in port. If so, he'd take refuge in spirits, anything but continue on this wildly foolish course he'd unexpectedly set for himself.

Margaret was at Gilmuir, and she would remain there another three weeks. In the meantime, there was no harm in the pretense. He might want revenge from Jeanne du Marchand, but he abruptly realized he had no idea what form it might take.

"Do you truly have a daughter?"

When had she learned to portray such poignancy in a question? She sounded almost sad, the words simple enough but layered with emotion.

"Do you doubt it?" he asked, turning and facing her.

"Then you're a widower."

"Yes." The lie came easily, but of the two of them, her conscience was more burdened. What was one of his simple falsehoods in comparison?

"Where is the child now?"

She looked around the room as if to find Margaret hiding behind a chair.

"Margaret's not here at the moment," he said, unwittingly amused. "She's away from Edinburgh."

"How odd that you require the services of a governess this evening."

"No more so than that you require a position, Miss du Marchand." He bowed slightly to her and held out a glass of sherry. She took it, their fingers brushing.

Retreating to the other side of the room, he watched her.

"My daughter is very intelligent," he abruptly said, understanding the irony of describing their child to her. "She wants to know everything, and I have been delaying hiring someone simply because I didn't want a stranger in my house."

She didn't speak, and Douglas found himself irritated at her silence. He wanted her to be curious, to ask questions.

"Perhaps you should not hire a governess, then."

He frowned at her. He'd not expected her reluctance.

"Perhaps you're not qualified," he said, goading her. To his disappointment, she remained silent. The Jeanne of his youth wouldn't have been so restrained.

"I was given to understand you're French. You can teach my daughter the language."

"I'm half English," she said. "I no longer speak French," she added, once again surprising him.

"Why?"

She shrugged, a gesture that further irritated him.

"Very well," Douglas said. "You can teach Margaret Italian, then. And a little mathematics. I presume you also teach the basics of a good gentlewoman's education? Watercolors? Pianoforte? Delicate needlework?"

"I do not excel in needlework," she said, evidently determined not to be hired.

"You do play the pianoforte?" he asked sardonically.

"Yes," she said shortly. "I can also dance well enough to

instruct. That is, if you wish to save yourself the expense of a dance master."

She'd danced with him once, beneath the weeping willow in the corner of the garden. They'd circled the trunk and laughed at the fact that they took turns humming a tune. He wondered if it was a memory she'd forgotten.

"I needn't worry about money, Miss du Marchand. In addition, I can pay you more than Hartley did."

"There are more important things than wealth, Mr. MacRae."

"Such as?"

"Safety."

Once again she surprised him, further annoying him. "What does that mean?"

"Is it your intent to make me your mistress, Mr. MacRae? I have no intention of leaving one position only to land in another similar circumstance."

"Why would you ask that?"

"Who hires a governess with no child in attendance?"

He surveyed her for a good minute. Finally, he spoke again. "I'm a great deal richer than Hartley, Miss du Marchand, and I do not doubt that I'm a better lover."

Jeanne had obviously expected a different answer. One laced with indignation, perhaps. Or wrapped in honor like twine. He wanted to warn her that where she was concerned, he had little honor left. Rage, yes. Even a reluctant curiosity. But not honor.

She played with the locket at her neck. The room was warm but that wasn't, he suspected, why her cheeks were pink.

"Are your governesses normally measured by their willingness to share your bed?"

"I've never hired a governess before."

"Nor have you now." She raised one eyebrow and studied him.

She gathered up the shawl around her shoulders. At first he thought she would stand and move toward the door. But she only inclined her head, stubbornly refusing to speak further.

"I've already sent Lassiter to bed. Shall I rouse him to show you to a guest chamber or will you allow me to do so?"

He didn't doubt that she was about to refuse when he raised his hand to forestall her words. "Tomorrow you can decide about my offer, Miss Marchand. Tomorrow is soon enough to plan your future." He forced a smile to his face. "Edinburgh at night is no place for a woman, even one so unwaveringly independent."

She looked as if she would still refuse.

"Shall I give you some type of guarantee that I am not the type to prowl at my servants' doors? Or an affidavit from my existing staff that I have not once made a nocturnal visit to their rooms? I furnish locks to my female servants, Miss du Marchand, a device necessary for their peace of mind, not because I'm afraid I'll be crazed by lust before morning."

"Have I insulted you?" she asked, looking genuinely curious.

He frowned at her. "It's raining outside. Do you want to stay or not?"

For a moment they shared a look, and he wondered if she could feel his confusion. He wanted to hate her, but she was weaker than he right now. He'd never taken advantage of a woman's vulnerability and wouldn't begin tonight.

He should let her leave. If he did, he needn't be bothered with her again. But she would be somewhere, interfering with his peace of mind. At least now he knew where she was and what was happening to her.

For two years he'd thought her dead and that was the only reason he'd been able to tolerate her memory. But Jeanne was very far from dead, and very far from forgettable.

Everything he had become, and was now, dated back in some way to Jeanne. Because of his love for her, he'd returned to France and found his daughter. Caring for Margaret had made him mature quickly, had focused his desires to be as successful as or more so than his brothers. Because of Jeanne he was no longer the young man he'd been in Paris. Nothing would ever make him as foolish again.

But in her presence he was reminded of that boy, of the artless wonder of those days.

She was a dangerous woman.

Chapter 12

⟨~~~∽◯◯∽~~~⟩

The strange surroundings should have disturbed her, but Jeanne slept deeply, dreams chasing her. She was in Paris again, and then at Vallans, with the ruins forming an odd and eerie background to a scene of unimaginable beauty. The palest yellow roses were blooming against the gold-colored bricks. The blue sky was clear and cloudless, and the breeze blew from the south, carrying with it the scent of lavender. She saw herself in one of her favorite dresses walking the path from the chapel to the summer gardens, a journey she knew well and had made often. Abruptly, the scene changed again and she was in Scotland standing on the doorstep of her aunt's home. Despite her frantic knocking, no one answered and in her dream she experienced the same desperate abandon she'd felt in her waking life.

A noise, the small click of a lock, made her restless, drew her upward from sleep. Pushing at the covers, she turned in the bed, one arm curled beneath a pillow, the other atop the heavily embroidered coverlet.

The touch of a finger on her hand incited her to wake,

but she kept her eyes shut. His hand smoothed from her shoulder to elbow and then to her fingers. Lightly, his fingers wrapped around her wrist in a living manacle. She didn't struggle or fight him. Instead she lay quiescent and pliant, perhaps even eager.

"You shouldn't be here," she whispered.

Douglas didn't answer, but she knew he wasn't going to leave. As long as she didn't open her eyes, she didn't have to banish him. He could be the youth of her heart, the boy she'd learned to adore through an awakening of their minds and bodies. He was the only one to teach her passion, the only one to debate and argue with her, the only one to exchange ideas as if they were fistfuls of gold, precious and to be excitedly examined.

She didn't move, anticipation harnessing her breath. Slowly, she pulled back her hand, feeling the gentle abrasion of the fine linen sheet against her palm. The tips of her fingers counted each individual stitch in the needlework of the coverlet, worked out the pattern in her mind. A rose, a leaf, a singing bird.

Speak. Please speak, and I'll know you're real and not simply a dream.

She dared not open her eyes, because to do so would be to approve of his presence. Or find that he wasn't here after all, that she'd only created him from dreams and half-formed memories.

Please be real.

That was a truly unforgivable prayer, wasn't it? The nuns at the convent had failed abysmally in their mission to rid her of harlotry, then. She was indeed doomed to perdition, as they'd predicted so often.

She heard the rustle of fabric and wondered if he removed his clothing. When she felt him sit on the edge of the bed, she stretched out her hand and encountered a naked hip. She jerked back her hand as if she'd touched fire and then extended it slowly again, allowing her fingers to explore.

His hand caught hers, fingers entwined, and then she felt a most surprising sensation as her hand was lifted. He kissed her palm in a lover's gesture, one he'd repeated countless times a decade ago. A soft exhalation, a gasp of pleasure, escaped her.

Touch me, she almost said and the words trembled on her lips, desperate to be voiced. *Touch me, Douglas, and make me forget.* She raised her arms, extending them around his shoulders. Gently, relentlessly, she pulled him down to her.

They lay there for a moment, silent and hushed, a thousand words unspoken between them. Yet they still had not kissed. In the darkness, in the silence, she kept her eyes closed, holding him, her cheek against his, listening to him breathe, feeling the texture of his skin beneath her palms. It seemed as if she were being granted a prayer after all. How many times had she wished for just such a moment? How many nights had she awakened from dreams of him longing only for a touch?

Please, do not let this be simply a dream.

But she could feel the pounding of his heart, the abrasion of his night beard, and the callused tips of his fingers. Her dream lover had never appeared so real before tonight.

If she had the power, if she could control the world and all within it, she would freeze this moment poised on the brink of discovery forever. Once they had hidden from the world. Now they hid from each other.

He pulled back and placed his palm against her cheek in a hauntingly familiar gesture, all the more powerful for the fact that it evoked so many memories.

"Are you crying?" he asked softly.

She only nodded wordlessly. She felt too much at that moment. Grief and wonder, sorrow and joy. He'd come to seduce and instead had incited her tears.

For years she'd been told that her mortal soul was irrefutably blackened, that hell waited for her with its gaping, scorched maw. She'd stood before her accusers and confessed to whatever sins they wished from her, accepting that she was flawed and fallible.

Temptation perched upon her bedstead now, waiting for her to refute it. But how could she deny her need? Or her loneliness? Or him?

She opened her eyes and cupped his face with her hands, peering intently into it as if she could see in the darkness. If she had been capable of words, she would have told him what a handsome man he'd grown to be. The boy had been striking with his blue eyes and black hair, but the man stopped her heart.

Seeing him two days ago had brought back so many memories—the loss of her innocence, the loss of her freedom, the loss of her child. Yet loving him had been the single most wondrous act of her life, and those months in Paris had been filled with enough recollections to sustain her for almost ten years.

She wanted more.

Give me more memories upon which to build my life. Give me something that I can remember in the long, dark hours until I die. Give me your kisses and the feel of your body, and the hint of a love once so strong that it changed my life.

The words were improvident ones, the truth too painful to utter. Instead, she would simply converse with her hands and her fingers and her lips and her limbs. In loving him she'd salute the memory of that girl who had given so much, only to lose it all.

But she would not trust him to be constant.

When he finally kissed her, she was sixteen again and the world was filled with summer. There were colorful flowers in the lush gardens, and she and Douglas had made their bed beneath the weeping willow. He'd spread a blanket for her, one she'd confiscated from the linen press. They'd lain together in the morning mist, their loving accompanied by the faint sound of rain drizzling from the branches.

He had taught her to kiss and she'd learned her lessons well. On that morning so long ago, she pulled away and asked him, "Do you love me, Douglas?"

He'd raised his head and smiled at her and she'd seen the answer in his eyes. "Yes," he said, bending down to kiss her again. "With all my heart." Another kiss. "With all my heart and soul." One more kiss. "With all my mind and heart and soul."

Love me, she said in her heart now, the words somewhat different but the desire the same.

She stood and removed her nightgown, grateful for the darkness as she bared her body. Taking the steps back to the bed, she knelt beside him. As young lovers, they had laughed and teased each other, taking turns in seduction. The lessons of her youth were not lost on her now.

Extending his arms around her, he drew her down atop him. Her breasts pressed against his chest, her thighs cradling his erection. They fit together perfectly, as if nature itself had designed one for the other.

She was the one initiating their kiss now, as her hands flattened against his cheeks, her palms abraded by his whiskers. She kissed him with all the longing of nearly a decade, all the loneliness of a thousand dream-filled nights.

His hands were large and warm, wandering over her backside, cupping her bottom, and pulling her even closer. Engrossed in his kiss, she didn't notice when he abruptly stopped touching her.

Slowly, he sat up and, reaching inside the drawer, unerringly pulled out a tinderbox containing flints, steel, and tinder. He scraped the flint against the steel and the sparks ignited the cotton fibers. The small flame was enough to light the candle on the nightstand.

She moved, gathering up the sheets in front of her, and backed up to the headboard, feeling the carved vines and flowers of the wood press into her skin. In that second the mood was broken, the illusion of a shadow lover destroyed, and in his place a Douglas with set face and angry eyes.

"Turn around, Jeanne," he said slowly.

She shook her head from side to side, silently calling herself a fool. She should have known what he would encounter. How could she have forgotten?

He grabbed her by the shoulders and turned her. She beat at his arms, but there was nothing she could do against his strength. Feeling the warmth of the candle flame inches from her shoulders, she could well imagine what he saw. One of the other penitents had treated her after the last beating, and had been shocked enough to whisper, "Oh, your poor back, Jeanne. They have scarred you so."

"What happened to you?" he asked.

She bowed her head. For a few moments she'd wanted to relive the past before all had been lost to her. What a fool she'd been to think that she could simply wish away all those years.

"What happened?" he asked again. He reached out his fingers and trailed them over her back, tracing the line of her scars.

She left the comfort of the bed, pulling at the sheet and wrapping it around her. Walking to the windows, she wished suddenly that she could simply fly from the room. She would be a bird and alight on a nearby tree and escape this questioning. But she was all too human, wasn't she?

A fact that he'd just discovered.

"I was sent to the Convent of Sacré-Coeur as a girl. They found it expeditious to enforce some lessons."

"By beating you?" he asked incredulously. "What did you do that was so terrible, Jeanne?"

She had questioned their edicts, smiled at a novitiate, been found weeping in the laundry. All such activities indicated to the nuns that she was still focused on her previous life and not the one that God had given her at the convent.

Instead of answering him, she remained silent. But Douglas wasn't content with that.

"Why were you sent there?"

"I did something that earned my father's displeasure." She had fallen in love, deliriously and deliciously in love. She ached for that long-ago girl and the boy she adored. She would not mention the other secrets of her life. Douglas had been granted too much by accident.

A moment later she felt him beside her. Slowly, he turned her again.

"Jeanne," he said, and she had never heard a more beautiful sound since the last time he'd said her name, a hundred years ago in a land far away. She felt tears come to her eyes and closed her lids, trapping one and letting the other escape to fall in a straight line down to her chin. She felt his fingers there as he captured it.

Did he hold her sorrow ransom?

Suddenly she could bear it no longer. She didn't want the intervening years to come between them; she didn't want anything to stay him from touching her. Let memory wait for an hour. Let her sin be forgotten for a span of minutes. Give her love now, perfect and joyous, enough to last for another ten years.

She extended her hands and placed them flat on his chest. "Love me," she whispered and the words seemed too loud in that silent room. "Love me, Douglas." The youthful

Jeanne reached out her arms and enfolded him, gently pushed him back on the bed, and hovered over him, teasing as she had not done for years. "Kiss me."

Abruptly, she was on her back. He said something that she didn't hear. Perhaps her name or an oath or some other word whose meaning was inconsequential for this moment.

"Love me," she whispered again, and now there was no doubt of his assent as his lips, warm and heated, covered hers.

She was always swept into a vortex when Douglas kissed her. Now there was only a deep darkness, and a tightness in her chest. He kissed as he always had with deliberation and delight, his tongue entering her mouth. Then he kissed her throat, his lips pressed against the base of her neck and just below her ear, spots where she was especially sensitive. They had not forgotten all the special places they had discovered together—his neck, her breasts, his lower back, behind her knees.

Time had made so many changes in him that she wanted to savor each one slowly and deliciously. His muscles were more defined on his shoulders and back as her fingers trailed a path across his skin, remembering.

He'd obviously learned more about lovemaking in the intervening years and she jealously wanted to know from whom and when. But she was engaged in a pretense, imagining with half her mind that she was the girl of Paris, the one without a care except the greatest one—that of meeting Douglas in secret.

The stubble on his beard gently abraded her breast and then his mouth touched her nipples teasingly. His hand pressed against her abdomen with a gentle pressure and moved up and then down in a slowly taunting circle. His fingers stretched lower with each revolution until she placed her hand atop his.

She couldn't seem to catch her breath, as warmth followed wherever his fingers lingered.

When his thumb finally found her damp and swollen, she made a small welcoming sound and spread her legs wider for him. As delicious as his kisses on her shoulders, the edge of her jaw and her temple, as heavenly as his hands and mouth caressing her breasts, what she truly wanted was for him to be inside her. She wanted to be stretched and filled; she wanted to feel him surging in her until she shuddered in his arms. Until the past and the present were fused together in passion and neither could tell the difference.

He raised himself over her, kissing her slowly, deeply, and an instant later entered her with the same deliberate passion. She found his gentleness almost too much and felt tears well up in her eyes again. His invasion of her was slow, complete, and thorough.

She arched beneath him in a wordless demand that he met with a tender kiss. Patience was not a word for this moment. She wanted everything now. She wanted to feel it all. If not forgiveness, then forgetfulness for a time.

He devastated her completely with a soft kiss, a gentle murmur. "Jeanne." Just her name and nothing more than that.

In that instant, she allowed him inside the most guarded part of her—not her body, that he controlled as he began to surge within her—but her heart.

The boy who'd loved her had promised her fidelity and yet had not been faithful. The boy she'd adored had vowed his constancy and yet had vanished. The man was a stranger, but in this act of passion he merged to become the boy she'd loved.

"Douglas," Jeanne whispered, as if to call him to her.

He bent and kissed her, hard, deeply, and she was caught

up in a maelstrom of sensation. Even her fingers tingled and yet he didn't move faster; he didn't seek to find his own pleasure before hers. He had always been a considerate lover but now he was a maddening one.

She gripped his shoulders and bit her lip and arched beneath him. His patience and endurance summoned her response from where it lay hidden all these years.

Wrapping her arms around his neck, she almost whispered the words that were forbidden between them. *I love you* lay muted on her lips as pleasure flooded through her. All the various parts of her separated in that instant as mind, body, soul flew away. When they rejoined, she felt weak, her hands trembling where they lay against his shoulders.

Her face was warm, her nipples erect and brushing almost painfully against his chest. She gripped his buttocks and pulled him to her and he acquiesced, surging into her deeper than before. A small gasp of surprise emerged from her as she climaxed again.

And then he exploded in her arms, and she held him, her arms wrapped around his shoulders as she felt him breathe harshly against her hot cheek.

Her eyes closed, the better to savor the tremors that resonated through her body. In the depths of her mind she spoke a simple benediction, comprised of only two words. Nevertheless, it seemed to be a prayer. *Douglas. Beloved.*

Chapter 13

Fluffy streaks of clouds colored pink and gray stretched across the sky. Lit from below, they formed a blanket for dawn, adding depth to a magnificent sunrise. Beyond, at the edge of the horizon, the sky was tinted the palest blue, while closer the hue was indigo.

Morning had come to Edinburgh.

Jeanne felt Douglas leave the bed. In a brief, unplanned entreaty, she stretched out her hand. His fingers touched hers gently before moving away. A confession without a word spoken, a way of telling her that perhaps he knew how she felt. Or maybe it was nothing more than a silent farewell.

The entire night had been a joining of memory and flesh. She had been the Jeanne of her youth for a brief matter of hours. In that time she'd felt no guilt or remorse. The world had been a kind place, giving her no reason to hate.

For a brief span of hours he'd given her back a sense of herself, a person the convent had tried so hard and so long to extirpate. She felt almost innocent, naïve and joyous, as optimistic as a child. She wanted to thank him in words, but somehow they wouldn't come. Now was not the time for speech or confession.

After hearing the door click shut, she opened her eyes. Her shadow lover was gone and in his place, the impression of his head on her pillow, the scent of warm bodies, and a hollowness.

Had it not been for the sweet feeling of lassitude in her body, she might have thought herself the recipient of a long and sensual dream.

What had she done?

If she were wiser, she'd leave. She would obtain a position as a scullery maid or shopkeeper's assistant. She should leave Douglas MacRae's house and go about the business of her life before he discovered things about her, or realized how weak she was when it came to him.

She didn't want to leave. Perhaps that was the true meaning of sin, to weigh the consequences of an act and still perform it, to laugh in the face of retribution, and to dare for the sake of pleasure.

Turning onto her side, she stared out the window. The room faced east and the sun was making its appearance on the horizon now.

She'd been labeled a harlot long before now and had paid the price during the last ten years for any number of sins. Let the world damn her again; she no longer cared.

Those months in Paris had been the most beautiful of her life, and last night had proven that her memory wasn't false. He touched her and her body trembled in awe of it. He smoothed his hand across her thigh and incited sensations she'd never felt before or since. Her flesh pebbled and her sigh encouraged the passage of a finger down to a knee and upward to a hip. She wanted his touch everywhere, to single out each separate place on her body and to mark it in a special way no man ever had.

The world was not the kind place it had seemed for a few

hours last night. Instead, it was filled with men like Robert Hartley. Here was safety, for a time, and pleasure, for as long as she wished it.

If the past months and years had taught her nothing else, they'd taught her the value of the moment. She should savor nourishment when it came, delight in beauty when it appeared, and treasure the absence of pain. Why should she not treat love the same and cherish it whenever it occurred?

Because it would bring incredible anguish when it ceased.

She was all too knowledgeable about despair and loneliness, and dreaded them both. Such familiarity should have made her stronger. After all, the limits of her endurance had been reached, stretched, and reached again. Loving Douglas would be almost like stepping beyond the boundaries one more time and testing herself further. All the while, expecting him to leave her once again, or banish her from his house.

A wiser woman would thank him for the gift of the night before, for allowing her to pretend for just a little while. A wiser woman would simply kiss him passionately one last time and take her leave. A wiser woman would stride away from this beautiful house and never look back.

But she had never been wise in regards to Douglas MacRae. If she had, she wouldn't have been so lonely in the past ten years.

When she'd first gone to the convent, she'd awake to the sound of the wind whistling through the corridors at night, the sound similar to a baby's cry. She'd shiver from the chill, and begin to cry, the tears like ice on her face. Two years had passed before she realized that no one was coming to rescue her. Slower still, she'd come to understand that her imprisonment would last until the day she died. Over time her tears came less until only her nightmares remained, confusing, chaotic expressions of her greater despair.

She no longer cared what they did to her at the convent, what punishments she endured, what she suffered from day to day. With her apathy had come a type of freedom and, in time, a release. She'd changed even further as the years passed, becoming stronger in her weakness than those who had once been the masters.

She also began to understand that there was nothing that could be done to cure the past. It was simply there, accusing and unremitting. Yet she still wanted it to be different with every breath she took and with every beat of her heart.

The house was waking around her, commonplace household noises marking the start of another day—maids walking down the hallway, the low murmur of conversation. Life was going on regardless of her participation. She felt outside of it at the moment, an observer. But then, she hadn't been part of the world for a very long time.

Standing, she walked to the basin, surprised to find that the water was warm. Evidently she had slept through the maid's arrival. Once that might have embarrassed her, but she was far removed from such petty concerns as reputation. If she had cared that much for the gossip of servants, she would have removed herself from the house the moment Lassiter saw her last night. She was not foolish enough to think that the elderly majordomo would remain silent. Even the most loyal of servants talked. She didn't delude herself into thinking that they were ignorant of what had transpired the night before.

She pulled out one of her dresses from the valise, smoothing the fabric repeatedly until most of the wrinkles were gone. Dressing took longer than it should have. Anytime a garment touched her skin, Jeanne stopped in remembrance of what Douglas's touch had felt like on that spot. A sleeve sliding against her arm recalled his teasing kiss. Fastening her bodice reminded her of his stroking fingers on her breasts. Her palm pressing gently against her throat recalled his lips.

As she fastened her collar she realized that something was missing.

The locket she'd worn since returning home to Vallans was gone. How had she left her mother's locket behind?

Twice she went through the valise that Douglas had carried to her room, certain finally that it was not there.

She had lost one of the last mementos of her former life.

Perhaps it was an omen.

Douglas was furious with himself. What the hell had he done? He'd lain with a woman he despised. He'd kissed her with gentleness, tenderness, and touched her as if he held some respect for her. Lust shouldn't have transformed him from a rational man to a beast, but it had. Dear God, it had.

Last night he'd paced in his room, thinking of her. He'd almost worn a path in the carpet before he lost the battle with himself, finding himself in front of the door to the guest room.

If Lassiter had discovered him, he didn't know what he would have told his majordomo.

Now Douglas entered his library and closed the door behind him, still conscious of the fact that the woman he had hated for ten years lay asleep above him.

She'd come into his home and he'd immediately lusted after her. She'd sat on his couch looking tired and what had he thought? Not that now was the perfect time to accuse her. Not that now was the opportune moment to avenge Margaret. Not that he would have the opportunity to punish Jeanne for past deeds. No, all he thought was that she'd been a pretty girl, but she'd matured into a voluptuous woman.

The night before had proven that he was a fool around her.

She had to leave. Now. Immediately, before his curiosity and his lust overwhelmed him again. And his curiosity.

I did something that earned my father's displeasure.

The words returned, softly spoken and stated in a voice that didn't ask for pity. She had stood straight and tall in front of him, clutching the sheet to her chest. But he had the impression that she would have been as filled with pride naked. There was something about Jeanne, some sense of herself, perhaps, that he'd never witnessed in another woman.

Or never wished to see.

He pinched the bridge of his nose, willing his headache away. He'd slept for a while, and then awakened holding Jeanne, all the memories of Paris he'd thought forgotten replaying in his mind.

He'd remembered their first kiss, the first time they'd loved, the sound of her laughter. She would bring books from her father's library and they would read together, and argue points of logic or philosophy. He'd see things during the day that he couldn't wait to tell her and would jot them down in a small book he carried for simply that reason. He'd stand outside in the street until the curtain slowly closed and then opened again, a sign for him to meet her at the entrance to the terraced garden.

They were as attuned physically as they were in thought. Last night her arm had slid across his chest and every pore on his skin had responded. She trailed a finger from his shoulder to his elbow and he shivered. When he'd entered her it was like coming home, the feeling so blissful that he registered it with a note of warning.

Why the hell couldn't he get Jeanne du Marchand out of his mind and out of his life?

Because he'd invited her into his house, offered her a position, bedded her with gentleness, touched her with restraint, and even now replayed the memory of cupping his hands around her beautifully shaped bottom and lifting her so that the angle of his thrusts would bring them both greater pleasure.

He halted, recognizing his own idiocy with some chagrin. Even now he couldn't stop thinking of how it had been.

Going to the fireplace, he looked above it to the painting he'd had commissioned of Margaret. She was seated not in the formal pose as was customary, but outdoors at a place they called Iseabal's Knoll. Behind her was the great fortress of Gilmuir, the MacRae ancestral home.

There were some in the family who said that Margaret resembled him and others who said that she looked more like Moira, his grandmother. But his daughter reminded him of his mother, Leitis, with her black hair and brilliant blue eyes.

But in nature she was as bright and curious as Jeanne had been. What had happened to the girl he'd known?

They found it expeditious to enforce some lessons.

He concentrated on the portrait of his daughter, banishing, with some difficulty, the memory of Jeanne's words.

Margaret was, from the moment he'd rescued her, the most important thing in his life. He had restructured his future for her, had changed his life's course in order to rear her. He'd even built this house for her, in a proper section of Edinburgh where she'd be known as a wealthy heiress to his fortune.

For her sake, and to prevent her from being labeled illegitimate, he'd started the rumor that he was a widower. Even his servants thought him a man who grieved for his long-dead wife.

His relationships with other women had been circumspect at first, then gradually declining. He hadn't wanted his behavior to taint Margaret's future. Only recently had he begun thinking of marriage, to the extent that he'd actually attended some events in the newly constructed Assembly Rooms. His requirements for a wife were remarkably simple. Not only must he love her but Margaret must love her as well.

The only reason he'd reacted so feverishly to Jeanne was because it had been a long time since he'd had the company of a woman. He was simply lonely.

Going to his desk, he sat heavily in the leather chair behind it. He stared at the wall, envisioning the night before. She always bit at her bottom lip and arched her body when she found her pleasure, the better to savor the sensation she was feeling.

"It's like the world is ending inside of me and beginning again," she'd said once.

They'd been young lovers together, perfectly matched in needs and desires. He'd never known a woman since then so responsive to his touch. Last night proved that nothing had changed between them.

As he sat there, he recalled every single moment, and knew he always would. He ached to reach out even now and smooth her bottom lip with his thumb. Or cup her face in his hand, or touch his lips to her nipples.

Douglas stood, deciding that there was only one way to end this. She had to leave.

He took the stairs two at a time, striding past his chamber, past Margaret's room located in the middle of the second floor. Finally, he came to the guest room. Before he had time to reconsider, he rapped sharply on the door.

Jeanne opened it quickly, as if she'd been standing there waiting for his summons.

For a moment, he forgot why he'd raced up here. Her cheeks were deep rose, her mouth still swollen from his kisses. He knew every inch of her body as he knew his own. To his surprise, he realized that the girl was only a faint rendition of the woman she'd become.

He'd fallen in love with the girl, but the woman attracted him as much as she confused him.

"Would you like to come in?" she asked, stepping aside. She looked at him quizzically and he realized he must have, indeed, been acting like an idiot, standing there speechless.

He shook his head.

"This won't do," he abruptly said.

She studied him with grave eyes. As a girl she'd been filled with enthusiasm. As a woman she was the personification of poise. Or was it coldness? After all, she'd sent a newborn infant away to be fostered, uncaring whether it lived or died.

"Have you given any consideration to my offer?" he found himself asking. They were not the words he'd intended to speak.

"I have."

He raised an eyebrow.

"It would be foolish for me to leave, I think." She shrugged, a gesture he'd seen Margaret make often.

"You don't seem very enthusiastic about your new post." The second eyebrow joined the first.

She smiled, startling him. He'd forgotten the charm of her smile, the teasing nature of it. When Jeanne smiled, even her eyes mirrored amusement. "But I am."

"Good," he said, nodding at her.

He turned without saying another word and retraced his steps, passing his daughter's room, acutely conscious that Jeanne was staring after him.

The chamber next to Margaret's was currently occupied by her nurse. Today he'd give orders that it was to be vacated for Jeanne. Up until now he'd refused to hire a governess only because doing so would indicate that his daughter was of a sufficient age not to need him.

What an irony that he'd just hired her mother.

* * *

"I love the sea, Aunt Mary," Margaret MacRae said, peering over the side of the ship. The current was swift and the newest of the MacRae fleet rode it easily, even at anchor. "It always looks different, depending on the time of day."

"Indeed it does, Margaret. You should see the ocean near Italy, or off the coast of Spain. There it changes color from green to blue and back to green again within the span of hours."

"Shall I ever see the ocean? I mean, now that I'm grown." She looked over her shoulder at Mary. "I would so very much like to, but Father always gets that frown on his face if I ask when we're going to sea again. Is it because I'm a girl?"

Mary thought for a moment, wondering how to say to the child that it wasn't her gender that no doubt caused Douglas to scowl but the question itself. Margaret was bright and energetic, and had a daunting desire for adventure. Not unlike her mother, if Douglas's tales were to be believed. Mary had begun to think that no one could possibly equal the adventurous Jeanne. Perhaps it was just as well.

"If he'll not take you," she said, realizing that it was a rash promise she offered the child, "then Hamish and I will one day."

"Truly?"

"Most assuredly," Mary said, moving from her perch at the bow. The day was beautiful as only a day in the Highlands could be—deep blue cloudless skies, with the sun shining so brightly overhead that it felt as if God Himself smiled on the Scots. The crisp breeze from the north ruffled the waters of the firth, carrying a hint of what an ocean might feel like beneath the hull of the *Ian MacRae*.

The MacRae ships were mostly named after the women

of the family, except this one in honor of its patriarch. Ian would probably have been amused at the irony, since he wasn't especially fond of the sea. Seven years ago, the ship carrying Ian and Leitis MacRae to Nova Scotia from Scotland had been lost in a massive storm. The newest ship from the MacRae shipyards was christened in a solemn and bittersweet ceremony, one that she and Hamish had witnessed from the firth.

Despite Hamish's assurances to her that she would bring no harm to those living at Gilmuir, Mary hadn't set foot on Scottish soil in ten years. Instead, she and her husband had sailed the world, expanding the MacRae trading empire, exploring the various ports, and accumulating all manner of treatments and medicaments.

Once she had been a healer, but had lost faith in her own skill. It was Hamish who had insisted that she begin again and use what she'd learned to help others.

She wouldn't, Mary thought, looking at the brilliant blue sky over Gilmuir, have traded any of that time with Hamish. Her husband had brought love and laughter into her life, and those years had given her back a confidence in her ability to heal.

Smiling at the young girl in front of her, she thought that Margaret was one of her greatest healing success stories.

When she'd first seen the tiny, emaciated infant, Mary had been certain that it was only a matter of hours until she perished. But there had been a spark of life in the child, something so persistent that it had struggled and won the battle against death itself. The journey back to health had been a long and difficult one, but Margaret had proven that will alone is sometimes the most formidable weapon against illness.

Now, all these years later, Margaret was a radiantly healthy child, with an active mind and a generous heart.

She was the closest Mary would ever come to having her

own child, but that realization was an old one. After all these years, she'd still not conceived and she'd stopped hoping. Occasionally she might long for a son for Hamish, and sometimes she would ask him if he missed having an heir. He would always frown at the question, which was an answer in itself.

"If we had a child, Mary, eventually we'd have to stay on land," he said the last time she'd asked.

"You wouldn't leave me there and sail away?" she teased.

Another frown, this one fiercer than the first. "Are you daft?" He studied her carefully. "Why do you keep asking, Mary? Is it something you wish?"

She always shook her head, the lack of a child never disturbing her overmuch. Not when she had Margaret to love, and all the other MacRae nieces and nephews.

Besides, Hamish was right, if she had a child they would have to curtail their current life, make arrangements to spend more time on land. The problem was, where would they ever settle down? Not in Scotland, surely. Nor England, since they shared the same crown. France? Not a palatable choice, given that more and more people were leaving France daily. America might do, but it was too far from the rest of the MacRaes, and Nova Scotia held only bittersweet memories now.

She'd been remanded for a hearing in Sheriff's Court in Inverness for the crime of killing her first husband, Gordon Gilly. While his death had occurred during her treatment of him, the truth was that the elderly man had died as a result of a tragic accident. Neither she nor Hamish had wanted to stay and let the courts in Edinburgh reason that out, not when they could have easily put her to death.

For now they were both happy to sail the world. As often as they could, Mary and Hamish came to Gilmuir, and every year they planned their visit to coincide with Margaret's summer trip to the MacRae fortress. For a month Douglas allowed her to visit with her cousins, his oldest brother, Alisdair and his wife, Iseabal, acting as guardians for the assembled brood.

"I wish Father would come soon," Margaret abruptly said.

"He's not due to arrive for three weeks, Margaret."

The girl sighed heavily. "I know, but it seems such a very long time."

"I thought you were having a good time."

"I am, of course," Margaret said, tracing a path on the rail with one finger. "My cousins are all very nice, and I love Gilmuir, but it seems so much better when Father's here."

The bond between father and daughter had always been strong, even during these summers. Yet she'd never seen the child as pensive as she was now, as if something weighed heavily on her mind.

Reaching over, she placed her arm around Margaret's shoulders. "Is there something troubling you?"

Margaret shook her head and then smiled, the expression such an obvious effort that Mary was alarmed.

"It's Cameron MacPherson," she said, sighing again. "He is such a bother." She propped her elbows on the railing and stared out at the narrow firth. "He's my cousin Robbie's best friend and the most aggravating boy."

"You must simply ignore him, then," Mary said, trying not to smile.

Margaret frowned over at her. "It is not that easy, Aunt Mary. He's everywhere. He lives in the village and he comes to Gilmuir all the time! His father is a stonemason and he's forever underfoot. Besides," she said, staring down at the churning waters of the firth, "he refuses to leave even when I tell him to go away. He calls me blackbird," she muttered. "And says that my eyes are a very odd color." She looked up at Mary again. "They are not. They're the same shade as Father's, and his are wonderful."

Mary smiled at that remark, carefully not commenting that Margaret thought everything about Douglas was wonderful. "Well, he sounds as though he amuses himself by teasing you. Perhaps if you just pretended he wasn't there?"

"He pulls my hair," Margaret announced. "And worse, when he's around, Robbie doesn't want to be bothered with me."

Mary couldn't imagine the cousins quarreling. Alisdair's son, Robbie, was only two years older than Margaret. They'd played together ever since Douglas had brought Margaret to Gilmuir for the first time as a toddler. Aislin, Robert's sister, was older by four years, and had a separate set of interests and friends. This summer, she'd been allowed to visit Sherbourne, her father's estate in England.

"Would you like to go sailing with us, then, lass?"

Mary turned to see Hamish standing there. He was the largest of the MacRae brothers, half a head taller than Alisdair, his oldest brother, and broader in the chest than any of them. There were scars on his face—and the rest of his body, although those were only for her to see—where he'd been tortured years earlier. Over the years the scars had faded, but a stranger still noticed them. She'd stopped seeing them the day after she'd met Hamish MacRae. To her, and most women—a truth she'd rather not admit—he was an arresting and attractive man, but never more so than now, attired in his white shirt and black trousers, with his thumbs hooked at his waist. His left arm did not move as quickly or as easily as his right. But that was a vast improvement from the time when the limb was nearly useless.

"Aunt Mary said that we might go sailing on the ocean," Margaret said, her eyes expectant.

"She did, did she?" he teased, his glance going to

Mary. "I was thinking of a shorter voyage, myself. Up to the mouth of the firth and then back. Will that be enough?"

Margaret looked disappointed, but she resolutely smiled and nodded. "Shall I go help the first mate, then?"

Hamish laughed and gestured to where Thomas stood. "Go and tell him I said you were to be shown the sextant. A good sailor must know where she's going as well as how to come back."

He walked to where Mary stood, looping his arm around her back, the two of them watching Margaret scamper over the deck, her braid coming loose and tendrils of black hair spreading over her shoulders.

"She reminds me of you," Hamish surprisingly said.

She glanced at him quizzically. "How so?"

"She's got a world of curiosity in those eyes of hers. So do you."

"I do?" She smiled at him, wondering if he was talking about her interest in healing or other, more sensual pursuits. They'd been lovers since a few days after they met, their need for each other instantaneous and fiery. Nor had the years dimmed their yearning for each other.

"I worry about her, though," Mary said.

"Why? She's an heiress, her father dotes on her, and everyone at Gilmuir adores her."

"And she doesn't have a mother. A mother is very important for a little girl of nine."

Hamish nodded.

"You'll just have to do the job, Mary."

"For now," she agreed. "Until Douglas marries."

He drew back, surprised. "You think he will?"

She smiled at him, reached up, and placed her hand flat against his cheek. "The MacRae men are very lusty," she teased. "He cannot help but find a mate soon. I only hope she likes Margaret and Margaret approves of her."

"A fierce requirement for any woman," Hamish said.

"Perhaps too much of one," Mary agreed and wondered if love would ever find Douglas MacRae again. Or was he destined to love only one woman, lost to him by both circumstance and hate?

Chapter 14

A fresh-faced maid with a charming, elfish smile nodded at her from the doorway. "Begging your pardon, miss."

Jeanne turned from where she stood by the window and smiled in response.

"Dinner will be served in the small dining room, miss. I'm to take you there, if you're ready."

Jeanne felt her stomach clench, but outwardly she didn't reveal any sign of her nervousness. "Yes," she said simply. "I am."

What, after all, did she need to do to prepare to meet with Douglas again? Comb her hair? She'd done that. Ready her attire? She'd smoothed as many wrinkles as she could from her dress. Her face was washed as well as her hands.

If her complexion was pale it could be blamed on the loss of sleep the night before. That, too, might be the reason her eyes sparkled entirely too much.

Tonight she wore her best dress, a deep blue with ecru lace at the neckline. If one looked closely it was possible to see that the lace had been mended in two places and the material showed wear at the cuff. But it was so much more ornate than anything she'd worn in the last decade that she prized it.

Now she adjusted her shawl and pretended that she was as poised as she had once been, while following the maid through the corridor and down the lovely soaring staircase.

Douglas had evidently built his home with comfort in mind, but he'd added decorative touches that surprised her as well. The walls had niches in them, small shell-like enclosures that framed a sculpture here and there. On the landing was another embrasure and inside it a strange-looking brass object.

"It's an astrolabe," the young maid said. "It's very old and very rare." She looked in both directions and then whispered to Jeanne, "And it's the very devil to dust."

"What does it do?"

"It's a medieval instrument, used for navigating," she said, frowning up at the ceiling as she obviously recited something she'd learned. "It's been replaced by the sextant."

Amused, Jeanne thanked her and didn't mention the fact that she was no clearer as to its use.

Douglas came from a family of men dedicated to the sea, a fact she'd once questioned. "Do you not wish to sail?"

"I want to see everything," he admitted. "I want to go to the Orient, and learn what I can there. And India, of course. There's a big, wide, wonderful world out there, Jeanne, and I want my share of it."

He'd been lying on his back, his arms folded beneath his head, staring up at the sky. She remembered the day as clearly as if it had occurred an hour ago. The spot was not conducive to lovemaking, being too public, but they had spent the afternoon talking.

Catching sight of a small cinnabar jar in yet another embrasure, she wondered if he'd been to the Orient after all.

There was so much she knew about him, details that were personal and private. Yet there was so much still a mystery.

She and Douglas were intimate strangers.

At the bottom of the staircase the maid turned to her right, leading Jeanne through another series of corridors. The house was huge, the rooms they passed all luxurious and well appointed. She'd not seen them the previous evening, and her day had been spent in circumspect and self-imposed isolation. She hadn't wanted to see Douglas, delaying that moment when they'd meet again. The encounter this morning had been confusing enough.

He'd looked as if he were angry with her, as if he wanted to punish her for what had happened between them. At the very least, he looked displeased that he'd offered her the position as his child's governess and then oddly relieved when she formally accepted.

She'd wanted to tell him that he shouldn't come to her bed again, that the post of governess should preclude the position of mistress. But she'd remained silent, surprising herself.

Perhaps because she was afraid that he might make a vow not to come to her room again, never to tap on her door demanding entrance. Not once would he cross the threshold, invade her bed, or place his hands on her or kiss her the way he had.

How could she bear that?

So she'd remained silent, the promise unsolicited, the vow unmade.

The young maid gestured to a doorway and then simply faded away. Lassiter appeared, as if she'd conjured him up to guide her the rest of the way. He bowed unctuously, his black uniform accessorized with a stiff white stock and spotless white linen gloves.

Jeanne, who'd been surrounded by hundreds of servants during her formative years, was suddenly uncomfortable in his presence.

"Good evening, Lassiter," she said. Her voice sounded unused and strange.

He only bowed in response before turning and leading the way inside the dining room. Stepping aside, he bowed once again before nodding to a footman, who drew out a chair. Douglas stood, waiting for her to sit. She did so, and he regained his seat to her left at the head of the table.

The room was a cozy one, the table small and square, and matching the sideboard on either side of the room. A small door connected to a passageway that no doubt led to the kitchen.

As intimate as the dining room was, it was still impressive in its show of wealth. The walls were covered in gathered folds of patterned silk, and a crystal chandelier hung over the table, lit with dozens of candles. More candles, pale yellow columns of beeswax, were arranged in silver holders atop the sideboard.

If Douglas wished to impress her with his wealth, he'd already done so. His home was a showplace and the treasures he'd collected no doubt worth a fortune. But she'd learned that the content of a man's character was more valuable than his wealth.

"I'm pleased you decided to join me," he said, dismissing Lassiter with a nod. The majordomo hesitated in the doorway, looking back at both of them. She wanted to assure the elderly servant that she would do nothing to Douglas that warranted such a last, concerned gaze.

"I have to eat," she said, a less-than-civil comment.

Once, she'd been adept at those social niceties required to make a guest feel comfortable at either Vallans or their Paris home. As her father's hostess, she was skilled at making a shy person feel welcome, and steering a garrulous visitor to an audience.

The past nine years, however, had stripped the gift of

conversation from her. Silence was a more comfortable companion.

"I think you'll enjoy the meal," he said, as if her surly response to him hadn't been followed by silence. "My cook is quite renowned."

"I'm certain I shall." There, she sounded almost civil.

"Did you have a good day?"

"A restful one," she admitted. She'd done nothing but remain in her room, waiting for him, if the truth be told. Yet truth wasn't a necessary component between them, was it? They'd shared many things, but nothing as brutal as honesty.

"I trust my staff has seen to your comfort." He inclined his head, ever the genial host.

She forced a smile to her face. "They've been exceedingly polite."

As the two of them were being polite. Yet anyone walking into the room could easily feel the undercurrents between them.

She raised her glass of wine and sipped from it.

"A good vintage," he said, "with a back note of oak."

She smiled politely, wondering if he remembered some of their earlier conversations. Vallans had had its own vineyards and she'd grown up appreciating the labor and skill necessary to transform the grapes into wine. Once, she'd even ventured the subject with her father with an idea of initiating some changes into the process. She'd been roundly reproached for even thinking of such a thing. The daughter of the Comte du Marchand did not indulge in wine-making, however old and venerated the tradition.

If Douglas remembered, he didn't mention it. Nor did he give any inclination that they were anything more than acquaintances. But she knew the shape of his shoulders beneath his fine shirt and exquisitely tailored jacket. She could measure the width of his chest with three hand spans, fingers splayed. He shuddered when she touched him and stroked his erection between her hands, and breathed an oath against her cheek when pleasure grew too much to hold silent.

She was a fool to be sitting here with Douglas. There were too many things left unsaid, too many conversations that lingered in the air between them, all memories of better times.

A sensual interlude was no substitute for honesty.

She smiled into her glass, thinking that, in addition to being a fool, she had also learned the skill of self-deception.

Very well, the truth. Those months in Paris had been the most joyous and the most beautiful of her life. She'd spent nine years paying for the sin of them. Was it so terrible to want to re-create them for a little while? Possibly. Last night had proven to her that she could revisit the past, if only for a fleeting moment. A span of hours, silent and hushed and replete with recollection.

Yet even last night there had been an edge to their lovemaking. She'd been afraid. She could not allow herself to be vulnerable again, and he was the one person who had the power to hurt her. Above all, she'd been frightened that she might confide the horror of those months at Vallans to him, and the tragedy of their child's death.

The word wasn't right. Tragedy was such a barren word, imparting a certain detachment. A carriage loses a wheel and the occupants are injured. An epidemic of influenza decimates a town. Both occurrences, tragedies, happen without the victims' foreknowledge or premonition.

What, then, did she call what had happened to her child? A horror, or perhaps even worse—an abomination. Even though she'd wished and hoped for her father to change his mind, she should have been prepared for his rage and for his cruelty.

Last night she'd not told Douglas the truth, leaving it sitting between them like one of the evil gargoyles of Notre Dame. Today, she was too cautious to reveal her most painful secret. They had not, in fact, admitted to each other a shared past. For that matter, they had not yet acknowledged the night before.

She studied him over the rim of the glass.

He'd shaved and changed his clothes. She'd bathed and had brushed her hair until it shone, had used a rag to polish her shoes. Both of them were intent upon presenting themselves at their best.

Should she also confess that she'd stared at herself in the mirror, seeking confirmation that ten years had passed? Her skin had aged, it was true, and was too heavily tanned. But that was from her escape from France and not the result of nine years within the convent walls.

There were several lines around her eyes that hadn't been there a decade ago, and one tiny commalike indentation near her mouth.

Her eyes looked the most changed, the expression in them no longer excited or enthusiastic. She looked sad, an expression she could not banish despite her grimaces and silly faces into the mirror. Sorrow was a part of her, like the odd gray shade of her eyes and the tone of her voice, personal markers to identify her as Jeanne.

If they could not discuss their youth and they dared not discuss the future, that left only the present, these moments softly lit by candlelight and interrupted by the sounds of crystal being set down on the table linen, a napkin being unfolded, the fluttering of a candle flame. Words were rare between them, as precious and cherished as pearls strung on a silken thread.

She had dined at Versailles, and her own home, Vallans, had been a showplace of excess. She was not impressed with surroundings, but she found this cozy room to be the most pleasant place she'd been for quite a while. What would Douglas think, to learn that she was content as long as she was warm and dry, with the knife-edge of hunger satiated? A far cry from the spoiled girl of her youth.

That Jeanne had been enchanted with this man. The woman was equally so, and therein lay the danger. She wasn't the same person she had been, and neither was he. There was an aura to Douglas that hadn't been there before, a slightly dangerous impression about him, some dark thread to his personality that intrigued her as it cautioned her.

"You've a beautiful home," she said.

"Thank you. I've been moderately successful."

"May I ask the nature of your business?"

How strange that she didn't know.

"I trade," he said, smiling. "I have a fleet of ships that bring goods from the Orient to England and Scotland."

"It sounds like quite a venture."

"It is," he said. "The MacRaes were once sea captains, but we've branched out in the last decade. Now we have interests in a variety of concerns. My oldest brother, Alisdair, continues to build ships at our family home of Gilmuir. James trades in the linen produced in Aylshire, where he's settled. Brendan is the head of a distillery in Inverness, and Hamish still sails."

"And you are the merchant of the family."

"I am," he said, studying her over the rim of his glass. "Do you find that distasteful, Miss du Marchand?" he asked, as if they'd never loved in the darkness. As if she hadn't begged him to finish the torment and let her feel him climax in her arms.

"Trade?" She smiled. "No, I do not. A man is known by his character, Mr. MacRae, more than his occupation."

"Then how do you judge my character?"

She looked directly at him and spoke the truth. "I don't know you well enough to come to that judgment."

He waited until the footman finished carrying the tureen to the table. After they were served, he nodded, a curiously imperious gesture that sent the young man from the room. Instead of challenging her remark, he asked a disconcerting question. "Why did you leave France?"

Because she'd been imprisoned for nine years, because she could not bear what they'd done to Vallans, because she wanted a new life, because there were too many agonizing memories there.

"I found that it was no longer safe," she said instead. Revelation might be good for the soul but it had a way of leaving a bitter taste in her mouth.

However, he seemed dissatisfied with her answer. He leaned back in his chair and surveyed her.

Twice she nearly spoke, to say something inconsequential, anything but allow the silence to stretch between them. She picked up her spoon and tasted the soup.

"Were you raised in France?" he asked finally.

So, it was to be that way? They were going to engage in pretense again. There was, however, a certain amount of relief in the game. A certain freedom in being someone else for a time, pretending to be a stranger he had just met and bedded. Very well, she would play and somehow convince herself that the pretense wasn't almost as painful as the truth.

"Yes," she answered. "I spent my early years at Vallans, our chateau some distance from Paris, before I was allowed to come to the city."

"An interesting city, Paris."

"Have you been there?" There, not too much interest expressed, just enough to give this silly game some reality.

"I spent some time there in my youth. All in all, I prefer other cities."

She concentrated on the meal in front of her, deliberately ignoring the emotion his words provoked.

"That's a pity," she said. "There are those who consider Paris the most beautiful of all cities. Before the recent troubles, I mean."

"How did you avoid the recent troubles? Were you at your family's country home?"

"No," she said. She rearranged her silverware, dabbed at her mouth with the napkin, and folded it into a small rectangle.

She didn't furnish information to him easily but wanted him to ask for it, a game within a game. If he asked, she would tell him. But if he sat silent, she wouldn't volunteer the information. This was not, she realized, a casual conversation. They learned of each other under the guise of politeness, hiding their interest beneath the structure of commonplace questions and answers.

"You were at the convent."

There, the first admission that he remembered last night. She nodded.

"It seems to me that it might be easier, or safer, to remain inside the walls of a convent," he said. "Especially given the climate in France of late."

She smiled. "Perhaps. My isolation quite possibly saved my life. I was hundreds of miles from Paris and not affected by the riots. When Vallans was razed, I wasn't there. I knew nothing about what was transpiring in France."

"When did you learn?"

She chuckled mirthlessly. "When I awoke one morning to find that the convent was deserted. The nuns had fled in the horror and the gates were left unlocked and wide open. It was the first indication that something was wrong."

"You were left alone?" Disbelief flavored his voice, and she wanted to tell him that that had not been the worst of it.

But that journey through France would be her secret, one that she would keep.

"There was no one left but a few of the novitiates." Girls like herself who had been virtual prisoners. But at least they were among the lucky ones. There were headstones among the graveyard that marked the last resting places of some of Sacré-Coeur's inhabitants, women sent to the convent in disgrace for infractions similar to Jeanne's.

She and two other girls had walked through the deserted convent not quite believing their sudden freedom. That afternoon they, too, left before anyone could return and reinstate their imprisonment.

For nine years the convent had been, if not her home, then the place her body had resided. As she stood on the hill that evening and looked back at the gray structure, it seemed to Jeanne that the mist obscuring the building was not unlike a blanket, hiding the past nine years.

Douglas didn't say anything for several long minutes, leaving her with the impression that he formed his questions with great deliberation. Perhaps she should use as much care in her answers.

"Where did you go when you left the convent?"

"Home," she said shortly, wondering if he knew that his questions had lost their subtlety. He was interrogating her. "To Vallans."

That had been a difficult homecoming. She hadn't known that Vallans had been torched until approaching the ruins. Only the foundations and chimneys of Vallans remained, a testament to the once-great house that had dominated the countryside. The ornamental lake had been blackened by soot, and even the air smelled of fire.

After she'd found her hidden cache, she'd risen, only to discover that a figure stood there surveying her. Tall and spare, with a crown of red hair, Justine seemed part of the ruins, as if she commanded them with the insouciance of a queen. She didn't move as Jeanne walked slowly around the mounds of debris to stand in front of her, but remained standing where she was, hands clasped together in front of her.

It was as if no time at all had elapsed since Jeanne had seen the woman, the last memory that of Justine taking her child. A decade disappeared in the blink of an eye, leaving only moments between that deed and now.

"You look well, Justine," she had said, surveying the former housekeeper. While it was true the gray dress she wore fitted her loosely, her hair was upswept in a style reminiscent of Paris, her nails clean, and through the soot Jeanne could smell the scent of roses.

Wealth was no longer judged by gold and silver, by heavily brocaded gowns or jeweled slippers. The truly fortunate had food to eat and water to drink. The blessed had the luxury of cleanliness. Justine had evidently managed not only to survive the difficult times but also to prosper in them.

Justine had smiled. "I wish I could say the same of you." The other woman surveyed her up and down, and then surprised her by turning and walking away. After taking a few steps, she turned and glanced at Jeanne, an unspoken summons. Curious, Jeanne had followed.

"I saw your Vallans once," Douglas said, a remark that summoned her to the present so quickly that Jeanne felt dizzy with it.

"When?" she asked, feeling her heart constrict. Had he come looking for her after all?

"A very long time ago," he said. "I was seeking someone I knew."

"Did you find him?"

"In a way," he said, a cryptic answer that she waited for him to explain.

Instead, he remained silent, and she smoothed her napkin over her lap again and wondered when this interminable dinner would be finished.

"You've eaten very little."

She nodded, agreeing. Determinately, she picked up her spoon, intent upon finishing the soup.

"It was not an order, Jeanne."

Once again she nodded. "I know that. It's better to eat when you can rather than when you wish."

A remark Justine had made to her that day at Vallans when they'd reached the gatekeeper's cottage. Justine had evidently made it her home, with small comfortable touches like the cloth on the square table and curtains on the lone window.

"You are looking at me as if I'd never done a kindness for you before," Justine said as she placed an earthenware bowl in front of Jeanne and filled it with soup. Jeanne was so hungry that the smell of food had made her light-headed for a moment.

"You haven't," she said, beginning to eat.

Justine smiled. "Circumstances change. People change."

"The last time I saw you, Justine, you were taking my child from me, and now you're feeding me and claiming you're kind. People do not change that much."

Justine sat opposite her, a small smile playing around her mouth. How strange that age did not diminish her beauty, only added a luster to it like patina on silver.

"He wanted her killed, you know."

Jeanne stopped eating, carefully placing the spoon on the side of the bowl. "He told me to take the baby and make sure she died."

Nausea suddenly overwhelmed Jeanne and for a moment she thought she might be ill.

" 'Put a hand over her mouth, Justine,' he said. 'Smother her in a blanket.' " She shook her head. "I didn't kill her, you know," Justine said. "I do not murder children, even for your father."

"What happened to her?" The words came slowly, measured by her pendulous heartbeat. The air felt thick, every sound muted. Jeanne forced a breath into her chest and then out, striving for a composure she didn't feel.

"I might have taken her to foster for myself. I've always wanted a child." Justine shrugged. "What an irony if I had been able to raise the Comte du Marchand's granddaughter as my own."

"Instead?" Her chest hurt with the effort of restraining her words.

Joy was a tinny little sound, an unfamiliar bell. It began as a barely decipherable chime somewhere deep inside her, began to gain strength and cadence until it matched the clamoring sound of her heartbeat. Jeanne clasped her hands together tightly in front of her.

"Instead, I found an old couple who agreed to care for her." She shrugged. "They were grateful for the money I gave them."

"Why did you never tell me?" The training of the last nine years was in her favor. Jeanne didn't reveal any emotion at all, neither hope nor despair and certainly not the boundless grief she always felt when thinking of her child.

Justine's look was not kind as much as pitying. "Because your father was right about one thing. You were young and foolish, and had brought dishonor to the du Marchand name."

"Where is she?" The question evidently startled the other woman. But surely Justine must have known that she would ask. For a moment her brown eyes were almost kind, her smile appearing absurdly benevolent. Jeanne could not fix this gentler, kinder woman with the terror of her youth.

"It doesn't matter anymore, Jeanne," the older woman said softly, almost pityingly.

Four simple words. That's all. And the chime suddenly stopped. The dawn of her soul turned to midnight again.

What a strange tableau they must have made, two women struggling in life, facing each other across a small square table. As odd as this one, she thought, glancing up to see Douglas looking at her with suddenly intent eyes.

"What happened when you reached Vallans?"

"Nothing," she said. "There was nothing left of it." The sight of Vallans scorched and ruined was one of her greatest nightmares. For the longest time, standing there, she'd felt as if she were part of the scene, as destroyed as the magnificent chateau. She was only a ghost on the landscape, as ethereal as the hint of soot in the air.

"Why did you go back?"

She shrugged. "There was nowhere else for me to go."

"So after Vallans, you left France."

She nodded.

"Have you any family in Scotland?" he asked, the tone of his voice dispassionate and almost bored, as if he were disinterested in the answer. It was as if he quoted from an invisible text in his mind. How to entertain a guest at dinner: Discuss the weather, inquire after absent relatives.

"I have no relatives at all," she said, equally as distant.

His glance flicked in her direction and then away again as if afraid of giving away too much interest.

How easily they pretended that they hadn't discussed their lives intimately, including their dreams for the future. How arrogant they'd been in their youth, how easily convinced that the days stretched out empty and waiting to be filled with precious memories. But men fared better at futures then women, didn't they? Her life in the last ten years had been a simple exercise of enduring the present. Living in the past was too painful and it was foolish to project herself into a future that looked too much like the eternal sameness of her days.

As the meal wore on, she realized he was studying her intently. She pretended not to notice, but he was not so easily ignored. He was simply there, like a thunderstorm, a force of nature so strong that the very air in the room seemed charged.

The last quarter hour they hadn't spoken to each other. Two courses were brought in and taken away but she couldn't remember eating. The food was unmemorable, and that had nothing to do with the cook and everything to do with the man at her side.

"Why Scotland?" he asked, as if there had been no lull in the conversation.

"I came to find my aunt. But I learned that she died a year earlier. I found myself needing shelter and food. The most commonplace way to do that is to be employed."

"You could have married," he said.

"Marry?" She was genuinely amused.

"Why not? It's been the answer to a woman's dilemma for thousands of years, has it not?"

"In my case, I do not believe it would suit."

"Why is that?"

The conversation had taken a turn that was uncomfortable. She wished, suddenly, for the silence they had shared during most of the meal.

"I have never met anyone who would inspire the emotion necessary for marriage," she said. An answer as good as any. Better the lie than the truth. *You were in my heart and marked your place there forever.*

"Is love necessary for marriage? I thought other things were more important. Income, connections, legacy."

"I had been reared to believe that all true. But I have no

legacy anymore, no connections, and my only income now comes from you." She smiled at him, wondering where she'd found her courage. "What else is left but love?"

"Should I feel guilty about last night?" he asked abruptly, surprising her.

She reached for her napkin below the table, twisting it between her hands. Several silent moments passed between them before she looked at him again.

"You mustn't," she said composedly. "You didn't, after all, force me."

She held his look, determined not to be the first to glance away. When he finally broke their gaze, she felt released, and looked down at her plate once more.

"Does that mean that you would care to repeat the experience?"

Where had he learned such control?

The Douglas she had known had been an impulsive, almost rash young man. He wanted to see the world just like his older brothers, and conquer it in a way that the other MacRaes had not. He'd had so many plans and it looked to her now as if he had accomplished all of them.

Only to become a man who was intimidating and slightly dangerous.

But she resented his attempt to control the conversation. She resented the fact that he sat here whole and healthy and hale opposite her, seemingly untouched by life itself.

"If you wish," she said, mimicking his offhanded manner.

To the casual observer, her response had no effect on him. But she knew him too well. There was a patch of color high on his cheekbones and the rim of his ears suddenly deepened in color, signs that Douglas MacRae was angry.

The emotion made them equals, and the meal abruptly more palatable.

"What did you do to make your father send you to the convent?"

She'd been wrong. They weren't equals at all. He held the upper hand. Taking a sip of her wine, she considered how to answer. She wondered what he would do if she told him the truth. *Because I bore your child. Because I was a whore.* A name her father had called her. Those months had been unbearably lonely and filled with sorrow. She remembered putting her hands on either side of her round belly and conjuring up what life would be like with all three of them as a family. But Douglas had disappeared, all thoughts of responsibility evidently terrorizing him.

The moment she'd learned she was with child, her body had ceased to be her own. There was another being sharing it, altering her shape, dictating her moods and wishes. She was more a vessel for this child than a person belonging to herself, and the sensation had been both unsettling and awe-inspiring.

A part of her had disappeared when they'd taken her child from her the day she was born. Another part died when she'd been dragged from Vallans, placed in a coach, and bound and muffled with a gag in case she screamed and shamed the du Marchand name.

Nor had she ever returned to herself.

Instead, she had her own secrets, didn't she? Reasons not to bring up the past and play this game with him.

"My father sent me to the convent because I'd disappointed him," she said, the only answer she was going to give him.

Again, he sought refuge in silence. The man was a great deal more mysterious than the boy had been, and more cautious with his words and thoughts.

"What were you doing while I was at the convent?"

"Living here," he said shortly.

"With your daughter."

"Yes."

He suddenly stood and bowed to her. "If you will forgive me, I've remembered some duties not yet attended to." With that, he was gone, leaving her staring after him.

Chapter 15

～∞～

Jeanne expected him that night, and waited for him to come. Attired in her nightgown, she sat in the chair by the window. Would she welcome him? Or sit silent, a chastising sentinel, when he opened the door? With her hands clasped on her lap she watched the candle burn down, casting the lavishly appointed guest room in shadow.

The red-lacquered chest on the south side of the room was adorned with a stylized dragon in black and topped with two blue and white porcelain vases. The bed hangings were red silk, the coverlet white with an embroidered scarlet dragon in the center. The furniture was quite obviously patterned after a French design with claw feet and turned legs. A writing desk sat in the corner, and on the opposite side of the room was a basin for washing. Talc, soap, and tooth powder were arrayed on a silver tray nearby.

A lovely chamber, and one that was unbearably lonely, but she'd had years of practice with that emotion.

Finally, she stood and walked to the window, watching the gray clouds chase a black night. She was in the mood for rain, for heavy storms, and pounding thunder. She wanted lightning and danger and wished, suddenly, to be out in it, challenging the elements. Perhaps she'd stand on the highest hill and dare God to send her a thunderbolt.

As if she had summoned the rain, it began pattering against the windows. When he entered and shut the door softly behind him, she didn't turn but kept her gaze on the night-darkened street through the rivulets of rain.

"I couldn't stay away," he said and it was a confession, one that she knew she'd never receive in the light of day.

"I know," she whispered and it was an admission of her own, an acknowledgment of their mutual weakness.

He came to her, placed his hands on her waist, and turned her until she faced him. He pulled her to him and kissed her, an open mouth and hungry kiss that replicated all that she felt and more. She wrapped her arms around his neck and held on as he lifted and carried her to the bed.

In this night of mist and thunder, he pulled the draperies closed until the bed was surrounded in silk. Only then did he speak again, his voice husky and low.

"You knew I would come."

"Yes," she whispered in an assent, or perhaps a confession.

"And you want me here."

How could she not? But instead of answering, she placed her hand against his cheek, her thumb brushing the edge of his smile.

Last night had been the first time they lay on a bed and loved. But their bower beneath a tree had been as magical and their trysting place along the river had been special and beautiful. She suspected that this night would be as rare and remarkable, and then wondered if it was wise to love him again. The question was fleeting and unanswerable, because he kissed her again and every thought vanished.

"Tell me what you want," he said, the question allowing no evasion.

"Everything." She could tell that her answer surprised him.

"That covers a dozen or so sins, Jeanne," he said, smiling.

The word amused her. "I've been punished for more than a dozen sins, Douglas. What's a few more?"

He reached out with one finger, traced her lower lip. "What shall I do first, then?"

"Kiss me again," she softly said. "I've grown accustomed to your kisses."

"And then?"

"Begin with a kiss."

"A small enough request," he said, acquiescing. Long moments later she pulled back.

"I want you to know me so well that I feel a part of you." She placed her hand on the curve of his face, her palm lightly cupping his jaw. Slowly her fingers moved to his neck and across to his shoulder.

She could feel the muscles bunching there where he supported himself. Unlike the night before he was fully dressed. Only his coat was gone, but he was still attired in his fine lawn shirt and trousers. Even his boots, she noted with a smile.

His look was difficult to decipher, almost as if he willed himself not to reveal any emotion at this minute. But his eyes glittered and there was a flush high on his cheekbones. The sight of Douglas, aroused, struck an answering chord deep inside her.

"I want you to be so close that you can't tell if it's my breath or yours." She placed her hand flat against his chest, feeling his heart beat strongly beneath her palm. "Or my heart beating or yours. My pleasure or yours."

She began undressing him, her fingers fumbling on the buttons. He smiled at her fevered attempts, not understanding that her desire was fueled by desperation. She had to feel in order to cease thinking, or her thoughts would overwhelm her.

Perhaps she'd be the instrument of her own downfall, confessing everything rather than bear the suspense.

"Are you trying to seduce me, Jeanne?" he asked, one corner of his mouth tilting up in a smile.

"Do you know that I was once punished for not being a virgin?" Startled, she stared up at him. She hadn't intended to say that.

He didn't respond, only covered her hands with his.

"As a woman grows, she enters into evil, taking into her body the strength of men until they are weakened and puny and easily led into sin."

Douglas drew back, frowning at her. "Who said that?"

"A nun I used to know," she said, wishing that the shadows were all-encompassing. Instead, the lone candle flickered on the bedside table, illuminating the sudden watchful look in his eyes. "Sister Marie-Thérèse would say that every night before my punishment. She stored the whip on the altar, a constant reminder that the God of her faith was a fierce deity. I used to try to prepare myself but I was always surprised by how much it hurt."

"Should you be quoting a nun at this moment?" he asked, his voice carefully expressionless.

"I can't imagine a better time," she said, savoring the exquisite irony of this moment. She began to smile, realizing that it was the truth. "She was a sour-faced nun who hated everything about me."

"She wouldn't be pleased to see you now," he said, beginning to smile as well.

"No," Jeanne answered, "she wouldn't."

"Then kiss me, Jeanne," he said. "And all sour-faced nuns be damned."

When he touched her in the faint light she opened her

arms, welcoming him into her heart with no more resistance than a sigh.

She felt tears come to the corners of her eyes when he kissed her neck and murmured something against her skin. No matter what had happened between them, whatever history they carried, they would always be hungry for each other.

But would that be enough?

He was suddenly naked and in a few swift moves her nightgown was tossed to the floor.

He sat up and drew her to him, his breathing more controlled than hers. Gently, he pulled her on to him so that she sat half on, half off his thighs, his erection brushing her intimate folds. She wanted him inside of her, but he wouldn't move farther, only remained just out of reach.

Her fingers began to tremble as well as the muscles in her abdomen. As if he were opium and she desperately needed the drug. Laying her cheek against his shoulder, she breathed deeply, exhaling against his neck.

"Soon, Jeanne, but not now."

He teased her with words, and with softly stroking fingers. She bit her lip and kissed his throat, feeling the heat rise both inside her body and on his skin. Reaching out one finger, she traced a circular path around and then down the length of his erection. Once, as a girl, she'd held him cradled between her palms and stroked him to fulfillment, absolutely amazed and delighted at his response to her touch.

"No," he said now, the word uttered from between clenched teeth. "You're not supposed to do that."

"I'm not?"

Their whispers were heated, their words soft and intimate, no one else to hear them in the cocoon of the bed. It might have been another world they created, silk-shielded and shadowed. Here they might be anyone other than who they were, and here they might love in unfettered pleasure.

"Stop me if you can," she said, teasing.

"You know I cannot. Besides, I would be a fool to do so."

She didn't know how long they tormented each other, but when he raised a finger and touched her breast, circling the nipple slowly, she placed a soft kiss against his throat and then another against his ear. He'd always liked it when she nibbled on his lobe and bit enough that he turned his head and kissed her once again.

That was all they allowed themselves—soft, gentle teasing touches, and chaste kisses—until she thought she might go mad with it.

Minutes passed, and then it seemed as though hours had transpired. Her breath grew more rapid, her blood felt hot, her skin fevered.

"Please," she said, whispering against his ear. "Please."

Suddenly the pillow was beneath her buttocks and he was lifting her higher for his mouth.

Her body arched without thought as pleasure swept over her, so fiercely that she bit her lip rather than cry out.

As she crested, he was inside her, fevered and impatient and wondrous.

"Forgive me," he said, an apology for his need. The sudden imploration was an unwelcome interruption. Her arms wrapped around his neck.

"Forgive me," she whispered, an echo of his plea. The words became a refrain, as the past entwined with the present. He inhaled her plea in a kiss and sent it catapulting somewhere where nonsense words and soft-voiced entreaties disappear.

"Forgive me," she murmured later.

He kissed her once more, not understanding, and she, coward that she was, sought pleasure and ignored the chance for revelation.

Chapter 16

❦

The next morning, Jeanne was awakened by a knock on the door. Glancing to the side of the bed, she realized she was alone.

Standing, she donned her wrapper before opening the door. The woman facing her was close to her age, with pale blond hair arranged in plaits on the top of her head. Her dress was dark blue, with white collar and cuffs.

"Good morning, miss," she said, smiling brightly at Jeanne. "I've just come to tell you that your chamber's been readied."

"You're the housekeeper," Jeanne said, only to receive a laugh in response.

"Oh, no, miss," the other woman said, her blue eyes kind. "I'm Betty, Miss Margaret's nurse. Not that she truly needs a nurse, being the great grown girl that she is." She smiled at Jeanne. "That's what she's forever telling me."

She took a few steps away from the door and pointed to a room down the hall. "I've moved my things. One of the maids and I have tidied it up right enough for you. I'd be pleased to help you move your belongings."

"I can't take your room," Jeanne protested.

"Oh, but it's really for the governess," Betty said cheerfully. "I'm already settled on the third floor." She bent closer, as if afraid that someone else might overhear. "In truth, miss, it's a little less formal up there. Not that I don't think the world of Mr. Douglas and Miss Margaret, but I'm looking forward to the change."

"Give me a moment," Jeanne said, "and I'll join you."

Jeanne donned her most severe and governesslike attire, a dark blue dress not unlike Betty's, ornamented with a white neckline and matching piping on the edge of the cuffs. She, who had been coached on how to direct retainers all her life, now looked every inch the upper-class servant.

She put her hair up in a style similar to Betty's. Perhaps the severe braid was more of an effort to modify her nature than her curls.

Betty led the way down the hall, with Jeanne following. The room was larger than she expected, with two tall windows facing east. On the west wall was a large four-poster bed hung with beige linen drapes. Along one wall was a heavily carved wardrobe and bureau, while a fireplace occupied the third wall. Underfoot was a lovely oval carpet in shades of gold and beige.

"That door leads to Miss Margaret's room," Betty said. "You can brighten it up yourself, miss. If you need any help moving your things, just give me a call." She pointed to the bellpull beside the fireplace. "It rings in the kitchen, but Cook can find me right enough."

"I'm sure I'll do fine," Jeanne said. "Unfortunately, what belongings I have can be easily put in a valise."

Betty's smile dimmed somewhat. "I know what you mean, Miss. The same thing happened to me once. But you'll find that you've come to a place you can easily call home." She hesitated for a moment. "Would you like a tray in the room, miss? Or would you care to take breakfast with the staff?"

Jeanne glanced down the hall. Douglas was gone; it was time for her to begin being a governess. How she behaved from this moment forward would dictate the tone of her stay at Douglas's home.

"I'd like to take breakfast with the staff," she said. "Give me a few moments and I'll join you downstairs."

Betty nodded.

Jeanne packed her valise with what few belongings she had. At the door she looked back at the room she'd occupied for only two nights.

Did the servants know that Douglas had spent the previous night with her? They probably did. Little of import happened in a house, even as large as this one, without the staff knowing. But, like all well-trained employees, they would probably not reveal how they personally felt.

In her new chamber she placed her valise in the tall armoire. After breakfast she would unpack. Now she surveyed herself in the mirror, smoothed her hair back at the temples. With some trepidation Jeanne walked down the hall and slowly descended the stairs.

Lassiter greeted her as she rounded the last curve. The elderly majordomo nodded slightly. No doubt the gesture was meant to be a bow but was modified somewhat for both his age and her new position as governess.

"Good morning, miss," he said, his voice sounding rusty and unused.

"Good morning, Lassiter," she responded. She hesitated, her hand still on the banister, as she considered whether or not she should ask about Douglas's whereabouts.

"Mr. MacRae asked me to give you his compliments, miss, but he was called away."

She nodded, hiding the fact that the news was surprising.

"I see. Will he be gone long?"

"I'm sure I don't know." There was that unctuous half
bow again. She had to commend Lassiter; he was adept at
conveying exactly what he thought while seeming to avoid
even a hint of insolence.

"Thank you," she said, straightening her shoulders.
"Could you tell me where I can find Betty?" she asked.

For a moment she didn't think he was going to answer her.

Sighing inwardly, she drew herself up and frowned
down at him. She might wish to forget that she was the
Comte du Marchand's daughter, but the role of two-thirds
of her lifetime was one she could easily and quickly as-
sume. "Well, Lassiter?" she asked.

He wiggled one of his white, bushy eyebrows at her. She
stifled her smile as she realized it was Lassiter's version of
surprise.

"This way, miss," he said. Bowing once more, he began
to shuffle down the corridor. She followed him to a large,
airy room in the rear of the house.

"Miss," he said, almost as if announcing her. He stepped
aside as she entered, and then simply melted from sight.

Lassiter was superb at disappearing.

The kitchen was a large open room with high ceilings
and windows located in two walls. Sunlight filtered
through white pots of herbs sitting on a series of shelves
across the windows. The effect was almost like a conservatory, with the sun creating leafy patterns on the green
walls. A large rectangular table stretched the length of the
room and was currently occupied by several people who
were enjoying what looked to be a luxurious breakfast.

A florid-faced woman standing at the stove turned as she
entered the room, her warm smile greeting her. Jeanne returned the expression as Betty stood and made room for
her at the table.

"Is it a French breakfast you'll be wanting, miss, or the English one?" Cook asked.

Jeanne glanced at the array of food piled in the middle of the table. "I'll just have a scone and some tea," she said, opting for a meal somewhere between the two extremes.

"You just sit there, then," Betty said, pointing to the head of the table. Jeanne hesitated, but Betty waved her to her seat.

"This fine gentleman is Stephens, the coachman," Betty said, beginning the introductions. "And Malcolm, who heads up the gardeners." She pointed to the stove and the plump woman standing in front of it. "That's Granya, our cook, and you know Lassiter."

Jeanne nodded and smiled a greeting at the three.

"Doesn't Lassiter eat with you?" Jeanne asked, wondering if she was taking his chair.

"He's only for a bit of oats in the morning," Betty said. "He doesn't eat as hearty as he should."

Going to the stove, she filled a pot with boiling water from a simmering kettle and returned to the table. "We haven't a housekeeper in place, Miss du Marchand. We have two maids who do the heavy work, and a few of Malcolm's boys who still live at home and arrive every morning."

"Don't forget the grooms, Betty," Stephens said in his gravelly voice. He turned to Jeanne. "I've three boys who sleep over the stable. Good lads, all. And two of Lassiter's footmen, although they're able to do a bit of everything."

"I'm surprised," Jeanne said, surveying them all, "that you manage a house this size with only the five of you."

Betty smiled. "It would be easier with more staff, but it's the way Mr. Douglas wants it. He doesn't like a lot of people underfoot."

"Have you been with him long?"

Malcolm answered her first. "Since the house was built, about seven years now. Before that, I was with Mr. Douglas's brother Alisdair."

Surprised, she turned to him. Malcolm's beard was closely shorn, with enough gray hairs mixed among the black to give him a grizzled appearance. His brown eyes were ringed with deep lines, but his smile was broad and charming.

"Most of us know the MacRaes in one way or another," Stephens explained. "I worked with Alisdair for years before Mr. Douglas set up this house. I bought his horses for him, and maintain his carriages. He's a rich man, but he's not a fool with his money."

The others nodded.

"I worked in Inverness," Cook said. "As well as Betty." She and Betty smiled at each other.

"I would have stayed there for the rest of my days had it not been for Mr. Douglas," Betty said. "I was a maid myself, working for one of Miss Mary's friends. Mr. Douglas came straight from Gilmuir one day, and asked me if I would like to be a nurse. I told him that I'd never had any experience but that I was willing to try. He told me that Miss Mary had recommended me." She smiled, evidently pleased by the praise. "She said that I had a good heart and that was all that he cared about. I've been with him and Miss Margaret ever since."

"Miss Mary?"

"She married Hamish, one of Mr. Douglas's brothers. Poor thing can never spend another day in Scotland." Betty shook her head from side to side but wasn't forthcoming with any details.

"She was married to an old man," Malcolm said, evidently determined to pick up the slack in the story. "He died and she was accused of his murder."

Betty sent him an irritated look but took up the tale in the next breath. "He was a very nice man but much older than Miss Mary. Up until he became sick Mr. Gordon was the nicest employer, but after he got ill a more crotchety man you could never find.

"Miss Mary tried everything she could to heal him." She glanced around the table, relating the story to all of them.

"She was a healer, you see." This comment from Malcolm, who'd evidently heard the story before.

"Anyway," Betty said, with another quelling look toward Malcolm, "Miss Mary was very sad when he died. She spent the next year being a good citizen of Inverness. If anyone needed her help and could not pay, Miss Mary still treated them. She spent many a night sitting at the bedside of a patient."

Betty chewed her muffin slowly, evidently thinking back to the days in Inverness. Jeanne folded her hands in front of her and took a deep breath, cultivating her patience. She'd had years of training from the convent in simply enduring, but periodically she reverted to that impatient girl of her youth.

"One day, one of the MacRae brothers came to her husband's place of business. Did I mention that he was a goldsmith?"

Jeanne shook her head.

"He was a very talented man. His apprentice was not so talented, but very clever."

"The man's here in Edinburgh," Malcolm said. "Charles Talbot. He should be ashamed of showing his face near decent folk."

Once again, Betty shot him a look filled with irritation.

"I believe I know the man," Jeanne interjected. "I've been to his shop myself."

"A shop he set up with Mary's money," Betty said loyally.

Glancing over at Malcolm and then at Jeanne, she stopped herself. "But am I getting ahead of the story?"

Jeanne had no idea where the story began or ended, so she only smiled.

"Tell her about Hamish," Malcolm suggested earnestly. His eyes never left Betty, and Jeanne had the feeling that it wasn't just the story that prompted his interest.

Betty nodded. "One day, one of the MacRae brothers came to the shop and said that his brother Hamish was wounded and needed treatment. The laird and his wife had always been customers of Miss Mary's husband, so she was eager to do what she could to help."

Betty smiled, her expression holding a touch of mischievousness.

"One thing led to another as things sometimes do, and Miss Mary and Hamish found themselves in love. But Charles had other plans. I believe it was then that he started the rumors that Miss Mary killed her husband. She was taken to court and bound over for trial in Edinburgh. But before she could be sent away from Inverness, Mr. Hamish spirited her away."

"That's why she can never come back to Scotland?" Jeanne asked. "Because she would be sent to trial?"

Betty nodded. "Everyone knows she had nothing to do with it, that Mr. Gordon's death was an accident well enough. She has a heart as pure as the angels. But Mr. Hamish won't take the chance. They went sailing off to see the world, they did, and only come back to Gilmuir once a year."

Jeanne accepted a plate filled with scones from Cook and murmured her thanks. She took one and began to eat.

"That's where Mr. Douglas is now, miss," Betty said. "It's time for the gathering." The other servants nodded, as if understanding what Betty had said.

"The gathering?" Jeanne asked.

"All the MacRaes, miss. They come together every summer to meet at Gilmuir. The brothers and their wives—Hamish and Mary, James and Riona, Brendan and Elspeth—all join Alisdair and Iseabal. And, of course, Mr. Douglas."

"It's a way of keeping close ties among the family, Miss du Marchand," Stephens said. "They want the cousins to know each other."

"They've a crowd of children," Cook said, her round face wreathed in a smile. "And Miss Margaret the queen of all of them."

"With Mr. Douglas the most doting father," Betty said. "No matter how long or hard he works, he's always home to tuck her into bed."

The rest of the conversation consisted of desultory things, places to shop, the weather in Edinburgh, and talk of people she didn't know.

All her life she'd felt separated from others, kept apart. As a child because her father believed her better and more exalted than others. In the convent she'd been isolated because she was the greatest sinner.

Seeing the world as an outsider rendered her detached from other people. She'd long since realized that the ability to feel, really feel, for another human being was a worthy trait. But even more so was the courage to be vulnerable.

As she sat and listened, Jeanne envied these people who had so easily made room for her at their table and now included her in their conversation. Once, she might never have noticed them, and now she was desirous of their camaraderie and respect.

The more she learned, the greater her regard for Douglas grew. He evidently treated people with fairness and with affection they both felt and appreciated.

Breakfast finished, she stood, smoothing her skirts down. She folded her hands in front of her. "Thank you," she said to Cook. The other woman nodded, and a moment later Jeanne left the kitchen and the warm and welcoming group.

What was she to do in the meantime? She didn't want to return to her room and remain there as she had all day yesterday. Turning, she walked down the hall, hearing her footsteps on the polished oak boards.

She stood at the entrance to the parlor, realizing that she hadn't truly noticed her surroundings when she'd been here before. The room was lovely. There was not one discordant note about the entire chamber, and it had evidently been decorated with comfort in mind. The damask curtains were draped from the top of the window to the floor, the material matching that of several pillows arranged along the upholstered furniture in front of the large marble fireplace.

Two blue and white Chinese urns flanked either side of the fireplace. Now, of course, there was no fire, since the morning was warm. But the room was saved from stuffiness by the two windows open to let in the breeze. Below her feet was a richly patterned carpet that reminded her of the Lalange tapestry that had hung at Vallans. A creation of unimaginable beauty and age, it had faded over the years, acquiring a rich patina of beige, soft blue, and rose.

The parlor was both modest and luxurious, small touches like the gold bibelot boxes on the table between the chairs attesting to the wealth of its owner. But as warm and hospitable as it was, there was nothing here that revealed Douglas's taste. Nothing that revealed anything intrinsically personal about him, and that lack was what she noticed the most.

She would have been surprised to see anything out of place, a pair of shoes under the table or a book carefully waiting for a reader, a half-empty cup.

Retracing her steps, Jeanne walked into the morning room. Smaller than the parlor, it boasted a wall covering of patterned silk in tones of pale yellow. A settee sat against one wall, while a chair sat adjacent to it, the two pieces of furniture separated by a heavily carved circular table. A sideboard sat against one wall opposite a row of windows. She went and stood there, looking out at the view facing the garden.

Not a garden, she realized an instant later, but rather a wild place filled with overgrown bushes and brambles and half-grown saplings. In the middle of the space was a tree, an oak with massive branches heavily laden with spring leaves.

There had been a tree on the convent property, set out in the field, all alone. There wasn't anything about it to mark it as unique from other trees—it wasn't appreciably larger, or endowed with more magnificent branches. Birds congregated there before a storm or at nightfall or daybreak and then flew away in a swift rush of uplifted wings.

But she could see the tree from her cell, and it had become a lodestone for her eyes, a way to mark the seasons. In winter it appeared stark, with its grayish-colored branches clawing at the sky. Spring saw it adorned with curling green leaves spiky with new life. Summer was the time of lush growth, when a canopy of sheltering leaves hid the branches from view. Autumn was the dying time of year, and the tree—her tree—seemed to grieve in the season. The branches hung lower; the leaves fell with a slow and solemn certainty in a soundless dirge as they covered the ground.

How strange to be reminded of that single, simple tree, and how sad that it was her only happy memory of nine years.

Turning, she walked back to the door of the morning room. A young maid emerged from behind one panel into the hall, startling her.

"Good morning, miss," she said, bobbing a curtsy. With her clanking bucket and scrub brush, she disappeared into the morning room, leaving Jeanne standing in the hall.

The door to her right was closed, the brass handle newly polished and shining brightly, almost a lure for her to open it.

The combination of curiosity and loneliness proved too difficult to ignore. Jeanne pushed the door open and stepped into the room, closing the door hurriedly behind her.

Heavy velvet drapes obscured the windows and darkened the room. Here was, if not the soul of the house, then the mind of it. Mahogany bookshelves filled with gilded leatherbound books lined the walls. A massive carved rectangular desk faced the door.

Standing in front of it, she reached out and touched the wood, her fingers sliding over the satiny finish. In the middle of his desk lay a leather blotter, all four corners adorned with tooled leather. At the edge sat a crystal inkwell and next to it a set of quills all sharpened for his use. To her right was a curious lantern fixed with a black shade. Bending down to examine it, she realized that the amount of light could be adjusted by moving the central metal cylinder up and down.

On the left side of the desk sat a branch of candles, each contained within a shapely glass globe, the better to maximize light while keeping any wax from falling on the surface of the wood.

Slowly, she circled the desk and carefully pulled out the tufted burgundy leather chair. Resting her hands on either side of her, she felt the lion heads at the ends of the chair arms.

Douglas sat here, resting his hands in the very same place.

The house felt lonely without Douglas, and this room especially. Leaning back in the chair, she closed her eyes and breathed in the scent of leather. A masculine room, one that mirrored Douglas more than the other chambers she'd seen.

When would he return?

Coming to this house, being with Douglas again, had already altered her life so that she felt caught between the past and the future, in some nebulous present that had no shape or form. Her mind counseled restraint—being here with Douglas was an interlude, no more. Yet her heart could not quite concur. Love didn't remain dormant for long; it struggled to survive or it died.

In all this time, it had never died.

Opening her eyes, she surveyed the darkened room. Opposite the desk on the far wall was a fireplace, and this one was as ornately carved as the one in the parlor. Brass fireplace tools sat on one side of the hearth, while a large copper urn sat on the other. An upholstered fender welcomed the chilly visitor, urged him to come closer and sit before the fire. Farther back were two wing chairs, each covered in a deep burgundy cloth. Between the chairs was a curiously carved table in the shape of a crouching lion. On the marble top sat another branch of candles.

She stood slowly and made her way to the fireplace.

Above the mantel was an exquisite portrait of a young girl. The artist caught her smiling, almost as if she were getting ready to burst into laughter and restraining it by the greatest effort. Her brilliant blue eyes were dancing with mischief, her black hair hung in ringlets to her shoulders. In one hand she held a basket whose contents were revealed by a pair of shining eyes. A girl and her kitten.

Jeanne found herself smiling up at the picture. Going to the window, she drew back the curtains. A shaft of sunlight illuminated the portrait and as Jeanne stared into the vivid blue eyes of the little girl, she realized that it could only be Douglas's daughter, Margaret.

The surge of grief she suddenly felt surprised her. Reaching out, she gripped the mantel to steady herself. The resemblance to Douglas was startling. The little girl had the same shade of hair, the same blue eyes, and his stubborn jaw. There was a tilt to her head that reminded Jeanne of Douglas, and even her mouth, formed in a smile, brought him to mind.

If she'd lived, her daughter would have been nine this year. The child in the portrait looked older.

Jeanne only had flashes of recall from the morning of her daughter's birth. She remembered lying there marveling at the wrinkled infant on her stomach, tenderly covering her with both hands so that she wouldn't be cold. Everything about her was perfect, from her wizened little face to the fists flailing in the air.

The midwife, however, had noticed something, some imperfection that she'd gleefully announced to the assembled women. "There's a mark on her leg," she called out. "A sign of the devil's touch. A sure sign that she was conceived in sin."

An indication of Jeanne's fall from grace, that none of the servants in attendance around her had chastised the midwife for her words. Even Justine, tall and spare and judgmental, had not ventured to silence the old woman.

Jeanne had ignored them all, so entranced with this miracle that she hadn't wanted anyone to sully it. True, there was a small birthmark, a crescent-shaped purple mark on her daughter's leg, but it would no doubt fade in time.

Time, one of those precious commodities she'd taken for granted in those halcyon days of her innocence. What a foolish girl she'd been.

As she stared at the portrait of Margaret, Jeanne felt as if she'd been knifed, the pain so real that she glanced down at herself to make sure she hadn't been wounded. She felt the same sense of horror standing there that she did on that morning so long ago. Only moments after Jeanne experienced wonder at the tiny creation she and Douglas had created, Justine had taken the baby, wrapping her tightly in a swath of linen and leaving the room. Jeanne's throat had been raw with her screams before she'd been force-fed a draught from the midwife.

Now she felt the same sense of helpless grief.

She stood there until her heart stopped pounding so hard and her breath came a little easier. The tears were more difficult to contain. Finally, she walked toward the window with the slow, heavy steps of an elderly person. Once the curtain was closed she stood in the darkness for several long moments, head bowed, trying to regain her composure.

Hearing a sound behind her, Jeanne glanced over her shoulder to see Betty entering the room. Before she could be chastised for being somewhere she shouldn't be, she asked a question. "Did you know her mother?" She nodded toward the portrait, suddenly desperate to know more about Douglas's wife.

When Betty didn't answer her, Jeanne turned.

"It's not a subject we discuss, miss," Betty said, her expression guarded. "From the stories I've heard him tell Miss Margaret, he loved her very much."

Jeanne brushed the fingers of both hands over her face, straightened her bodice, and forced a smile to her lips. "Thank you, Betty," she said, once more composed. "I shouldn't have asked."

The nurse nodded.

"You should enjoy this holiday," Betty said. "Mr. Douglas said you were to be treated like a valued guest in his absence."

"Then I shall," Jeanne said, feeling herself warm at the comment. She left the room with Betty, deliberately not glancing at the portrait again.

*   *   *

Charles Talbot made his way to the Hartley home, returning the silverware he'd repaired. The bill was also discreetly attached, and he fervently hoped the housekeeper was prompt in paying it.

His most important reason for this errand, however, was to meet with the Comte's daughter. If he was fortunate, he could convince her to allow him to handle the sale of the ruby without involving her father.

Five years ago, Talbot had married a lovely woman, a widow who was as charming as she had been wealthy. She had sickened and died a year ago, leaving him a rich man. Or so he'd thought. The interview with her solicitor had been startlingly simple and disconcerting.

"You're not listed in her will," he'd said, looking too amused for Charles's peace of mind.

"I was her husband," he'd protested.

"She left her estate to her sister."

"But she can't do that." But to his amazement, Charles had discovered that she could.

These last years had not been prosperous ones. With the influx of French émigrés, he'd been hard-pressed to charge as much as he had previously for one of his designs. He'd had to dismiss two of his apprentices, and kept one only half days. Even that arrangement looked doubtful in the future unless he came up with a way to make some money.

The Somerville ruby might be exactly what he needed.

He didn't, however, trust the Comte du Marchand, which was why he was here, knocking on the kitchen door of the Hartley home.

A young maid, her hair trapped in a starched white cap and her round face watchful as she bobbed a curtsy, opened the door to him.

He explained his errand, was directed to the housekeeper. Once he'd turned over the silverware and had his

work approved as well as his bill, he returned to the kitchen
and asked a question of the same young maid.

"Is Miss du Marchand available?" he asked.

She frowned at him but answered nonetheless. "Oh, no,
sir, she don't work here no more. She left."

He stared at her, uncomprehending. "What do you
mean, she left?"

"She just walked out. No one knew until they went to her
room. She wasn't there." She glanced behind her and then
looked both ways as if afraid of being overheard. "I've
never seen Mr. Hartley so angry," she whispered.

"Where did she go?"

She shrugged, and then shook her head. "No one knows.
Not a letter, not a word."

Had the Comte du Marchand gotten to her first? He
withdrew a coin from his pocket, one he could scarcely afford to part with, and smiled at the young maid. "Take
this," he said, putting the coin in her hand. "If you hear
anything, send word to me, and I'll match that coin with
another."

She bobbed another curtsy, her eyes wide. "I will, sir,"
she said. "I promise."

He gave her his name and address, and left the house,
annoyed and dispirited by the fruitlessness of today's errand. Not only was he desperate to locate the Somerville
ruby, it now appeared that he also needed to find the
Comte's daughter.

Chapter 17

The sky was deep blue and cloudless. The wind came out of the north, blowing him home to Gilmuir. Douglas stood at the bow of the ship and watched as they approached the fortress, recalling, as he always did, his first sight of the restored structure his brother Alisdair had brought back to life.

He'd been seventeen, recently recalled from France by his father. The elder MacRae had been annoyed at the length of his youngest son's stay in Paris and more than willing to take Douglas to Scotland. Ten years ago, aboard the ship with his mother and father, Douglas had looked up and seen, as he did now, the great golden rock topped with a magnificent edifice. Towers on all four corners marked the perimeter of the peninsula on which it stood. Closer to the loch was the priory, its arched windows gleaming with stained glass.

Six years ago, they had held the memorial for their parents in that place, and it had felt hallowed, almost as if he were standing in the shadow of God. All five MacRae brothers had been there, solemn and adult, yet all of them feeling bereft and abandoned.

The journey down the firth was a slow one. It took three days to reach Gilmuir by land from Edinburgh, and only a day by water. But he still had hours in which to view the sights before him, time enough to wonder at the fact that he'd escaped Edinburgh and was at Gilmuir a week early. He chose not to think of Jeanne. Instead, his memory conjured up his first visit here, when he'd been seventeen and miserable. He had known, then, that Jeanne was with child, but that was all the information he had. He had gone to see her one last time before he was due to meet his family. He'd wanted, fool that he was, for her to come with him. An elopement, if the Comte would have it no other way.

Instead of seeing Jeanne, however, he had only met Justine.

He'd finally divulged the story to his parents, and they, in turn, had sought fit to spread the entire tale to his brothers. The MacRae family had, as they always did, banded together. If hurt was imposed on one, it was felt by all. A few weeks later, he'd left Gilmuir with his brother Hamish and Hamish's wife, Mary, determined to return to France as soon as he could.

The ship, one of his own fleet, rode the currents of the firth with ease. Alisdair had designed the *Edinburgh Lass*; the MacRae shipyards had created it. Now he braced his legs apart, his hands behind his back, easily keeping his balance while his mind recalled his one and only visit to Vallans.

Seven months, four days, and three hours after he'd vowed to return to France, he'd reached the du Marchand chateau, only to discover that Jeanne was gone. He'd spent a week trying to find out what had happened to both Jeanne and his child. A young stableboy had finally succumbed to a large bribe, telling Douglas what he'd seen. Jeanne had left Vallans weeks ago for an unknown destination, but the child was located nearby.

The memory of finding his daughter would remain with him forever. The woodcutter's hut was located not far from Vallans, on the edge of the forest. The doorway into the cottage was so low that Douglas had to stoop in order to enter. After his eyes grew accustomed to the darkness he realized that the space was even smaller than it had appeared from the outside. The bricks were loose in several places, allowing patches of light, the only illumination in the hovel. The furnishings were sparse, a rough-hewn wooden table, two chairs, and a sagging cot located behind a curtain.

"What do you want?" a quavering female voice had asked. She was pressed against the brick wall, gripping her apron with her fists, a look of fear on her face. Beside her stood a stoop-shouldered man clutching a pipe between both hands as if it were the greatest treasure of his life.

He'd not expected the inhabitants to be so old.

"You have a child here, the daughter of Jeanne du Marchand. Where is she?"

The couple glanced at each other, but neither moved to speak.

"Is your silence worth dying for?"

He heard Mary's surprised gasp, but didn't move to reassure her that he had no intention of killing the old woman and her husband. If they didn't produce his daughter he might kill them after all.

"We were given the child," the old woman said, sending him a quick, appraising glance.

"I'm taking her back."

"She's like our own daughter."

"She *is* my daughter."

The old man began to sidle away. A tiny mewling cry from the cot alerted him, and Douglas pushed back the curtain and stared down in revulsion at the sight that met his eyes.

He bent closer, a wave of nausea passing over him. He had not been around many infants in his life, but Douglas knew that what he was looking at was unnatural.

The infant was little more than a skeleton. The flies that buzzed around her face no doubt weighed more. Tufts of black hair covered her tiny head, and when she blinked up at him her MacRae blue eyes silenced any doubt he might have had about her parentage.

Mary came to his side and would have reached out and scooped up the child in her arms had he not stopped her.

"No," he said, nearly incapable of speech. Emotions flooded through him—joy that his mission had succeeded, horror that his daughter looked as if she would not live the night. Above all, he was filled with rage for Jeanne du Marchand, who had left Vallans with no thought for her child.

"I'll carry her," he said and gently lifted the infant, ignoring everything but the look in her brilliant blue eyes. She fixed her gaze on him as if she knew he was saving her. Her head was too big for her body, and as he stared at her emaciated form in disbelief, one tiny hand reached out and almost touched him. He cradled her in his arms, bent his head and kissed the tiny fist.

She couldn't be more than a month old or maybe two and lighter than a breath; such a small and weightless burden that when she closed her eyes he thought she'd died. His heart pounded in a rapid, panicked beat until she moved again. Only then did he lift his gaze to the old couple.

"Did you never feed her?" His voice sounded calm, almost rational, a remarkable feat considering that he wanted to kill both of them.

"She's a picky eater, sir," the old woman said. She bent her knees in an awkward curtsy. "And the money the woman gave us ran out. We couldn't hire a wet nurse."

Mary used her kerchief as a makeshift blanket, covering the baby in his arms.

"Can we save her?" he asked, glancing at her.

His sister-in-law's look was too compassionate, her brown eyes revealing the truth.

But then the baby blinked her eyes and looked up at him. There, in his daughter's face, he saw the shadow of his parents and his brothers. She was a MacRae and he prayed that she had the strong will of all MacRaes.

"Live," he whispered to her. "Please, live."

She was his child, but he had never expected to feel the overwhelming sense of protectiveness that he did at this moment. Nor had he thought to love her instantly and completely.

"We'll save her," Douglas said to his sister-in-law. "We will."

Instead of speaking, instead of giving him countless reasons why such a miracle would not happen, she only nodded, tears swimming in her eyes.

"What is her name?" he demanded of the couple.

The old man merely shook his head while his wife shrugged, the outline of her bony shoulders showing beneath her shawl.

"We've never named her," she said. "But you can, if you wish, sir," she added, grinning at him, revealing the brown stubs of her teeth.

He shook his head in disgust. Settling the infant in his arms more firmly, Douglas headed for the door.

"You can't be taking her, sir," the old woman said, clearly alarmed. "What if someone finds out that she's gone?"

"I doubt anyone will come looking for her."

Anger for everything French nearly overpowered him. He hated the country, the people, even the language.

Everything except for the child he cradled in his arms, so slight that she might have been a ghost of herself.

A moment later he emerged from the dark hovel to the sunlight, Mary following. The old woman followed them to where his brother Hamish stood beside their horses.

"Pay them," Douglas said and waited until Mary mounted before handing up his daughter.

Hamish withdrew a small leather bag from his waistcoat and tossed it to the woman. She opened it quickly and gasped at the amount of gold coins resting inside. There was enough money to keep her and her husband for the rest of their lives.

"You don't deserve it," Douglas said, glancing over his shoulder. "But this amount will buy your silence. Tell anyone, if they bother to ask, that she died. I doubt anyone will want proof."

The old woman nodded eagerly.

"Bless you, sir," the old man called from his position by the door.

Douglas didn't turn at his words. Instead, he mounted and then held out his arms. Mary reached over and gave him his daughter.

"It's a miracle she's alive," Mary said, one hand smoothing his coated arm, the other resting lightly on the kerchief covering his daughter.

Weeks had passed before they'd known if she would survive.

Douglas had never considered that he might hate as deeply as he loved. Not until the moment he'd taken his daughter into his arms and looked down at that tiny, wizened face. He'd known then that he would forever hate Jeanne du Marchand for what she'd done.

Where had that hatred gone?

As if he'd summoned Margaret with his memories, he saw a movement out of the corner of his eye. The blur became a green dress and flowing black curls as she raced across the glen, followed by two bigger boys.

He felt the door to his heart creaking open once again.

Watching impatiently as the sailors lowered the anchor, he waited until they approached the dock like a lumbering and cautious tortoise. Before the ropes were lowered and tied off, Douglas swung himself over the side and climbed the rope ladder down to the pier.

Margaret had disappeared, but he knew where she would be, the same place she always was when he came to take her back to Edinburgh.

He didn't have the affinity for Gilmuir that Margaret had. She reminded him of his mother, and the tales she'd often told of the old fortress when he was a boy. Or perhaps she was more like Moira MacRae, his grandmother, who'd been a skilled horsewoman, married an English Earl but still returned every summer to her home in Scotland.

Sometimes, when Margaret spoke of the fortress, her eyes lit up and her face glowed. To his daughter, there was no place in the world as grand as Gilmuir.

Alisdair had spent years restoring the ancestral home of the MacRaes. Douglas often suspected that Gilmuir was more magnificent now than it had ever been.

Every summer, the brothers, their wives, and their children united at Gilmuir. All of the MacRaes made a point of coming together for a month in order to strengthen familial ties. None of them wanted to forget the legacy that had brought them home to Scotland.

James returned from his village of Ayleshire. Brendan and his brood traveled in two coaches from Inverness. Even Hamish and Mary scheduled their voyages in order to return to Scotland in time. Because Mary would never set foot on Scottish soil, they made a point of meeting aboard Hamish's ship to greet her, a reunion Douglas never missed. He would always be grateful to Mary, certain that Margaret was alive today because of his sister-in-law's knowledge and skill with healing.

· Although he saw his brothers often during the year and their wives occasionally, returning to Gilmuir was special. Douglas always felt a surge of memory—recollections of his parents, his great-uncle, and all the tales he'd been taught as a boy growing up in Nova Scotia. His MacRae heritage was here in the soil, the very air of Gilmuir.

He left the dock and took the cobbled path. To the right it wound up to the top of the hill and to Gilmuir. Straight ahead lay the trail to the land bridge and the glen. Below him was the necklace of rocks, a chain of massive blackened stones emerging from the bottom of the loch. Beyond the rocks was a cove once kept secret but now used to test new hull designs for the MacRae shipyards. The sunlight glinted off the deep blue water, the reflection striking the cliff walls.

Chips of silver embedded in the stone reminded him of Jeanne's eyes.

Once, he'd wanted to punish her, as if by inflicting pain he could right the wrongs she'd caused. As the years had passed, gratitude for Margaret's survival and love for his daughter had softened his rage, only to have it return at the sight of her.

Before he left Edinburgh he and Jeanne had not yet admitted their past to one another, as if each knew what must follow if they did so. Jeanne would have to confess what she'd done, and he would have to destroy her.

He should have held her at arm's length. Instead, he'd bedded her not once but twice. She'd proven to be such an irresistible lure that he'd found himself fleeing from her, arriving at Gilmuir before he was expected.

She was there in his mind, however, so strong that she might have stood beside him, her hand on his arm. In fact, when Alisdair suddenly stepped into the path to greet him,

Douglas was surprised that his older brother didn't remark upon her presence.

"You look tired," Alisdair said, clapping him on the back. "You've been working too hard, Douglas. Don't we have enough money?"

He smiled in response to Alisdair's familiar quip.

"Mary will have you drinking all sorts of possets and potions to keep up your strength."

"They're here?" he asked, surprised.

Alisdair nodded. "They're as early as you."

The years had been kind to Alisdair. His hair had a little more silver at the temples, his face bore a few more lines, but other than that he didn't look appreciably older. Iseabal, his wife, had the same good fortune. Her hair hadn't changed color, and only a few lines appeared at the corners of her eyes, a testament to her habit of smiling often.

Alisdair reminded Douglas of their father, capable of achieving a commanding presence without speaking a word. Perhaps it was because he was the oldest brother of five. Or maybe because he'd inherited their father's title, and was an English Earl in addition to being master of Gilmuir.

He assumed responsibility easily and was a born leader. His only mistake was in occasionally attempting to lead his brothers, all of whom were possessed of the same strong personality.

"Margaret is about," Alisdair said, scanning the glen for signs of his niece.

"I know where she is," Douglas said, looking ahead. Across the land bridge that connected the promontory of Gilmuir to the glen was a hill they called Iseabal's Knoll. Over the years a path had been carved in the glen and through the forest and he took it now, bidding Alisdair farewell for a time.

A small green scarf had been wrapped around a sapling,

a clue that he was correct in assuming Margaret was there. His mother had often spoken of this hill, telling stories of how his great-uncle had dared the English by playing his pipes here.

The hill had been the first place he'd brought Margaret on their very first trip to Gilmuir. She'd been two years old, still too thin but healthy. He'd held her up so that she could see everything in front of her. "It's Gilmuir, Meggie. It belongs to you, and to every MacRae."

Although Alisdair had rebuilt the fortress, using a substantial portion of the legacy from his English inheritance to do so, he had insisted on altering the ownership of Gilmuir after the memorial service for their parents. The brothers had signed the papers in front of a solicitor, taking ownership of a share of the ancestral estate. Despite the fact that each of them had created homes in other parts of Scotland, they were now linked to Gilmuir legally.

The forest was shadowed even though it was noon and the sun directly overhead. The cool air was redolent with the heavy, sharp scent of decaying leaves and musty earth. Moss growing on one side of a few sapling trunks attested to the fact that it had been a damp spring.

He continued upward, the stillness of the forest a balm to his spirit. He found himself relaxing, the concerns he brought with him from Edinburgh being lost in the greater expanse of nature around him.

He took a deep breath and felt some of the tension leave him. Being at Gilmuir relaxed him, or perhaps it was only that he was going to see Margaret soon. This year she'd begged to be able to spend some extra time with Mary and Hamish and he'd allowed her a three-week visit before the Gathering began. His life, carefully proscribed, had continued without her, but there was something missing in Edinburgh, some sense of happiness, of rightness.

It was not strictly for Margaret that he worked so hard as

much as it was his sense of himself. He had obligations, true, but his driving ambition urged him to continue thinking, advancing, and conquering one obstacle after another. Even when he had sailed with Hamish, acting as captain aboard his brother's ship, he'd pushed himself to learn all that he could. Now Douglas owned a fleet of MacRae-built vessels.

There were times, like now, with the journey to Gilmuir fresh in his mind, and the glint of the sea visible through the towering pines, that he still yearned to be at sea. When Margaret was three, however, he'd traded living aboard ship with a rolling deck, imminent threats of fierce storms, or becalmed seas for a more conventional existence in Edinburgh.

He had created a happy life for himself and his daughter, at least until he'd seen Jeanne du Marchand again.

Douglas stopped, looked around him as if to ascertain that only the squirrels and foxes and other feral creatures were witness to his confusion. There she was again, in the midst of his mind. Just when he thought himself free of her, she had popped in, diverting his thoughts, leading him from relaxation to irritation.

Go away, Jeanne.

He could almost see her in the filtered sunlight. She was standing there, an ethereal figure, a ghost of his imagination. She held out one hand as if to entreat him to follow her. Where? To perdition, no doubt.

He closed his eyes and shook his head, the better to banish her. Margaret was waiting.

Swiftly, he began walking again, cutting across the path to a less-well-known trail that led past a shadowed cave to his left. The cave, too, featured prominently in his parents' tales.

He found it difficult to remember that an English fort had stood beside Gilmuir on the promontory. But it had been picked clean, dismantled brick by brick after the English had left MacRae land. Traces of it weren't even visible anymore, since Alisdair had constructed part of the new Gilmuir over the ruins.

That's what he should do with his life—build something on the ruins of it. Perhaps he should marry. Find a woman who suited both him and Margaret and create a new existence, one not dependent upon memory.

Out of the corner of his eye he thought he saw a flicker of material. Or a ghost again?

Go away, Jeanne. Take your sad eyes and hint of mystery and leave me alone.

Pushing through the thick growth of trees, he emerged at the top of the hill. Here, he'd been told, a large pine had once stood. Over the years, the earth had been flattened by wind and rain and was now covered in a thick layer of pine needles.

She wasn't there, but he knew she was nearby. He heard a giggle and smiled. Margaret never walked when she could run, and never simply smiled when she could laugh. She was so filled with life that Douglas felt energized in her presence.

"Papa!" Suddenly she was hurtling herself toward him. He opened his arms and grabbed her and was enveloped at the same time in a smothering embrace, her arms wrapped around his neck, her warm cheek pressed against his. She squeezed tightly as if to never let him go.

A moment later she pulled back and glared at him accusingly. "You took so very long to get here."

"I took the right amount of time, Meggie," he said. "In fact, I'm early."

She frowned at him, her entire face revealing her displeasure. Her mother's beauty was in the shape of her nose and the curve of her chin. She had Jeanne's hands, long-fingered and elegant even though her nails were filled with dirt at the moment.

Margaret was, despite the resemblance to either of her parents, quintessentially herself.

"Yes, but it just seemed so very long. You cannot measure how long something *seems,* Papa."

He set her down on the ground and she immediately placed her hand in his. She was taller than most girls her age, a fact that occasionally caused her some discomfort.

"It's because I was a picky eater as a baby," he'd heard her say once to a group of teasing cousins. "They fed me and fed me and fed me. I couldn't help but grow tall, could I?"

"It seemed long for me, too," he said now. "Have you enjoyed your summer?"

She looked at him, eyes shining. "Oh, yes, Papa, it's been the most wondrous time."

Suddenly she reminded him of the girl he'd known in Paris. Jeanne had such vivacity, so much enthusiasm for life. Where had that personality gone? What had life done to Jeanne that had subdued her so very much?

He remembered the scars on her back, and her words about the convent.

I did something that earned my father's displeasure.

Had the Comte discovered her actions? Had he, too, been sickened by what Jeanne had done?

He wanted to hate her for being complex when she should have been uncomplicatedly evil. He wanted to hate her for piercing the armor of his self-restraint, and his façade of indifference. He wanted to hate her for weeping, for being scarred, for her aura of sorrow, for his unexpected and unwanted curiosity about those missing ten years. Above all, he wanted to hate her for the fact that she made him care.

"It feels like we're on the edge of the world," Margaret said, staring out at the vista before them.

Her hand tightened within his and he felt a surge of protectiveness for her. When he was little more than a child himself, he had held her within his arms, feeling revulsion for what her mother had done. Now that revulsion was directed at himself. He had made love tenderly and with great passion to a woman who had cared so little for her own child that she had sent her to her death.

Now that child looked up at him worshipfully, confident that he could order her world and make everything right for her.

He would die trying.

"It does feel as if we're on the edge of the world, doesn't it?" he said. "Or at least the only world that matters."

"I wish we might be able to live here forever," Margaret said, her voice holding a note of wistfulness.

"Unfortunately, we cannot."

She nodded quickly. "Because your business is in Edinburgh."

"And our home, don't forget that."

"But couldn't you build something here?" Her glance encompassed the far glen. The prosperous village seemed to expand up the hillside every year. The road leading to Inverness had once only been a track but was now paved. Upward of two hundred people lived at Gilmuir, a great many of them employed at the shipyards.

"I'm sorry, Meggie," he said. "But I have business in Edinburgh."

"You always have business in Edinburgh," she said, sighing deeply to let him know she wasn't pleased.

He hid his smile.

"I'd like to come and see Gilmuir in winter, Papa. Robbie says the ice hangs all over the trees and the forest looks magical. I want to come back then. Could we, please?"

It was the first time she'd ever expressed a desire to return to Gilmuir in the winter.

"The winds are cold and bitter in winter," he said, having made the journey more than once.

"I don't care. The fireplaces at Gilmuir are huge. They'll keep us warm."

"We'll see," he said and she sighed again, sending him an admonitory glance.

He grinned, placed his hands beneath her arms, and hoisted her up until they were eye level. He kissed her soundly on the nose, his heart lighting at the sight of her grin.

"Do try, Papa," she said somberly. She tilted her head back and studied him, and in that instant he saw her mother in the child's face.

Go away, Jeanne.

The ghost in his mind only smiled.

Jeanne dressed and, as she usually did, rearranged her neckline so that her mother's pendant wouldn't show. Her hand flattened against the base of her throat as she remembered that she'd left it behind. Although not an especially pretty piece of jewelry, it was a last link to her mother, the last link to Vallans, and perhaps even to her past. As much as she valued it, however, she wouldn't be so foolish as to return to the Hartley home, not when she'd taken such pains to escape it.

At breakfast the staff was in their usual talkative mood, the conversation turning, as it usually did, to Douglas and Margaret.

"When do you expect them to return?" Jeanne asked when, one by one, the staff dispersed. Her heart beat quicker as she waited for Betty to answer.

"The Gathering lasts a month, so they'll be back then. Mr. Douglas never takes more time away from his business. Even though," she added, "Miss Margaret often stays longer. This year, for example, she went with Mr. Hamish and his wife three weeks early. Very close with them, she is.

"The time will pass quickly enough, you'll see," Betty said, as if she knew how discomfited Jeanne was by that information. "Cook is practicing some new recipes for Miss Margaret and I'm busy with my own set of errands. One day they'll be back and you'll wonder where the time went."

"Is there anything I can do to help?" Jeanne asked, looking around the immaculate kitchen. Even at the convent she'd been given tasks to accomplish. The unoccupied hours since Douglas had left had given her too much time to think about him.

"Oh, no, miss, we have it all in hand. You should enjoy your free hours. There's a sweet little park on the corner. You might wish to take a walk and enjoy the day. I myself have plans to do the very same. Have you ever noticed that the air is so much clearer after a storm?"

Jeanne watched as Betty wiped down the already spotless table, washed the rag, and spread it out to dry. "Would you be going toward town?" she asked. "If so, I have a favor to ask."

Betty glanced at her curiously. "What is it, miss?"

"I've left my locket where I used to work. I need someone to retrieve it for me."

"Used to work?"

Jeanne clasped her hands before her, wondering if it was a wise thing to mention the necklace. How much else would she have to divulge? "I was employed as a governess to Robert Hartley's oldest child."

"I had no idea you'd been in service here in Edinburgh," Betty said. The other woman had perfected the art of revealing nothing. Her round face was carefully devoid of expression and her eyes held no emotion at all. "Mr. Douglas only told us you were from France."

Jeanne took refuge in silence. Betty had been friendly to her from the first, but there was a decided chill to the air now as she twisted the rag she'd just smoothed across the work surface.

"You've the time to go yourself if you wish, miss."

Jeanne stood and walked to the window. A series of shelves stretched across the view of the tiny garden. For a moment neither woman spoke, but the interval wasn't peaceful. Instead, the silence seemed to hum with questions.

"I'd rather not return to the Hartley home," Jeanne said finally.

Betty glanced at her sharply.

Jeanne took a deep breath and faced the other woman. "I had no choice but to leave, Betty. Or perhaps I did," Jeanne corrected. "I chose to leave rather than to stay under difficult circumstances."

"And what circumstances would those be?" Betty's eyes narrowed.

"Is that important?"

Betty didn't glance away. "Are these circumstances any better, miss?"

In that moment Jeanne realized there were no secrets in this household. Not only did the servants probably know that she had shared Douglas's bed but they'd given their tacit approval. At least, until this moment.

She felt her cheeks warm under Betty's continued scrutiny. Finally, Jeanne answered her. "I will welcome a man to my bed or refuse him, Betty. It is my decision and mine alone. I will not be forced into it." And that was it, wasn't it? Not whether or not she was considered virtuous, but whether it was her own choice. For years, she'd had that luxury taken from her. She had vowed never to be a prisoner again, even if it was only of the will.

Betty surprised her by nodding, as if she agreed. "Will you be leaving us as well?"

Inherent in the question was another one that wasn't voiced: *Will you be leaving Douglas?* Evidently, it wasn't prudery but loyalty that stiffened Betty's back and made her voice sound like ice.

"When I'm no longer wanted," Jeanne said, offering Betty the hard-won truth.

Betty nodded again. "Give me the directions," she said. "I'll fetch your necklace this afternoon." A moment later she was out the door, leaving Jeanne in the empty room.

"When I'm no longer wanted," she said again in the silence. How many nights had she lain awake, thinking of just that? How many hours had been spent reliving those moments with Douglas? She knew that she would stay until he sent her away, but she would not leave first. How odd to suddenly understand the enormity of her need for him.

A wiser woman would have been frightened. Instead, she only smiled faintly, thinking that, despite her care and caution, she had become a prisoner after all.

Chapter 18

Douglas looked around the clan hall, relieved that he'd finally begin the journey home tomorrow. He'd stayed the full time, even though there had been plenty of reasons to leave Gilmuir early. Negotiations were under way for a new warehouse site in London. In addition, two ships, the *MacRae Maiden* and the newly refitted *Moira MacRae*, were due in from India. Men who had been boyhood companions in Nova Scotia captained both ships and he anticipated seeing them again.

If his impatience to return to Edinburgh was based partly on the fact that Jeanne was there, it was an admission Douglas had no intention of making to another human being.

Moving through the clan hall, Douglas nodded to a few villagers. Finally he sat at the table, a replica of one that had been here for generations. After the '45, Gilmuir had been put to the torch before being razed by English cannon. Nothing had been left of the old castle but a few walls, a corridor, and the ruins of the priory. Alisdair had gradually rebuilt the fortress, adding on two wings and several towers.

The hall was an impressive chamber. Three stories tall, it was festooned at the ceiling with replicas of banners the MacRaes had possessed through the centuries. Small metal lanterns sat inside yellow-painted embrasures, casting intimate circles of light over the hundred or so people gathered here. There was enough festivity and laughter that no one noticed his silence.

Margaret, like the other children, had been sent to sleep in the loft on the third floor. None of the parents truly expected their children to fall sleep easily. There was too much excitement during this last night, too many conversations to listen to, and too much activity to witness.

Someone passed him a tankard, and he drank appreciably, savoring Brendan's newest batch of whiskey. His brother had married Elspeth nine years earlier and a few years ago had taken over her father's distillery.

"I'll take a hundred barrels," he said as Brendan sat beside him.

His brother laughed. "If you'll take two hundred, I'll throw in my brother-in-law to help you over the winter."

Douglas raised one eyebrow. "Trouble in Inverness?"

"Jack needs a diversion," Brendan said in a low tone.

He remembered Brendan's brother-in-law from a previous visit to Inverness. Newly married and working at the distillery, Jack had been a happy young husband. Circumstances changed a year later when his wife died in childbirth.

"Elspeth thinks he needs a change of scenery," Brendan said, looking fondly across the table at his wife.

"She looks tired," Douglas said. Like most of his sisters-in-law, she'd done too much to prepare for this event. Since he'd arrived, he had a chance to witness exactly how much work the gathering required.

"She's expecting again," Brendan confided.

Douglas took another sip of his whiskey. "What does

that make, six children? Are you single-handedly trying to repopulate the Highlands, Brendan?"

His brother grinned but didn't answer. Leaving the table a moment later, he went to sit beside his wife. Douglas couldn't hear their whispered conversation but he could imagine it. Brendan would be urging her to rest while Elspeth reluctantly agreed. She wouldn't go, however, until Brendan joined her.

Concern and caring, togetherness, a respite from loneliness, love—that's what he'd witnessed in the MacRae marriages this past month. He'd never before been envious of his brothers, despite the fact that by the time he was born they were nearly men. He'd not had their camaraderie when he was a boy, but he'd had something they had not—the undivided attention of both his parents.

While his older brothers were sailing the seas or building ships, he was growing up in Nova Scotia, living a life appreciably different from theirs. The contingent of Scots who had emigrated from Gilmuir nearly fifty years ago had lived in hardship. His youth, however, had been spent in relative comfort. His brothers had been educated either by his parents or a Jesuit priest who had taken refuge among the émigrés from Scotland. Douglas, however, had wanted to attend the Sorbonne in Paris and had done so.

It was the loss of their parents that had brought the five brothers closer together and strengthened their bond. Over the past seven years Douglas had grown to know them, respect them, and consider his four brothers his best friends.

But he had no intention of telling any of them about Jeanne. He doubted any of them would really understand either the circumstances or what he felt. He wasn't entirely certain he did.

The festivities were increasing in volume. Douglas leaned back against the wall and watched the dancing, feeling oddly as if he were simply an observer at this most familial of occasions. Alisdair's wife waved to him and he forced a smile to his face for Iseabal's benefit.

Across the room he saw Hamish, and slowly he made his way to his brother's side, greeting those people who called out to him. For three years he and Hamish had sailed together, Douglas learning a great deal about being a ship's captain under his brother's tutelage. Hamish had also taught him a great deal about life as well, those lessons learned through observation. His older brother had taken him on when he was seventeen years old, angry, heartsick, and feeling belligerent toward the world. Despite the fact that Hamish was newly married and no doubt had wanted to be alone with his bride, he'd given him patience, understanding, and enough work that he'd fallen exhausted into his bunk at night. When the time had come, Hamish had also listened, given him advice, and unfailingly assisted Douglas when he was determined to return to France to find his child.

"Is Mary ready for visitors?" Douglas asked.

"She's had all hands on deck this afternoon cleaning," Hamish said with a smile.

Every year at the Gathering all the brothers and their wives met aboard Hamish's ship. The children remained at Gilmuir, tucked into their beds while the adults made the journey down to the firth. The event was an intimate one filled with recollections and laughter, and occasionally some solemn moments.

He excused himself and mounted the stairs to the loft. In moments he found Margaret's pallet, and sat down on the edge of it.

"Wouldn't you be more comfortable in your own room?" he asked his daughter. Each of the cousins had his or her own room in one of the wings Alisdair had added to Gilmuir. If Brendan's brood kept growing, however, his brother would be forced to add to the fortress.

She shook her head vehemently from side to side, sending her black curls swinging. "Please, Papa, no. Everyone is looking forward to tonight." She pulled on his sleeve until he bent down to hear her whisper. "Robbie has promised to tell me the story of Ionis the Saint."

"A very great tale indeed," he said, remembering one of the stories that swirled around Gilmuir. The priory, it was said, had been built on hallowed ground, a place where pilgrims had once come to pray.

He looked around the large loft. It was evident from their appearance that the children were related. Black hair was predominant, and in a few faces he saw the MacRae blue eyes. He doubted, for all the presence of blankets and pillows, that there would be much sleep going on tonight.

Iseabal was tapping Robbie's nose with her finger, a gentle admonition that her youngest child no doubt required. Riona, sitting beside her own two children, smiled at him and he smiled back.

Margaret followed his gaze, her eyes suddenly becoming pensive.

"Would you tell me a story, Papa?"

He knew, without asking, what story she wanted to hear. Amid all this maternal affection she would naturally feel the loss of a mother more acutely. Several of her cousins glanced at him with interest, and he suddenly realized that the tale was not going to be for her ears alone.

"Please Papa?" she said, scooting down on the pallet. He covered her with the sheet and tucked it below her chin.

"Once," he began, "I lived in Paris."

"When you were going to school," she interrupted.

He nodded, hiding his smile. "Yes, when I was going to school." The story was one he'd told her since she was a baby. But then, he'd never thought to see Jeanne du Marchand again. Now he wished he'd invented a little more, and depended on the truth a little less.

"You were studying philosophy," she said.

"Who is telling this story?" he teased.

She only smiled at him and for the moment was content to let him continue.

"I was studying philosophy," he said. He had been so filled with himself back then, so certain of the world. Everything had been either black or white, with no grays in between. If he wanted something, all he had to do was reach out his hand and grasp it. He had never failed, never been denied anything, had never felt pain. Later he looked back and winced at what a naïve, gullible, and impression-istic fool he'd been.

"And you saw her one day," Margaret prompted.

At his nod, she clasped her hands together over the sheet, so obviously impatient with him that he smiled.

"I saw her walking to her carriage with her maid at her side." Too easily, his mind replayed that instant. "She was the most beautiful creature I'd ever seen." She'd laughed at some-thing her maid had said, in such an unrestrained manner that he'd been captivated. This was a fulsome laugh, not the polite titter used at the French court or the embarrassed chuckle an Englishwoman might employ, half covering her mouth with her hand as if to hide her less-than-perfect teeth. Jeanne had laughed with such great abandon that he'd stopped and watched her, smiling at the sound of her amusement.

Margaret had the same lust for life.

He glanced at his daughter. "She smiled at me just then," he said. Suddenly he was no longer only a student in Paris. He could have been a courtier from a bygone time, a suitor in medieval Italy. She had the capacity to render him both more and less than he was simply with a smile.

"And you followed her home."

"Yes," he admitted, "I followed her home." Only to find

that she was the daughter of the Comte du Marchand, and so well guarded that he'd despaired of ever seeing her again. "I watched and waited for her," he said, abruptly conscious of the audience to his tale. Iseabal leaned against the wall and smiled at him, and he realized she had probably never heard the story before.

"There was a stone fence around her Paris home. I climbed it one day, and sat there debating what to do next when I saw her. She was walking through the gardens, a book in her hand."

He'd jumped down and gone to her. Jeanne had turned at his approach, so startled that she'd dropped the book to the ground.

"I picked up her book and handed it to her."

"And that's when you knew that you loved her." Margaret smiled, satisfied.

"Yes," he said. "That's when I knew." As simple as that, he'd fallen in love, the emotion coming to him in a way it never had before and probably never would again, suddenly and cataclysmically. He'd not expected to find himself enchanted by a pair of fog-colored eyes and a pink mouth that curved into such a delightful smile. Immediately, he'd wanted to reach out his hand and feel the silken texture of her hair, let the tendrils wrap themselves around his fingers. Then he would pull her gently to him and kiss that surprisingly seductive mouth.

She had smiled at him, however, asking him in French if he was a trespasser or a burglar.

"Neither," he'd said in his very bad French. "Only an admirer."

"Of me?" she'd asked, changing to English so quickly that he could only stare at her in stunned amazement.

"Dear God, yes," he said, an answer that made her frown at him. "I'm sorry, but you're so beautiful," he tried to explain.

She'd laughed then, her amusement further ensnaring him. "You shouldn't be here," she said a moment later, banishing him with a slight smile.

"Probably not," he'd replied, feeling reckless. "But I've been brought here against my will. By you."

She'd laughed again, and he'd laughed with her.

"What did she do then?" Margaret prompted, bringing him back to the present.

"She wanted to know my name."

"The very next day," Margaret added, "you began to meet in the garden."

"Yes." He smoothed his hand over the sheet in an effort to organize his thoughts. Every day for months they had met in the secluded garden at the rear of the house. There, he'd loved her, beneath a venerable tree near the corner, a secluded bower that had become their first trysting place. He could still recall that time as if he had just left her, the memories of her so poignant and perfect in detail that they would no doubt forever rank among the most precious of his recollections.

"A few months later you asked her to marry you," Margaret said impatiently. "Of course she said yes."

He realized he was faltering in his tale, so he continued. "Yes, we married," he said, unabashedly lying to his only child. The story was one he'd concocted a few years earlier, never realizing that it would appeal to Margaret's sense of drama and adventure. "But we had to steal away, because her father did not approve."

"He was a mean old man, but she was beautiful like a princess," Margaret announced, a little louder than necessary. No doubt the words were meant for her cousins, most of whom were listening.

He bent over to kiss her on the forehead. He smiled at her but that didn't soften her sudden frown. She could be very critical of his storytelling abilities, so he continued with his fabricated tale. "We sailed around the world until we discovered that you were going to be born."

"Were you very happy?"

"Very happy," he said, glancing up to discover Iseabal and Riona looking at him. Their compassion was surprisingly painful, so he concentrated instead on Margaret's intent face. She had her eyes closed and he wondered if she was imagining her mother.

"She had black hair just like mine, didn't she, Papa?"

"She did." *And does, a thick mane that gleams in the sunlight and in the soft glow of candles.* He still, even now, wanted to thread his fingers through her hair and feel the softness of it.

"Were you very much in love, Papa?"

"With all my heart," he answered and that part at least was true.

"But she died," she said, an ending to the story she'd never added before, making him wonder if she did so for her cousins' benefit. "And I got sick and wouldn't eat. Do you think it's because I missed her?"

Douglas welcomed the spurt of anger. He should continue to remember happier days and not the more recent ones in Edinburgh. Or even when he'd rescued his daughter. "No doubt," he said. "But now it's time for sleep, Meggie."

She nodded, but he knew she'd be up and about the moment he left the loft. But he wasn't in the mood to be a disciplinarian. The summer month at Gilmuir was the time to be adventurous and daring. There was time enough when they returned to Edinburgh to be proper.

A lesson for him as well.

Charles Talbot stood watching the MacRae house in the darkness, waiting for signs that the young maid at the Hartley home had been correct. "Miss du Marchand's working for the MacRaes, sir. She sent one of their maids to the house for her locket."

"Are you sure of this?" He'd reluctantly parted with the last of his coins, wishing there was some way that the information hadn't proven to be so costly. He hoped that du Marchand would pay him well for the information.

She bobbed a curtsy and was out the door before he could question her further.

The house was a large one, situated on the end of the square. The Comte's daughter had come up in the world, it seemed. As he watched, an elderly manservant came out of the front door and lit the lamps beside the steps. However, there was no sign of the woman.

He waited for another quarter hour before resigning himself to the fact that he wasn't going to be able to verify her presence for himself.

If she had been there, he might have approached her himself, possibly even suggest that the sale of the ruby could make her future secure. But if she truly had stolen the ruby, then ownership of it would be in doubt, enough that he couldn't sell it to a reputable buyer. Perhaps it was better to allow the Count to secure the stone.

However, he didn't trust du Marchand, and it had nothing to do with the Frenchman's arrogance and everything to do with the look in his eyes. He'd seen contempt before; he'd been subjected to that expression from his neighbors in Inverness before he'd decided to move to Edinburgh. There was that emotion, but added to it was a cruel glint in du Marchand's eyes, a hint that the man would stop at nothing to achieve his aims.

Charles had often felt the same. Now it was only a simple question of which of the two of them would achieve what he wanted.

Chapter 19

The nine years at the Convent of Sacré-Coeur had been marked by deprivations. Jeanne had grown used to one meal a day, to the stark emptiness of the cell she'd been assigned, and even the paucity of conversation. One of her greatest pleasures, that of reading, was prohibited because of the scarcity of books. Even if she had been allowed the time and the luxury, she wouldn't have been able to discern the words on the page. Her precious spectacles had been hidden in the secret niche at Vallans. Now, however, they perched on the end of her nose as she sat engrossed in a novel by Mr. Henry Fielding. Numerous times she closed the book and stared at the spine, then opened it again, so fascinated with the tale of *The History of Tom Jones, a Foundling*, that she could not put down the book.

Jeanne had spent countless afternoons in the sunny yellow parlor in front of the cold fireplace, her feet propped up on the needlepoint footrest, her mind adrift in a fascinating world. Reading had helped the time pass until Douglas returned, and had kept her occupied. Otherwise, she would no doubt have roamed through the house aimlessly, feeling the emptiness of his home and missing him beyond measure.

Sometimes Betty would bring her tea and stay to talk, but mostly Jeanne was left alone. Today, however, Betty rapped on the doorframe, interrupting her. With some difficulty, Jeanne pulled herself from Sophia's protestations and blinked at the maid.

"You have a visitor, miss," Betty said, peering into the parlor. "Lassiter wanted to announce him but I told him I'd let you know."

Lassiter didn't quite know how to treat her. As a governess she wasn't subject to his regulations, so it would have been perfectly natural for him to ignore her. However, Douglas had evidently given orders that she was to be treated as a guest in his house, which meant that Lassiter had to consider her well-being, ask her preferences for meals, and appear willing to serve. The confusion of roles left him frowning at her when he wasn't being overly obsequious.

"A visitor?" Jeanne asked, standing. She placed the book she was reading on the table and removed her spectacles, blinking at Betty until she came into focus. "I don't know anyone who would visit me here," she said, confused. The only people she knew other than the Hartleys were those in the émigré community, but none of them knew she was here.

"Well, know him or not, he seems a very proper gentleman," Betty said. "He's wearing a very fancy suit with a vest embroidered with gold thread. He's got a cane in his hand and I thought he was going to strike Lassiter with it, so impatient is he to see you."

"I truly don't know anyone like that," Jeanne protested.

"Shall I bring him into the parlor?"

Jeanne nodded, smoothing her hands over her skirt, then

from her temple to her nape, wishing that she had a chance to look in the mirror before greeting an unexpected guest.

Who was coming to call on her? Robert Hartley? Surely not. Taking a deep breath, she faced the door and clasped her hands together in front of her.

As the visitor was shown into the room, she sat abruptly, staring at him as if he were a ghost.

He should have shown more signs of dissipation, some wear, considering his age. True, there were more lines around his eyes, and his blond hair had whitened considerably. But his face was tanned, and the fact that he left his hair unpowdered suited him.

His attire was less ornate then she remembered. Although his vest was embroidered, his waistcoat was an almost somber brown. There were no jewels in his shoe buckles, no rings on his fingers, yet he managed to appear both immaculate and prosperous. Not an easy feat for an émigré.

"Hello, Father," she said, remaining seated.

He tilted his head in acknowledgment of her rudeness.

"Jeanne. You're looking well."

"You're looking magnificent, considering you're dead," she said with no effort at humor. "How did you manage to resurrect yourself?"

"A rumor put out to assuage the mobs, my dear. I merely became a citizen of France."

He bowed slightly in a sardonic gesture.

The last time she'd seen him he'd been ordering her into a carriage bound for the Convent of Sacré-Coeur. He'd ignored her pleas as if she were nothing more than a tiresome stranger, and then gave the orders for her to be bound and gagged.

"Why are you here?" she asked, deliberately refusing to offer him a chair. She would not play the hostess. He could die of thirst and hunger before she lifted a hand to offer him refreshments.

"Such a cordial greeting, daughter," he said, smiling benevolently at her. She noted, however, that his eyes didn't change. They were still watchful, still predatory, the expression of a hawk or a falcon. Glancing at the empty chair beside her, he said, "Are you not going to offer me a place to sit, Jeanne?"

"You're not welcome here." She didn't stand, thinking of all the days in the convent when Marie-Thérèse had made her kneel on the rough-hewn floor of the chapel and confess her sins aloud, including the shame she'd brought to her family, and her disobedience toward her father.

"I can see that," he said, tapping his walking stick on the floor. "However, I came to see my only child. To wish you well and offer my felicitations. Perhaps we could compare notes on your escape. How did you manage that?"

"How did you even know I was in Scotland?"

He smiled. "Perhaps I learned from a mutual friend."

"Justine?"

He looked surprised and it was her turn to smile, an expression that lacked humor. She remembered only too well her last encounter with Justine at Vallans.

Jeanne had never felt the emotion she was experiencing now, a loathing so deep that she felt cold with it. She stood, finally, but didn't approach him.

He raised one eyebrow and looked imperiously at her. "Are you still aggrieved about that incident? You're not the first aristocrat to find yourself with child. What I did was for your own protection. Don't be so naïve as to believe the world accepts bastards, Jeanne. You were never that provincial." He laughed, a titter that was an affectation at court and sounded even more brittle and false here in this lovely parlor.

At least he didn't pretend to be other than what he was.

If once he had loved her it was because she had either amused him or resembled him. She had been a perfect child until she'd erred and then she was tossed away with no more regard than her baby daughter.

"Get out," she said, surprised that she could manage the words at all, but hatred evidently made her both resolute and strong.

"I would have thought the convent taught you respect," he said, his mask of geniality beginning to slip.

"They taught me a great deal, Father. However, I endeavored to forget those lessons the moment I left."

"A pity," he said. "You might have become a more tractable woman. A man does not admire a woman of rough temper, Jeanne." He looked around him at the room with its hint of luxury. "However, you've managed to do well enough for yourself. Another post as governess? Or something else entirely?"

She felt her face warm, and cursed both her embarrassment and his knowing smile. But before she could answer, he raised his walking stick and pointed it at her throat.

"I want your mother's necklace," he said, surprising her. "Give me that and I'll not trouble you further." Smiling, he added, "I'll be dead to you again, a reasonable arrangement, do you not agree?"

Her hand closed over the locket. "Why?"

"Because it belongs to me." The mask of gentility slipped completely even as his face seemed to age, the grooves on either side of his mouth deepening. "Everything at Vallans belonged to me. You stole it."

She smiled. "I hid it before you sent me away," she said, grateful for the strength to appear amused. "And found it among the ruins. Do you want my spectacles and journals as well?"

"I want the necklace," he said, his gray eyes wintry.

"No."

Walking to the fireplace, she pulled the bell cord beside it, summoning Lassiter. She and her father wordlessly stared at each other until the older man entered the room.

"The gentleman is leaving," she said. "See him to the door, Lassiter. If you need any assistance, summon one of the stable lads."

One thing for which she could not fault the majordomo was his instant recognition of the circumstances. He bowed slightly, his voice low and respectful. "Sir," he said. "If you'll follow me."

Her father stared at her. "I want it, Jeanne, and I'll have it," he said, before turning toward the door.

"You'll get nothing else from me," she said as he left the room. As she stared after him, she whispered, "You've taken too much as it is."

Chapter 20

ᕤ◯◯ᕥ

Douglas scooped his sleeping child into his arms and left the carriage. Margaret had fallen asleep as soon as they'd reached land. Smiling down into her face, he walked up the steps to his house, dismissing the coachman with a softly voiced command.

Margaret mumbled something in her sleep and curled her cheek against his chest, much as she had done as a baby.

In that moment he felt as though the past and the present were pulling him in two. He wanted to visit Jeanne and yet at the same time Douglas knew that it would be safer to condemn her to perdition and get on with his life.

A month must have dampened Jeanne's allure. He wouldn't be as enthralled with her as he had been before leaving Edinburgh. The time apart would have acted as a sanity-inducing respite.

Nevertheless, when he opened the front door of his home to be greeted by a sleepy Lassiter, the first question he wanted to ask was about Jeanne.

"Is all well, Lassiter?"

"Very well, sir. Welcome home."

"It's good to be back," he said.

Bless the instinct of well-trained servants, he thought a moment later when Lassiter turned and led the way to the stairs, casually remarking, "The young lady has been asking when you would return, sir."

"Has she?"

Lassiter only nodded, and the subject was exhausted, which was just as well. Douglas didn't know what else to say.

"She had a visitor when you were away, sir," Lassiter said.

Douglas glanced at his majordomo. "Who?"

"I don't know, sir," Lassiter said. "A Frenchman. He carried a gold walking stick and had blond hair. Not a young man, but not old, either. Near to my height."

"How long did he stay?"

"A few minutes, no more. He looked decidedly put out when he left. Nor did the young lady seem pleased at his appearance."

The Sherbourne estate in England, his father's boyhood home, boasted a chapel complete with a set of clarion bells. Each one of them was ringing in his mind even now.

He walked upstairs, depositing Margaret in her bed. Betty bustled around him, helping to undress her.

Bending down, he kissed his daughter on the forehead. "Goodnight, Meggie."

She looked up at him, rubbing her eyes. "Are we home, Papa?"

"We are. But it's late, and you should go back to sleep."

She nodded groggily at him and he didn't doubt that she would soon be asleep again.

"Should I stay with her tonight, sir?" Betty asked, bobbing a small curtsey.

"I don't think so," he said. "But tuck her in well, Betty, it was a rough journey."

The seas from Gilmuir had been choppy, yet the summer storm they encountered had made Margaret laugh. He had been slightly less euphoric, thinking that their ship could be easily dashed on the rocks. But the only casualty on their journey had been a sail that had come loose and wrapped around the mainmast. It would be repaired tomorrow at Leith.

After he left Margaret's room, Douglas walked down the hall to his own chamber. Closing the door, he went to the fireplace to light a candle. The flame flickered and then caught, and he placed the holder back on the mantel and shrugged out of his jacket.

He'd never considered hiring a valet, and now he was doubly grateful that there wasn't anyone bustling around him. There were times when his life was simply too busy, when the demands of his company, his family, and his responsibilities pressed in too much. He exempted Margaret from that sense of duty simply because she was the one for whom he worked so hard.

Nor, surprisingly enough, did he put Jeanne in the category of obligations. She brought back his youth, his past, a feeling of being young and too excited about life to be wise. She was his glorious error, his profligacy, and his imprudence.

And a temptation he didn't want to ignore.

He pinched the flame out between two fingers and left his darkened bedroom before he could change his mind. His conscience surprisingly did not speak during the long walk down the hall to Jeanne's chamber. Placing his hand flat against the door, he wondered if she had locked it against him. There would be none in this house who would dare disturb her, so if the latch was engaged, it would be a signal to him alone.

He pushed on the handle and the door swung open easily, almost in invitation. Closing the door quietly, he stood with his back against it, waiting for a sign of either welcome or repudiation.

A lone flickering candle on the bedside table was the only illumination. Jeanne was sitting up in bed, attired in her threadbare nightgown, her knees drawn up and her arms around them.

"I heard your carriage," she said, her look direct and unflinching.

Fool that he was, he answered her with too much truth. "I was away too long."

She only nodded in response, as if afraid to reveal her vulnerability. But she had never been fragile as a girl.

Standing, she came to him, took his hand, and led him back to her bed. He allowed her to mount the steps and sit on the edge of the bed, and slowly untie his stock.

"Did you miss me, Jeanne?" he asked, the words like jewels in the silence, each one as precious as a ruby or diamond.

"Yes."

She halted in the act of undressing him and looked at him, her eyes hiding nothing. He had the discomfiting thought that if he stared long enough he might unearth the contents of her soul and all manner of secrets.

"It's been a long time since I had a woman companion," he said, deliberately crude. "I should have a mistress."

She hesitated for a moment and then resumed her efforts, his stock finally untied. With deft fingers, she began unbuttoning his vest.

"Should you?"

How calm her voice sounded, and yet he had the feeling that it was difficult for her to speak with such aplomb.

He reached down and tilted up her chin with one finger.

"I haven't asked you to be my mistress," he said.

"Don't now," she said, reaching out and placing her fingers against his lips. "Please, don't say such things. Later, after we've loved, there will be time enough to wound one another."

Startled, he drew back from her touch, gripping her hand tightly. Immediately he realized he'd been too forceful and bent and placed a kiss on the inside of her wrist in a wordless petition for forgiveness.

"Do we wound each other, Jeanne?" he asked softly.

Once again, he had the feeling that he would be safer leaving her. He wanted to be around her more than was wise. When he was separated from her, it felt as if his very soul ached.

She placed her hands flat on his chest, surprising him. In the candlelight, her look was somber. He should have guessed her next words. "Why are you here, Douglas?"

He placed his palms against the backs of her hands, thinking that they felt soft and warm, almost fragile. She was trembling, but he couldn't have discerned that from her steady look.

Did he terrify her as much as she did him? How strange that they were going to be lovers again, fearing each other so much.

Why was he here?

She had forced him into looking at his own motives. He stepped away from the bed, turning and walking toward the window. He should have left the room, but as difficult as this moment was, he still didn't want to leave her.

He didn't want her comfort, although physical pleasure wasn't something he'd willingly forgo. He didn't want forgetfulness—there were some memories that could never be expunged from his mind. Nor did he lie to himself and hide behind the pretense that he wanted to avenge his daughter.

Why was he here?

Not even because she was his past. He had been a boy and was not one any longer. But the man could fall in love with her as easily as the boy had. Perhaps that emotion would last longer than before and be twice as destructive.

"For forgetfulness," he said finally. "For a bit of comfort in the night." Twin lies that he offered up to her to hide his own confusion.

He wanted to ask her why she'd done what she had to their child, but that was a question that could not have a good answer. Instead, he concentrated on the view of the park, the wrought-iron gate with pointed spears and benches arranged in strategic spots. A lantern on all four corners illuminated the park and was kept lit by a man paid to patrol the area.

Money guaranteed him privilege but it didn't assure him peace of mind.

Douglas realized that he didn't want to invite the past into this room. It had no place in his life at this moment. He wanted an hour or two of Jeanne. Of pleasure. Of love.

God help him.

He turned to find her standing beside him. Her smile was enchanting and utterly damning. This was the woman who had tried to kill his child. But even that accusation sounded wrong, as if he were missing part of the puzzle of Jeanne du Marchand. He made a decision, in that moment, to wonder about it later. Now he wouldn't think.

"The world is filled with fools," he said cryptically. "And I'm just one of them." A statement he didn't mean to make. But then, he had not meant to bed her the first time or the second, and he should not have come to her tonight.

Slowly she unfastened his shirt, before placing her hands flat on his bared chest, her thumbs meeting and her fingers splayed wide, as if to claim him with her touch. His hands remained at his side, the one part of his body that was obeying. His erection, however, was rampant and rebellious, seeking an escape from the tight confines of his trousers.

He removed her hands from his chest and picked her up and carried her to the bed, arranging her so that she sat on the edge, her feet dangling. He gripped her worn nightgown in the middle of the neckline and slowly began to tear it down the middle.

She didn't utter one word of protest, her silence an aphrodisiac of its own. As if he needed one at the moment.

Jeanne sat until he finished, until the frayed edges of the material framed the perfect globes of her breasts. He placed his hands on her waist and pulled her to him. He wanted to kiss her but he wouldn't, not yet. Not until her eyes were dark with desire, and her breath was nothing more than a gasp.

He bent down and tasted one nipple, his tongue tracing a path first around the aureole. She shivered in response and made a sound deep in her throat. He smiled as she wound her hand around his neck to flatten on the back of his head. Her fingers pressed against his scalp and urged him closer.

Teasing her instead, he touched only the very tip of her nipple with his tongue. She placed her other hand beneath her breast. This time he succumbed to her urging, tasting the whole of her nipple, sucking her until his cheeks hollowed and her indrawn breath was expelled in a sigh.

Separating the gown, he looked at her illuminated by the candle. Her eyes were closed and her hands clenched the sheet on either side of her.

"Look at me," he said softly.

Slowly, she opened her eyes.

"I want you to watch what we do."

She nodded, her eyes never leaving his as he reached out and caressed her breasts with both hands.

"You're very responsive." His thumb brushed over a nipple, felt it grow tighter, and he bent down to lick it in praise.

"Am I?" Her voice sounded choked.

He placed both hands at her waist and helped her from the high bed. When she stood before him, he gently turned her.

"Lift up your hair."

She hesitated for a moment before moving, holding her hair up from her neck in a thoroughly feminine gesture. Her hair wasn't long, only shoulder-length, and he realized that it was because of her years at the convent.

When she bent her head, he saw her scars once again. *I did something that earned my father's displeasure.* Had the Comte sent her there because of their love? Because she'd met him countless times in secret assignations? Because she'd borne a child?

The questions begged to be asked, but the moment they were, more revelations would follow. He didn't want to hate her tonight. He didn't, God forgive him, truly want to know.

One by one he kissed her scars before turning her. She stood in front of him, her eyes pooling with tears. When had she learned to show so much emotion in her eyes? He didn't want her grateful or sad. He wanted her needy and desperate with it.

Wordlessly, he helped her to the bed again, pulling her so that she sat on the edge, her feet dangling. Pulling off his stock completely, he wound it around one breast and then the other, framing them with the white cloth.

"It's silk," he said when she only looked at him, surprise banishing her tears. "Do you like the feel of it?"

She nodded, and he was grateful she didn't speak. He didn't want to hear her voice if it was laced with any emotion other than lust. He pulled on the ends of the stock and both breasts were gently constrained. He pulled harder and she closed her eyes.

With the fringed ends of the stock he brushed a nipple,

still impudent and tight. He blew on it, and it seemed to lengthen beneath his ministrations.

"Do you want me to kiss you there?" he asked.

She nodded.

He ceased moving until she opened her eyes.

"Do you want me to kiss you there?" he asked again, and this time she spoke.

"Please," she said, her voice throaty and seductive.

"Why?"

She looked confused for only a second before a small smile curved her lips. "Because I like the way your mouth feels on my breasts."

They had teased each other years ago, and she'd not forgotten the game, it seemed.

He kissed her breast, drawing out the nipple between his lips. She sighed again, and he wanted to be in her, now. But he delayed, knowing that the pleasure to come would be greater for not being easily gratified.

Gently his hands stroked over every inch of her body. Tenderly, he touched her, making her sigh or gasp. This woman alone of all the women he'd ever met confused him and delighted him and made him behave with such reckless abandon that he should have been worried for his immortal soul.

"You're a beautiful woman," he said as his fingers touched the curly, soft hair between her legs.

She licked her lips as he spread her legs, unsurprised to find that she was damp at his touch. She'd always been receptive and passionate.

"Do you think so?" she asked, too breathlessly for composure. He stroked a finger down a delicate fold, hesitating where the flesh looked puffy and swollen. She closed her eyes and moved her legs wider, an unspoken entreaty to continue.

"Yes, I do," he said, as if they were conducting a civil conversation within earshot of others.

Another stroke.

"Has no one ever told you?" He bore down with one tender fingertip, found the one place he sought, and gently circled it. She made a slight sound in response.

He pulled on the stock with his free hand and it slid across her breasts, further stimulating them. Inserting a finger, then two, into her, he stroked her with his thumb. Brushing a palm over her sensitized nipples, he leaned over and kissed her. His fingers kept up a rhythm of fast, and then slow, repeating the motion until her hips arched. He inhaled her soft sounds as she climaxed, held her as she shuddered in his arms, moved his fingers gently to prolong the sensation.

Winding her arms around his neck, she held on to him, trembling. Sighing against his cheek, she whispered, "Come in me, Douglas. Please."

So much for restraint.

In record time, he'd thrown off his clothes and freed his erection. She reached out to touch him, her hands stroking him tenderly.

He was both the winner and loser in the game of seduction. Suddenly he realized it didn't matter anymore, they were so equally matched in lust that they were both winners. And if they lost, perhaps it was only a sense of themselves.

She stroked him between her palms and looked entranced as he grew harder and longer under her ministrations. He spread her legs with both hands on the inside of her thighs and lowered himself over her. She widened her knees still farther so that he could have easy access to the core of her.

All he could feel as he entered her was Jeanne, not vengeance or retribution, only the pleasure she effortlessly offered and he selfishly accepted.

He moved closer and bent over her, bracing himself on his forearms. Only then did he kiss her again, a deep drugging kiss that sent his mind spiraling in delight.

Her hips arched as she surged upward, granting him a sensation of dizzying pleasure. He prayed for control and found it only with the greatest of wills, thrusting into her again and again. Breathing hard against her throat, he repeated her name over and over as if the sound of it granted some power beyond that which he'd ever known.

"Douglas." She shuddered around him, pulling him to her. When he climaxed, it felt as if he'd expended all his life force into her. She returned it to him in an exclamation, a soft crying gasp that made him surge forward repeatedly.

He thought he might actually die in that moment when his breath raced in the same frantic patter as his heart. His vision darkened and his memories faded, leaving only Jeanne and then simply nothing.

Long moments later, he roused to find that his weight was fully atop her. He drew back and she moved her hands over his shoulders as if to keep him with her.

"I'm too heavy."

"No," she said softly, sweetly, her voice low and seductive.

A soft sheen of perspiration was on her chest and her face. A rosy glow transformed her torso, and her eyes were languorous. If he could have, he would have commissioned an artist to paint her just that way, pleasured and flushed. He knew in that instant that he would never satiate his lust with her. She would resurrect it with a smile, a kiss, or a look in her eyes.

Standing, he donned his clothes again, slowly so that his mind might have an opportunity to catch up with this body.

The only solution to his dilemma was to send her away.

Instead of dressing, she sat up with her legs to one side, one hand braced on the mattress, the other draped on her thigh. Her head rested against the headboard as if she had been wearied by seduction. He glanced at her once and then away, thinking that the sight of Jeanne naked was too tempting. He wanted to join her on the bed, tease her with his fingers and his lips. Make her sob with pleasure until she was hoarse.

"I missed you," she said, the words little more than a whisper.

He wanted her again.

"Did you?" he asked, thinking that it would be just as easy to strip off his clothes and join her. He'd wake in the morning, before the servants were up. No one would know that he'd spent the night in decadent pleasure with Jeanne.

"I did," she said, her voice sounding throaty and passionate.

He removed his trousers, and then his shirt, uncaring where they landed. Naked, he went to her and embraced her, bending down to kiss her again.

"Show me how much."

Chapter 21

J eanne woke in the night to find that Douglas had left
her, which was just as well. She didn't know what to
say to him. They had not yet admitted the past to each
other. Yet each time they met and loved, they stripped another layer of pretense away.

A glance at the clock on the mantel made her sigh. Only
three-fifteen. But she knew that she wouldn't fall asleep
again.

Just then, she realized that the connecting door to Margaret's room was ajar. Donning her wrapper and slippers,
she pushed open the door to see Douglas sitting on the
edge of a bed in a room created for a princess.

The bedroom was unlike Davis's spartan chamber.
Margaret's furniture was constructed in scale for a child.
The four-poster bed was hung with shirred white silk, the
coverlet monogramed with two *M*'s intertwined. A flow-
ered carpet in shades of blue and pink stretched from the
bed to a miniature mahogany armoire topped with an
arched pediment.

A little girl sat in bed propped up with at least four pillows, all of which were covered in a thick crocheted lace. Her black hair hung loose around her shoulders in a cloud. The candle on the nightstand sent shadows around the two of them.

"Just remember, Meggie," Douglas said tenderly, "that nightmares can't hurt you."

The little girl's gaze was fixed on her father as if he were the center of her universe.

"But it was coming after me, and it was making me run. Why?"

"I don't know," Douglas said, smiling lightly. "Nightmares aren't supposed to make sense. When I was a little boy I used to dream about a bull. It was coming through the fence after me, and chasing me into my mother's parlor."

"A bull? That's silly, Papa. A bull can't come in the house."

"Neither can a wolf."

"But it had big long teeth," she said, protesting.

"It's not here now. Shall I check to make sure?"

She looked away and then back at him, the beginning of a smile on her face. "Please, Papa."

He made a great show of looking under the bed and in the armoire. As he turned, he glanced at Jeanne, but didn't say anything to alert Margaret as to her presence.

"No wolf here, Meggie."

She slipped down farther beneath the covers and nodded.

"Could you stay just until I fall asleep?"

"Of course I can," he said easily. "And after that, Betty will be here with you if you like."

Just then Margaret glanced toward the door, and Jeanne almost gasped aloud. The child's eyes were the most beautiful that she'd ever seen. Like Douglas's, they were blue but much lighter than her father's, giving her an almost ethereal appearance. Coupled with her pale skin, Margaret looked not unlike a fairy princess. The portrait had not done her justice. But then, she doubted any artist could have captured the child's beauty.

"Who is that, Papa?"

Douglas glanced at her. "Your governess, Margaret. Miss du Marchand."

Jeanne didn't know whether or not to stay where she was or enter the room. Margaret herself ended her confusion by slipping from the bed and coming to the doorway.

She pulled the door open all the way and then presented the most perfect of curtsies to Jeanne.

"How do you do, Miss du Marchand? I'm Margaret MacRae. Are you truly my governess?"

Jeanne exchanged a quick glance with Douglas.

"Yes," Jeanne said. "I am."

"I have never had a governess before. Papa says it's because I was too young. I read a great deal, however. I've educated myself, but I don't suppose it can be a good thing to do that."

Startled, Jeanne smiled down at the child. "I don't suppose it can."

"Do you know Latin?"

"A smattering of it," Jeanne confessed.

"I would very much like to learn it. And geography as well. I'm an heiress, you see, and I must know as much as I can before I become wealthy."

"Tomorrow is soon enough, Margaret," Douglas interjected, "to ascertain your governess's strengths." He patted the coverlet and she returned to the bed, clambering up beside her father.

He stood and then leaned down to kiss her on the forehead. She scooted beneath the covers without another word, smiling up at him in perfect trust. The picture they presented made Jeanne's heart ache.

"It's time for you to go to sleep, Margaret."

"You said you would stay with me."

"And I will, but I have something to do first. I'll return in a moment."

"She's very intelligent," Jeanne said, when Douglas came to her side. He left the lantern lit for Margaret and escorted Jeanne back to her room.

"She's very much like her mother," he said.

She wanted to ask about this nameless, faceless woman but pride held her tongue.

"I didn't mean to intrude," she said. "I couldn't sleep."

"Guilty conscience?" he asked lightly, his gaze intent on her face.

"Perhaps," she said. "Or memories."

He didn't respond to her remark, only smiled. "My sister-in-law recommends Chinese tea for sleepless nights. Shall I have some prepared for you?"

Before she could state that she didn't want any servants awakened on her behalf, he added, "I was going to make some for myself."

"If it isn't any trouble."

"Not at all," he said.

How exquisitely polite they were to each other. She followed him down the corridor. At the head of the staircase, she watched him descend the steps. His dressing gown was dark blue, the exact shade of his eyes, and she wondered if a woman had picked out the fabric.

"You mustn't come to my room again." She hadn't meant to blurt it out in quite that fashion, but it needed to be said.

He glanced at her over his shoulder. "Why is that?" Without waiting for her answer, he continued walking.

Irritated, she could only stare at his back. "Because your child is in the house. You didn't think I would be your mistress and her governess as well?"

Again, he didn't respond.

At the bottom of the stairs he waited for her. She stopped at the first step so that she was level with him, refusing to have him tower over her. Pulling her wrapper even closer, she belted it tighter with a firm tug. He smiled at her gestures, as if knowing that the filmy material was no barrier to his will or even to her needs.

The staircase around them echoed sound, so she whispered, "You mustn't come to my room." Even as she spoke the words she could hear the longing in them. It seemed as if he did as well, because he trailed one hand, fingers splayed, from her waist to the base of her throat.

In the past few hours they'd loved twice. But her body readied for him with that simple touch.

"Is this something you truly wish, Jeanne?"

"It is," she replied, wishing that the words sounded less tremulous.

"Then that's what you shall have," he said casually. "I won't come to your room until you invite me."

She wished that he were not so handsome or that his charm was not so effortless. At this moment he reminded her of the boy she'd known, reckless and daring and wild.

"Please," she said and she wasn't entirely certain what she was asking for. He seemed to sense that as well because when he looked at her there was compassion in his eyes, as if he knew how foolish she was around him and pitied her for it.

Holding out his hand for her, he waited until she placed her own in it before leading her through the corridors of his night-darkened house. At the Hartley home, a footman had been assigned to stay awake during the night in case one of the family needed assistance. In Douglas's house, all of the servants retired to the third floor at night.

When they entered the kitchen, he closed the door behind them, going immediately to a cupboard where the candles were stored. He lit one with a length of twisted paper stored in a container near the stove. Before putting the cover back over the glowing embers, he fanned them into flame. Filling a small kettle with water, he placed it atop the stove.

Jeanne sat at the end of the table, her customary place when the staff was dining, and watched him.

"You're quite adept in a kitchen," she said, surprised.

"I didn't always employ people to obey my every whim, Jeanne," he said, his smile softening the words.

"Do you cook as well as make tea?"

"Rudimentary meals," he said. He arranged two cups and saucers on a tray and then suddenly left the room. A moment later he was back, carrying a decanter she recognized from his library. He poured a small amount into each cup before replacing the crystal stopper.

"I've never had whiskey," she admitted.

"It will help you sleep."

"I trust you do not administer the same remedy to Margaret?"

He shook his head, evidently not realizing she was teasing.

"Does she often have nightmares?"

"Often enough," he said shortly. The tone of his voice altered, as if he didn't like answering questions about his daughter. The protectiveness he demonstrated startled her, and made her envious in a way that shamed her.

Why should she be jealous of a child? Or was it more than that? Did she envy the mother, the nameless, faceless, adored woman who had given birth to Douglas's child and then died?

She realized that she resented the fact that this woman, however long dead, had somehow sullied Jeanne's memories of those days in Paris. Now, when she remembered that time, she would also recall her current doubts.

Had Douglas even loved her? Had he lied when he told her so? Or had she simply imagined his affection all this time?

"Tell me about her mother," she said and there must have been something about the question that startled him, because he turned and stared at her.

"Why would you want to know?" he asked, frowning at her.

"Is it something I shouldn't have asked?"

"She was a spoiled and willful woman. Cruel, and used to getting her own way. Is that what you want to know?"

Yes, blessedly, it was. The look in his eyes betrayed his emotions easily enough. The woman had the power to enrage him still, to anger and possibly even repulse him. His expression hadn't softened when he spoke of her and his voice had a hard edge to it.

"And yet, you loved her."

He picked up the tray, holding it so tight that his knuckles were white. Returning to the table, he placed the tray down on the scarred wooden surface with more force than was necessary.

"I'm sorry," she said in the face of his silence. "I shouldn't have said that."

"You have a way of cutting me to the quick with a few words, Jeanne. But then you always have." He smiled lightly.

She felt herself grow cold, then hot as she realized the import of his words. "I was wondering when you would say something, Douglas." She reached for one of the cups and noticed that her hand was trembling. "Or have you just now remembered me?"

"I might ask the same thing of you," he said. Sitting beside her, he watched as she poured their tea. Anyone seeing them would be unaware of the deep and dangerous currents that swirled around the room or the fact that they were speaking so lightly of things that mattered so much.

Her heart felt as if it rested at the base of her throat. Her breath was constricted as if someone had tied a string around her chest and was pulling it tight. And all the while she was pouring tea and acting as hostess. All she needed to make this moment thoroughly ridiculous was to have her father stroll into the kitchen.

Humor was unexpected and not entirely welcome. But she had the sudden, absurd wish to laugh. After all this time, this conversation seemed anticlimactic and almost unnecessary.

"I never forgot," she said, softly. "Never."

"Not even during those years at the convent?"

"How could I, when I was punished for even thinking of you?"

He looked startled.

"I confessed, you see," she told him. "Perhaps I was feeling rash, but I once told one of the nuns that I had dreamed of you. They began punishing me both in the morning and the evening just to ensure that my dreams remained chaste."

He didn't say anything for a moment. When he spoke, his voice was low and almost hesitant, as if he framed the words as he said them. "What did you do?"

She laughed, grateful for his question, and her sudden amusement. "What was I to do?" She endured it because there was no other alternative, just like this moment as well.

"You've changed a great deal."

"Ten years have passed," she said. "You can't imagine that I would have remained the same. For that matter, you've changed as well."

"I've grown more cynical," he said, his eyes never leaving her face. What was he searching for?

This conversation was dangerous. She felt perched on

the edge of a precipice. One false move and she could go hurtling off into the darkness. She didn't want to reveal anything to him, and yet, paradoxically, she wanted him to know everything about her.

"Drink your tea," he said, much in the same way he would to Margaret. Startled, she glanced up at him.

Tonight was not the night for revelations, it seemed. In silence and some sort of peace, she sat and sipped at her whiskey-laced tea.

"Is your tea hot enough?"

"Yes, it's fine."

"Is the whiskey too strong?"

"No," she answered.

"Are you hungry?"

"No, thank you."

Finally, the silence lengthened between them and she realized that it was not an uncomfortable moment. They sat together almost as friends, or lovers who had accidentally discovered some other link in their lives.

"Margaret is waiting," he said, standing and moving toward the doorway. "I've given my word to stay with her until she falls asleep again."

"You're a very good father," she said, unsurprised. She had always thought him constant, someone upon whom she could depend. Until, of course, he never came for her, never looked for her. Now his child needed him, and he was there.

Like Jeanne had not been for her daughter.

She sipped at her tea and surveyed the empty room, determined that sadness would not ruin the rest of this night.

Chapter 22

❧❧❧

Before a week had passed, Jeanne's routine as a governess had been established. In the mornings, she gave Margaret her lessons in the small schoolroom at the top of the house. In the afternoons, the two of them took a walk followed by a few hours of dance, music, or painting classes.

The ballroom where they practiced dancing was quite cool in the hotter time of day. Likewise the small room that Douglas had suggested they use for Margaret's painting class. Sometimes it felt as if the entire house had been given over to Jeanne with the express intent of making Douglas's daughter happy.

Margaret was a precocious child, one who seemed to revel in the world around her. Every day was an adventure. She was a natural mimic, and quickly learned the Italian phrases Jeanne taught her. Her greatest affection was for painting, however, and it was evident that the child was talented. Margaret had already gone beyond her meager talents, and Jeanne made a mental note to discuss further lessons with Douglas.

Douglas's interest in his daughter's day surprised her.

He supervised her diet, her exercise, and her lesson plans. He was the one who suggested that Margaret might wish to learn Greek.

"Only if you wish to teach it, of course," he said to her. "Or Latin, if you prefer."

"Do you think she'll have any need for it?"

"Do you only espouse teaching a subject that might have value? I remember discussing your lessons with you, and your education didn't seem at all practical."

"Not for the convent," she quickly answered before she could bite back the words. "I learned independence of mind and spirit, Douglas, and that the world is a kind and a just place. Neither one of those lessons has been of value."

"If her curiosity leads her to places she shouldn't go, Jeanne, perhaps her wisdom will keep her from acting foolish."

"So you think that no education is ever truly wasted?" she asked.

He smiled. "Any good teacher would think so."

She had never once considered that he might be iconoclastic in regards to his daughter. Or that he might be forward-thinking. He had no prejudice whatsoever for the fact that Margaret was female. Nor had he ever expressed dissatisfaction or disappointment in that fact. In addition, Jeanne had the distinct impression that she served as Margaret's governess only to enhance the child's learning, not to change or alter the essence of Margaret herself.

Unlike Jeanne's father, who had her educated so that she might be a reflection of his good taste and his erudition, Douglas thought Margaret was, simply put, perfect.

Jeanne didn't know what she had expected Margaret MacRae to be like, but it wasn't a child who had such a well-developed sense of herself. She was unlike Davis the way a butterfly is different from a stone. In addition, she had a quick wit and a facile mind.

Today they were studying the history of the Empire, a subject that was as new to Jeanne as it was to Margaret. Neither one of them was overly interested in the topic, but it was a necessary part of the child's history lesson.

Jeanne sat at a small desk on a raised portion in the front of the schoolroom, while Margaret sat in front of her. The morning had been one of storms and now a fine rain was falling. She'd opened the two windows to let in some of the balmy air and kept the door ajar so that the cross currents would allow some type of breeze. But the time passed in a desultory fashion, and both teacher and student were obviously indifferent to their studies.

"Do you think God can be seen, Miss du Marchand?" Margaret abruptly asked. She propped her elbow on the table she used as a desk, and leaned her chin on her palm, staring out of the window to the gray-hued horizon. There wasn't a hint of fair weather in the sky. Instead, it appeared that it might rain all day.

"Where did that question come from?" Jeanne asked, looking up from her desk and surveying the child.

Margaret shrugged, her gaze still directed toward the view.

"I don't believe so," Jeanne answered. "I believe you're supposed to believe in God without seeing Him."

Margaret looked unimpressed. "Do you believe in God?"

"I do, yes." She waited for more questions, hoping that Margaret wouldn't peer too closely into her governess's faith. The years at the convent had soured her as to religious practices.

"Is Heaven supposed to be invisible as well?"

"Are you thinking of your mother?" Jeanne asked gently, holding her breath, and wondering what reaction that question would engender.

Margaret shook her head. "No, my cat."

"Your cat?" Jeanne asked, surprised. "I didn't know you

had a cat." The moment the words were out, she remembered the portrait in Douglas's study and the kitten who'd been painted into the scene.

"She died, Miss du Marchand," Margaret said patiently, glancing at her.

"I'm very sorry, Margaret. I didn't know."

"You couldn't have, of course. It happened a year ago."

Jeanne folded her arms and waited.

Margaret didn't disappoint. "Do you think there's a cat heaven and a dog heaven and a people heaven?"

"I think there are some questions that you should ask your father," Jeanne said in self-defense.

"He said to ask you."

He would.

"No," she said firmly, "I do not believe that Heaven is invisible. Not to its inhabitants. I do not think the living can see it, however. As to animals and humans, surely God would be merciful and open the gates of heaven to those we love, whoever and whatever they are."

Margaret looked slightly mollified. "That's what Papa said."

"You mustn't do that, you know," Jeanne said, impatiently tapping her fingers on top of the desk.

"Do what?"

She wasn't fooled by the innocent smile the child gave her. "Ask each of us a question and pick the answer you like the best."

Jeanne didn't know what Margaret might have said to such an accusation. At that moment the door swung open a little, revealing Douglas standing there.

"You should feel privileged to be so solicited, Miss du Marchand," he said, smiling and entering the room.

She hadn't seen him for a few days, and as usual the sight of Douglas made her heart beat faster and her breath feel tight.

His attire was simple, the clothes expensive but un-adorned. The lace on his cuffs and at his throat was not an elaborate pattern. His shoe buckles were silver squares. His vest was sedately embroidered with silver thread on the black silk, while his breeches were tan. He was the very picture of a prosperous businessman, an individual sober of mien and intensely focused.

Ever since she'd issued her decree, he'd not visited her once. For that fact she told herself she was profoundly grateful. In her mind she portrayed him as nothing more than a parent of her student, a delusional thought that she was able to continue for hours at a time. Until, of course, she saw him or Margaret spoke of him, which she did of-ten. And then her pretense would come tumbling down like a flimsy structure of blocks, to lie jumbled on the floor.

She missed him. Intently. At night she'd sometimes awaken and lie staring at the ceiling, clenching the sheets with both fists. Once, she'd even awakened at the end of a particularly sensual dream, on the precipice of release. She'd called his name into her pillow and beat on the mat-tress, but it didn't eradicate the need or ease the loneliness.

"I've come to invite you to the warehouse," he said to Margaret. "There's a ship due to arrive from the Orient, and I know you'd like to see the treasures for yourself."

"May we really, Papa?" Margaret asked. She glanced at Jeanne. "Please, Miss du Marchand, say yes, and we can spend the whole afternoon there."

A temptation? Or a foolish idea? Perhaps even a danger-ous one. Jeanne folded her hands in front of her and looked at Douglas inquiringly.

"You should plan on visiting the MacRae empire, Miss du Marchand. You can see our vault of gold ingots."

"We have so much more than that," Margaret said, standing and going to her father's side. She turned and looked at Jeanne. "You should see the warehouse, Miss du

Marchand. It's like the most enchanted place in the entire world. Please, may we go?"

His look dared her to refuse. Did he know that she was feeling rash—or was it lonely—enough to take his dare? Foolish man, she'd thrust her fist at God Himself. She was more than capable of declining Douglas MacRae.

"We have our lessons," she said softly.

Let him command her, and then there would be no assent on her part, and no responsibility for what would inevitably occur. Or perhaps it was only what she wanted to happen. But he remained silent, watching her, refusing to order, relinquishing his role of employer for that of tormenter.

Ask me, and I'll come. Tell me, and I'll be the first at the door. But still, he said nothing.

Disappointed, she turned to Margaret. "We need to finish up our study of history today," she said.

Douglas looked down at his daughter's frowning face. "We'll do it some other time, Meggie." He glanced at Jeanne. "I'll leave you to your lessons, then," he said, placing his hand on his daughter's head. He did that often, a benediction of touch that was gentle and almost unconscious, as if he reassured himself that she was near. Margaret, in turn, always smiled up at him—the two of them in harmony with each other.

It was a perfect familial moment, one that made Jeanne's stomach clench.

After he left, the room seemed less bright, as if the storm had intensified or the gray day suddenly dimmed even more.

Jeanne turned to Margaret. "We have an hour before luncheon. Shall we make the best use of our time?" She forced herself to smile brightly at the child.

Margaret frowned at her, but returned to her desk and picked up her slate nonetheless.

"You know you wanted to go, Miss du Marchand," she said a moment later.

Jeanne glanced at her, surprised.

"My cat was like you sometimes. I'd give her a piece of fish but she'd pretend not to like it. Papa said it was her pride that was hurting. She'd wanted to catch the fish herself."

Jeanne stared wordlessly at Margaret, unable to decide what was worse: being likened to a cat or the fact that the child was extraordinarily perceptive.

The stairway was fetid and close, the smell of refuse and unwashed bodies emerging from the depths.

Nicholas, Comte du Marchand, held his lace handkerchief firmly against his nose and tried not to breathe as the stench increased.

"This is your idea, Talbot?" he asked the man in front of him.

The goldsmith turned, his unapologetic grin illuminated by the lantern in his hand. "Where else do you expect me to find a man to do your bidding, Count?"

"My title is an ancient one," Nicholas said, pinching the handkerchief close to his nose. "Pray do not offend me by using it like a club."

Talbot only grinned again, and descended another of the slippery steps. "Mary King's Close dates back to the seventeenth century, your lordship," he said mockingly. "Almost as old as that title of yours, I'd venture."

Nicholas's ancestors had helped finance the Norman invasion of England, but he didn't bother attempting to educate the goldsmith.

The pit they descended into was a series of streets that had, for some odd reason, sunk into the ground not long after they were cobbled, creating a settlement beneath the city. Beyond the darkness, he could see a flicker of torch-light and lantern, and could hear the echo of laughter.

"Don't be afraid, your lordship. Those aren't ghosts."

Nicholas frowned at the younger man, wishing that he'd tumble down the steps into the darkness. He doubted anyone would ever find the body.

"Don't be absurd," he said between clenched lips. "I'm not a child, to be afraid of the dark."

"There's more down here than the dark," Talbot said. "There's a tale that plague victims were walled up in here. You can still hear their screams if you keep quiet."

"A gruesome history," Nicholas said dryly. "Do you not know any more pleasant stories?"

"Queasy, your lordship?" Talbot's laughter echoed against the soot-covered brick.

Nicholas took a step forward and placed the head of his cane against the man's back. "Did you know, Talbot, that there is a blade located inside this walking stick? A short jab and you'll be one more corpse." He glanced around, surveying the blackened bricks and deep shadows. "I'll venture that more than one body has been left here over the years."

Talbot stepped forward, and glanced over his shoulder at Nicholas. "My pardons, your lordship, I meant no disrespect." Before Nicholas could comment, he disappeared into the shadows. "Don't step on any old bones, your lordship," he said, his amused voice disembodied and echoing.

Nicholas followed his path, by necessity placing his hand on the slimy brick wall and picking his way down the steps. The glow of the lantern abruptly disappeared from view, leaving him in total darkness.

The skittering sound around him increased, punctuated by high-pitched squeaks. He detested rats.

"Have you lost your way, your lordship?" Talbot said,

suddenly appearing at the bottom of the steps surrounded by a nimbus of light.

"Is it absolutely necessary to come to this . . ." He hesitated for a moment, knowing that there was no appropriate word for this dungeon. "Place?"

"It gets easier a few feet up ahead, your lordship."

Nicholas grimly smiled, thinking that once he had the ruby, he would never again be forced to consort with the goldsmith.

The floor abruptly sloped beneath his feet, rendering him momentarily disoriented. He stopped and focused on the light ahead. As he walked downward toward it, he realized that Talbot had entered a tavern.

He ducked his head below a low-hung lintel, and entered a wide smoke-filled room. A corpulent man dressed in a stained shirt with rolled-up sleeves was tapping a keg that sat on rockers on the bar's surface. He looked up at their entrance and studied them for a moment before nodding at Talbot. Nicholas fingered the neck of his walking stick and reassured himself that he was somewhat protected.

He never underestimated the situations in which he found himself. Neither did he believe in the goodness of his fellow man. His cynicism had kept him alive these last few years when the society he'd known had disintegrated around him, leaving only anarchy and mob rule.

Several men hunched over the bar with elbows planted firmly on the wood and hands cupped protectively around chipped tankards. One man was attired in a low-slung cap, and boasted a few days' worth of beard. But it was his foul-smelling clothes that had Nicholas pressing his handkerchief to his nose again and wishing he'd brought his lavender water with him.

Talbot whispered something to the tavern owner and the man responded with a jerk of his chin. Nicholas followed as Talbot wended his way through the smoke-filled room toward a table in the rear. A single man was seated there and at Talbot's appearance he kicked out a low-slung stool to his left and gestured toward it with his hand.

Talbot sat and a moment later Nicholas did as well. Folding his hands over the top of his walking stick, he studied the man to his right.

His face was round, marked with scars and small pustules. The flesh hung in folds to his chin, as if he'd recently lost a great deal of weight. His eyes were brown and badly bloodshot, either from the liquor, smoke, or illness. The hands that clutched his tankard were large, fleshy, but his nails were surprisingly clean. Most of his teeth were missing but those that remained were brown stubs.

He looked exactly like what he was—a man who would kidnap or kill, depending upon the amount paid him.

"I hear you want an errand done," the man said, his burr of accent so thick that Nicholas could barely understand his words.

"Yes," Nicholas said, leaning forward. He told the man exactly what he needed.

When he finished, the man stared into his tankard, and then slowly nodded. "I'll do it."

"How much?"

When the man answered, it was Nicholas's turn to remain silent. He was running out of money, but it seemed as if he had no other choice. If only his daughter had been the biddable girl she'd once been, he would not have had to resort to such tactics. Finally, he nodded in agreement.

The price decided upon, Talbot ordered them each a tankard. Nicholas was wise enough not to refuse, but at the same time he wasn't going to drink anything in this foul place.

A few minutes later, he gave the man the information to

carry out his assignment, and then stood, carefully hiding his disgust. It would never do to alienate those he needed.

Turning, he made his way from the tavern, leaving the haze and smoke behind. As he began to climb the steps he had the unwelcome feeling that he had just left the pits of hell.

Chapter 23

"My father thinks you're very beautiful, Miss du Marchand," Margaret said one day.

A proper governess would chastise Margaret for her comment, or explain that it was not polite to offer an opinion about a person's appearance. After all, it was character that counted more than beauty. But she didn't say those words. Instead, she only stared at the child. "What makes you think that?"

"He said it," Margaret said, concentrating on the book in front of her. A small smile tilted her lips and Jeanne studied her for some moments in order to ascertain whether or not Margaret was being mischievous. But it seemed as if she wasn't, after all, because a moment later she spoke again and the topic was different.

"The dressmaker's coming tomorrow, Miss du Marchand. I'm to tell you that I need the afternoon free." She glanced over at Jeanne, an earnest expression on her face. "Would you please tell Papa that I really shouldn't be taken from my studies?"

"Why?" Jeanne asked, confused. It was not the first time

she'd been relegated to monosyllabic replies around the child. Jeanne shook herself mentally. "Why, Margaret? Do you not like the dressmaker?"

"I like her as a person well enough, Miss du Marchand. It's just that I have no patience for new clothes." Margaret sighed heavily. "I would very much like to be able to click my fingers together and have my clothes be ready for me. Instead, I must stand there for hours and hours and be fitted. They measure and they poke, and they take so long, Miss du Marchand."

"You should be grateful that you have a father who is wealthy enough to provide lovely dresses for you." Jeanne looked over her spectacles at Margaret and tried not to remember when she'd felt the same as a child being pinned into her court dresses. Hours had seemed like years. But time had a way of speeding up the older one became. Months now felt like weeks, and a day only an hour.

"Is that why you only have three dresses, Miss du Marchand? Were you poor as a child?"

She really should do something about the child's ability to render her speechless so often.

"No," Jeanne said. "My father was quite wealthy. But circumstances change, Margaret. One should always be grateful for what one has at the time."

Margaret nodded. "Perhaps it would be bearable if you would go with me," she said. "Wouldn't you like a few new dresses? Papa wouldn't mind."

"But I would," Jeanne said, frowning at her charge. "I could not accept them."

"It could be part of your salary," she said, her smile so beatific that Jeanne studied her for a moment.

"You haven't said anything to him, have you?"

Margaret shrugged.

"Margaret MacRae," Jeanne said, irritated.

"He said you were beautiful, Miss du Marchand. Beautiful." Margaret sighed heavily, such a dramatic and overwrought performance that Jeanne almost smiled.

"That was very nice of him, Margaret, but it still does not change the fact that he should not be buying me dresses. I can afford them well enough on my own."

"Then you'll go with me?"

Jeanne shook her head.

Margaret frowned at her, obviously disappointed, and studied the book in front of her again. This time, Jeanne noticed that she was squinting.

"Are you having trouble seeing, Margaret? Are the words like little tadpoles across the page?"

Margaret looked up, her eyes sparkling. "I don't believe I've ever seen little tadpoles, Miss du Marchand. What are they?"

"Are the words swimming across the page?" Jeanne said instead.

"No, they don't," Margaret said seriously. "Occasionally it seems as if they're very far away. But that's only when I'm tired or the light is dim."

Jeanne pulled off her own spectacles and handed them to the child. "Here," she said, "try these on and see if they help."

The frames were too large, but Margaret managed to entwine the ribbon earpiece around each ear. Balancing the book with both hands, she stared at the page. A look of utter wonder came over her face.

"I can see everything," she said, her voice filled with awe. "Every single thing."

She looked up at Jeanne as she removed the spectacles. "Why don't you wear them all the time, Miss du Marchand?"

Vanity. Not a confession she'd make to the little girl. "The older I get," Jeanne said instead, "the less it seems I need them." Not a large lie, in the scheme of things.

Margaret studied the frame, the gold wire that held the glass lenses together. "They seem to be a wonderful invention."

"I thought the same when my governess discovered that I needed help reading."

Margaret smiled up at her. "And now you've done the same for me, Miss du Marchand."

There was something oddly reminiscent about Margaret's smile. Jeanne fingered her locket, wondering why her mother came so strongly to her mind at this moment.

"Are you certain that you can spare me for the dressmakers, Miss du Marchand?" Margaret asked one last time.

"Absolutely certain," she said, smiling and making a mental note to take the opportunity of Margaret's fitting to discuss her vision problems with Douglas.

"Are you very, very certain? I think I should practice my tables, don't you?"

She frowned at the little girl. "You will go."

Margaret sighed heavily again. "If I cannot go to the warehouse, Miss du Marchand, why should I have to be fitted for dresses? The first is educational, while the second is only a bore."

Jeanne shook her head, thinking that the child did have a point.

"We've done well this week," she said. "Shall I tell your father that we'll go and see the warehouse?"

"May we?" Margaret's face was wreathed in a sudden, blinding smile. "Oh, yes, Miss du Marchand. I'd very much like to go."

"Then we shall," she said. "As a reward for enduring the dressmaker."

Margaret sighed and rolled her eyes, but Jeanne noted that her smile didn't fade and she didn't protest the arrangement.

"You'll truly enjoy it, Miss du Marchand."

"I'm sure I shall," Jeanne said decorously, quite capably hiding the fact that she felt as young as Margaret at that moment, and as excited.

Hamish MacRae watched his wife treat one of the men from Gilmuir and smiled as he heard her instructions.

"You'll wash that wound every day, Peter. I've told Iseabal about your injury and she knows to check it."

She wound a bandage around the man's hand, frowning at him while she did so.

Hamish wasn't entirely certain he believed in destiny, but he knew that he'd been given a blessing the day Mary came into his life. He had vowed, when taking her from Scotland, to give the world to her, and she surprised him by being as eager as he for adventure. Now, nearly a decade later, what he'd promised had come true. They'd seen the African continent, Egypt, and the Orient. He'd taken Mary to his boyhood home of Nova Scotia and even become embroiled in a skirmish between an English ship and an American vessel.

Hamish had watched as Mary learned medical treatments in nearly every country they'd visited. Aboard his ship was a storeroom set aside for medicines alone—jars of ginseng, Chinese herbs, and a host of remedies Mary now used to treat an impressive list of ailments. Never had he valued her talents more than in this past year, when they'd embarked on another series of voyages—across the English Channel and back again.

In the past months their rescue missions to France had increased, and it seemed to Hamish that there were always more troubled souls needing help. Mary's talent at healing as well as her nurturing spirit were evident every time she sat at the bedside of an ill patient or anguished about a sick child.

In a few weeks they would sail for France again. Another message had come and he and Mary would sail into a secluded harbor, their potential cargo a few dozen terrified, exhausted people.

Every time Hamish looked at his reflection, the scars on his face and body brought back the recollection of his year of imprisonment. Every time he felt the twinge of a muscle ache or a bone, he remembered feeling as lost and alone as the French people they rescued. And for Mary, the fact that she couldn't set foot on Scottish soil was an adequate reminder of her own days of terror.

They each did what they could to help, even though they each knew there was more to be done. A country was in peril, and they saw it on the faces of the men, women, and children who fled from France in desperation.

Hamish stepped forward, glancing at Peter and sending him a commiserating look. He'd been at the receiving end of Mary's strict pronouncements himself.

"You're better off just doing what she says," he said in a low voice as the man passed him.

Peter grimaced, glanced at his bandaged hand and then back at Mary, evidently having already come to that conclusion on his own.

Hamish grinned as he reached Mary's side. "You should let the man leave with his dignity, my love. Don't chastise him so well that he crawls away."

"I'll leave him his hand, instead," she said angrily, staring after Peter. "He almost let the wound putrefy, Hamish."

Before she could continue with a gruesome litany of the man's symptoms, Hamish grabbed her and kissed her soundly. A few minutes later, he pulled away, whispering a thoroughly decadent remedy for a wound of his own.

"It's very swollen," he said, wiggling his eyebrows. "And needs some tender care."

"What kind of ministrations did you have in mind?" she asked, her face turning a delightful shade of pink.

"A touch of a hand, perhaps? A tender kiss?"

"I'll have to see this grievous injury," she said, taking his hand.

"And I'm more than willing to show it to you," he said, grinning, letting her precede him to their cabin.

While Margaret was occupied with the dressmakers, Jeanne visited Douglas. She entered the library after receiving a summons to her knock.

"I believe Margaret needs some spectacles," she said without preamble.

Douglas looked up from the papers he was signing and frowned at her. "What do you mean, she needs spectacles? She sees perfectly well."

She wondered if he was going to be as obtuse about the subject as her own father. A du Marchand had no flaws, according to him; therefore she had no need for any device to assist her.

"She can't see as well as you think," she said firmly.

He put his quill down and sat back in the chair, surveying her. Instead of arguing further, he surprised her by remaining silent.

"I believe that I could contact someone who might be able to make her a pair. I've heard that there is a very good firm in London, but I'm certain that Edinburgh must have a company who can provide spectacles for her as well."

"Why do you care?"

Taken aback, she could only stare at him. "She's my charge. You've hired me to be her governess. Should I not care for her?"

Again he startled her by not doing what she expected. Instead of answering her, he asked another question, one even more disturbing than the first. "Who was here when I was at Gilmuir?"

"Who was here?" she repeated. Of course someone had told him. Some member of his loyal staff must have mentioned her visitor. "Why didn't you ask before now?"

He smiled. "I told myself that you would volunteer the information. But you didn't. Then I told myself it didn't matter, but I find that it does. Who was it, Jeanne?"

"My father," she said and had the unique pleasure of seeing Douglas MacRae at a loss for words.

"I thought he was dead," he said finally.

"He did a credible imitation of being alive," she said, her hand closing so tightly over the spectacles in her pocket that she nearly broke them. Carefully, she loosened her grip and withdrew her hand.

"What did he want? Shall I offer to employ another French émigré?"

"I doubt my father would take advantage of your offer, Douglas. He has yet to understand that France has changed, and with it, the world. He still sees himself as a grand man."

"But you see it differently. Why is that?"

"My father would tell you it's because I'm half English."

"I don't care what your father would say. What do you say?"

She shrugged. "Perhaps nine years in a convent altered my thinking, Douglas."

"Then what did he want with you, Jeanne?"

She gave him the truth and wondered what he might do with it. "I don't believe that my father cares anything about me. I ceased to be a true du Marchand many years ago." She fingered the locket and smiled. "He wanted my mother's necklace."

"Why?"

Her smile broadened. "Not for any sentimental value. I

thought at first that he might want to show it to the Somerville family, to prove his relationship to them. But they are as decimated as the du Marchands. A distant cousin to my mother has inherited the title."

He frowned. "Still, you could have sought a home with him."

"Perhaps," she said, agreeing. "But I decided that it would better to seek my own life than to be indebted to anyone else. I've developed a certain obstinacy of will from the convent. No doubt the nuns would be horrified."

He stood and rounded the desk and walked toward her. "As they would by your conduct, no doubt."

Her smile was rueful agreement.

"You're more beautiful now than you ever were as a girl," he said softly, startling her. "Sometimes I can't believe how truly beautiful you are and I tell myself that my eyes are playing tricks on me. Until I see you again and I'm captivated once more."

He reached out and brushed the back of his hand against her heated cheek. "There is no one who has such creamy skin as yours, Jeanne. Or that faint flush that looks like the most delicate rose at dawn."

He traced a finger over her upper lip and then her lower, as if he were memorizing the shape of her mouth. "Your lips are made for kissing. Every time you speak I have to force myself to listen to the words and not concentrate on the way your mouth moves."

Bending down, he breathed against her lips. "As if you're hinting for a kiss," he said softly before he placed his lips on hers.

Her arms reached up and entwined around his neck. She was lost in the kiss for long moments before she deliberately stepped back and turned, walking to the window. Her composure had been destroyed with a kiss. Did he know how easily he had done it? Or how charmed she was by

him? If he crooked his finger at her and bade her lie on the
carpet and await him, she'd no doubt do it, and feel a thrill
of anticipation.

"I have a present for you," he said, his voice wrapping
around her.

She glanced over her shoulder at him, surprised. "A
present?"

He went to the bookcase behind his desk and withdrew
something from the cabinet at the base of it. Returning, he
handed the box to her.

Placing it on his desk, she carefully unwrapped it,
glancing at him occasionally as she did so. The ribbon was
a length of lavender gauze that she carefully laid aside before taking off the top of the box. Inside was a nightgown
of diaphanous linen, the top and sleeves crafted of intricate
lace.

Even in Paris she'd never seen such a beautiful garment.

"I destroyed yours, I believe." A softly voiced confession, one that made her shiver to recall that moment.

"Do you not miss me, Jeanne?"

Oh, yes.

"I said that I wouldn't come to you, but I've been waiting for you to say the word. Why have you remained
silent?"

She glanced up at him to find him smiling.

"I would think that you don't enjoy our lovemaking," he
teased.

Enough to lose her mortal soul, but this, too, she
didn't say.

"Why did you stay with me?"

The question was so unexpected that she stared at him.
"Why did I stay with you?" she repeated.

He nodded.

She wasn't wise enough to lie. "Because those months
in Paris were the most beautiful of my life," she admitted.

"Because I wanted to feel that way again." But the greatest reason, the greatest secret, was one she kept hidden. *Because I love you, and even after all this time I can't turn my back on love.*

Over the last ten years she'd come to realize that the flesh was nothing. She could be hurt and abused, and as long as her spirit was intact very little could truly affect her. But this man, with his sardonic smile and his intense blue eyes, had the power to wound her deeply without seeming to try.

Jeanne had realized his power over her the day she'd left Paris and he still had not appeared. She'd stared at the sky, at the brilliant yellow, blue, and purple colors of the dawn. The mist had risen from the river, obscuring the base of the hill of Montmartre. The church of St. Pierre de Montmartre stared out as if to send her on its way, its Gothic style a fitting last glimpse of Paris.

He never came. No one did, and when she was sent to the convent, no one ever rescued her. Circumstance alone had released her from her votary prison.

The question trembled on her lips now. Why had he never tried to find her? Why had he never left word?

Deliberately avoiding looking at him, she picked up the box, stepping back and away.

"Will you think about the spectacles?" she asked in a voice that quavered. With some force of will she turned and faced him again. He was studying her, his blue eyes narrowed. "Margaret loves to read," she continued. "It's a shame that she cannot because of her father's pride."

He strode across the room, but hesitated at the door and turned back to her.

"Of course I'll get her the spectacles, Jeanne. She's my daughter. But even without them Margaret can see better than her mother."

He left her there staring after him.

Chapter 24

❦

Margaret peered inside the schoolroom. "Cook promised to prepare us a lunch, if you'd like to eat outside, Miss du Marchand."

"Outside?" Jeanne looked up from the slate in front of her.

Margaret walked to the window and pointed to the meadow beside the house. "Right there," she said, pointing to the large and venerable oak Jeanne had noticed before. "It's the perfect place for a meal." She turned and smiled at Jeanne. "We have to eat, after all, do we not?"

In her smile was a hint of the charm her father had so often used to his advantage. Jeanne found herself no more successful in denying the daughter than she was in refusing the father.

"Yes, we do at that."

As she descended the steps, Jeanne smiled at the young girl on the stairs industriously dusting the spools of the banister. Her employment at the Hartley home, however short-lived, had educated her about the life of servants. They were not often as concerned with the mistress and master of the house as they were with their own lives. Doug-

253

las's staff, however, surprised her. They seemed to share a camaraderie, yet they worked as hard as any people she knew. She doubted that in the kitchens of Vallans there had been such a general enjoyment of life, or, for that matter, a liking for their employer.

When she shared a meal with the servants, she sat and listened, and when conversation did, occasionally, turn to Douglas, she was not aware of looks directed at her. She could only credit Lassiter for their discretion, or perhaps the staff simply liked Douglas enough not to comment upon his actions. For whatever reason, she was grateful for their restraint.

Betty stood at the bottom of the stairs holding a basket with both hands. Jeanne took it from her, nearly sagging from its weight. "It feels like a great deal more food than we need."

"Cook is forever feeding Miss Margaret. Ever since she was a baby, people have been trying to get her to eat."

At Jeanne's questioning look, she added, "She was nearly starved as a baby."

Before Jeanne could ask any further questions, Margaret called out to her. "Miss du Marchand?" The child stood at the door, obviously impatient to be out on a very fine Edinburgh day.

Thanking Betty for her assistance, she followed Margaret out the front door and then to the left, along the path to the meadow.

"Do you have your book?" she asked.

Margaret nodded, a copy of *Praise of Folly* in her hand. "Must we have Erasmus, Miss du Marchand? He seems very dour."

"We must," she said firmly.

Margaret sighed again, but didn't demur.

Jeanne hid her smile. As much as she enjoyed teaching the girl, she was very conscious of Margaret's will. In that, Margaret was not unlike Jeanne herself. She'd been a tyrant, of sorts, as a child, her arrogance partly a result of who she was—the daughter of the Comte du Marchand must be obeyed. What Jeanne had accomplished with her rank, however, Margaret achieved with a smile.

"You'll find that he has a great deal of interest to say," Jeanne said, refusing to give way.

"Most adults do," Margaret said.

Surprised, Jeanne glanced at her.

"At least my uncles do," Margaret amended. "And Papa, of course." She looked at Jeanne and smiled, the expression impish. "And of course you, Miss du Marchand."

She was being teased, and it was such a novel experience that Jeanne felt a surge of warmth. "I'm pleased that you think so, Margaret. That will make Erasmus much easier to bear."

Margaret smiled back, conceding Jeanne the victor in this mild skirmish of wills.

They continued to follow a path through the dense overgrowth. The landscape had been transformed into a scene of wild beauty by the recent storms. Crimson wildflowers brushed against the brambles and saplings, vying for attention. Oak trees had budded early; their branches were now heavy with leaves. Somewhere, the longing call of a bird seeking its mate conveyed repose and tranquility, while the bright sky hinted at a warm and peaceful day.

Abruptly, the brambles and saplings disappeared and the land leveled out. The path they followed now was nothing more than a depression in the earth, but it was evident from the ease that Margaret took it that she'd come here often.

"Papa is having this area landscaped," she said, glancing at Jeanne over her shoulder. "He has a layout of terraces he wants built, and hedges and flower beds."

"It seems a shame to change it," Jeanne responded. "Although the park you described is no doubt very attractive," she hastened to add.

"You should see Gilmuir," Margaret said. "It's a truly lovely place. I wish Papa would live there, but of course he can't. Not with his business at Leith."

"I can't help but wonder why he settled in Edinburgh," Jeanne said.

"It's because of me," Margaret said, halting beneath the oak tree. Jeanne spread the blanket on the ground near the trunk.

"Why because of you?"

Margaret smiled. "Papa said that he wanted to create an empire for me to inherit. He said that I should be an heiress." She giggled, instantly banishing any hint of autocracy from that statement. "I would much rather have remained aboard ship, but Papa says that he wanted to choose a place on land that would be safer for me."

"So he picked Edinburgh?"

"Uncle James is in Ayleshire, Uncle Alisdair is at Gilmuir, Uncle Brendan is in Inverness, and Uncle Hamish is aboard ship."

Jeanne smoothed the corners of the blanket. "In that case, I can see why he chose Edinburgh."

"It was the only place left without a MacRae," Margaret said, shrugging.

They ate lunch leisurely, a meal of meat pies followed by fruit tarts adorned with slices of apple. When they were finished, Jeanne handed Margaret her own spectacles.

"We really should read Erasmus," Jeanne said.

Sighing loudly, Margaret nevertheless placed the loops of ribbons over her ears, opened the book, and began to read from where she left off this morning.

"Nature, more of a stepmother than a mother in several ways, has sown a seed of evil in the hearts of mortals, especially in the more thoughtful men,

*which makes them dissatisfied with their own lot and
envious of another's."*

The recitation was so very close to her own feelings of
late that Jeanne was startled.

"Do you think that's true, Miss du Marchand?" Margaret asked, holding her finger at her place and closing the
book. "I couldn't imagine wanting someone else's life."

"Then you should consider yourself blessed," Jeanne said.

Margaret seemed to consider that, and then nodded.
"Papa says that life can be a blessing or a curse, and it's a
man's attitude that decides the matter."

Was Douglas to be considered a font of wisdom in all
things? Margaret seemed to think so.

"There are circumstances that may occur to a person
that have nothing to do with attitude," Jeanne countered.

"Papa says that it's not what happens to you that's important, but how you react to it." Margaret's look was intent and thoughtful and too adult for Jeanne's peace of
mind.

"I can't say that I totally agree," she said carefully, realizing that she was treading on shaky ground. Margaret quite
obviously adored her father. But Douglas wasn't a god, and
Jeanne had no intention of treating him like one. "Death
happens, despite our wishes. For example, my mother died
when I was about your age. Yet I didn't encourage it with
my thoughts. And my reaction was grief and loneliness."

Margaret nodded, but didn't say anything in response.

"There are some events in life that must simply be endured, Margaret. When they come, and they most certainly
will, it's not your ability to think of good thoughts that will
sustain you, but faith."

"In God?"

"In yourself," Jeanne said firmly.

She thought about this for a moment. "Do you ever think of your mother, Miss du Marchand?"

The question was so unexpected that Jeanne hesitated. "Very often," she said. "Especially when I need advice. I wonder what she would tell me. Sometimes I think I can hear her in my mind."

Margaret nodded. She leaned back her head and stared up at the branches of the tree. "I think of my mother so often that I just know she's near me." She glanced at Jeanne. "Is that a bad thing, do you think, to believe in angels?"

Jeanne shook her head. "I cannot think so. But then, I'm not an expert on theology. Have you asked your father?"

Margaret shook her head. "Papa says he doesn't mind talking about her, but I can tell it makes him sad."

She shouldn't ask, but then she shouldn't have done a great many things concerning Douglas MacRae. "Do you remember her?"

Again Margaret shook her head. "No. She died at my birth. It's a very strange feeling, causing your mother's death."

"You did not cause it, Margaret," Jeanne said, reaching out and cupping her palm gently against the child's cheek. "It simply happened, that's all," she said softly. "One had nothing to do with the other." Sometimes a lie was more palatable than the truth.

"That's just what Papa says, Miss du Marchand. Whenever he tells me the story of how they met I think he must still love her. His voice gets very low and soft."

Jeanne busied herself in putting back the luncheon items into the basket, trying not to feel the pain Margaret's words evoked. An inner voice—wisdom or conscience—warned her not to continue, but she disregarded it.

"What did she look like?"

"Like a princess, Papa said. She was French, like you, Miss du Marchand."

There, payment for her curiosity.

Margaret was younger than her own child would have been, which meant that Douglas had not lost any time finding another woman to love. A woman who probably still lived in his heart. Why else did he only mention her cryptically and in passing?

How long had he waited? A few months? A year? Was that why he'd never come for her? He'd been in love with someone else by then, and she was only an afterthought. A faint memory. Oh, yes, Jeanne du Marchand. What a silly girl to think herself in love.

There, that was the reason to hate him, a way to diffuse the love that was growing stronger every day. How horrible that it didn't seem to matter.

"Sometimes," Margaret said, sitting back against the base of the tree, "I want to talk to her so very much." She looked at Jeanne. "I want to ask her if she ever misses me as much as I miss her. Do you think an angel ever remembers what it's like to be a person?"

Jeanne glanced at the young girl, seeing the pain in Margaret's eyes and remembering her own. Reaching over, she placed her hand on the girl's knee. "I think they must remember very clearly," she said, recalling only too well her feelings of abandonment when her own mother died. "I know that she must miss you very much."

"Do you truly think so?"

Jeanne nodded.

"Papa has this material at his warehouse. It comes from India and is white and gauzy with sparkles in it. It looks as if it might be made from angel wings." She smiled, her expression somewhat brighter, Jeanne was pleased to see. "Perhaps you'll see it tomorrow."

"The warehouse seems like a very profitable venture," Jeanne said, grateful that Margaret had changed the subject. She didn't truly wish to hear any more of angels and women who made Douglas sad even now.

How horrible to be jealous of a dead woman.

"Oh, it is. I overheard my Aunt Iseabal say that Papa was the most marriageable man in Edinburgh. Do you think that's true?"

They had gone from one unpalatable subject to another, it seemed.

"I wouldn't know," she said, standing.

Jeanne smoothed out the material she had clenched between her fists, decided that she truly could not bear any more talk of Margaret's mother or other women. Nevertheless, she found herself asking yet another question about her. "Are you named for her? For your mother, I mean?"

Margaret shook her head. "No, I'm named for my Aunt Mary. Her middle name is Margaret, too. My first name is too difficult for most people. It's Mireille."

"That's French for miracle," Jeanne said, surprised.

Margaret nodded. "Isn't that the prettiest name? Papa said it's because I was a miracle." She stood and brushed down her skirt. "I nearly died when I was a baby, you see. I wasn't supposed to live. But I did, and that's why they named me Miracle."

"It's a beautiful name," Jeanne said. And Margaret was a charming child. There was no doubt that she was loved, and that Douglas was a fond and affectionate father.

She shouldn't feel the bite of envy, or the peppering of tears. Such emotions were foolish, as was the wish that her own child might have lived. Regret would only poison the day.

Chapter 25

Douglas had never thought himself a man needing to bolster his confidence by boasting, but he found himself ordering his best barouche to be readied. Ever since Jeanne had sent him a carefully worded note, he'd been preparing for this outing. The journey to his warehouse was neither a difficult nor a long one, and could easily have been accomplished in a lesser carriage. But he wanted to impress her, only one symptom of losing his mind.

He had found reasons to go to the schoolroom often. A precaution, he told himself—as a girl, she'd turned her back on Margaret. But the governess seemed to genuinely care for her young charge.

The two sides of her character were not easily fit together, and he had some bad moments attempting to do so.

It was as if she knew, somehow, that every word she said and every act she performed was measured against a memory. The Jeanne of his youth in many ways matched with the woman she had become now. But there was still something wrong, and that disparity was keeping him awake at night.

Who was Jeanne du Marchand?

The girl he remembered had wanted to know every-thing. She was genuinely curious about his studies, and they argued vociferously about certain points of Immanuel Kant and other philosophers, finding themselves equally matched in education and intelligence. This Jeanne was more circumspect but just as curious. He'd discovered that she'd borrowed several books from his library, subjects that he found himself wanting to debate with her.

The younger Jeanne had loved with abandon, and so did this woman, shrouded as she was in mystery and an almost palpable aura of sorrow.

At times, though not often enough, this woman had the same tilted sense of humor, seeing the ridiculous and glo-rying in the absurd, not unlike the girl she'd been.

The discordance came when he attempted to understand her actions. Once, he'd thought her heartless and uncaring, but now he could see the warmth and gentleness she evinced when she taught Margaret. She'd been as nurtur-ing with Hartley's child, he remembered.

Then what had happened ten years ago? Had he been wrong all this time? The longer he spent in her presence, the more questions were unearthed, until Douglas wasn't entirely certain what the truth was.

He gave them a quarter hour, consulting his pocket watch from time to time and pacing in front of his house. The day was a fine one, the air warm out of the north, the breeze such that he could almost imagine himself far from Edinburgh and its thickly populated streets.

Hearing a sound, he turned to find Margaret racing down the steps, a bright and expectant smile on her face. A surge of love overwhelmed him and he opened up his arms. She jumped into them, just as she had since the time she learned to walk.

"One day you'll get too big for this, Meggie," he said,

knowing that he should expect much more decorous behavior from her. But there was time enough for growing up, a hundred years from now when he could bear the thought of losing her to adulthood.

She wrapped her arms around his neck and gave him a big kiss on the cheek. "Sometimes," she said, sighing, "I think I'll never grow up."

"Do not hasten the years, I beg you, Meggie," he teased. "I do not wish to be acquainted with the prospect of old age quite yet."

She tilted her head much like an inquisitive bird. "You shall always be the most handsome man in the world, Papa, even with white hair and a beard trailing down to the floor."

He laughed, wondering when she'd become so adept at flattery. "You are hinting at something, I think," he said, settling her on the step. "Could it be because it's your birthday soon?"

Mary had chosen her birth date, both of them uncertain exactly when she was born. With a touch of irony, he realized that the woman standing there so silent and demure was the one person who knew the correct date.

"How old will you be, Margaret?" Jeanne asked. "Ten?"

Margaret only giggled. He studied Jeanne as she smiled down at his daughter, and wondered why she couldn't see what was so obvious. Reaching out her hand, she brushed her fingers over Margaret's shoulder. A telling movement, an almost protective gesture.

Surprisingly, it infuriated him.

He speared a hand through his hair and told himself that he was being an idiot. He should be pleased at Jeanne's show of affection, and her solicitousness toward Margaret. Instead, he wanted to go to ask her why it had taken her so long to feel protective about her daughter. Why had she never done so before? Why had she nearly killed her?

She was the only person in the world who could push

him past the boundaries of his restraint. She had that power when she was a girl, and she still retained it. Perhaps that's why he was suddenly enraged.

He was not some poor dumb beast to be led to the slaughter. But he was acting the besotted fool, vacillating between lust and irritation. Entering the carriage, he sat with his back to the horses, surveying the two of them.

Anyone would know, seeing them, that they were related. Although Margaret looked more like his side of the family, she had gestures that reminded him of Jeanne, a quick upturn of her chin, a bright white infectious grin, and a laugh that was strangely echoing of her mother's.

Sometimes he thought Jeanne was willfully blind to her own child.

He frowned at her but she didn't look in his direction. She had never, until a few nights ago, discussed the past. Nor had she once mentioned the child she had carried. He couldn't help but wonder, though, if she was ever awakened with nightmares like Margaret. Did she ever feel the pinch of her conscience? Did she never once wish that she had acted differently, with more regard, with more compassion? With more charity?

"What are we going to see, Papa?"

"You'll have to be patient," he said, forcing a smile to his face.

She turned to Jeanne. "The last time I went, there were these beautiful carved masks, Miss du Marchand. And balls that sounded like the wind when you shook them."

"I believe they had sand in them," Douglas contributed.

"There are skins from lions and tigers, and great tusks from elephants. But you must take care, Miss du Marchand, never to get lost," she said, repeating the very instructions he had given her on her first visit to the warehouse. She had been five, he recalled, and overwhelmed with the sheer size of the buildings. Now, however, she knew every single nook and cranny of them.

The sound of the horses' hooves on the cobbles was oddly loud. There wasn't that much traffic in this part of the city. They traveled west on Princess Street, the thoroughfare seeming unbalanced because there were buildings only on the south side, giving the residents an unfettered view of Edinburgh castle.

New Town was comprised of straight streets, crescents, and squares, carefully planned in order to provide spacious surroundings for the more affluent of Edinburgh's inhabitants. Those who could not afford the Palladian structures lived in the narrow streets and closes of Old Town to the southeast.

As he watched, Jeanne smiled at something Margaret said and pointed to Edinburgh Castle nestled on the hill above the city. He didn't hear her words, but it was no doubt some bit of lore or legend she imparted. Her eyes were lively now, and her smile quick. No mystery surrounded her, no sadness. The role of governess fit her well enough, while that of mother had, no doubt, proven too difficult.

The more he knew about her, the more confused he became.

•

Chapter 26

Leith was Edinburgh's seaport, a bustling scene of both oceangoing and coastal vessels. The MacRae docks took up a sizable portion of the harbor, and today a series of ships sat ready to be offloaded. Nearby, the warehouses had MACRAE BROTHERS painted on the roofs in black letters large enough that they could be seen for miles.

There was no doubt that the MacRaes were a presence in Leith and the whole of Scotland.

The newest goods were stored in the far warehouse to the right. Fifty-seven clerks employed by MacRae Brothers worked in the building to the left. The middle structure was set aside for sorting the offloaded cargo. Some items would be stored and other merchandise would be delivered to shopkeepers and individuals who had preordered it. The most precious freight, including gold bars and silver ingots, was kept locked in the vault in Douglas's second-floor office.

Douglas had always believed that the success of MacRae Brothers was based, in large part, on the seventy-odd men who worked for him. Each individual, Douglas

267

believed, wanted two things in his life—some measure of contentment and his freedom. He provided a portion of the former by providing a decent wage for a decent day's work.

Once, he'd thought that sailing with Hamish had taught him the lessons he'd needed to know about men and life. But the last six years had become a schoolroom for him, and his establishment of MacRae Brothers a daily lesson. The Edinburgh community had looked on some of his ideas with surprise and occasionally some criticism.

When a man was experiencing financial hardship, Douglas felt he should offer a helping hand. After learning of a man's loss of his home, Douglas had established an emergency fund available to any man in his employ who needed it. Surprisingly, it was rarely touched except in cases of extreme hardship.

Additionally, Douglas began a rotating schedule, making it possible for a man to earn a day's pay without working from dawn to dusk. An employee could choose his own hours within a certain framework of time. Sundays were always holidays, and if a ship arrived, it waited to be offloaded until the next working day.

He gave a man time off when a child was born or a loved one ill, innovations that were not replicated elsewhere in Edinburgh or Leith. He attended every wedding, funeral, and christening for family members, and had been named the godparent of nine children in the last six years.

The changes he'd instituted had not only led to a stable work force but a feeling that MacRae Brothers was a large and friendly family. Men did not leave his company, and when there were positions posted, it was normal for a hundred men or more to apply.

The barouche halted in front of the middle building. Douglas exited the carriage first, followed by an impatient Margaret and, lastly, Jeanne. He held out his hand to help her from the carriage, and she laid her gloved fingers upon it. He could feel the heat of her hand through the linen and wondered if the rest of her was as fevered to the touch. Paradoxically, he was glad she'd dressed with such restraint today, and yet wished she had not. Not one button was undone, not one tress of hair loose. Even the ribbon of her bonnet was tied with a tight little knot beneath her chin.

A proper woman, past the first blush of youth, perhaps. But a woman with knowledge in her eyes, wisdom, and other emotions that he couldn't decipher. She was a mystery, a riddle, and an irritant.

They shared a look and then she withdrew her fingers. Not quickly as if she were offended, but one by one, drawing them across his palm in an almost taunting gesture.

He squeezed the tips of her fingers, noting her quick look of surprise. Her gaze dropped, shielding her eyes from him. Only the sudden bloom of color on her pale cheeks revealed her reaction.

Releasing her hand, he stepped back, turning and leading the way.

Margaret, however, had another. idea. She tucked her hand into his, and then grabbed Jeanne's until they walked three abreast. The fact that Margaret linked the two of them disturbed him on an elemental level. His daughter, unknowing, was replicating the truth.

Of the three of them, Margaret was the only innocent. She held nothing back, revealing to the world a lexicon of emotions. When she was excited, enthusiastic, or joyful everyone knew it. Nor was she shy about letting anyone know she was in pain or hurt, whether it be a physical ailment or an ache of the heart. He never wanted to dampen that great joy she felt about life, nor did he want to force her into hiding her emotions like her mother so ably did.

The convent had done that to Jeanne, or perhaps life itself. He'd never asked her about those days and now he wondered if she would have told him. There was a reticence to Jeanne that his curiosity couldn't shatter.

"Good afternoon, sir," a man called out from a booth in front of the center warehouse. Douglas approached him, smiling.

"Good morning, Jim."

The man who greeted him had a tanned face filled with wrinkles and neatly queued white hair. His bearing was that of a much younger man, with level shoulders and a ramrod-straight back. Jim was proud of his military past, having served for many years in one of the Highland regiments.

"Good morning, Miss Margaret," the older man said. "Have you come to see the new goods?"

"I have, Mr. McManus," she said, slipping her hand from Douglas's grip and waving to him. "This is my governess, Miss du Marchand." She pointed toward the dock. "Is that *The Sherbourne Lass*?"

Jim tipped his hat to Jeanne, and then turned to answer Margaret. "It is, miss. Came in a few hours ago."

"Jim is our watchman," Douglas said in an aside to Jeanne. "He performs security for the company. Jim guards the warehouse and makes sure no one enters who should not."

"Then I should feel fortunate to have been invited."

"I never thought you a thief, Jeanne."

She glanced at him curiously.

"Is Henry about?" he asked Jim.

"He is, sir. He'll be at the pilot's house. Do you want me to fetch him?"

"No," he answered. "I'll find him if I need him."

"I'll tell him you're here, sir."

"Do that," he said. "And say hello to Paulina for me."

The other man nodded, evidently pleased. "I'll do that, sir. She asks about you every time I go home."

"Jim's wife," he explained to Jeanne. "She's a sweet lady who bakes me tarts."

"Does she?" she asked, looking amused.

An archway topped the two massive doors of the warehouse. As he pushed open one of the doors, he saw Jeanne read the Latin inscription. A moment later, she smiled.

Her education had been eclectic and extensive.

"I speak the English of England and the German of Germany," she'd said once.

"Is that why you don't have an accent?" From the beginning he'd been fascinated that she sounded as proper as a duchess when she spoke English.

She had nodded, looking serious and sober, and altogether too kissable. "I'm not to have one," she'd replied. "To have an accent is to offer insult to the person with whom you're speaking. Besides, my mother was English, although my father would rather forget that fact. And my nurse was German."

"What about Latin?" he teased.

"You know as well as I that no one speaks it anymore. The closest I come is Italian."

She would be able to easily translate the motto inscribed in the stone above the door. The five MacRae brothers had taken the original clan motto of FORTITUDE and expanded it to OUR FAMILY, OUR STRENGTH.

He stood aside as Margaret entered the warehouse, followed more sedately by Jeanne. At first the place was dark, a sweet-smelling cave of unimaginable riches, of pungent aromas and shimmering fabrics. After his eyes adjusted to the dim light, Douglas led them down the center aisle.

"Do you not employ anyone here?" Jeanne asked.

"It's lunchtime, Miss du Marchand," Margaret said. "Everyone's in the dining hall."

"Do you think me a poor employer?" Douglas asked at

Jeanne's look of surprise. "I value the people who work for me. Or did you expect to find people in chains?"

She shook her head but didn't say anything, which was, to him, a thoroughly unsatisfactory response. He wanted to impress her, another clue to his mental instability around her. He wanted her to stop and stare around her in wonder. Seven years ago MacRae Brothers hadn't existed and he had built it all with his own sweat and sleepless nights. Although any of his brothers might have assisted him had he asked, he had preferred to accomplish his goal by himself, a certain independence of spirit that characterized him as a MacRae.

She didn't realize, of course, that he'd never brought another woman here. Only his sisters-in-law, and their opinion of him and what he'd accomplished, while valuable, wasn't as important as hers right at this moment.

Another reason to be irritated, he discovered. Because in the next few moments she didn't say anything, didn't exclaim in wonder, didn't even look appreciably impressed. After all, she was the Comte du Marchand's daughter, and used to the finest of everything.

Margaret was asking him a question, and he shook himself mentally, directing his attention toward his daughter.

His mood had soured, and that further irritated him. These outings to the warehouse had always been filled with amusement and Margaret's delight. He didn't want anything to spoil that, not even his disappointment at Jeanne's reaction.

He watched both of them as Margaret accompanied Jeanne down the main aisle of the warehouse. His daughter exclaimed over the various things she saw, new acquisitions since her last visit.

"Look, Miss du Marchand." Her fingers trailed over the surface of an intricately woven carpet. "Look at all the colors," she said, her eyes sparkling.

His daughter was a born merchant, her eyes lighting with interest on the shipment of silk. But she stopped in front of the ironwork, newly imported from West Africa, her small fingers trailing over the filigree.

Huge sacks of pepper perfumed the air as they passed one aisle. Crates of carved ivory and finely worked iron fishhooks led to a row of curiously wrapped articles.

"What are those, Papa?" Margaret asked.

He unwrapped the brightly patterned cloth, revealing a weapon worked in iron.

"It's a short sword," he said, reaching for another, taller wrapped bundle. "This is a spear," he said.

"It's not from Benin in Africa, Papa?" Margaret asked, evidently recalling his lectures during other visits to the warehouse.

"No," he said, proud that she remembered. "Although the workmanship is similar."

Margaret nodded before peering around him. "Papa doesn't trade with Benin, Miss du Marchand. No one who sails for MacRae Brothers is allowed to trade with them."

Jeanne looked inquiringly at Douglas.

"The major economic activity of Benin is slavery," he explained. "They make raids on their own people, and then sell them to Europeans."

"MacRaes don't buy slaves, Miss du Marchand," Margaret said, sounding far more advanced than her years.

Jeanne smiled at Margaret, and it appeared to Douglas that her look was filled with approval.

"Uncle Hamish was a slave once," Margaret confided to Jeanne in a voice that was meant to be a whisper, he was certain. Nevertheless, he heard her well enough, and turned to give her a censorious look. "Papa doesn't like to talk about it." Another confidence. This time, he didn't bother glancing at her.

"Benin seems a barbaric country," Jeanne said.

He smiled thinly. "Do not think Scotland so free of barbarism, Miss du Marchand. Dissent is not allowed here. And France has not proven itself to be civilized of late."

And what about her form of barbarism? Now was not the time for a confrontation, but he found himself wanting to ask why she'd acted as she had, handing over her newborn infant to be fostered when it was so evident that the child wouldn't survive. How dainty of her to commit murder with no blood on her hands. But it wasn't the place, especially with Margaret looking at the two of them with such unabashed interest.

He replaced the spear and short sword, making a mental note that they should be unwrapped and polished before delivering them to the collectors who'd ordered them.

Edinburgh was a wealthy city. Curiosity about other cultures and a desire to collect items from other countries had led to the continued success of MacRae Brothers. Originally, the warehouse had held only the staples and necessities of life. In the last five years, however, their inventory had increased to incorporate the odd and the unusual.

Turning, he led the way deeper into the building, Margaret at his side. When he didn't hear footsteps behind him, he glanced over his shoulder to see that Jeanne had stopped and was looking about her with interest. Several large rugs were arrayed on top of bundles of hemp and large kettledrums.

"You really do import everything, don't you?"

"Wait until you see the spice locker, Miss du Marchand," Margaret said. "And the tea chest. It's a huge room with hundreds and hundreds of tiny little drawers. And the gold vault."

Douglas laughed and placed both hands on Margaret's shoulders. "Perhaps your governess is not as fascinated as you or I, Meggie."

She tilted back her head to look at him. "Oh, Papa, how could anyone *not* be?"

"There you have it," he said, glancing at Jeanne. "You are hereby commanded to be enthralled."

"But I am," she said, smiling at both of them. She looked at Margaret. "What do you think I should see next?"

His daughter seemed to consider the matter. It would be the gold, he knew. She was fascinated by the array of ingots, not for the wealth they represented but their color and heaviness. He waited until she spoke, and when she announced her decision, he hid his smile.

"The vault, I think. The gold first and then the spice locker."

"The vault it is," Douglas said.

He turned and led the way to the stairs. This staircase was wide, the steps deep, purposely designed this way to make it easy for the workers to transport heavy merchandise up to the second floor.

"Why do you have the vaults upstairs?" Jeanne asked when he led them to the locked area.

"Flooding," he said, glancing over his shoulder at her. "We're next to the docks, and it's been known to happen. This way, both the tea and spices are safe from water damage."

"And the gold?"

"It's impervious to most disasters," he said. "Except theft. The vault has been especially designed to discourage even the most determined thief."

At the top of the steps was a series of doors. One led to his office, the middle to the gold vault, and the far left to the tea and spice locker.

Margaret led the way, opening the door and glancing back impatiently at both of them. Unerringly, she went to the larger wheel door and waited for him to open it. When he did, she was the first inside. The room was small due to the reinforcement of brick and stone around it, a precaution in case of fire.

The wealth represented here not only belonged to him but to his brothers. Shelves lined the room on three sides, and were filled with an array of small gold ingots. Bags of gold dust filled the far wall, and on the bottom shelf were a series of small drawstring bags, each one marked with Margaret's name.

"You've put another one there," she said, surprised.

"You've a birthday soon," he said. Every year he marked another bag with her name as one of her birthday gifts. Douglas carefully selected Margaret's main present, wanting something that would incite her imagination and give her a special memory of that year. For a long time he wasn't sure she would survive, which made her birthdays even more special, a true day of celebration.

This year he'd picked out a tiny chest from the Orient, a box so perfectly carved from ivory that it was a work of art. Inside he'd placed a length of ginseng he'd found. The wizened and withered spice resembled a dancing figure with arms outstretched. Once, he'd seen Margaret in that same pose, and the figure reminded him of her. There were those in the Orient who believed it good fortune to keep a ginseng root that resembled oneself.

"May I show Miss du Marchand the spice locker now, Father?"

"Perhaps your governess isn't interested," he said, glancing at Jeanne. She returned the look, the first time she'd done so since they'd climbed the stairs.

"If you'd rather I wait in the carriage, I shall," she said calmly.

"Why would you think that?"

"You seem to think I'm bored."

"Aren't you?"

"I can assure you that I'm not. I've learned a great deal in a short time."

"What have you learned, Miss du Marchand?" His tone was too rough; he could hear the edge of his words. She looked at him levelly, never glancing away. But then, he'd never faulted her courage.

He bit back any further comments because Margaret had turned and was looking at them curiously again.

Walking the short distance to the far wall, he jerked on the bell cord that he'd had installed in case anyone was ever trapped in the vault.

When the young man assigned to help Jim arrived, he instructed him to find Henry Duman.

Henry was the most senior of his employees, a grizzled veteran of the war with America. Because he was one of the most trusted of his employees, Henry performed many sensitive duties, including his most recent visit to London. Douglas had sent him as an emissary to negotiate for a plot of land on the Thames. Henry was tactful, resourceful, and above all, loyal.

A moment later a tall man stooped below the lintel to enter the vault. Although his jacket fit correctly, his arms seemed curiously too long for his body. His legs, likewise, seemed out of proportion, almost as if he were perched on stilts. He looked as if he had been stretched on the rack. Even his face was elongated, a graying beard softening the line of his jaw. But when he smiled, as he did now, the expression lit up his face, giving him a charm that made people forget about his appearance.

Margaret squealed in delight and ran to him. "Henry, you're back!"

For some odd reason, one Douglas didn't quite understand, his daughter had been fond of Henry from the first moment she'd seen him. She'd been five at the time, and had gone to him without hesitation. For his part, Henry had been bemused by the attention. Douglas often wondered if Henry had been isolated for most of his life because of his appearance. If that were the case, his life had changed the minute Margaret met him. His daughter was acutely protective of Henry, asking that the older man and his wife be invited to dinner at holidays, making Henry a present for his birthday. In turn, Henry always brought back a small surprise for her from each of his journeys. In that, he spoiled her as much as Douglas probably did.

"Do you have a present for me?" Margaret asked now.

"Margaret," Douglas said, reprimanding his daughter with a look. She glanced up at him and smiled her most beguiling smile, evidently not the least chastised.

"I do," Henry said, smiling and looking to Douglas for permission.

"Go ahead," Douglas said, watching as Margaret walked down the stairs with Henry. The older man's office was in the administration building, adjacent to the clerks. When Henry was not traveling as an emissary of MacRae Brothers, he was an excellent accountant.

Douglas knew from past experience that his daughter would perch in the chair in front of Henry's desk and proceed to tell him everything that had happened in her life since the last time they met. His daughter's distraction would give him some time to talk to Jeanne.

The moment had come. Finally. Irrevocably.

He turned and addressed Jeanne, bowing slightly. "We can either have this discussion where anyone can overhear, or we can do it in relative privacy. Your choice, Jeanne."

Her frown had the effect of irritating him further. "What is wrong, Douglas?"

"You," he said sardonically. "All my problems ultimately come down to one person—you."

Her frown intensified but she didn't say anything.

Douglas left the vault, glancing behind him to see if she

was following. In front of his office door, he wondered if this was the wisest decision. Although this confrontation had been coming for days, if not weeks, once the words were said they couldn't be taken back. He would have a choice—to banish her from his life, or hate himself for not sending her away.

She hesitated for a moment, and then left the vault, her hands folded demurely one over the other at her waist, her bonnet very properly at the perfect angle, her soft green dress the same one she'd worn when he'd first seen her at Hartley's home. There was little about her to recall the girl she'd been. There was no gaiety in her half smile, only forbearance. Her once expressive face was now impossible to read. Her posture was straight, perfect, and utterly rigid.

In all ways she appeared the proper governess.

However, in her gaze was a look of sorrow that shadowed her occasionally. He caught sight of it sometimes, so pervasive that it seemed as if a veil surrounded her, one constructed of the finest silk and nearly imperceptible to the eye.

Suddenly he wanted to banish that expression from her face, and make her laugh with Margaret's abandon. He wanted, for a few hours, to change her into the girl he had once known. He, who abhorred pretense but who had engaged in it these last few weeks, decided that a few more hours would suit him well enough.

Perhaps they might love together again tonight, after he convinced her to allow him to visit her chamber. Or perhaps he would urge her into his. He would love her not as a man, surfeited with confusion and curiosity, but as he had as a boy, with the purity of first and best love.

The air seemed to shimmer between them. He wanted to touch her, but he dared not. He wanted to shake her, but it would end in an embrace. He wanted to force her to confess all manner of sins, perhaps with a kiss.

God help him, but he still wanted her.

Chapter 27

O pening the door to his office, Douglas stepped aside, allowing her to precede him.

Instead of entering, Jeanne wanted to leave. If she had any wisdom at all, she'd find her way to the French émigré couple who had given her refuge before and might again today. When, however, had she ever been wise around Douglas?

A wall of mullioned windows dominated the room, the view of the sea and busy port of Leith. At the far side of his office, facing the panoramic scene, was a large mahogany desk supported on all four corners with carved dancing dolphins. Seated here, Douglas would be able to see the vessels bobbing on the ocean currents. Did he dream of far-off places, or was Edinburgh enough of an adventure for him?

In front of the windows, perched on a tripod, was a long brass object. She walked to it, reached out her hand, and touched a metal wheel connecting the device to its support.

"What is it?" she asked.

"A telescope. With it you can see objects that are far away."

She nodded, wanting to ask him to demonstrate. Now was not the time, however, for wonders of science or for delving into his interests. He had something on his mind. All afternoon he'd been acting oddly, glancing at her from time to time as if expecting her to change before his eyes. Something was bothering him, but she wasn't entirely certain she wanted to know what it was.

"You can't see the past, however," he said.

She glanced over her shoulder at him and then turned to stare out at the docks. A beautiful ship, painted white, sat at the end of the wide wooden pier. The two tall masts, black against the brilliant blue of the sky, were devoid of sails. The hull swept forward, as if the ship itself were impatient to be on the waves again. The name, THE SHERBOURNE LASS, was painted on the side in red, swooping letters.

He was right, the past was obscured, but she could still feel the pain of it, even now.

"I should find Margaret," she said.

"Margaret will be occupied for a good quarter hour, Jeanne, which will give us time to talk."

She didn't want to talk. Every time they met, she revealed a little more of herself.

Her past had been hinted at but not exposed. He'd seen her scars, but she'd never told him that she'd used his name as a comfort, biting down on the sound of it to muffle her screams during the beatings. She'd told him of returning to Vallans, but she'd never disclosed that she'd been nearly starving. He knew she'd escaped France, but he didn't know what that terrible journey had truly been like.

Nor did he know the greatest secret of all—that they'd had a child together.

Tell him. Tell him and then leave. Tell him what had happened all those years ago. Once she'd purged her conscience and unburdened her soul, she should ask him why he'd never come for her.

But the words wouldn't come. She didn't want to leave him. Or Margaret. The little girl had burrowed into her heart and remained there, firmly fixed.

She finally turned and faced him. Douglas stood in front of her, the sun illuminating his carefully expressionless features. However, she knew him well enough to know when he was angry.

His anger didn't frighten her. Only the truth did.

"I have to leave," she said, shocking herself. Yet it was easier, wasn't it, to deny him rather than be refused? She would be the one to walk away.

"After we've talked about Paris."

"No," she said. She didn't want to talk about the past. "If you would ask the coachman to take me back to your house, I'll pack my belongings and leave."

"I went to see you in Paris," he said, as if she hadn't spoken. "I went to tell you my parents had come, but instead of you, Justine was there."

She shook her head and held up one hand. Revelations would destroy her. The past was part of her, but the weakest, flimsiest part. She was held together with wishes and hopes and the barest breeze would shatter her. The last memory of them together should not be one of her weeping to him, begging him to understand.

"She told me you were with child."

It was beginning, the endless questions, the look of contempt, and the horror.

She closed her eyes and breathed deeply, wishing that there was another entity other than God to whom she might pray. The God of Sacré-Coeur was alternately vengeful and inattentive, flicking a finger in her direction as if to punish her for even being alive. She'd begun to think of him as a celestial Comte du Marchand, with powdered hair and a shiny golden suit sewn of sunbeams.

She opened her eyes and forced a smile to her face. "Are

you so angry at me because I wouldn't let you into my bed?" she demanded, turning on him. "Is that what this is all about?"

She strode toward him, and her smile broadened.

His expression altered, his frown changing to surprise.

"Very well, come tonight." Halting a few feet from him, she smiled, deliberately taunting him. "Or now. Here." Turning, she glanced at the expanse of his desk.

Walking toward it, she began untying the ribbons of her bonnet. She tossed it to a chair on the other side of the room and watched, uncaring, when it fell to the floor. She pushed his blotter out of the way and sat on the edge of his desk. Never moving her eyes from his, she began unfastening her bodice with both hands.

"What do you think you're doing?" he asked. His tone was harsh, his voice raspy. She had succeeded in disconcerting him but she'd also deflected his questions.

"Readying myself for you, of course. Do you require that I remove all my clothes, Douglas, or should I just tip up my skirts? I like it when you kiss my breasts. But please don't rip my chemise. I only have one."

"Stop it, Jeanne."

"Stop?" she asked, feigning dismay. Her fingers didn't hesitate, however, opening her bodice until she separated the fabric, revealing her stays and below it her threadbare chemise. She felt daring and wicked, and thoroughly brazen. When she was a girl she had delighted in loving him, had done so in the bright light of morning. What she was experiencing now was less bravado than an almost desperate wish to forestall his questions.

"Do you not want me?" she asked.

"More than is wise," he said, coming to stand in front of her. "If I didn't, I would send you away. I would have sent you away long before now."

The truth had a way of wounding her, but she pushed that thought away.

"Then perhaps we should simply rejoice in that, Douglas, and ignore everything else. It's a harsh world, and there isn't enough passion in it. Shouldn't we feel blessed with what we have?"

She reached up with one hand and curled it around his neck.

"For a moment?" she asked. "Just a moment of forgetfulness."

They had always been physically in tune with each other in a way that was magical and frightening. She wanted him to kiss her and make her forget. Perhaps in his arms they could revert to who they had been, and not the people they were now.

Make the years go away. Make the circumstances change. A command she didn't voice to Douglas because God had already heard and ignored her. But if she had a wish granted it would be that they would each feel free enough to love, and brave enough to love as they had once.

He stretched out his hand and touched her face, a soft and exploring touch that made her heart ache.

Holding out his hand, he waited until she took it and then he helped her from the desk. She turned, wondering if he was repudiating her, and that's when she saw the curio cabinet. Five feet long and easily that high, it was fronted with glass. Three shelves held an array of distinctive objects.

Walking to stand in front of it, she stared at the statues on the three shelves. Some were small, barely a hand span. Others were busts, and some were only sculptural fragments of reliefs.

And each of them looked like her.

"What are these?" she asked faintly.

For a long time he didn't speak. When he did, his words

came hesitantly. "A hobby of mine," he said. He moved to stand beside her.

"Where are they from?"

"All over the world."

The bust on the top shelf, a pale gray rendition of a young girl, had paint flecks on various places on the face.

"Phoenician?"

"Greek," he said.

The hairstyle was a simple one, gathered at the back of the head with ringlets escaping at the temples. She'd worn her hair that way the morning she first met Douglas.

On the first shelf, a smaller statuette was posed in a contemplative state, her head tilted slightly as if hearing a sound from far away.

But it was the face of each statuette or bust that stripped the breath from her. Although the ages ranged from ancient to more modern, each face was slightly similar, the heroine almost fragile-looking. Jeanne had changed in the intervening years; her face had matured. But at one time, she'd had the same look about her.

She reached up and touched the glass, obscuring the face of one particularly poignant statue. The girl was dressed in a diaphanous garment, holding out one edge of her skirt with one hand, as if she heard the sound of flutes, or felt the wind and was just in the act of beginning to dance to it.

Jeanne had done that once, and when she'd stopped twirling and dancing to the breeze, she had found him standing there leaning against a tree, arms folded and a particularly intent look on his face. That day they had made love for the first time.

"You did remember," she said, softly and with great difficulty. Her throat felt constricted, and the effort to speak was almost too much.

"Yes."

She whirled, facing him. "Why?" she demanded. "Why would you do that? Why collect all those things that look like me?"

"Because those memories were the most precious of my life."

Perhaps God did grant some of her prayers.

Standing with her fingers interlocked, she willed herself to move. But she couldn't. Not even when he reached out and touched her face, trailing a path from her temple to her chin with one soft and stroking finger.

"What happened to the child, Jeanne?" he asked.

Instead of answering him, she asked a question of her own. "Who is Margaret's mother?"

The question evidently discomfited him, because he only stared wordlessly at her.

Reaching out, she placed her hand flat on his chest. "You see, Douglas? Questions can hurt us," she said. "And the truth could destroy us."

"So you would rather live with falsehoods instead?"

"Yes," she told him honestly. "If not falsehoods, then let's be guilty of the sin of omission. We shouldn't tell each other everything. We shouldn't reveal the contents of our hearts and souls to each other."

"I have nothing to hide."

"While I do," she admitted freely. "But the convent has taught me to loathe self-abasement. So I won't reveal everything I am or have done simply to confess."

"I'm not certain I can accept your type of ignorance," he said. "There are some truths that need to be voiced."

She shook her head vehemently. "No, there aren't. For example, would you feel better or worse to know that I was kept in my room at Vallans, that I was never allowed outside for six months? I sat at the window watching the sky and the earth, desperate for the touch of a leaf or a blade of grass, or the soft, velvety feel of a flower petal on my palm.

I breathed in the air and longed for my freedom. That's truth for you, Douglas, but knowing it doesn't make life better, nor does it negate the past."

Her gaze never veered from his face. "I used to weep when you didn't come. The days passed, one after the other, and still you weren't there. I thought that you must have been horrified at the thought of becoming a father. And yet you must have been somewhere else, already celebrating the birth of your first child. What a precocious lover you were. Tell me, did you leave any children behind in Nova Scotia?"

"Not that I know of," he said, frowning at her.

"You were quite a rooster in France," she said. "Margaret's mother was French, was she not?"

She turned and walked in the other direction, pacing the length of the room. Nervous energy made her keep moving.

"You see, that's the truth, and it hurts." She smiled. "I don't want the truth," she said, shaking her head. "There are some things that should never be said, some confessions that should never be made."

"And some that must be."

She turned and looked at him. "Tomorrow," she said. "Tomorrow, we'll plan on wounding each other with words and memories."

Reaching him again, she wound both hands on the back of his neck, interlocking her fingers tightly. "Give me today, Douglas, that's all I ask."

Tomorrow she would leave him, but first she'd tell him the truth he so obviously wanted. She'd tell him about leaving Vallans and going in search of the couple that had been given her child. She'd tell him the whole horrible story, one she recalled all too often in dreams. But first, give her this; she would ask nothing more of Fate or an inattentive God.

Gently and determinedly, she pulled his head down for a

kiss. "Kiss me," she murmured against his lips and slowly
they opened. He tried to draw back, but she wouldn't allow
him. "Please," she said. Perhaps he heard her soft whisper
against his lips, or only felt her desperation. An instant
later his kiss deepened as his arms wrapped around her and
pulled her close to him.

There was something magical about Douglas's kisses.
They took her out of herself, transported her to a different place and time, and made her a different person.
Pleasure swept through her, from the tips of her fingers
to her toes. He was an opiate, and she was the poor de-
mented fool who would sell her soul for a few moments
of bliss.

He pulled away and began unfastening his waistcoat.
Removing his coat, then his vest, he began opening his
shirt, and all the while he never looked away, only stared at
her solemnly. As if what they were about to do was something grave and momentous, more so than any time they'd
ever loved.

These weeks with Douglas had taught her one thing
above all, that she could never replace him in her mind or
her heart. Every other man in her life would be measured
against Douglas and be found wanting.

"This is neither the time nor the place, Jeanne," he said
softly, but even as he condemned her eagerness, he toed
off his boots.

"No, it isn't," she agreed. "But your door has a lock on
it, does it not?"

He nodded.

"Then lock it, Douglas. Let's do something that isn't
wise or adult." She stood and walked to where the sun
made a brick-like pattern in the middle of the floor.

She held up her skirts and twirled in a circle, not feeling
as lighthearted as she wished, but mimicking an action that
she had performed as a girl. She wanted, for a few minutes

at least, to replicate that time. Or at least pretend that there were not secrets, hurtful and crushing, between them.

"Please," she said, dropping her skirts and placing her hands flat against the material. A second later she held them out, palms up. "Come and join me."

He strode past her and for a moment she thought he was going to leave the room, but then she heard the click of the lock and turned to find him standing there unwrapping his stock.

This time he didn't speak, didn't try to argue her out of lust, and neither did she. Because at this moment there was no one else in the world other than him, and there were no circumstances more important than the touch of his hands on her naked body.

The memory of him had kept her sane and being with him now made her want to live. He was simply necessary to her, just as air, water, and food were necessary. He was the blood that flowed through her body, the heart that beat in her chest, her lungs, and her limbs. He was her unfinished sentence, her half laugh, an unformed thought. He was life itself.

He returned to her, standing in front of her, a conjurer with sorcery in his hands. He moved them down her body and her clothes loosened, and stroked them over her skin and she began to tremble.

Douglas was as fevered as she. Her fingers flew over his clothing, burrowing past folds of cloth to touch his chest, pulling at the loosened stock, his shirt, until she could touch him.

Her dress was over her head, thrown a few feet away. His nimble fingers loosened her stays, let them fall heavily to the floor.

Suddenly she was on the floor, Douglas leaning over her. There were no questions this time, no teasing rejoinders, only a hunger on his face that was no doubt mirrored on hers. Where before there had been patience, now they were wild for each other.

He lifted her, knelt between her naked thighs. Reaching up, she pulled on his arms.

"Now, Douglas," she said, arching up beneath him. "Now, please."

She had to have him inside her, had to feel complete and whole one last time.

He surged within her. The discomfort of his possession eased a moment later when he hesitated, allowing her to become accustomed to his size.

Wrapping her arms around his neck, she clenched her eyes shut. The sun blazed behind her lids, the warmth flushing her face. But her world had narrowed to become only him.

The pleasure centered where they joined, spread outward, and harnessed her breath. Her heart raced, her blood rushed through her body hot and fast. When he rose up, she followed, holding on to him tightly. When he surged within her, she bowed beneath him.

In that sunlit room, they loved. Not with finesse as much as passion and an eagerness and desperation to forget for just a little while. When it was done, when she drew her breath again in a calm manner, and when her heart slowed its frenetic beat, Jeanne felt tears come to her eyes. Tears of joy and loss, so equally mixed that she couldn't separate the emotions.

Chapter 28

Douglas left her, standing and gathering up his clothing from where it was scattered over the floor. She lay there for a moment watching him. He was truly magnificent, with his muscled thighs and well-developed chest and arms.

He glanced at her but didn't smile. Instead, his solemn look warned her that they'd only delayed the inevitable by their loving.

Sitting up, she began to dress. She had to leave. If she didn't, there was every possibility she'd begin to weep, and crying would lead to confessions, and confessions would only lead to disaster. Tomorrow was time enough.

Her hair was askew, but instead of trying to tidy it up into a bun, she began to braid it. She'd tuck it up beneath her bonnet, a good enough style that would last until she reached her room.

Finally dressed, she grabbed her reticule and headed for the door.

"Where do you think you're going?" Douglas asked from behind her.

"I have to leave," she said. "Now. Please don't try to stop me. Don't ask me any questions, Douglas. Just let me leave."

"I'll tell the coachman to take you home," he said tightly.

Home, what a simple word, but that's what it had become. Without her being aware of it, she'd become accustomed to his house, the shape of it, the feeling of belonging inside it. She knew the staff and liked them, even Lassiter. The rooms were familiar; she knew the floor plan. But mostly, the occupants of Number Twelve Queen's Place—Douglas and Margaret—had made it feel like home. Family.

How would she bear leaving them?

She hurriedly walked through the door, down the steps, and into the perfumed wonder that was his warehouse. Twice she had to stop because she couldn't see and she impatiently wiped the tears away.

Passing the little booth that housed Jim the watchman, she waved and lowered her head, intent on reaching the coach.

"Please take me home, Stephens," she said in a choked voice, beating back her tears only through the greatest of wills.

He looked to the warehouse and then to her. "I can't, miss. I have to wait for Mr. MacRae."

"It's all right, Stephens," Douglas said from behind her. "Take Miss du Marchand home."

She whirled, startled that she hadn't heard him following her.

"You can come back for us."

Stephens nodded.

Douglas reached beyond her to the carriage door, opening it and then standing aside. "We'll talk when I return," he said.

"No," she said. "Tomorrow. Give me that at least." One more day. Just one more day.

He didn't respond, and she didn't glance at him.

Blindly, she pushed past him, entering the carriage and pulling the door closed after her. A few moments later the carriage finally moved, heading back for the MacRae residence.

After the coachman left her in front of Douglas's home, he turned around and returned to Leith. Jeanne looked at the steps in front of her as if they were insurmountable. Slowly, she took them one at a time, feeling as if she were climbing a mountain. Nodding to Lassiter, she made her way to her room, carefully closing the door and standing with her back to it.

Only then did she allow her tears to fall unchecked.

Toward evening, she took out her valise and opened it, putting it on the bed. She didn't want to leave, but there was no other alternative. She knew that from Douglas's face when he'd asked her that one question.

What happened to the child, Jeanne?

Betty knocked on the door. "Miss?" she called out when Jeanne didn't answer.

She finally opened the door, and the maid glanced at her, but didn't comment on Jeanne's tear-stained face or her reddened eyes. Her lack of comment was, in itself, a form of compassion.

"Mr. Douglas would like you to join him and Miss Margaret for dinner, miss."

A treat for Margaret. Since Margaret had returned to Edinburgh, Jeanne ate her meals in the nursery with Betty, who then returned to Margaret's room, helped her undress, wash, and prepare for bed. Jeanne would hear them, Margaret chattering on and on about Gilmuir, and the other topics of conversation dear to her heart. With Margaret, one never knew what would interest her. Yesterday it had been the shape of a raindrop. The day before the sound a frog made deep in his throat.

"Not tonight," she said, forcing a smile for Betty's sake. "Please tell him that I'd prefer a tray in my room."

Betty frowned, but her only comment was, "I'll tell Cook."

"Thank you," she said and closed the door softly behind her.

She ate her solitary dinner a little while later, sitting at the table beside the window, staring out at the night dotted by street lamps and the glowing bobbing lights of carriage lanterns. A few houses in the square were illuminated, and she wondered at the silhouettes against the draperies. Did these people live lives of quiet joy, or were they silent and despairing? Did they love or were they lonely?

How odd to think that someone like her might be sitting just as she was and wondering at the world outside her window. Who had said that grief shared was grief divided? Whoever it was had been wrong. Nothing about this pain could be shared or mitigated. It simply existed and would, she suspected, until the day she died.

What would her life have been like if she'd never met Douglas? She would never have felt the peaks of joy, but she wouldn't have been plunged into despair, either. She might have had a pleasant life, forever wondering about what she was missing. Occasionally, she might yearn for more adventure, more emotion, but she doubted that she'd feel as if her heart were breaking in two.

A knock on the door announced Margaret. She peered into the room from the connecting door. "May I come in, Miss du Marchand?"

Jeanne nodded.

She entered the room attired in a silvery pink gown that was a miniature version of the style a very fashionable woman might wear. A fichu of lace adorned with small pink rosettes reached to her neck, the lace duplicated at her wrists.

"I didn't have a chance to show you what Henry brought me."

She stretched out her hand to reveal a lovely miniature painting of Gilmuir.

"He had sketches of it from Aunt Iseabal, Miss du Marchand. Someone in London painted it for him. Isn't it the loveliest thing?"

Jeanne peered at the miniature. Even with the elaborate gold frame it was no bigger than Margaret's palm.

"It's very nice," she said. "Thank you for showing me."

Margaret went to their connecting door, but hesitated before entering her room. "Miss du Marchand?"

"Yes, Margaret?"

"Have you been crying?"

"Yes," Jeanne said, wondering if it was wise to be so truthful to the little girl. "I'm afraid I have."

"Do you miss your home? And your family?"

"Yes," she said, another truth.

"This can be your home, Miss du Marchand. And Father and I can be your new family."

She almost started weeping at the child's earnest look.

"Thank you very much, Margaret. That is very sweet and generous of you."

"My mother might have been like you, Miss du Marchand," the little girl said unexpectedly. "Father even said so at dinner."

"Did he?"

Margaret nodded. "But he didn't have that sad look in his eyes this time, Miss du Marchand. I think that's because of you."

Startled, she could only stare at the little girl and then at the connecting door as it slowly closed.

Chapter 29

J eanne heard Margaret whimper, the sound rousing her
from an uneasy sleep. She donned her wrapper and
slippers and pushed open the door to Margaret's room.
Placing her candle on the table next to the little girl's bed,
she sat on the edge. Gently, she shook Margaret's shoulder.
The child was crying in her sleep, a sight that caused her
own heartache.

"Margaret," she whispered, and the little girl's eyelids
fluttered. "Meggie," she said, using Douglas's endearment
for his daughter. "It's all right; it's just a dream."

The little girl sighed heavily in her sleep. A moment
later she moved closer to Jeanne, grabbed her hand, and
pulled it beneath the covers, cradling it against her cheek.
Jeanne smiled and used her free hand to push back the
damp tendrils of hair from Margaret's face.

"Sometimes it helps to talk about a dream," she said gently, knowing the child was awake. "Can you remember?"

"No," Margaret said softly.

"Was it the wolf again?"

Margaret shook her head, took a deep shuddering

breath, and exhaled slowly. Jeanne smoothed the covers around her, tucking them beneath her chin.

"Would you like me to stay with you until you fall asleep again?"

"Yes, please."

"Is there anything else I can do?"

"Please don't bring me any of that Chinese tea like Betty does." Margaret made a face, her eyes still closed. "I pretend to be asleep when she comes back from the kitchen," she confessed. "Anything but drink that horrid tea."

"I can promise you that I won't give you any Chinese tea," Jeanne said. "I was thinking of rubbing your back. Or finding a favorite doll."

Margaret slitted open one eye. "I haven't played with dolls in ages, Miss du Marchand," she said loftily.

"My error," Jeanne said, hiding her smile. "I forgot what an advanced age you were."

"I'm going to be nine, Miss du Marchand," she said.

Surprised, Jeanne glanced at her. "Nine? I thought you were turning ten." Most children advanced their age, counting themselves another year older after reaching the half-year mark.

"When I can't sleep, Papa makes me chocolate," she hinted.

"Oh, does he?"

She'd never made chocolate in her life, a confession she made now to Margaret. The little girl's eyes opened wide but then she smiled at Jeanne.

"I could show you how," she offered.

"Could you?"

"We would have to be as quiet as mice."

"We can make it an adventure," Jeanne said. It would be the last night with Margaret, the last time the little girl would amuse her or delight her with her intriguing questions.

Margaret slid her feet out from beneath the covers and sat up, releasing Jeanne's hand.

"Shall we go down to the kitchen, then, Miss du Marchand?" She looked excited, her eyes sparkling and the nightmare far from her mind.

Jeanne pulled back the covers, and then froze, her hand trembling as she clutched Margaret's blanket. The little girl's nightgown had ridden up and bared her leg. There, on her thigh, was a purplish birthmark in the shape of a crescent.

"You needn't bother, Jeanne," Douglas said.

She glanced toward the door to find him attired in his dark blue dressing gown holding a candle. "I'll make the chocolate for Meggie."

His features were blurry in the shadowed darkness, yet it wasn't her vision that made him difficult to see but the sudden sheen of tears. Her mind realized the truth before her heart.

Reaching out one hand, she warded him off rather than beckoned him closer. Standing, she took a step away from Margaret and another from him, hearing a roaring in her ears as she looked from one to the other.

Margaret was looking at her curiously, but Douglas's gaze was somber, his eyes flat. He walked to the side of the bed and pulled the bell rope for Betty.

Jeanne wanted to scream at him, but the words wouldn't come. She looked at Margaret again and it was as if she saw her for the first time. The little girl's vision problems, the gestures that were so similar, the feeling of déjà vu whenever the child smiled. Of course—it all made sense now.

Jeanne clasped both hands over her mouth tightly and an instant later held them together at her waist so that she wouldn't make fists of them and strike him.

"I saw her grave," she said helplessly. Sound was oddly muffled and she felt as if she had to shout in order to be heard. Her heart seemed to beat in her ears, and her throat was constricted. "I saw where she was buried."

He took a step toward her, and she backed up hurriedly, placing both hands flat against the wall on either side so that she wouldn't fall. She curved her fingers into the wall-. paper, felt her nails gouging the pattern, but still nothing felt real about this moment.

She must be dreaming.

"I saw her grave."

Douglas frowned, as if he hadn't expected her comment. "Somehow, you missed the evidence in front of your eyes."

"You knew," she said. "All this time, you knew."

There was too much emotion. None of it could be encapsulated into a word, a sentence. English didn't make sense, but even French could not adequately communicate what she was feeling.

"Betty, take Margaret to your room," he said, addressing the nurse who had entered the room without Jeanne noticing her.

Jeanne turned toward the wall, concentrating on the pattern of beige silk on which multicolored nosegays had been embroidered. A very expensive wall covering, but nothing was too costly for Margaret. Meggie.

She closed her eyes and forced herself to breathe.

"You wanted to know who Margaret's mother was." Douglas said, his voice oddly flat. "You are."

"I would have known," she said, speaking to the wallpaper in perfectly lucid tones, in carefully enunciated words. "I would have known my own child. You must be wrong."

"I found her not far from Vallans," he said, coming closer. "She'd been given to an old couple who almost let her starve to death. For days I thought she had died with each breath she took."

"I saw her grave," she said, tasting her own tears. She didn't know she was weeping until she placed both hands on her cheeks. Opening her eyes, she blinked at him to clear her vision.

"The old woman led me to her grave. No one had even made a marker for her." Her heart was being torn out telling him these things. She waited for him to condemn her, to hate her for not being strong enough to keep them from killing their child. "She died," she said, anticipating the grief that bowed her body each time she thought of that moment. But it didn't come. Instead, there was a curious lull in her mind, as if her thoughts had simply stopped.

"All this time, you knew," she said, leaning her forehead against the wall. She took a deep, shuddering breath. She felt as if her bones were breaking, and every muscle in her body contracted in an effort to hold herself together. If she didn't guard herself closely, she'd begin to scream.

"You knew," she said, and this time the words emerged as a whisper. "You knew, and never told me."

She turned and looked at him.

He frowned at her as if not expecting her accusation.

"Why should I? All this time you never mentioned her. Even today. When I questioned you, you refused to answer."

Placing her hands over her eyes, she willed him away. If she were lucky, if she were fortunate, she'd find herself back at the Convent of Sacré-Coeur. Let Marie-Thérèse punish her for these lascivious dreams. Perhaps she was dead, and this was hell, an endless circling torment like the one she'd been promised for her multitudinous sins.

"She'd been left to die." Douglas's voice was too loud, the tone one God might use.

All she had in her own defense was the truth. But she wouldn't tell him of that terrible morning of Margaret's birth, how she'd seen her daughter taken from her and screamed until her voice cracked. She wouldn't tell him how she'd been determined to survive the convent, if only to find her child. She wouldn't speak of that hideous day at the woodcutter's cottage when she'd seen the grave on the edge of the forest and known her daughter had been dead all these long years. She'd knelt there, wanting to die herself.

But she hadn't died, had she?

Jeanne held herself tightly, wrapping her arms around her midriff to still her shaking. She had been given her heart's desire and yet it felt as if God had slapped her in that instant. *Here, you wanted your child alive, but I give you Douglas's hatred and loathing as payment for all your sins.*

She had vowed on the day she had walked out of the convent that no one would ever make her beg again. Nor did she now, but Douglas would never know how close she came. As he turned at the door, she stretched out her hand. It trembled in the air. As he stared at her, she made a fist and drew it back to hold it tightly against her chest.

In that instant, she wanted the power of magic or sorcery. If she closed her eyes for a span of seconds and opened them again, perhaps the world would change. There would be no death or destruction or cruelty. Douglas would be a man who adored her and she would be the woman she'd always wanted to be. And the past would simply vanish. But there was no such thing as magic, and even prayers were specious things.

For a long wordless instant they stared at each other and it seemed to her that the past shimmered between them as deep as an ocean.

Not an ocean, she realized as he left the room, but tears.

Margaret waited until Betty fell asleep and then made her way to the stables. Jeremy, one of the stableboys, had whispered to her that he was going home for his half day off, which meant that the horses would be unguarded.

She debated using a saddle and then realized that even if she could manage to open the tack room lock, she wouldn't be able to sling it over the horse's back. Instead, she opened the door of one of the stalls and spoke softly to Nolly, the gentlest of the carriage horses. A quarter hour later, she'd finally accomplished the most difficult feat of all—getting the bridle and bit on the large horse.

She led Nolly out of her stall, stepped onto the mounting block, and climbed on her back. As odd as it felt being without a saddle, it was comforting, too. There was nothing between the animal and her but Nolly's surprisingly scratchy hair.

Slowly, she led Nolly out of the stable, grateful for the full moon and the kitchen lantern. Still, it was dark and too quiet, almost frighteningly so. She bent low over Nolly's back, grabbed the reins, and gave her a little slap on the neck. The horse obediently began a bone-jarring trot.

As a precaution, she'd taken a few coins from the strongbox in her father's library. She would be considered a thief, of course, for taking the coins and the horse, but she reasoned that at least she'd be punished all at once instead of stretching it out over an extended period of time.

She knew the way to Leith well, having made the journey often with her father. But it had never seemed quite so far, nor had she ever made the trip in the dark.

But as lonely as it seemed, and as frightening, the dark was still not as scary as her father could be when he was angry. She knew very well that he was going to be very angry at her for leaving. But what she learned tonight was so disturbing that she had to talk to someone about it.

Not her father, however.

She loved him very much, but he sometimes treated her as if she were an infant. She could put together things well enough in her mind, and what she had divined tonight was either the most improbable tale or the truth. She needed to talk to someone about what she suspected; someone who hadn't lied to her all these years by telling her a story that she now knew was false.

Nor could she talk to Miss du Marchand, especially since Miss du Marchand was the source of the problem. Was her governess really her mother?

Aunt Mary, therefore, was the logical answer. Except, of course, that Aunt Mary was aboard a ship at Gilmuir.

Just then, she saw the shadow of the warehouses, and hoped that Henry would be working late. She'd heard him complain often enough about all the paperwork necessary when a MacRae ship came into port. Suddenly someone grabbed the reins of the horse and Margaret almost fell off Nolly's back.

A man moved, holding up a lantern, and revealing a face that anyone might consider frightening.

Margaret told herself to be brave as the man reached for her.

Twice Douglas almost went to her, and twice stopped himself. He couldn't forget the look on Jeanne's face, and it haunted him.

She hadn't confessed as he'd expected. Nor had she pleaded with him to understand her actions. Instead, she seemed genuinely shocked, as if Meggie had truly been resurrected from the dead. Nor had she said one word in her own defense. Shouldn't a guilty woman have tried to convince him of her innocence?

For years he'd wanted something horrible and hideous to happen to Jeanne in order to repay her for her abandonment of her own child. Only to suspect, now, that he had been wrong all this time.

Why had she been sent to the convent? Only one of the

questions he needed to have answered. Yet Jeanne had never sought his compassion or elicited his pity.

Do you know that I was once punished for not being a virgin? A comment he suspected she'd not meant to make. *I confessed, you see. Perhaps I was feeling rash, but I once told one of the nuns that I had dreamed of you.*

His thoughts were beginning to be acutely uncomfortable.

She'd been genuinely caring of Margaret, wanting her to have spectacles, laughing at her comments. She'd been gentle and understanding, amused and tolerant. Even protective. Not the actions of a cruel woman.

Douglas felt as if his world were tumbling around him. He had the distinct and disturbing feeling that everything upon which he based his life in the past ten years was wrong. But if she wasn't guilty of sending their daughter to her death, why had she never told him what had happened?

I saw her grave.

The third time he made the journey down the hall and stood in front of her room. Placing his hand flat on the surface of the door, he willed her awake. Then, as if he were a conjurer, he heard her muffled sob.

Sadness disturbed him; it was the one emotion for which he was never prepared. People could be talked from rage but there was no defense for sorrow. Besides, what could he say to her to make up for what he'd done?

Turning, he walked back to his room and shut the door, knowing that it would be a sleepless night.

Chapter 30

Moving to the windows, Jeanne pulled back the drapes. Dawn was approaching on the horizon softly and shyly, as a bride might greet her new husband.

She felt estranged from the sight before her, as if she'd never before seen a dawn, as if even the hills of Edinburgh were alien to her. The only home she knew, the only safe and welcoming place, was inside her mind.

Closing her eyes, she felt the hot surge of tears, wondering how long she could cry. But she wept not in grief or anguish but a relief so deep that she felt weak from it. Taking one deep shuddering breath after another, she tried to regain her equilibrium, enough to stare out at the vista before her until it slowly began to make sense.

There, below her, was Princess Street and over there was Queen Street. She could see the corner of the small park in the middle of the square. A carriage was pulling up in front of one of the townhouses, and a wagon trundled noisily through a street farther away. Edinburgh Castle was perched on the hill above them, looking malevolent and regal all at once. To the left were the gardens, where work was finally beginning on the plan Douglas had devised. It would be a wonder of nature created especially for Margaret.

Margaret.

Her heart seemed to stutter.

Releasing her grip on the curtains, she smoothed the wrinkles she'd made with her hand. She turned and crossed the floor, the need to see her daughter instinctive and necessary. She had waited during the long night, but now she wanted to sit and watch as Margaret slept until she knew it was true, that the daughter she'd grieved for all these years was alive.

Slowly she opened the door between the two rooms. The chamber was as it had always been, fit for a princess. But now the princess was her daughter.

But she wasn't there.

Thinking that she must still be with Betty, Jeanne went to the third floor, tapping on the nurse's door. Betty answered a few minutes later, attired in her wrapper, a large frilly cap covering her hair. She needn't rise at dawn like some of the other staff, and Jeanne was quick to apologize for the intrusion.

"Is anything wrong, miss?" Betty asked, peering into the corridor.

"No," Jeanne answered, realizing that it was suddenly true. Nothing was wrong. For the first time in a very long time nothing was wrong. She began to smile.

"I'm so sorry to disturb you, Betty, but I need to see Margaret. Is she still asleep?"

"I don't know, miss," Betty said. She stepped aside, revealing a small but tidy chamber. "She went back to her room sometime in the night."

"She's not there," Jeanne said.

That was the only warning she was given that something

terrible had happened at Number Twelve Queen's Place.

A few moments later the two women stood outside Douglas's chamber, having visited Margaret's empty room.

"Do you think we should rouse Mr. Douglas, miss? She might be anywhere about the house."

Jeanne shook her head, trying to tamp down the panic she was beginning to feel. "Go and fetch Lassiter," she suggested. "Perhaps the two of you can mount a search through the house. Wake the other servants as well. And Stephens," she added as Betty began to walk quickly down the hall.

Fifteen minutes later, however, Margaret had still not been found.

Lassiter bowed slightly before Jeanne as she stood before Douglas's chamber.

"If you would like to return to your room, miss, I can notify the master."

Margaret was her daughter, and she wouldn't abdicate this responsibility to anyone. As little as she wished to see Douglas right now, someone would have to alert him. Who better but she?

"That's all right, Lassiter," she said. "I'll tell him."

He wiggled his eyebrows at her, but stepped back as she strode forward, rapping on the door with a peremptory knock.

When Douglas came to the door he looked rumpled, cautious, and thoroughly appealing.

"Margaret is missing," she said as a greeting.

He ran his fingers through his hair and stared at her. "What do you mean, she's missing?" he asked, frowning.

"She's not with Betty and she's not in her room. We've searched the house. Where does a child of nine go at dawn?"

He stared out at the servants arrayed behind her. Without

a word he turned and left the doorway. She followed him, realizing that she'd never before been in his chamber. The room was the length of the house, and lavish. The furniture was constructed on a large scale, a huge bed dominating the longer wall.

He was standing in front of an armoire on the far side of the room. Reaching in, he pulled out a shirt, donned it, and tucked it into his trousers. At her appearance he looked startled.

"Why didn't you tell me?" she asked abruptly, the anger she'd tamped down the night before surfacing once again. "When you saw me again, why didn't you tell me our child was alive?"

He looked at her solemnly for several long moments. "As far as I knew you'd abandoned her. Why didn't you once mention her?"

"Because I considered myself a murderer," she said flatly. "Because I never stopped grieving for her. Because I couldn't bear to remember what had happened. Because I couldn't bear for you to hate me."

He only looked at her intently, as if judging the truth of her confession. She wanted to tell him that it would have been easier to lie, but then, there had been too many lies between them.

"Why didn't you ever come for me?"

There was no way to ask the question without it seeming laden with pathos. She should have withdrawn it, but for the sake of the young girl who'd yearned for him so desperately, she let it remain between them.

Once more he gave her a considering look, as if debating whether or not to deliver the truth. "At first I hated you," he said, "for what had happened to Margaret. Later, I thought you were dead."

She wanted, suddenly, to ask him if he still hated her, but that was not an answer she could bear at the moment.

Turning, she walked back to the door.

"I'll be with you shortly," he said.

She nodded, glancing beyond him to where a tapestry hung on the far wall. Douglas was not done with his surprises, it seemed. She remembered the tapestry, recalling when she was a little girl and had been entranced with the scene, a procession winding down from a golden castle on a hill, a princess with black hair with her hand holding the bridle of a unicorn.

"The man I bought it from said it had come from Vallans," he said.

"I remember it hanging in the hall to the right of the grand staircase. I didn't know anything had survived."

"I bought it for Margaret. I wanted her to have something of her heritage."

All thoughts but one vanished. "Where could she be?" she asked.

"I don't know, but we'll find her."

"She's a very obedient child," Jeanne said.

He smiled lightly as he sat on the edge of the bed and donned his shoes. "She has a mind of her own. But I can't see Margaret leaving her bed before she has to."

Jeanne knew that well enough. A few times, her charge had been late to the schoolroom, and in the mornings Margaret was often querulous and uncommunicative. It was only after a few hours of being awake that her usual sunny personality surfaced.

She left Douglas to finish dressing. When he joined her they rechecked the public rooms and the rest of the downstairs together but found no sign of Margaret. Douglas conferred with Lassiter some moments later, and when they separated he appeared less sanguine and more concerned.

"What is it?" she asked.

He looked grim, his mouth thinned, his eyes carefully devoid of expression.

She stood in front of him and folded her arms, determined to get an answer. "You can't withhold information from me. Not now."

He looked as if he would like to argue with her, but then relented. "One of the downstairs windows is broken," he said. "It looks as if an intruder has made his way into the house."

"You think someone has taken her," she said, the dread she was beginning to feel too familiar.

He didn't dispute her reasoning. "Yes," he said shortly.

She had a leaden feeling in the middle of her stomach. Margaret was missing.

"My father," she said without hesitation.

Douglas looked startled.

"My father," she repeated.

I want it, Jeanne, and I'll have it.

She felt as if she might faint, and her legs were suddenly too weak to support her. Reaching out, she grabbed the back of the chair and sat heavily.

"Your father?" Douglas asked, frowning. "Why would you think that?"

"Because he's ruthless and arrogant, and wouldn't hesitate to do anything, however vile, to get his own way."

Releasing the clasp, she held the necklace out to him. "He said he would do anything to get this."

He took the locket, hefting it in his hand. "It's heavy, but then it's gold."

She nodded. "It was a present from my mother."

He looked at her and then the necklace. She knew what he was thinking. "It *is* ugly, isn't it?"

"What's inside?"

"I've never been able to open it," she admitted. "I didn't force it because I didn't want to ruin it."

"May I?"

She nodded.

He left the room, Jeanne following. Entering the office, he went to the window and opened the draperies. He dropped the necklace in the center of his desk and sat, looking in the right-hand drawer for something.

A moment later he found it, a small metal implement that had a thumbscrew on the top and looked like calipers. The tines were bent outward and then back into a curve before meeting at the ends.

"What is that?" she asked.

"A tool my sister-in-law Mary uses to extract splinters," he answered. "I borrowed it one day and never returned it." He glanced up at her. "I've been meaning to, but it always slips my mind. Maybe there was a reason for that."

"Shouldn't we be doing something else?" she asked.

"Like what?" he asked, concentrating on inserting the tool between the overlap on the rectangular case.

"Like finding Margaret," she said.

"I am," he said and gave her an irritated look. "I want to find out why the Comte du Marchand wanted this locket badly enough to steal my child."

"You don't understand," she said, the ticking of the clock on the mantel adding punctuation to her words. "If he has her, he won't care what happens to her."

His hands stilled as he looked at Jeanne.

"Who do you think would have been just as pleased if she'd died taking her first breath? Who do you think told Justine to kill her?"

He didn't say anything for a moment, and then he looked down at the locket. With more force than necessary, he pushed the tool into the case, bending it.

She moved to stand in front of the desk, curious. Slowly the back began to move. Finally the case separated, revealing a folded cloth.

He handed the locket to her. "Do you want to see what it is? After all, it belongs to you."

The ecru color of the cloth had originally been ivory.
She could tell that from the color of the folds as she unwrapped it. Stunned, she stared down at the jewel nestled
in her palm.

"What is it?"

She held out her hand for him to see.

"It's the Somerville ruby," she said slowly. "I remember
my mother showing it to me when I was a child." The
heart-shaped ruby was a deep red shade, the color of
blood. As a child she had been fascinated with the stone
and the history of it. She would inherit it, just as her
mother had, and her mother before her. Generations of
Somerville women had guarded the ruby, kept it in trust for
their daughters. "I thought it was gone, like everything else
at Vallans." She smiled, but there was no humor in the expression. "At least now I know why he wanted the locket."

"I thought he was wealthy enough on his own."

"There was never enough money for my father," she said
sardonically. "It was a matter of pride to him. His horses
were the best, and his houses were the most lavishly decorated. Everything with which he surrounded himself was
the epitome of perfection."

"Even his daughter?"

She glanced at him and then away, wondering if he'd always been so perceptive. "Yes, even his daughter," she admitted. "But the last few years can't have been easy on
him, not with the loss of Vallans."

Handing him the stone, she closed up the locket and fastened it around her neck once more. "The price I paid for it
has been too high. I wouldn't give it to my father and now
he's taken Margaret."

"I'm a wealthy man on my own, Jeanne," he countered.
"Margaret might have been abducted because of who I am."

She looked at him, knowing that he said what he did to
ease her anxiety. But her fears were part of her now, as

much as her breath or her heartbeat. She knew what her father was capable of, and what he'd do to accomplish his aims.

"It was him," she said, knowing it was true.

He placed the ruby on the top of his desk without saying anything further.

"Then I'll find him," Douglas said.

She nodded, moving to stand at the window. He came to her side as she stared at the horizon, now blurred through her tears.

"I'm frightened," she said, startling herself with the revelation. Not that she admitted to the fear—it had been there from the moment she'd first realized that Margaret was missing—but that she'd actually spoken the words aloud. She'd hidden her true emotions for years, and the only honest thing between them of late had been passion.

"So am I," he said gently, placing his hand on her shoulder.

They stood for a moment, linked by circumstance and emotion, until Jeanne turned.

"What happens now?" she asked, brushing away her tears.

"I'm going to enlist help," he said. "Edinburgh is a big city, and I'll need people to help me find Margaret."

"I'm coming with you."

"No," he said. "I need you here."

"You can't expect me to simply remain in the house as if nothing's happened."

"What if word comes? Someone needs to be here. One of her parents."

His words had the effect of silencing her. She nodded reluctantly.

Chapter 31

⟨⟨⟨◦◦◦⟩⟩⟩

"What are you going to do?"

"I'm going to the warehouse," he said. "I employ over seventy men, and today they're going to help me look for Margaret."

She nodded, making no comment.

"Why do people band together and help in the midst of despair, Douglas? Why don't they identify more with gladness?" The words were spoken so slowly that he wondered what they cost her in effort. "Is it because they feel better about their own lives when someone else is weeping about theirs?" She shook her head.

He led her to the chair beside the fireplace. He'd order a fire built even though it was summer. The warmth would help take the chill off her skin.

"We'll find her, Jeanne."

"Yes."

She sat as proper as a dowager empress, yet too young to have acquired the poise of age. There was something in her eyes that spoke of life experience, a look that sistered her to the women who'd been rescued from France by Hamish

319

and Mary. She appeared lost and haunted, disbelieving his words yet refusing to concede.

She was the strongest person he knew. Her fingers probably trembled but she'd kept them clasped tightly together. A muscle flexed in her cheek as if to keep her lips from quivering. But she'd not been able to hide the look in her eyes. Fear always surfaces in the eyes.

"Please find her," she said, the request so quietly spoken that he almost missed it. Her lips barely moved, but her eyes deepened in color, their gray shade turned leaden by unshed tears.

Part of him didn't want to be needed. He didn't want her depending on him so deeply. The responsibility was too great and failing too difficult to contemplate. But this was Jeanne, and he had no other choice.

"I will," he said and it was a promise he gave her. "I will," he repeated and she seemed mollified, nodding.

"You mustn't worry about me," she said, almost smiling. He didn't question her ability to divine his thoughts. Women had the power to surprise with their innate intuition. Or perhaps it was simply because they studied people more carefully than men, in tune for half-hidden emotions and thoughts.

Worry accompanied his journey to the warehouse. When he arrived, he rounded up every single employee and addressed them in the yard at the back of the buildings, a drab and dull place that someone, perhaps Henry, had ordered enlivened by a planting of flowers. Now those flowers waved gaily and unknowingly in the morning breeze.

As he stared out at the sea of faces, he realized that until this moment he'd never felt different from any of them. But there was every possibility that Margaret had been taken because he was the owner of MacRae Brothers and a wealthy man.

He would have traded every cent of his fortune for Margaret's safety.

As he began to address his employees, he watched as their faces changed from curiosity to anger.

"This morning someone entered my house and took my daughter," he told the assembled crowd. After a gasp that seemed to travel through the men, each face turned toward him. "I need your help to find her."

Margaret was a favorite here. During the annual meeting of families, she played with their children as if she were one of them and not the owner's daughter. She didn't care if a boy's father was a wagon driver or laborer or a clerk. If she disliked someone, it was because of his personality, not because of his place in the world.

Although he secretly agreed with Jeanne that the Comte was probably responsible, he didn't mention that possibility to the men assembled in front of him. He might well be wrong.

He knew every single one of these men, had hired each personally. He knew the stories of their families and their individual triumphs and failures. All of them were good, hardworking men whose labor had made it possible for MacRae Brothers to prosper.

"If you will form four lines," he said. "We'll give out the assignments." Some men would be sent into taverns to see if they could learn anything. Others would be sent to various places throughout Edinburgh where criminal activity was prevalent or to talk to prosperous merchants in locations where crime was never a factor.

He stepped down from the impromptu podium and made his way through the crowd, accepting the well-wishes and prayers of the men who clapped him on the back. He answered them all as best he could.

Tables had been set up as per his earlier instructions to

Jim. The watchman had set aside four tablets, one for each of the lines, and had selected four clerks to keep a record of which man was assigned and where.

"Where's Henry?" he asked, when he scanned the crowd and couldn't find the older man.

"I thought you sent him back to London, sir," Jim said.

He nodded, thinking that the older man might have gone before learning of Margaret's disappearance. If he had, it was too late to call him back now.

Sitting at the table, Douglas sketched out a rough map of Edinburgh. The general shape of the city was that of a large circle. He divided it into quarters, giving a section leading from Leith south to the center of Edinburgh to one group of men. Another section from the west near Queens-ferry Road ended at Majesty's Court. The other two quadrants, south and east, led from St. Johns' Road around to Craighall.

"Give me something to do, sir." Surprised, Douglas turned to find Lassiter standing there, his usual formal attire replaced by workingman's jacket and trousers. So surprised was he by his majordomo's appearance that Douglas didn't say anything for a long moment.

"I may look infirm, Mr. MacRae," Lassiter said, "but I can assure you that I'm as able-bodied as any man here."

"I don't doubt it, Lassiter," he said. "But did you ever think that I need you at home?"

"Miss du Marchand is in command, sir." He stood stiffly at attention, as if he were still in the infantry and fighting one of England's many battles in America.

"Very well," Douglas said, knowing that the worst thing he could do for the old man's pride would be to send him home after he'd volunteered to help. He assigned his majordomo to the south quadrant. "It's a rough area," he cautioned, "but I have no doubt that you'll persevere."

"Indeed, I shall, sir."

"We'll find her, Lassiter."

Lassiter nodded. "It is my fervent hope, sir."

When? The question hung between them, demanding an answer. Unfortunately, Douglas didn't have one.

There was little sun today, the overcast sky a mirror to his mood. The view before him was of the Firth of Forth and beyond to the North Sea. The world lay out there, exciting and challenging. But his existence had always been marked by the width of a raven-haired little girl's smile.

And now its depth was measured by the track of one woman's tear.

He mounted his horse and returned to Edinburgh to begin his own search, beginning at Queen Street and slowly widening the circle. Hours passed with him asking every passerby if he'd seen a little girl with black curls and a radiant smile. No one answered in the affirmative. Nor did he find any further clues as to where Margaret might have gone—where she might have been taken. His mind shied from that thought.

Jeanne's despair about Margaret being missing was real. Had she felt the same when the infant she'd borne had been taken from her? Jeanne's words kept coming back to him. *Who do you think would have been just as pleased if she'd died taking her first breath?*

For years, anger had left a rut inside him, a pitted road where nothing else could travel. He'd felt only rage when thinking of Jeanne du Marchand. Yet even that emotion wasn't pure hatred. Instead, it was mixed with desire, confusion, and a curious sort of despair.

Last night he'd begun to suspect he was wrong, only to realize it firmly this morning. Now he felt as if he'd been released from the past and presented with the chance of a future. All he had to do was sort out the present.

Jeanne went back to her room, but she didn't change her clothes right away. The pitcher had been filled with hot water and she washed her face, wishing she had cold water to reduce the puffiness around her eyes. After blotting her face dry with the towel, she stared at herself in the mirror over the bureau. Her eyes were red, her face too pale. Even her lips looked bloodless. She folded the towel and hung it on the rack beside the basin.

Moving to the window, she stared out at the advancing morning. She felt on edge, nervous. Twice she looked back toward the door, and twice turned away. Finally, she clasped her hands together, trying to stop her trembling.

A noise made her turn, but there was nothing there. Moving to the door, she opened it and looked both to the right and left. There was no one in the corridor.

She was being foolish, but she felt as if she were being observed. Slowly, she closed the door, and that's when she felt the breath against her neck.

Jeanne didn't have a chance to scream. Two hands were suddenly wrapped around her throat so tightly that she could barely breathe. Her assailant threw her up against the door until her cheek was pressed flat against the intricately carved panel.

"Where's the ruby?" a harsh voice demanded.

She tried to speak but all that emerged was a choked gasp. Her arms flailed, hands clawing at the fingers that cut off her air.

"Where's the ruby?" The grip around her throat tightened.

She made a sound, a half moan to acknowledge the darkness surrounding her. She was going to die before she could speak.

Abruptly, he released her and jerked the locket from

around her neck. She winced at the pain and sagged against the wall, both of her hands encircling her neck.

"Is it in here?" he asked, twisting the necklace around his hand. He opened the loosened case and, finding it empty, threw it to the floor.

She sank down slowly to her knees, her breath coming in deep, hoarse gasps.

"Where's the ruby?" he asked for a third time. Her only response was to weakly shake her head from side to side.

Leaning her head against the wall, Jeanne turned to see the man who'd invaded her bedchamber. His face was pocked, his teeth blackened. Thinning hair fell to his shoulders, and his face was larger and rounder than his skinny frame warranted. Behind him was the open door of the armoire. How long had he hidden in there, waiting for her?

"Tell me or I'll kill you."

"Kill . . . me . . . and . . . no . . . ruby." Each word was punctuated with a wince.

He seemed to consider the matter for a moment. "There are other things I could do to you."

She shrugged.

Her reaction seemed to surprise him. Scowling at her, he dragged her to her feet with a punishing grip on one arm. "Give me the bloody ruby."

"I don't have it."

She didn't see his hand until the blow struck her. She fell to her hands and knees again, tasting blood.

"I don't have it."

He swore, a particularly foul oath.

Jerking her to her feet again, he breathed whiskey fumes into her face. "Then you'll just have to find it, won't you?"

He dragged her to the wardrobe, reached in, and grabbed a stocking, stuffing it into her mouth.

"If you even try to scream, I'll choke you again," he threatened. Her throat hurt so badly that she was incapable of making more than a faint sound. Screaming seemed an impossibility.

She nodded and hoped he would believe her.

He took another of her stockings and wrapped it around her wrists. The knot was too tight and her hands tingled.

No one was in the corridor. It seemed as if every single servant had left the house, intent on searching for Margaret.

He dragged her through the deserted kitchen and out to the back. Hedges were planted on either side of the drive and he pulled her through one of them, uncaring that the branches were filled with tiny, piercing thorns. A carriage was waiting on the other side. He reached out, opened the door, and threw her inside. She fell to her knees but righted herself quick enough.

"What the hell is she doing here?" a voice demanded.

"She wouldn't talk."

"Take off the gag," the man said. "A du Marchand is never treated like a common prisoner."

That's all she ever had been, Jeanne realized. Not a person but a thing, a daughter, a du Marchand, an object of some value only because of its ancestors and not because of its own worth.

She rubbed her mouth, staring at the man opposite her. Her lips were numb but she managed a greeting nevertheless.

"Hello, Father."

He looked, as usual, impeccable and immaculate.

"She doesn't have the ruby."

Her father studied her, his eyes narrowing.

"I think she does." A moment later he spoke to her abductor. "Leave us," he said, and the man vanished to the outside of the carriage. No one disobeyed the Comte du Marchand. Even as an émigré, he had a force of will that was surprising.

But so did she, a discovery she'd made years earlier.

She faced him, leaning back against cushions of the carriage. "I don't have the ruby," she said, her voice still sounding unlike her. She massaged the base of her throat. His glance went to her neck and then he looked away. She wondered if the man's fingerprints were embedded in her skin.

"Where's my daughter?"

He stared at her, confusion flickering in his eyes just for an instant.

"Your daughter?"

"You know who I'm talking about. Margaret MacRae. The little girl you took from her home. Where is she?"

He flicked an imaginary speck of dust from his sleeve. "I haven't the slightest idea what you're prattling on about, but you disappoint me in all this talk about your bastard. Have you never learned discretion?"

He looked so irritated that she almost believed him.

"Where's the ruby?" he asked, leaning back against the cushion and fixing her with a cold look.

"Douglas has it," she said, almost smiling.

Anger pinched his features and made him ugly.

The journey home was marked by Douglas's impatience and punctuated with his prayers. He hoped that by the time he reached his house word would have come about Margaret. Or, even better, she might be home.

I didn't mean to worry you, Papa, she'd say. But that was as far as his imagination could carry him. There wasn't a situation he could envision that would take Margaret from home. She wasn't the type of child to be disobedient.

Lassiter had still not returned from his assignment, but a tall young footman had taken his place. He opened the door and bowed too deeply as Douglas entered.

"Is there any news?"

"No, sir, nothing."

Douglas walked into his library and closed the door behind him. For a moment he simply stood there before walking to the fireplace. He looked up at the portrait. The curtains were still closed but a shaft of light from between them struck the fortress of Gilmuir, almost making it seem inhabited. The glow made Margaret's eyes sparkle and once again he realized how much his daughter resembled the picture of his grandmother, Moira MacRae.

"Wherever you are, Margaret," he said solemnly, "be safe. Be safe."

He couldn't tolerate the thought that she might be in danger, or that she might be hurt somewhere or ill. The idea that someone might have taken her was one that he couldn't bear to entertain. There are some thoughts that a parent was not meant to have.

Suddenly he needed to be with Jeanne. He needed to understand how she had endured nine years of uncertainty. How had she made it through one day? One week?

He should have protected Margaret more assiduously. He should have ensured that the lock on the window was stronger. Or that there was a guard posted at night.

His thoughts stopped. There were some things he could never prevent; he knew that well enough. He gave himself the illusion of safety within the walls of his home, but even that had been breached. Yet he'd done everything he could to provide a secure and safe place for his daughter. The fact that it had been violated not only angered him but made him feel culpable.

A moment later, he was knocking on Jeanne's door. When he received no answer, Douglas turned the handle only to find that room was empty. The armoire door was wide open, and a few of her garments were in disarray, but other than that there was no sign of her.

He pulled on the bell rope, greeting the tall footman with a question when he arrived a few moments later.

"Where is Miss du Marchand?"

"I don't know, sir. Shall I ask the staff?"

"Do that," he said impatiently.

Douglas went back to the armoire and hung up her garments neatly, stacking her much-darned stockings in the bottom. Her clothes smelled of lilies and he wondered why that was. His fingers trailed across the sleeve of one of her two dresses before he finally closed the door.

He'd never investigated her chamber as he did now, violating her privacy in a way that he knew was wrong but could somehow not prevent. She had few possessions, nothing more than could be packed in a small valise. There was something intrinsically wrong with that fact. She'd come from an old family, a wealthy, respected name in France, but she had less than the poorest inhabitant of Edinburgh.

Who Jeanne was could be found in her eyes, not in what she owned.

On top of the nightstand was a book and resting on the red leather cover were her spectacles.

He held them in his hand. Her fingers had spread the hinged temples wide and placed the ribbons around her ears. She had pressed the covers of the book apart and read the words printed there. He opened the red leather book at random and only then realized that it was a journal.

I'm going to have his child. I can't believe my joy. Part of me knows it's wrong to be so happy, but I can't wait to see Douglas and tell him. I can't wait to see my child. I must betray my happiness every time I speak because I cannot stop smiling.

He closed the book, holding it between his hands for a moment before opening it again. Half of the book was blank and he searched for the last page where she'd written something. It was a day ago, the handwriting appreciably different from her earlier script. This writing was not so effusive; there were not so many curls and swooping letters.

I see him with Margaret sometimes, and my heart feels as if it's breaking. This, then, is the real punishment for my sin, that I should see what can never be mine and endlessly want it. My beautiful daughter, heaven's greatest angel, I miss you.

"Sir?"

He turned and glanced at Betty. Slowly, he returned the book and the spectacles to the top of the nightstand.

Something shiny caught his eye, and he bent to pick up the locket.

"Has Miss du Marchand gone looking for Margaret?" he asked before she could speak. He threaded the necklace through his fingers, wondering at the fear that suddenly speared him.

"I don't think so, sir. When I came back a few hours ago, I knocked on the door, and she wasn't here."

He stared at the nurse and behind her the footman.

Douglas felt his temper edge up one more notch at their blank expressions. "Is there something strange about this house? Is there a magic cave beneath the stairs where people disappear? Why is everyone suddenly missing?"

Betty's eyes widened.

Douglas pointed his finger at the footman. "How long have you been here?"

"At the door since two, sir," he said, his Adam's apple bobbing nervously.

"And when did you get back?" he said, pointing at Betty, the gesture having the effect of making her eyes even wider.

"About the same time, sir," she said, bobbing a curtsy.

"So you don't know how long she's been gone?" He'd

left the house about eight, which meant that Jeanne could have been missing for hours.

He rubbed his hand across his forehead.

An unwanted thought struck him, one that seemed perfectly plausible. What if they were together? What if she had left him and taken Margaret? It would be a punishment he probably deserved. But there was something wrong about that idea.

Jeanne didn't possess his capacity for cruelty.

Chapter 32

"**W**hat are you going to do?" Jeanne asked her father.

"Do not think that, because of our attachment, you have any right to speak to me in that tone."

"What you don't understand, Father," she said, talking despite the pain in her throat, "is that I gave up any fear of you a long time ago. There is nothing you can do to me that you haven't already done."

"A pity that your punishments didn't teach you anything, then."

"Oh, they taught me a great deal. Shall I tell you what they taught me?"

"The journey will hopefully not be that long, Jeanne," Nicholas answered, "that I will be forced to espouse an interest in a subject that would, essentially, bore me."

For a moment she didn't say anything, merely studied him.

"You're not going to let me go, are you? Do not pretend otherwise, Father. I wouldn't believe you, regardless."

"You might have been a source of pride, Jeanne. But,

like most women, you're ruled by your emotions. It made a whore of you."

"At least I am not willing to sacrifice everything for the sake of my name. Edinburgh is littered with people who used to be important, whose names were ancient in France. But they're still going hungry."

He looked at her with derision. "I have no intention of being reduced to hiring myself out."

"Your actions have brought more shame to the du Marchand name than anything I've done. What type of man wants to kill a child?"

"Bastards do not litter our family tree."

"No," she said in contempt. "Only murderers."

Eyes closed, Douglas pressed his thumb and forefinger to the bridge of his nose. He was getting a headache. His library, usually a sanctum, felt almost like a prison at the moment. Standing, he left the room, making his way to the rear of the house only to be hailed by the officious footman.

"Lassiter is back, sir. Would you like me to get him for you?"

He turned and stared at the footman. "Let Lassiter rest."

"Can I help you, sir?" the footman asked.

"Unless you can saddle a horse, then no," Douglas said shortly. "Return to your post."

He was halfway to the stable when he was hailed again. This time he stopped, took a deep breath, and prayed for patience before answering. But it was Lassiter this time, still dressed in his workman's clothes.

"Sir!" Lassiter called.

"You should be resting," he said when the older man reached his side. His majordomo wasn't a young man, but Douglas was willing to bet that he'd worked as hard as one today.

"Sir, this just came for you." Only then did he see the envelope in Lassiter's hand.

He took the envelope, slipping a finger beneath the flap. "Who brought it?"

"One of the street boys. He's waiting in the foyer."

"He probably doesn't know anything," Douglas said, scanning the words. The message was succinct.

If you want to see her again, bring the ruby.

He crumpled the letter in his hand, obscuring the signature of the Comte du Marchand.

"I took the liberty of questioning the boy myself. I believe you're right, sir. He was given a coin to bring the envelope to you and to direct you to an entrance to Mary King's Close. It's not a place I would recommend you go alone."

"My daughter's been taken, Lassiter, and now Jeanne. I don't have a choice."

There had been occasions in his life when he had been surfeited with rage: the rescue of his infant daughter, seeing Jeanne in Robert Hartley's home, and now.

He wanted to hurt the Comte du Marchand. He wanted to kill him, slowly, and watch as the breath left his body. Only then would he feel a sense of vindication. Not only for Margaret, but for what the man had done to Jeanne.

"Shall I accompany you, sir?" Lassiter asked. "I have some acquaintance with fisticuffs."

He smiled at his majordomo. Lassiter looked like he would blow away in a high wind, but there was a fierce look on his face that warned he was not to be taken less than seriously. Only today, he'd demonstrated how loyal and determined he was.

"You continually surprise me, Lassiter."

"A man is not solely his occupation, sir." The majordomo bowed slightly and smiled, the fierce look on his face softening only somewhat.

"I appreciate the offer," Douglas said. "I'm not such a fool as to go into a lion's den without reinforcements."

The fact of the matter was that there were few men left to accompany him. Everyone else in his employ was scattered throughout Edinburgh, which left the young footman or Lassiter. Of the two, he'd choose Lassiter.

"Then shall we go, sir?" Lassiter straightened his workman's jacket, adjusted the pitch of his cap, and squared his chin.

A strange moment to feel amusement, but it faded just as quickly as Douglas rounded the house and nodded to the boy who'd been sent as his guide.

"He won't come," Jeanne said, her voice still hoarse.

"You had best hope he does, my dear," Nicholas said, putting the lantern on the small table. The room in which they sat was made of four brick walls and an opening, and was small enough that it could be called an alcove. The man who had abducted her had led them down to this dark and damp place and then disappeared as soon as her father paid him a few coins.

"Or you'll do what?" she asked. "Kill me? Justine isn't around to carry out your orders, Father. Have you someone else to do your bidding?"

"The convent changed you," he said. "I'm surprised; I would have thought you less courageous, not more so."

"Freedom does that," she said. "Tell me, did you ever regret your decision to send me there?"

He seemed to consider the question for a moment.

"No, you shamed the du Marchand name. I considered that you were simply receiving a justly deserved punishment."

She could not fault him for his honesty or for his consistency. "Tell me where Margaret is."

Instead of answering, he leaned back against the chair and regarded her with some interest. "You remind me of your mother, Jeanne. I find the resemblance quite extraordinary. My dearest Hélène wasn't quite as . . . English as you've become, however."

"How would you define being English?" she asked.

Nicholas raised one eyebrow but he answered nonetheless. "A certain arrogance of speech," he replied. "A lack of tact, perhaps."

"A certain independence of spirit?"

"Exactly."

"Perhaps I'm Scot."

He sent her a disgruntled look before moving the chair back into the shadows. He then adjusted the wick on the lantern until the light was barely enough to illuminate the space. Sitting again, he rearranged his walking stick so that the blade was drawn from its holder just enough to allow him to use it quickly.

"You've overestimated my worth to Douglas MacRae," Jeanne said.

"I don't think so. I think MacRae values you very highly. After all, does he not remember you from Paris?"

Surprised, she clasped her hands tightly together, trying not to reveal any emotion at all. "How did you know?"

"I made it my point to discover the father of your child. I might have demonstrated the extent of my irritation with that young man had he not left France so soon."

"When you have the ruby, will you go back to France?"

His expression turned sour. "Not now. Perhaps after the madness has eased, when a man is recognized once more for his lineage."

She was grateful for being able to see him as he truly was, a man of middle years who had been privileged from birth. Circumstances had stripped him of his rank and fortune but he still clung to the notion that he belonged to a rarefied group, that he was unique and somehow blessed above other men. Commonsense rules and normal behavior had never applied to the Comte du Marchand. For that reason, he could send his granddaughter to her death and imprison his daughter and never feel a pinch of contrition.

"So, will you kill me, Father? Or simply leave me here?" She stared at the rats huddled in the corner, their black and shiny eyes looking like tiny shards of ebony. They appeared avaricious and hungry. "And allow them to do the job for you."

"Now, that would be a solution, would it not?"

She turned at the sound of footsteps, thinking to shout and warn Douglas that it was a trap. She knew her father had no intention of letting him leave this place alive. But to her surprise, it wasn't Douglas at all, but the goldsmith, Charles Talbot.

"I knew you would cheat me," he said.

"What are you doing here?" Nicholas asked, standing.

"A question I might ask you, Count. The kidnapping was planned for tomorrow."

"I changed my mind and didn't see the necessity of informing you."

"You're going to sell the ruby without me, aren't you? Have you already lined up a buyer?"

Jeanne looked from one to the other. How had Charles Talbot become involved in her father's plans?

"Where is Margaret MacRae?" she asked, jerking away from her father.

Both men turned to her, anger etched on their faces.

"What have you done with her? You have me; you no

longer need a child. If you let her go, I'll get the ruby for you."

Talbot raised his hand and sliced it through the air as if to cut off her words. "I don't know anything about a child. All I know is that your father is a French weasel. He'll cheat anyone."

"Am I supposed to feel badly because you have a low opinion of me, Talbot?" Nicholas asked dismissively. "If so, you're wrong. An insult from you is indeed a compliment."

He glanced at Jeanne. "You've been rattling on about that brat for hours now. I don't have her, but if I'd known you had such fondness for the girl, perhaps I would have planned differently. But you're going to give up the stone easily enough, daughter. As I recall, you're not too fond of pain."

She stared at him, feeling as if someone had stopped her on an Edinburgh street and introduced himself, claiming a fatherly bond. She didn't hate her father but neither did she like him. She didn't know him. Nor did she want to. He was a travesty, an aberration, a monster that she was somehow related to by blood. It was worthless to wish that her mother had been unfaithful and that she was the daughter of another, when she and Nicholas, Comte du Marchand, shared the same features—the same color eyes, the same shaped nose, the same half smile.

Talbot glanced in her direction. "Do you have the ruby, Miss du Marchand?"

She shook her head. "Not with me. But I know where it is."

"Don't tell him anything else," her father commanded.

She ignored him and edged closer to Talbot. "If you release Margaret, I'll give it to you."

"I regret that I don't know what you're talking about. But perhaps we can come to some kind of arrangement."

She'd sooner bargain with a snake, but Jeanne kept a smile on her face.

Behind her, Nicholas moved along the wall toward Talbot, so slowly that she wondered if the goldsmith noticed. Or did he see that her father held his walking stick behind his back like a club?

She felt a frisson of horror knowing what her father was going to do.

"You never intended to let me sell the ruby for you, did you?"

"Of course I did," Nicholas said. "However, contrary to what you believed, it was not going to benefit you."

"You're a damned fool, Count, if you think I'll let you cheat me."

"You're impertinent, Talbot. A base merchant."

The lantern illuminated Talbot's smile, one that did not quite reach his eyes. They were narrowed as they looked at her father. "This isn't France, Count. And I'm not one of your flunkies."

"A pity, that," Nicholas said. "I would have you killed if we were in France."

The goldsmith didn't have a chance to answer. Her father's arm arced over his head. Jeanne screamed out a warning as she heard the hiss of a blade.

Shockingly, a gunshot reverberated in the small space, the sound ringing in her ears.

Her father twisted around, a look of surprise on his face. Slowly, he fell, landing heavily at Jeanne's feet.

Douglas heard a gunshot and then the sound of Jeanne's scream, felt his heart catapult in his chest, experiencing fear like he hadn't known since those early days of Meggie's life. The steps were slippery but he barely noticed them as he half tumbled, half flew down the steep staircase.

His blood chilled as Jeanne screamed again, and then his heart seemed to stop as he entered the doorway and saw her. Her attacker was a man of middle years, a stranger to

Douglas. When he raised his arm to strike Jeanne again, Douglas threw himself on the man.

For a moment he was insensate, incapable of rational thought or reasonable action. All he wanted to do was to destroy the man who dared raise his hand against Jeanne. He felt the touch of a hand on his shoulder, pulled away, and then felt it again.

"Douglas."

Only then did sounds begin to penetrate. He heard the gasping wheeze of the man on the ground beneath him, the soft pulpy sounds of his fists repeatedly striking the man's face, and above it all, the sound of Jeanne's soft, imploring voice.

"Douglas." Just his name, and like a siren's call it had the effect of pulling him back from madness.

Rational thought came slower. He was atop the body, his knees braced on either side of the older man's chest. And he was beating him senseless.

Douglas took a deep, steadying breath, forcing himself to calm. Jeanne's hand on his cheek was a cool, soft touch. He turned toward it and looked up at her. She knelt beside him and framed his face.

"It's all right, Douglas," she said, her words seeming to come from very far away. It wasn't, of course, but he somehow managed a half smile and was rewarded for his effort by her gentle kiss on his lips.

She stood then, holding out her hand for him. He placed his own bloody fingers against her palm, allowing himself to be led away from the silent, recumbent form on the stone floor.

"Have I killed him?"

A moan a second later reassured Douglas that he had not.

"He hurt you," he said, taking her in his arms. He felt her tremble against him, breathed into her hair, exhaling as he fought down his anger.

"It doesn't matter."

"What a foolish thing to say, Jeanne," he said gently. "Of course it matters. *You* matter."

He pulled back and surveyed her in the faint lantern light. There was a red mark forming on her cheek that would soon lead to a bruise. Her eyes looked haunted, the shadows accentuated below her eyes. His thumbs traced over the fragility of her lovely face. How could his happiness be so contained within this one woman? How could she be all that he needed?

"It doesn't matter *now,*" she amended.

"Does it hurt?" he asked, gently circling her reddened skin.

"No," she said, shaking her head.

In the distance, Douglas heard the faint sound of laughter, and nearby came the skittering sound of rats.

"I don't think he knows where Margaret is," Jeanne said.

"Who is he?" Douglas asked, glancing at the man who still lay huddled on the floor.

"Charles Talbot, a jeweler."

The name was familiar to him, but he ignored the niggling memory in favor of leaving this place.

As they headed for the door, Jeanne turned and looked at the far wall and that's when Douglas saw the other body.

"My father," she said. "If he knew where Margaret was, Douglas, he didn't say." She looked at him helplessly. "What do we do now?"

"Get out of here," he said, taking her arm and leading her up the steps.

He turned, still holding an arm around her, and surveyed this small room. In this dimmest of dungeons, in this place of horror, he had almost lost her again. How many times could a man resurrect himself without hope?

How had she done it?

He glanced at her, realizing the depth of her strength.

Even now, when most women would have been justifiably in hysterics, she was calm. She didn't tremble. Nor did she cry, and as he looked, the expression in her eyes softened.

"I almost lost you," he said, and he didn't just speak of tonight's adventures.

She nodded, and it was as if she understood the depth of his horror. "No," she said softly and curled her fingers around his bloody hand.

He led her up the stairs into the clean night air. At the top, he glanced up at the sky and the sparkling stars. The world was too large, the universe too vast. One little girl could so easily become lost.

If they didn't find Margaret, he would need to borrow some of Jeanne's strength.

Chapter 33

L assiter was given the task of turning Talbot over to the authorities, which he looked pleased to do. When she and Douglas returned home, he led her to his library.

"How do you feel?"

Moving to the sideboard, he poured them both a glass of sherry, and then brought both glasses to where she sat and placed them on the lion table between the wing chairs.

She smiled. "I don't know," she told him honestly. "I thought him dead, and seeing him alive was a shock. But I don't know how I feel about his death. Isn't that odd?"

He studied her, a look that was particularly intense.

"You've not realized it completely, I think," he said, handing her one of the glasses. She stared at it for a long moment before she finally began to drink.

"I don't mourn him. I hated him for too long for that. I thought he had Margaret," she said. "If I regret anything, it's that he didn't tell us where she was."

He nodded. "I'm sending some men into Mary King's Close. I can't overlook the possibility that Margaret is there."

"She could be anywhere," Jeanne said, beginning to tremble.

Douglas set down his own glass before taking hers and placing it on the table. Slowly, he pulled her into his arms. She leaned against him, wishing that she could absorb some of his strength. As she gave a shuddering sigh, he tightened his embrace.

Douglas. Even his name seemed to give her comfort.

Wrapping her arms around him, she flattened her hands against his back and placed her cheek against his chest.

"We'll find her, Jeanne. We'll find her."

She nodded, and prayed that his words weren't simply meant to be reassuring. Let them be a portent, an omen. Or even a prayer.

A little while later he led her to the chair and then bent and laid a fire.

"You've done this often," she said, watching his easy movements.

"Often enough," he said, smiling back at her.

"I wondered what you'd done for ten years," she admitted. "Now I know. You were making fires, tea, and a fortune."

"I sailed for the first three," he said, returning to sit beside her. "Until I decided that a life aboard ship wasn't the best for Margaret."

She leaned back against the wing chair, staring into the fire. Although it was the middle of summer, the room felt chilled.

"Tell me about her," she said, turning and forcing a smile to her face. "I want to know everything."

For the rest of the evening, they kept a vigil as they waited for word to come from the hundreds of people still looking for Margaret.

She already knew that her daughter had a quick mind, but as the hours passed, Jeanne learned of Margaret's love of sailing, apples, and Chinese puzzle boxes. Besides

Gilmuir, she liked James's home of Ayleshire, and visiting the dolphins outside Inverness.

Together they sat in the wing chairs facing the fire, Douglas talking while Jeanne listened. Toward midnight, he replenished the fire. He was solicitous of her, providing a footstool, plying her with endless glasses of wine. She took a few sips from each, thinking that it might be pleasant to maintain a fogginess from drink. But nothing would mitigate the sense of loss she felt, so deep and pervasive that it mimicked the day they took baby Margaret from her.

Occasionally, Douglas would stand and begin to pace, stopping by her chair to pat her shoulder or brush the back of his hand against her cheek. It was the first time that they had felt a freedom to reveal their deepest thoughts to one another, and yet they did so without words.

She would grab his fingers and place a kiss against his knuckles, wondering if he knew how very much she loved him. The words were too difficult to say. The last time she'd done so, her life had altered in terrible ways. She was twice shy about revealing herself so completely yet again.

"What do we do next?" she asked, crossing her arms over her chest and cupping her elbows in suddenly cold palms. The evening was cool, but that wasn't the reason she felt chilled.

Standing, she moved to the fire, stood watching the blaze as it suddenly wavered, a blur of gold, orange, and blue flames.

"Tell me what happened," he said, and she knew suddenly what he wanted to know. Not her abduction, but an older story, one of a spoiled yet innocent young girl.

The tale wasn't long, and he remained silent while she spoke.

"I never believed that he would take her from me," she said, speaking of the day Margaret was born. "I thought he would let me go somewhere with her, someplace where they didn't know the du Marchand name." She laughed a mirthless laugh. "I had suggested America or England, and he seemed to agree.

"But once the baby was born, everything changed. He had Justine take the baby away and had me sent to the convent and I was a prisoner there, too."

She glanced at him. "The first thing I did when I left the convent was return to Vallans. I thought that there was a chance that I could find her." She smiled at her own foolishness and hope. "I found the place where she had been taken. The old man had died a few years earlier, but his wife was still alive. She was terrified of me, and my questions, but she finally told me what had happened."

The small misshapen cottage on the outskirts of the woods had been a place of horror, not charm. Jeanne could remember everything about that foggy day, the feeling of every breath she'd taken, and every scent she'd inhaled of that foul place rife with decaying wood and slimy leaves.

"She led me to a grave," she said, her voice trembling. "I stood there and knew that I had failed my child. My actions had led to her death."

The ground had felt spongy beneath her knees as she'd knelt there, weeping until her eyes were dry.

"I should have been stronger," she said now at his silence. "I should have found a way to protect her."

"You were only seventeen," he said.

She smoothed her damp palms over her skirt. "Yes," she said, "I was only seventeen." She looked at him, startled to discover that his eyes hadn't left her. His quick appraisal was less one of masculine appreciation than it was of concern.

"Jeanne, you were no match for him."

She smiled, again grateful to him for attempting to ease

her self-reproach, to absolve her of any culpability. "I didn't want to see, Douglas. I didn't want to know." There, the greatest sin of all. She hadn't wanted to believe the worst could happen. But it had.

"But she's alive," he said.

"Yes," she said, turning to him and holding out her hands. He pulled her into his embrace. "You saved her. And me." He'd restored her soul by saving their child when she could not. *Please, God, let Margaret be found. Let her be safe.*

She continued with her tale. "That morning when I saw her grave, I decided that I would die. There was nothing to live for anymore."

Closing her eyes, she felt his arms tighten around her. She spoke against his throat, grateful that he was so close.

"I didn't want to live. But I did. I gradually made my way to Scotland." She smiled at the thought of the ruby safely tucked away in her locket. The sale of it might have made her journey easier. "I didn't have any money, but it didn't seem to matter because I truly didn't care what happened to me. I existed simply because I didn't die.

"Until I saw you. Then everything changed. I was terrified you would find out what had happened and despise me as much as I despised myself." She stretched out her hand, touched his face, smoothing her palm along his jaw.

"I thought you didn't care all this time," he said. "That you didn't want Margaret. Or even me."

She shook her head. "And I thought you never tried to find me because you discovered I was going to have your child." She smiled faintly. "We've been hiding from each other all this time."

He wrapped his arms around her, speaking the words next to her cheek. "Forgive me," he said, the words sounding as if they'd originated from deep inside him. "Forgive me."

"I do," she said, finally.

Together they would heal, but only if Margaret was found. *Safe,* she added in a silent, fervent prayer.

Toward dawn, Jeanne fell into a fitful doze, sitting upright in the wing chair. She was awakened when Douglas placed a coverlet around her, tucking it over her knees. Sleepily, she thanked him as he bent and placed a kiss on her forehead.

She opened her eyes and their gazes locked. In that moment she felt as if she had opened the door of her soul and allowed him inside, wandering where no one else had ever ventured. She almost wanted to whisper for him to take care so that he didn't disarrange anything, or shatter something lovely like an illusion.

But he said nothing at all and only reached out his hand to trail his fingers across her face with the most gentle of touches. He brushed her hair back behind her ear before bending down to place a kiss against her lips.

She felt her heart slowly break at the tender look on his face.

"We'll find her," he said. "I promise."

There was nothing at all certain about the future. Everything was tenuous and they each stepped across a narrow bridge to each other, one built of glass. A tremble, a brush of a hand, or a flick of a finger, and it may come tumbling down. But it was as if they each knew it, and took greater care of one another.

She began to count the hours, one after the other until a dozen had passed and then a dozen more. A day was gone, and then two, the dawns and sunsets ponderously similar.

Douglas traveled routes through Edinburgh every day, making contacts with people he knew, going to his warehouse. There, a selection of employees came to him with reports, none of them positive so far.

Each night he shared her bed, but only to hold her. She

lay with his arms around her and still felt cold, as if this loss of their child were again her fault. Once, she tried to tell him how sorry she was, but tears tightened her throat and made her incapable of speech.

He'd tightened his arms around her, and breathed the words against her cheek. "We'll find her, Jeanne. Believe me."

She could only nod.

On the third morning, when one of the maids called out that she had her breakfast tray, Jeanne dismissed her. When she knocked on the door of her room again a few moments later, Jeanne didn't bother answering. A minute later she heard the door open and close softly.

"I don't want any breakfast," she said. She stood at the window staring out at the gray and overcast day.

"Do you intend to stay up here until she's found?" Douglas asked.

"No," she said, turning and looking at him. "I am going with you today. And tomorrow, and the day after that. I can't simply remain here and wait for news."

For ten years she'd been strong, and it was time she was strong again. They would find their daughter, but together.

"I would welcome the company," he said, coming to stand beside her.

She leaned against him, closing her eyes, grateful when he extended his arms around her.

"I have to do something," she explained. "Otherwise, I think I'll go mad. I'm angry at the entire world. How am I to live through this, Douglas? The first time I lost her nearly killed me."

He kissed her softly, a gesture meant to be more comforting than passionate. "Together, we'll live through it."

He wasn't looking at her, but at the far horizon, as if he were remembering something particularly grim.

A knock on the door preceded one of Lassiter's footmen. The majordomo insisted upon searching with the other employees every day. Therefore, his normal duties went to an assortment of young men, each of whom was terrified of doing something wrong. This one looked particularly harried, bending in an awkward bow that looked even more stilted since he was so tall.

"You've a visitor, sir. A Mr. Hamish MacRae. He says he has important news about Miss Margaret."

Douglas preceded the footmen out of the room. Jeanne grabbed her skirts in both hands and raced down the stairs behind him, only to halt at the landing.

"Where is she?" Douglas asked a tall, broad-shouldered man standing in the foyer.

Hamish was the same height as Douglas, but was older and carried more weight. A few scars marred his face, but didn't detract from his appearance of strength. His brown eyes appraised Douglas quickly, and then his gaze traveled up the stairs to rest on Jeanne.

"Where is she?" Douglas asked again and Hamish must have heard the underlying worry in Douglas's voice because he held up his hand.

"She's well," Hamish said, smiling. "She convinced Henry to bring her to Gilmuir."

"Gilmuir?" Douglas threaded his fingers through his hair and stared at his brother.

Jeanne held on to the banister and slowly descended the stairs, feeling as if her legs wouldn't support her.

Hamish nodded. "She needed to see Mary, she said."

Jeanne and Douglas exchanged a look, both slightly bemused. They had never considered that Margaret might have left Edinburgh of her own free will.

"She's only nine," Jeanne said, reaching Douglas's side. He put his arm around her.

"But determined." Hamish's glance encompassed her.

"You must be Jeanne," he said, his smile broadening. "Remember, she's your daughter. You both strike me as being more than a little stubborn."

"But she's all right?" Douglas asked.

"She is, even though she isn't sure she wants to talk to you," he said to Douglas. "And she doesn't know what to say to you," he added, directing his attention to Jeanne.

She frowned at him, perplexed. "Why not?"

"It seems that Margaret has been able to piece together that Jeanne is her mother." He nodded at Douglas. "She believes that you betrayed her. While you," he said, glancing at Jeanne, "lied to her. I don't think she's altogether displeased that you're her mother," he added. "She's just a little confused."

"But she's safe?"

"Safe with Mary at the moment."

The relief that Jeanne felt was suddenly so strong that she thought she might faint from it. She reached out and Douglas enfolded his hand over hers and together they stood, strangely enough almost in the pose of a bride and groom.

For the third time they exchanged a glance and this time they didn't bother to look away. And then, in front of his brother and the gangly footman, Douglas bent and kissed her, so sweetly that Jeanne felt tears slip from her eyes.

The nuns of Sacré-Coeur were wrong. There was no further need to make reparations to save her immortal soul. The tears she'd already shed were payment enough.

Chapter 34

The only time Jeanne had been aboard a ship was on the miserable voyage crossing the English Channel. The waves had been choppy and the winds high. Each time the bow of the ship pointed skyward and then tilted down on the next trench of wave, she was sure they were going to be pitched to the bottom of the sea.

She had been exhausted, hungry, and cold. Going from nine years of imprisonment to being responsible for herself in a world not disposed to care much for solitary women had also left her feeling vulnerable and frightened.

The voyage from Leith to Gilmuir, however, was different. Douglas had commandeered one of the MacRae ships waiting at his dock when Hamish announced he was returning to Gilmuir later.

"I make it to Edinburgh so seldom, Mary's given me a list of supplies she wants," he'd said, shaking his head.

This vessel, designed for crossing the oceans of the world, felt as though it were flying across the glassy water. The sea was calm, the winds brisk but gentle, but Jeanne was just as afraid as the time when she'd left France.

"Are you certain she's all right?" she asked Douglas again for the hundreth time.

He stood beside her and, at her query, extended his arm around her, pulling her tight. "If Hamish says she's fine, she is. I've never known him to lie." He smiled slightly, one corner of his lip upturned. "Not even to spare my feelings."

She wouldn't feel reassured, however, until she actually saw Margaret, until she could ascertain herself that her daughter was safe and unharmed.

"What ever made her do such a thing?"

"I'm afraid we'll have to ask Margaret that," Douglas said, staring off at the far horizon.

"What am I going to say to her?"

He glanced down at her, his smile disappearing. "Tell her the truth."

She shook her head. "Maybe one day," she said, "but not now. She's only nine."

"Eight," he corrected with a smile. "Her birthday's not for ten days."

She shook her head. "Do you remember the night at Robert Hartley's home?"

He nodded.

"That was Margaret's real birthday." Nine years ago on that day she'd given birth to her child.

He looked bemused by the knowledge. She curved her arm around his, leaned her head on his shoulder. "Margaret is such an English name," she said.

"What did you choose?"

"Genevieve," she said. She'd never told anyone that. Nor had she spoken that name for nine years. "But Margaret suits her better."

For long moments they stood there, feeling the current of the ocean beneath the ship. The wind stirred her hair loose from its bun, and caressed her face. She felt her heart swell as Douglas pulled her closer, a sense of joy sweeping through her so powerfully that it felt as if lightning traveled from her head to her toes.

Despite her trepidation, she was happy. Purely and deliciously happy in a way that she couldn't remember being for so very long. For the first time in what felt like a hundred years, there was no discordance between the girl she had been and the woman she was. True, she was a little more experienced, but she felt completely like herself. Jeanne du Marchand. Lover, friend, mother.

She reached out and took his hand, holding it between hers, studying the shape of it. His hands were so large compared to hers. They were calloused and rough in spots, evidence that he worked hard for a living. He had created an empire and she knew it would continue to grow and expand under his leadership. He was a man other men admired and emulated.

He was capable of so many things that she felt as if she had wasted her life in comparison. As if it had been taken from her. But, in that moment, instead of feeling deprived, she knew that she was the most fortunate woman on earth.

She had been given a new chance. She and her daughter had both been resurrected from the dead, a gift more precious than any she could imagine had been given to her.

"There," he said pointing with his right hand to a sight in front and slightly above them. "That's Gilmuir."

She straightened and stared up at the structure, feeling as if her heart had clenched tight in her chest and then resounded with a beat so fierce that her ribs trembled with it.

"It looks like Vallans," she said and then realized that the resemblance was fleeting. The brick was the same color as her home, and the shape of the fortress was the same as the chateau. The four turrets were similar, also. But Gilmuir was so much larger and so much more impressive in comparison.

Vallans had not been used as a fortress for centuries, but

she could easily imagine Gilmuir remaining a defensive structure for as long as a MacRae would wish it. Built at the end of a promontory, it seemed to sit on its haunches like a great wild beast.

"No wonder Margaret loves it here," she said. "What a glorious place."

"You know that?"

She nodded. "Gilmuir is one of her favorite topics of conversation. That, and Cameron, of course."

"Who is Cameron?"

She glanced at him, noting that he didn't look the least pleased. "I think perhaps it's better if Margaret told you," she said, smiling.

Ahead of them, in the firth, was a large building jutting out over the water.

When she pointed to it, Douglas explained. "It's part of Alisdair's shipbuilding company. There are a few other buildings sprinkled around the glen where they treat the wood and build parts of the ship. But the final construction is done there, while the hulls are tested in the cove. I'll show it to you one day, as well as the secret staircase."

"A secret staircase?"

"You sound as excited as Margaret," he teased. "Wait until you see Ionis's Cave."

"Who is Ionis?"

"Hundreds of years ago a man was isolated to this promontory. Below, in a cave we've named after him, are the works of his lifetime, portraits of a woman he adored."

"What became of him?"

"He was made a saint because of his years of penitence," Douglas said. "And the promontory became a place of pilgrimage, at least until the first MacRae claimed it."

She studied him, wondering if that first MacRae was anything like his descendant. Douglas had the temperament and the courage of a man who would found a dynasty and create a place like Gilmuir to protect it.

They slowed their progress into the firth and navigated the last curve. There, sitting on the water like a magnificent swan at rest, was the *Ian MacRae*, Hamish's ship.

Jeanne felt herself beginning to tremble and held herself tight as they weighed anchor.

"Meggie is there," he said gently.

She nodded, hoping that he wouldn't ask her to stay behind. But he said nothing of the sort, and when the rope ladder was strung over the side, he turned to her. "I'll go down first and steady the ladder."

As he put one leg over the side, she held out one hand to stay him. He halted, looking at her in puzzlement.

She reached his side in a few steps, leaned over, and tenderly kissed him. "Be careful," she whispered against his cheek. "I don't know what I would do if anything ever happened to you."

"I do," he said. "You would survive. You're the strongest woman I know."

He reached out and grabbed her hand and placed a kiss on the center of her palm. "You are as precious to me, Jeanne," he said, his words replicated in his gaze. Regardless of the presence of the sailors around them, she kissed him again.

A minute later, he swung his other leg over the side and disappeared. She leaned over the edge and watched him. He made the descent look so easy. A feat that wasn't as simple to replicate, she discovered when she used the rope ladder herself a few minutes later. She couldn't seem to find the rungs with her feet, and twice she lost her grip with one hand. Every so often she couldn't help but give a little squeal when the ladder began to sway from side to side.

She was very grateful to make it halfway down. Douglas

reached up, grabbed her around the waist, and helped her down the rest of the way.

"We have to do it again," he said in a muffled voice. "At Hamish's ship."

Only then did she realize he was laughing.

She turned, wound her arms around his neck, and shifted her weight from one leg to another, sending the boat careening from side to side.

He only grabbed her tighter around the waist and smiled down into her face. "Are you trying to send us into the firth, Jeanne?"

"I think you deserve it, for laughing at me."

He nodded. "Perhaps I do. Forgive me?" He lowered his head, their foreheads touching. "Forgive me, love?"

They kissed again, and she could feel his smile.

A few moments later they sat and he removed his jacket, tossing it to her. She folded it and put it on her lap, her hands stroking the material as he reached out to take the oars and began to row.

The closer they came to the *Ian MacRae*, the larger the ship appeared. When she said as much, Douglas smiled. "It's built for the China trade. It's the largest vessel in the MacRae fleet, and it's a good thing. It's Hamish's and Mary's home."

Douglas ascended the rope ladder first, leaving her to make the journey upward with even less grace than her first attempt. But he didn't say anything as he helped her over the side, and if he thought her amusing, there wasn't a ghost of a smile in evidence.

A woman stood a few feet away, attired in a dark green dress that seemed to accentuate the red highlights in her brown hair. Her dark brown eyes appeared kind, and her smile was equally pleasant. Her hands were clasped together in front of her, giving Jeanne the impression that she had infinite patience.

They approached her, but she spoke first. "I'm Mary MacRae," she said softly. "You must be Miss du Marchand."

Her smile grew brighter as Douglas extended one arm around Jeanne's shoulders.

"Is Margaret here?" Jeanne asked, her voice tremulous.

Reaching out, Mary took Jeanne's hand in hers. "I think it would be better to let Douglas talk to her first," she advised. "I have some wonderfully relaxing tea in my cabin. Would you care to join me?"

The very last thing she wanted at this moment was tea, but it seemed as if she didn't have a choice. Mary grabbed her hand and led her across the deck. Jeanne sent a last, helpless look at Douglas but he only smiled, turned, and walked in the other direction. Only then did she see the small figure at the bow of the ship staring relentlessly out to sea.

Douglas didn't know what to do first, hug Margaret or scold her. He settled for the first, picking her up bodily and extending his arms around her. She didn't hug him in return but remained stiff and unrelenting.

Meggie, angry, was a formidable sight.

Lowering her to the deck again, he stood and stared down at her.

"Mireille Margaret MacRae," he said sternly, "what have you got to say for yourself?"

She looked mutinous, her bottom lip pushed out into a stubborn pout that he'd rarely seen from her.

"I'm a thief, Papa. I took the money from the strongbox, and borrowed a horse to take me to Leith. Henry didn't want to, but I told him that if he didn't bring me to Gilmuir, I would simply find another way."

"Where is he now?" Douglas asked, thinking that he needed to have a very long talk with his employee. On the one hand, he applauded the man's loyalty to his daughter.

But on the other, he thought that Henry might have found another way to remedy the situation other than bringing her to Gilmuir.

"I sent him back to Edinburgh," she said. "He didn't want to go but I promised him that nothing would happen to him."

"You did, did you?" he asked wryly.

She glanced at him. "I gave him my word, Papa, and you always said that a person's word is his promise."

"What do you think I would have done?"

"Fire him," she said with a small sigh. "But he truly loves his job, Papa. In addition, his wife isn't well, you know."

He concentrated on something other than Henry's fate. "Do you know all the bad things that could happen to you by traveling in the middle of the night, Margaret?"

"That's exactly what Henry said," she said, sighing again. "He was angry with me." She looked up at him, blue eyes wide. "I'm sorry, Papa. I know it was a bad thing to do. But I was so very vexed with you."

"But you aren't now?" he asked, folding his arms and staring down at her. He tapped his foot against the deck and waited to hear this newest revelation.

"I don't think so," she said, evidently considering the matter. "I'm not entirely certain. Aunt Mary told me how much you loved my mother, so I can only think that you lied to me for my best benefit, even though you have often said that a lie benefits no one."

It was a disconcerting experience, having his words thrown back in his face, especially by his own child.

"There was a reason for my lie, Meggie."

She looked doubtful, but she didn't argue with him. Instead, she sighed again and reached out to take his hand. Douglas had the discomfiting feeling that he was being reprimanded without a word spoken.

Chapter 35

⟨◦◦◦⟩

Jeanne sat at the table in the captain's cabin of the *Ian MacRae,* her elbows placed on the wooden surface, the palms of her hands pressed against her eyes. Not because they hurt, but because she didn't want to see the woman in front of her. Or envision the sights she so calmly described.

It was her own fault. She'd asked Mary to tell her about those early days when Margaret had been found. Although Jeanne didn't want to hear of the abuse her daughter had suffered, of the terrible sores on her body, of the months of careful nursing that it had taken to save her life, she didn't halt Mary's soft words. She was grateful for one thing—that her father was now enduring a celestial judgment.

"Douglas spent the first three years of Margaret's life hovering over her," Mary said, smiling at the memory. "I finally told him that he was going to give Margaret an exaggerated view of her own importance. Or make the child fearful, which was just as bad. At first he wouldn't let her go anywhere without him. I've never seen anyone so miserable the first time she remained at Gilmuir without him."

She poured more tea and pushed the cup across the table to Jeanne.

"Margaret was six and having the time of her life, but Douglas imagined every single horror that could happen. Colds, lightning strikes, influenza." She gently laughed. "He's much better lately. The years have proven to him that Margaret is a survivor."

She smiled again and Jeanne was struck by how beautiful the expression was on Mary's face. It lit up her eyes and imparted a sense of profound joy.

"It's your turn now," Mary said. "Tell me what happened to you."

She told Mary the entire story, from the moment she'd been called into her father's library until the day before when they'd despaired of finding Margaret. Certain details, such as sharing Douglas's bed, were omitted, but Jeanne didn't doubt that Mary could piece together that part of the tale as well.

Jeanne stood and walked to the rear of the cabin. A row of windows stretching the width of the space revealed the firth and, beyond, the fortress of Gilmuir. "I've never loved anyone but Douglas," Jeanne said softly. "I can't imagine ever loving anyone else."

"And you paid dearly for that emotion."

Jeanne nodded only once.

A moment later she felt Mary's hand on her shoulder and glanced at the older woman. "You cannot erase those years, my dear, but you can build on them. Incorporate the good memories into the person you've become. Learn something from those experiences and then put the bad memories away."

"I have so much to thank you for," Jeanne said, turning and holding both of Mary's hands in her own. "Thank you for saving my daughter."

Mary only smiled and led Jeanne to another window.

There, standing at the bow of the ship, was Douglas, and beside him, Margaret.

A buoyancy began in Jeanne's toes and swept upward to settle in the middle of her stomach. Everything that she ever wanted in her entire life, every sort of happiness, was encapsulated in the two people in front of her.

"It's time," Mary said.

Jeanne nodded, leaving the comfort of the captain's cabin and making her way to the front of the ship. Each footfall made a smart tapping noise against the solid wooden deck. Two sailors, as if sensing a confrontation, glanced at her and then picked up their buckets and left, tipping their hats to her in an almost salute.

Before Jeanne reached them, Margaret turned, releasing her father's hand.

She stared intently up at Jeanne. "Papa used to tell me a story about my mother. Was it true?"

Jeanne glanced at Douglas, uncertain.

"It's mostly true," he answered.

"Are you my mother, Miss du Marchand?"

Jeanne nodded, overwhelmed. Words wouldn't come, but they must. How did she explain to Margaret what had happened?

"Yes, I am." It was the first time, she realized with shock, that she acknowledged it publicly.

"And you're not an angel," Margaret said.

That acerbic comment surprised a smile from Jeanne.

"I can guarantee you that I'm not."

"Then where have you been?"

Jeanne suddenly knew what she had to say.

She turned and walked some distance away and sat on a ledge next to the railing. She didn't beckon Margaret closer, only waited. The child stared at her solemnly for several moments before walking slowly toward Jeanne.

Before her daughter could speak, Jeanne began. "I've already told you that my mother died when I was young."

Margaret nodded cautiously.

"I've always cherished the one thing that she left for me." Jeanne withdrew the locket from around her neck. Douglas had had it repaired and had given it to her before they had boarded the *Ian MacRae*. "It's not a very pretty necklace," she said. "But it held a secret in our family, the Somerville ruby." She opened it now and showed Margaret the stone.

"My life would have been easier if she'd told me about the secret," Jeanne said. "But perhaps she had her reasons."

"Just like you and Papa?" Margaret asked.

Jeanne nodded, wondering how Margaret had developed her perceptiveness.

"We didn't mean to hurt you," she said. "Do you believe that?" Before Margaret could answer, she draped the locket over the little girl's head.

She bent her head and studied it intently. "Is it mine?"

Jeanne nodded. "I can't explain everything, Margaret. All I can tell you is that I've always loved you."

"You have?" She fingered the locket, seemed to consider the matter, and asked one more question. "Is the ruby mine, too?"

Jeanne smiled. "Yes, it's yours."

Margaret sighed heavily. "It's a very nice present, Miss du Marchand, but I like getting a mother better." She narrowed her eyes and stared at her. "Are you very certain you are?"

Jeanne nodded.

"Do I have any brothers or sisters?"

"Not yet," Douglas said, coming to her side.

Jeanne glanced up at him and he returned her look solemnly. Margaret surprised her, however, by reaching out and hugging her. This time Jeanne didn't try to hide her tears.

"You mustn't cry," Margaret said, drawing back concerned.

"I'm just happy."

Margaret looked doubtful about that answer and glanced at her father, who smiled down at her. "Why don't you go tell Aunt Mary that I need to send a message to Gilmuir?"

The little girl didn't look the least pleased to be sent on an errand but, after studying her father's face, evidently decided against rebellion.

Before she left them, though, she asked another question of her mother. "Will you continue to be my governess, then?" she asked, frowning. "It doesn't seem entirely proper."

"Margaret." Douglas shook his head at her.

She sighed and reluctantly made her way to the captain's cabin, leaving Jeanne alone with Douglas.

He turned and faced the firth, arms crossed in front of him, affecting an intense scrutiny of the water and the far horizon where the sea met the sky. She waited for him to speak, and when he did, it was softly.

"It took an instant to find you, an hour to love you, a week to know that I couldn't live without you. It took ten years to realize that I'd never be able to forget you." He faced her. "Will it take a lifetime to convince you that I love you?"

She shook her head.

"I love you with all my heart," he said. "With my soul, quite possibly. You occupy too much of my mind. My present is indelibly woven around you, as was my past."

His hands fell to his sides. Jeanne had the strangest feeling that he stood there unguarded waiting for her to repudiate him. But he was Douglas, her youthful lover and forever friend, the man who occupied her thoughts, and the father of her child. Her love.

"Marry me, Jeanne. Be part of my future."

She studied him, grateful for this instant in time. She would never forget his look at this moment, just as she had never forgotten the memories of Paris. Now those recollections were forever freed of their sadness, of their tinge of grief.

Did she have the courage of that girl? She smiled, thinking that she did, and more. She'd been tested and strengthened by what had happened to her. She could survive without Douglas, but life with him would be so much richer and more complete. In the end, it wasn't courage that made her stand and go to him, but a feeling that doing so was simply right.

Winding her arms around his neck, she stood on tiptoe to brush a soft kiss against his lips. "Yes, I'll marry you. I love you, Douglas. I always have, sometimes to my detriment, mostly to my blessing. Do you think that's how love is?"

"I think, perhaps, that we have the rest of our lives to study it," he said, pulling her closer to him.

Epilogue

There was a hush in the priory, but unlike the last ceremony to be held here, there was no grief in evidence, and no sound of muffled tears.

The time of the ceremony had been chosen with care in order to show the stained-glass windows at their best. Now shafts of jewellike light colored gold, scarlet, emerald, and indigo illuminated the faces of the congregation, danced upon the altar, and pooled around the couple standing with hands linked at the front of the priory.

The magnificence of the scene would cause some of the worshipers in the Scottish Reformed Church to say it was reminiscent of popery. But should that comment have been made to anyone at Gilmuir he would have demurred and said that it was only history he witnessed and nothing more.

Generations of MacRaes had stood in this same spot over the centuries. The room itself, one of the largest at Gilmuir, had been rebuilt, but only as it had once been. The arches had been restored, the slate floor replaced. While it was true that the shape of the priory had been altered, that was only done to allow for the passage through the secret staircase.

Although this holy place had been rebuilt with the past in mind, the ceremony held here was very much one of the future. The whole of the clan was here, if not in physical form, then in spirit.

Jeanne Catherine Alexis du Marchand was marrying Douglas Allen MacRae. Standing behind them was their daughter, Margaret, a look of irritation flitting over her face as she caught sight of her nemesis behind a pillar. She frowned at him, while Cameron only grinned back at her.

Alisdair MacRae recalled when Douglas was born a lifetime ago. As an adolescent he'd been shocked and appalled at the travail of birth, so much so that the two times his darling wife had been brought to bed with a child he'd been awed by her courage.

James MacRae remembered when Douglas had been an angry seventeen-year-old, desperate to return to France, and longing for the woman he was now marrying a decade later.

Hamish had witnessed Douglas's emergence into manhood, and had sailed with him for three years. He wasn't surprised at either the success his brother had become or the strength of character he possessed.

Brendan remembered Douglas as a younger brother, when he'd been annoying and mischievous. He sent a cautionary glance toward his two older sons, who immediately subsided and stared straight ahead, afraid of further angering their father.

Mary MacRae, standing on Scottish soil for the first time in more than ten years, witnessed the marriage with a feeling of rightness and completion. She had given her life to healing, but she knew sometimes that wounds were never truly mended until the heart was engaged. She witnessed the glance between Douglas and Jeanne, feeling almost like a usurper seeing such tenderness. Tears came to her eyes and at that moment Hamish turned his head, looking down at her. She smiled to reassure him, but he only looked puzzled. In the quiet moment, she clasped his hand and squeezed it. He responded by bending over and tenderly kissing her.

The wedding finished, the vows exchanged, the bride smiled at the groom and the groom at the bride. The wind blew gently against the priory and the sun blazed even brighter as if in celestial approval. The priory was filled with joy, and if there were tears spilled they dried atop smiles.

Margaret extended her hands to her parents, one on each side.

"Now," she said, very firmly and very loudly, as if addressing both corporeal and spiritual entities, "we're a family."

The five MacRae brothers smiled as one at the little girl so much like Moira MacRae.

A murmur began in the rear of the priory, and carried forward, growing in volume. One by one the members of the convocation raised their right fists in a gesture mimicking that on the clan badge.

The cry, which had been used in war, in battle, in despair and loss, almost shook the building. As it was repeatedly shouted, it subtly changed, becoming an acknowledgment of celebration, a victory over circumstance and time itself.

To the MacRaes! Our family, our strength!

Author's Note

~~~~~~~~∞~~~~~~~~

Mary King's Close, or street, is a real place and the origin of it as depicted in the book is true. Plague victims were, indeed, walled up there, and tours now take place where guides tell of seeing apparitions and hearing the faint echo of long-ago screams.

Edinburgh is a fascinating city whose character can't be adequately conveyed within the covers of a novel. Instead, it has to be felt to be truly appreciated. Like Edinburgh, Paris is rich with the aura of the past. As a teenager, I was fascinated with Montmartre, and used to stand on the steps watching the sunsets over Paris. If there are such things as ghosts among us, they linger in enchanted cities and special locales.

Unfortunately, the treatment Jeanne received at the Convent of Sacré-Coeur is based on truth. Having a child out of wedlock was considered a grievous sin in the eighteenth century, and the child was often sent away to be fostered and forgotten.

The Terror that gripped France actually began about two years after the book ends. But the beginning of the social upheaval started much earlier. People began leaving France with what possessions they could, as if knowing what would happen a few years later.

Spectacles have been around since the thirteenth century. A thousand years earlier than that, glass bowls filled with water were used to magnify print.

Writing the series about the MacRaes and Gilmuir has been a bittersweet labor of love for me. Even after leaving them I want to know what happened. Did Margaret and Cameron repeat history? Did Aislin choose to live at Sherbourne? Did Malcolm ever declare his feelings to Betty? What effect did the French Revolution and the Terror have on Hamish and Mary? I can only imagine all these things, and hope that you will as well.

Coming in August from Avon Books, romance so sizzling it will burn up the pages!

A WANTED MAN by Susan Kay Law
An Avon Romantic Treasure

Laura Hamilton has spent her life sheltered by her tycoon father's protectiveness, until she finally takes a bold step toward independence—a trip that will lead her to Sam Duncan. Sam's steely nerves have made him one of the most famous hired guns in the West, but can he react to Laura's allure fast enough to save his heart?

THE DAMSEL IN THIS DRESS by Marianne Stillings
An Avon Contemporary Romance

Soldier McKennitt, detective-turned-bestselling author, is just trying to find out who is panning his books in the *Port Henry Ledger*. His trail leads him not to a nasty shrew but to charming Betsy Tremaine, and suddenly romance comes down off the shelf—but first they've got to get Betsy safely out of the path of a stalker who has "true crime" in mind . . .

Also available in August, two beautifully repackaged classic Julia Quinn love stories

MINX

When untamable Henrietta Barrett's guardian passes away, her beloved home falls into the hands of William Dunford—London's most elusive bachelor.

BRIGHTER THAN THE SUN

The dashing—if incorrigible—Earl of Billington needs a bride before his thirtieth birthday if he hopes to earn his inheritance. And the vicar's daughter, Miss Eleanor Lyndon, needs a new home.

REL 0704

Avon Romantic Treasures

Unforgettable, enthralling love stories,
sparkling with passion and adventure
from Romance's bestselling authors

Avon Romances—
the best in exceptional authors
and unforgettable novels!